‘*Control Point* is *Black Haw*... ...st- ... is ... Cole's war- ti... gritty reality of army life and in the exploration of patriotism as the protagonist wrestles with the line between the law and what he sees as right’

Peter V. Brett, international bestselling author of *The Desert Spear*

‘Hands down, the best military fantasy I’ve ever read; *Control Point* is a chilling, enthralling story. Myke Cole just might be a wizard himself’

Ann Aguiree, bestselling author of *Enclave*

‘Cross *The Forever War* with *Witchworld*, add in the real world modern military of *Black Hawk Down*, and you get *Control Point*, the mile-a-minute story of someone trying to find purpose in a war he never asked for’

Jack Campbell, *New York Times* bestselling author of *The Lost Fleet* series

‘It’s impossible to blow up so much in such style between two covers and not have a hit. I'd watch it in 3D’

Mark Lawrence, acclaimed author of *Prince of Thorns*

‘A thrill ride from the first page until the very last. *Control Point* had me hooked’

Shiloh Walker, national bestselling author

‘Oscar Britton is an action hero with brains and a heart and a conscience. Combined with a compelling plot, this is a “one more chapter” book’

Robin Hobb, international bestselling author

‘Cole mixes supernatural powers with military experience, giving us a world in which magic and technology are used with equal effectiveness and precision . . . He’s found that perfect recipe’

Tor.com

‘An intense masterwork. *****’

The Ranting Dragon

‘Myke Cole takes you down range where the bullets fly and the magic burns with precision-guided ferocity that’ll put you on the edge of your seat before blowing you right out of it’

Chris Evans, author of the *Iron Elves* series

‘A non-stop thrill ride . . . bunker down as the fireballs fly with the bullets and enjoy one of 2012’s most exciting debuts. *****’

Fantasy Faction

‘An action-packed thrill ride . . . had me hooked from the start’

SciFi Chick

‘Everything I could hope for and more . . . if you are looking for a new voice, you better make sure Myke Cole is on your list’

Paperless Reading

‘*Control Point* is an absolute blast . . . my advice is to run, don’t walk, to your nearest bookseller and buy a copy’

Staffer’s Musing

‘Simply awesome. A mix of military might and old-school wizardry’

The Founding Fields

‘A really kick-ass premise’

SFF World

‘One of my favourite new books and a possible contender for 2012 book of the year’

Fantasy Book Review

‘If you aren’t excited yet for this book, you should be . . . I can’t wait to get my hands on *Fortress Frontier*’

Fantasy Book Critic

‘A modern, relevant and highly gripping read’

SF Signal

‘Beware, if you pick it up, you may not be able to do anything until you finish . . . possibly the debut of the year’

Only the Best Science Fiction and Fantasy

‘Intense, on-the-edge-of-your-seat thrilling . . . the action is superb, and better than any I’ve read before. It’s awesome, and everyone needs to read it’

Civilian Reader

CONTROL POINT

MYKE COLE

CONTROL POINT

headline

First published in 2012 by
HEADLINE PUBLISHING GROUP

1

Cataloguing in Publication Data is available from the British Library

ISBN 978 0 7553 9397 8

Typeset in Zapf Elliptical by Avon DataSet Ltd,
Bidford-on-Avon, Warwickshire

Printed and bound by CPI Group (UK) Ltd, Croydon, CR0 4YY

Headline's policy is to use papers that are natural, renewable and recyclable products and made from wood grown in sustainable forests. The logging and manufacturing processes are expected to conform to the environmental regulations of the country of origin.

HEADLINE PUBLISHING GROUP
An Hachette UK Company
338 Euston Road
London NW1 3BH

www.headline.co.uk
www.hachette.co.uk

As a security contractor, government civilian and military officer, Myke Cole's career has run the gamut from Counter-terrorism to Cyber Warfare to Federal Law Enforcement. He has done three tours in Iraq and was recalled to serve during the Deepwater Horizon oil spill. A lifelong fan of fantasy novels, comic books and Dungeons and Dragons, Myke now lives in Brooklyn, New York. This is his first novel.

www.mykecole.com

Twitter: @MykeCole

A glossary of military terms, acronyms and slang can be found at the end of the book.

Dedicated to the soldiers, sailors, airmen, marines, and coast guards of the United States armed services and the combined-forces men and women (British, Canadian, Australian, Georgian and others too many to mention) who I have served alongside. If I have ever been even a little bit brave under fire, it is only because I didn't want to let you down.

Flight

'Latent' has become part of the magical jargon. It used to mean folks who were channeling magic but hadn't yet realized it. Now everyone from the Unmanifested to the professional military Sorcerer is considered 'Latent'. It's the catchall for anyone touched by the Great Reawakening and a sign of how quickly we've adapted to this new reality.

– John Brunk

Staff Research Associate, *Oxford English Dictionary*

Chapter One

Assault

. . . coming to you live from the Lincoln Memorial in Washington, DC, where we have just been informed that a Selfer incident has collapsed the memorial with an unknown number of tourists trapped inside. A SOC intervention team is inbound, and we will continue with regular updates as the situation unfolds . . .

– Alex Brinn, SPY7 News, Washington, DC
Reporting on the Bloch Incident

They want me to kill a child, Lieutenant Oscar Britton thought.

The monitor showed a silent video feed from a high-school security camera. On it, a young boy stood in a school auditorium. A long-sleeved black T-shirt covered his skinny chest. Silver chains connected rings in his ears, nose, and lips. His hair was a spray of mousse and color.

He was wreathed in a bright ball of fire.

Billowing smoke clouded the camera feed, but Britton could see the boy stretch out a hand, flames jetting past the camera's range, engulfing fleeing students, who rolled away, beating at their hair and clothing. People were running, screaming.

Beside the boy stood a chubby girl, her dyed black hair matching her lipstick and eye makeup. She spread her arms.

The flames around the boy pulsed in time with her motions, forming two man-sized and -shaped peaks of flame. The fire elementals danced among the students, burning as they went.

Britton watched as the elementals multiplied – four, then six. Wires sparked as the fire reached the stage. The girl's magic touched them as well, the electricity forming dancing human shapes, elementals of sizzling energy. They lit among the students, fingertips crackling arcs of dazzling blue lightning.

Britton swallowed as his team shuffled uneasily behind him. He heard them make room for Lieutenant Morgan and his assaulters, who entered the briefing room and clustered around the monitor, still tightening straps on gun slings and slamming rounds into their magazines. They loaded armor-piercing, hollow-point, and incendiary ammunition. Not the standard ball or half charges normally used on a capture mission. Britton swallowed again. These were bullets for taking on a dug-in, professional enemy.

The video went to static, then looped for the fifth time as they waited for the briefing to start. The boy burst into flame yet again, the girl beside him conjuring the man-shaped fire elementals to scatter through the auditorium.

Fear formed a cold knot in Britton's stomach. He pushed it away, conscious of the stares of his men. A leader who voiced fear instilled it in his subordinates.

The mission briefer finally took up his position beside the monitor. His blue eyes were gray flint under the fluorescent lights. 'It's South Burlington High School, about seven klicks from our position. We sent a Sorcerer to check out a tip on an unreported Latency, and these kids decided to tear the place up once they knew they were caught. The local police are already on the scene, and they're going to refer to me as Captain Thorsson. I'll need you to stick to call signs. Call me Harlequin at all times.

'The helos are undergoing final checks outside, and you should be on deck to assault the target in fifteen minutes from jump. South Burlington PD and a company out of the Eighty-sixth have evacuated the civilians. We should have it totally clear now, so the order's come down to go in and bring order to the chaos.'

'Looks like Pyromancers, sir?' Britton asked.

Harlequin snorted and gave voice to Britton's fears. 'You honestly think a fifteen-year-old girl would have the control it takes to move even one elemental around like that, let alone half a dozen? Those flame-men are self-willed.'

'Just great!' Private First Class Dawes whispered loudly enough to be heard by the whole room. 'A Probe! A fucking Elementalist! Jesus fucking Christ!'

Warrant Officer Cheatham turned to his man. 'So, she's a Probe! Prohibited school's no more dangerous than a legal one to a real soldier!'

'It's okay, Dan,' Britton said, gesturing to Cheatham. Dawes was the youngest member of their team and prone to the histrionics of youth.

Britton could feel the terror in the room. Morgan shifted uneasily, drawing glances from his team.

'I don't like it any more than you do,' Harlequin said, 'but the law is clear. All Supernatural Operations Corps runs inside the United States must be integrated with regular army support. That's not my call. That's by presidential decree.

'But you are on perimeter, cordon, and fire-suppression duty. This is a SOC op, and you will let us handle the actual target.'

Target, Britton thought. *So that's what you call a fifteen-year-old girl and her boyfriend*.

'What are you going to do, sir?' Britton asked.

'You gonna put a tornado down on 'em, sir?' Dawes asked.

The corner of Harlequin's mouth lifted slightly. 'Something like that.'

If anyone else had said it, the men would have laughed. But Harlequin was a commissioned Sorcerer in the Supernatural Operations Corps.

He meant every word.

'Sir,' Britton said, trying not to let his uncertainty show. 'With my bird in the air and my boys on the ground, that's not an acceptable risk. Copters and tornadoes don't exactly mix.'

'Your concern for your team is noted,' Harlequin said, 'but if you stick to your positions and do as you're told, you won't get hit by any stray magic.'

Supporting the SOC *and* taking on a Probe. Lieutenant Morgan's voice finally broke, along with his nerve. 'You've got to be kidding me.'

Britton felt the fear leap from the lieutenant to his troops. His own team was fracturing before his eyes, the terror eating into their professionalism. He knew he should be holding them together, but he had just seen kids burning to death in the halls of the very high school he used to attend. In a few minutes, he would be landing his team on the roof where he first kissed a girl, supporting a SOC unit turning its magical might against two teenagers.

The boy, they might take alive. Selfers were sometimes pardoned for past crimes if they took the oath and joined the SOC.

But the girl had no chance. She was a Probe, and only one thing happened to those who Manifested in Prohibited magical schools. They were gunned down or carted off, hooded and cuffed, never to be seen again.

'Sir, I just want to confirm that this is a capture mission, right?' Britton asked.

Harlequin shrugged. 'Of course. Rules of engagement are clear: if they engage you, escalate to deadly force. Err on the side of protecting your people.'

'They're scared kids, sir,' Britton continued. 'Maybe they'd surrender? Have we gotten in touch with their parents to see if they can talk them down? I know it sounds silly, but . . .'

'It does sound silly, Lieutenant!' Harlequin cut him off. 'And we don't have time for hand-wringing right now. Those kids had a choice. They could have turned themselves in. They didn't. They chose to go it on their own. Remember, you're only a Selfer if you run.

'Now, any other questions?' Harlequin asked, glaring at the assembled teams.

There weren't any.

'Good,' Harlequin said. 'Get geared up and get your asses in the air. I'm jumping now. Morgan! You're on the ground manning relief. Britton! You jump with me. Co-ords are already in the bird. I'll meet you on target.'

He leaned in to Britton as he left. 'Look, Lieutenant. The law may require me to take you along, but you keep your men out of my way and out of the fight. You're not trained for this. And if I ever again catch you putting doubt in the minds of an assault force about to go hot, I will personally fry your ass.'

Harlequin threw open the door and leapt skyward, flying quickly out of view.

'Sir.' Dawes tugged Britton's sleeve. 'Can't they get another team? I don't wanna work with no Sorcerers.'

'They're on our side, remember?' Britton forced a smile. Terror curdled in his gut. 'SOC's still army.'

Sergeant Goodman, carrying the support weapon for Britton's team, snorted and nervously tapped the safety on her light machine gun.

'Sir, it's a high school,' said Dawes, sounding high-school aged himself through his thick Arkansas accent.

'Selfers or not, they're just kids,' Goodman added.

They're reading my mind, Britton thought, but he asked 'Why do we call them Selfers, Goodman?'

She hesitated. Britton took a step forward, glaring at her. She might have a point, but she had to believe in this mission if she was going to carry it out. They all had to. 'Why?'

'Because they don't think about how their magic puts others in danger,' she gave the textbook response. 'Because they only think about themselves.'

'Absolutely right,' Britton said. 'There are thirty-four American corpses buried in the rubble of the Lincoln Memorial because of kids like this! Who knows how many kids, hell, or even some of my former teachers, are down there right now? If you can't do this, say so now. Once we go dynamic and hit that roof, I need everyone in the game. I give you my word; I won't hold it against you. If you want out, now's the time.'

He gave them a moment to respond. No one said a word.

Britton had to get his team moving. The more they stood around, the more the fear would take hold. 'Okay, you heard the man, and you know the plan!' he called out. 'Let's show the SOC how the Green Mountain Boys get the job done! We're going to be up to our assholes in elementals up there, so gear for it. Fire suppression for the pyro. There might be lightning elementals, too, so I want everyone to suit up in as much rubber insulation as the armorer will dispense. Move with a purpose, people!'

As his team hurried to comply, Britton looked back at the looping video and suppressed a shudder.

The world's gone mad, Britton thought. *Magic has changed everything.*

Even if he wasn't required to do the deed personally, he knew what Harlequin and his men intended.

Britton sat behind the helicopter's controls and looked at the man floating in the sky.

Harlequin stood in midair, flight suit rippling in the breeze. Over a thousand feet below him, South Burlington High School glowed in the party colors of spinning police-car lights.

Behind Britton, four army assaulters looked down between their boots, dangling over the helicopter skids, shifting flame-retardant tanks and body armor out of the way for a better view.

Harlequin swooped down to land on one of the Kiowa's skids, rocking the helicopter and forcing the assaulters to pull their feet back inside. The rotors beat the air over the Aeromancer's head, stirring his close-cropped blond hair.

The assaulters looked nervously at Britton, and Warrant Officer Cheatham shifted in the copilot's seat. Britton, at least twice Harlequin's size, turned to face him. The Aeromancer was not impressed.

'All right,' he shouted loudly enough to be heard over the Kiowa's engine, his blue eyes hard. 'You're to hold position here while we do our job.'

Britton's brown skin concealed an angry flush. Harlequin might be a Sorcerer, but the assault order came down from on high for all of them. But the real rage came from the sense of relief. No matter how badly he didn't want to do this, he still had to. Holding position would be tantamount to dereliction of duty.

'With all due respect, sir,' he called out over the whine of the rotors, 'I have to follow the TOC's orders. "Big army" has to run shotgun on this raid.'

'That's crap,' Harlequin responded. 'We're not in the damned briefing room anymore, and I don't care what Tactical

Operations Command says. This is a real fight, with real magic. I don't need regular pukes fucking it up. You will hold your position here until told otherwise. Is that perfectly clear?'

Britton sympathized with Harlequin's desire to avoid unnecessary loss of life, but that didn't change the fact that he'd flown onto Britton's helicopter and insulted his team.

And it didn't change the nagging feeling that if there was any chance at all those kids might be saved, Britton had to be there to make sure he saw it through.

'Negative, sir,' Britton said. 'My orders are to accompany you to the target and deploy my team. That's what I intend to do.'

'I'm giving you an order, Lieutenant,' Harlequin said through gritted teeth. He stretched an arm outside the helicopter. The brilliant stars winked out as shreds of cloud unraveled over the rotors, thudding against thickening air.

Britton's stomach clenched as thunder rumbled, but he did his best to look unimpressed. He toggled the cockpit radio. 'TOC, this is support. Can someone put me through to Major Reynolds? I'm being ordered to . . .'

Harlequin conjured a gust of air that toggled the radio off. 'Fucking forget it!'

Britton sighed and listened briefly to the radio static. 'Sir, my orders come directly from the colonel, and last time I checked, he outranks you.'

Harlequin paused, his anger palpable. Britton gripped the controls tightly to keep his hands from shaking. He felt the tremble in the rudder pedals as the rotors spun up, slicing through the summoned clouds.

'We're moving, sir,' Britton said. 'Are you riding with us or with your own team?'

Harlequin cursed, dropped backward off the skid, righted himself, and flew off, outpacing the helicopter easily. The cloud cover around the Kiowa instantly wafted apart.

'Holy crap, sir,' Master Sergeant Young leaned in to shout over the Kiowa's engine. 'I've never seen anyone talk to a Sorcerer like that.'

'Seriously, sir,' Sergeant Goodman added. 'The SOC don't give a fuck if they get court-martialed. They'll just zap you.'

'The army's the army,' Britton said with a conviction he didn't feel. 'Latent or not, we all follow orders.'

'Thank you, sir. Seriously,' Cheatham said, 'I wouldn't want anyone talking to my people that way.'

Britton nodded, uncomfortable with the praise.

The Supernatural Operations Corps bird, another Kiowa, sleek and black, came into view as they descended. Its side was blazoned with the SOC arms – the Stars and Stripes fluttering behind the eye in the pyramid. Symbols of the four elements hovered in the corners representing legal magical schools: Pyromancy, Hydromancy, Aeromancy, and Terramancy. The red cross crowned the display, symbolizing Physiomancy, the most prized of the permitted schools. The banner beneath read: OUR GIFTS, FOR OUR NATION.

The high-school roof materialized below them, a pitted atoll of raised brick sides stretched with black tar paper. A single, brick-housed metal door led into the building.

Britton set the Kiowa hovering and nodded to Cheatham to take the controls. He turned to the assaulters.

'Okay. You all got the brief,' he shouted. 'Two targets barricaded inside. Keep the perimeter secure and the fires under control. Remember, one Pyromancer and one Probe Elementalist.'

'They're Selfers, sir,' Goodman said. 'Why can't we just bomb the building? Why's it worth risking our lives?'

'Our orders are to take them down and bring them in for justice,' Britton replied. 'If the rules of engagement change, and we have to kill them, then we will. Until then, we're on a capture mission. Everybody square?'

It's a damned lie, he thought. *Those kids are dead. Harlequin has no intention of capturing anybody.*

He made eye contact with each member of his team. None looked away.

Satisfied, he nodded. 'Okay, double-check your gear and let's do this.'

He barely had time to retake the Kiowa's controls before the commlink crackled to life with Major Reynolds's voice in the TOC trailer on the ground below. 'Full element heads up!

Support element, this is TOC. Go hot. I say again, go hot and prep for entry on target.'

'Acknowledged. Support element is hot,' Britton said into the commlink. 'You heard the man!' he called to his team. 'Weapons free and eyes on target!' He heard the click of safeties coming off on Dawes's carbine and Goodman's machine gun. Hertzog and Young hefted their flame suppressors. A quick glance confirmed the assaulters' sighting down their barrels at the roof.

Oh God, he thought. *I didn't sign up to fight children.* He tried to push his doubts away. The law was the law. You didn't negotiate with unregulated magic users.

'SOC Element,' came Reynolds's voice over the commlink. 'This is TOC. Aero-1, sweep perimeter. Pyro-1, go hot.'

Harlequin dove from the SOC helicopter and rocketed around the school. A figure leaned out of the SOC Kiowa, pumping his fist. His arm erupted in bright orange fire.

Harlequin's voice came over the commlink, 'Aero-1 pass complete. All's quiet. South Burlington police have the perimeter secure.' A pause, then, 'Pyro-1 is hot and ready. SOC Assault-1 and -2 are good to go.'

'Roger that,' Reynolds said. 'South Burlington SWAT has been kind enough to provide perimeter and entry from the ground. I'm patching them through now.'

A short crackle was followed by a thick New-England-accented voice. 'This is Captain Rutledge with South Burlington PD tactical. Perimeter is secure. Students and faculty are clear, fires are out, and we've got the first two floors locked down. Your Selfers are above there somewhere. My men are withdrawn under sniper cover. You're good to go when ready.'

'Roger that,' said Reynolds. 'Okay, Aero-1. Your show. Call 'em out.'

Harlequin streaked over the roof and lit gracefully on the SOC helicopter's skid. He reached inside and produced a microphone.

'This is Captain Thorsson of the US Army Supernatural Operations Corps,' his voice blared over a bullhorn mounted beneath the Kiowa. 'You are accused of unlawful magic use in violation of the McGauer-Linden Act. You have thirty seconds to surrender yourselves. This is your first and only warning.'

The only sounds that followed were the roaring engines of the Kiowas.

'Christ,' Cheatham whispered. He had two high-school-aged girls of his own.

'We have to do this,' Britton said, his voice hollow in his own ears. 'They're walking bombs.'

Cheatham set his jaw, 'They're probably hiding down there, scared as hell.'

Dawes was scared as hell, too. Britton put his hand on Cheatham's shoulder. 'Dan. I need you focused.'

Cheatham didn't look at Britton. 'I'll do my job, sir.'

'"You're only a Selfer if you run," Dan,' Britton parroted Harlequin's words. 'They could have turned themselves in. They had a choice.'

Cheatham framed a reply, but was cut off by Reynolds's voice blazing over the commlink. 'All right! That's it! Element! Go dynamic!'

'To arms, Pyro-1. Let's smoke 'em out,' Harlequin's voice crackled over the channel. 'Spare the good Captain Rutledge's men and light her up, stories three and higher.'

The Pyromancer stepped onto the helicopter's skid, the bright fire extending to engulf his entire body. He raised his arms, and the flames curled in on themselves, shifting from red to orange to white. The air shimmered around them, then folded in on itself as the Pyromancer thrust his arms forward. The flames rocketed outward with a roar that competed with the helicopter engines.

The fire struck the building just above the second floor, punching through the windows. A moment later, the remaining glass burst outward. Flames arced upward to paint the night sky. The SOC Kiowa circled the building as the Pyromancer continued his strike until the entire floor burned brightly.

Britton shuddered. If the kids weren't burned alive, they'd have the choice of fleeing downstairs, under the guns of the police snipers, or out to the roof, where the Kiowas waited.

'Reel her back a bit,' Harlequin's voice came over the commlink, amused. 'We want to give them a chance to surrender. Okay, Support! It's your big day! Let's get on that roof. There's one egress. Think you can cover that?'

Britton pushed the rotors as hard as he dared. He cleared the roof sides with inches to spare and felt his bones jar as the helicopter made a textbook hard landing. The four assaulters leapt off – Goodman and Dawes covering the entrance. Young and Hertzog were already coating the roof with foam to keep the fire from spreading. The rotor wash peeled the tar paper back, sending the thick gravel beneath skittering across the rooftop.

The metal door flew open, and the boy and girl from the video raced out, coughing and beating at their smoldering hair.

'Contact front!' Young called, then screamed at the kids to get down.

Britton pulled hard on the collective, adjusting the rotor pitch to get the Kiowa airborne. The girl broke from the doorway, reaching out toward the helicopter. The dancing gravel shuddered, spun, and coalesced into a humanoid shape, the stone stretching and flowing together into a man-shaped stone creature, eight feet tall. The tar paper lowered as the gravel beneath drew up into the giant form, its huge shoulders reflecting the flickering firelight from veins of quartz. The rock elemental gripped one of the helicopter skids with a gravelly fist, yanking down hard. There was a roar, a whine of metal, and the Kiowa lurched to one side. Britton heard successive bangs as the rotors collided with the rooftop, breaking into pieces. The helo's body grounded against the roof, shielding the team from the splintering blades, which sounded against its metal cabin with sharp reports.

Cheatham sagged in his safety harness, punching at the release. 'I'm stuck, sir.'

Britton could see the girl continuing to gesture. The wind, whipped into dusty funnels by the breaking rotors, coalesced into human shapes, plunging among the assaulters, who cried out, firing as they fell back to the roof's edge. The air elementals spun among them, their flexing tornado forms spinning shreds of tar paper, broken gravel, and spent ammunition casings. Dawes squeezed off two shots that punched through one of the creatures harmlessly before it swatted him with a gale that knocked him flat against the roof's lip. He slammed against it hard, the thickness of his body armor protecting his spine and saving him from going over the edge.

They had landed to take on two Selfers. Within moments, they faced a small army.

Britton knew that to stop the elementals, they'd have to take out the girl. *Whether Harlequin wants it or not, he thought, we're in the fight now*.

'TOC! We've got sentient elemental conjuration up here! We're pinned down!' Britton shouted into the microphone, yanking his pistol from its holster.

'Goddamn it!' Harlequin said. 'I knew this would happen!' Britton heard more gunfire, then a deafening explosion from the direction of the shooting. He looked over Cheatham's shoulder to see the boy wreathed in a tornado of flame. Bullets pocked the wall around the Selfer, tore holes in his chest and legs as he thrust his hands forward and arced the burning funnel towards Dawes with such force that bricks went flying. The blast flew wild, but the edge caught Dawes as he dove to the side. The intense heat ignited the helicopter's side, the metal sparking white as it burned away in patches, mixing with the dripping remnants of the windscreen. The fuel tank kicked outward with a bang, the blast catching Dawes as he sprawled on the roof. Cheatham's flight suit smoldered, but the Kiowa's shell shielded him from the blast. The tar paper vaporized, the gravel beneath heated white-hot, the stones exploding like gunshots.

One of the SOC assaulters had rappelled to the roof and leveled his carbine at the girl. She glanced at him, and the lingering flames erupted, spawning three man-shaped figures. They launched themselves at him, pounding with flickering fists. He screamed as his helmet melted, the covering of his armor burning away, ceramic plates beneath turning white-hot. Young and Hertzog turned the fire suppressors on them, drowning the elementals in foam. The creatures stayed on the assaulter, burning him even as they diminished under the flame-retardant chemicals.

Dear God, Britton thought. *It's the girl. If I don't stop her, she'll fry the whole team*.

Britton finally punched out of the restraints and fell out of the helicopter, his shoulder striking the roof hard enough to jar his teeth. He aimed his pistol at the girl, squeezing the trigger as a rock elemental stepped between them, the bullet whining off the shifting stone.

The misshapen head drove forward. Britton dodged, but it only moved him into the elemental's arms, which pinned his own, squeezing hard. Britton dropped the pistol and gasped for breath, his ribs flexing. His vision began to gray.

Harlequin's boots landed on the roof with a thud.

The Aeromancer lifted his arms, and dark clouds spun around his hands, pulsing with angry electricity. Lightning burst forth in a dazzling arc, tearing off the elemental's head and missing Britton by inches. Electricity pulsed through the thing's shoulders, grounding through the gravel so that Britton only felt a slight twinge of electric current. Rock flowed up to form a new head as the elemental turned to face the new threat, releasing Britton, who sucked down air, cradling his battered ribs.

One of the air elementals, its vaguely human outline marked by swirling dust, leapt over the helo toward them. Harlequin extended a hand, and a gale swept into it, its shape blurring as it was blown apart, scattering dozens of bullet casings swept up in its funneling form.

'That's one you owe me, Lieutenant,' Harlequin said, as Britton scrambled to his feet and retrieved his gun. 'I told you you'd just get in the damn way.' He leapt into the sky, turning toward the girl, only to be caught by another air elemental that had formed itself into a spinning funnel. Harlequin spun into its recesses, cursing, battered by gravel caught in the funnel's center. The air elemental contracted on itself, spinning the Aeromancer dizzy, and both swept over the side of the roof.

The rock elemental, its head restored, stormed toward the rest of the assault team, who battled the small army of elementals. Goodman turned the machine gun on the creature, funneling the heavy-caliber rounds until they ripped a sizeable hole in its torso, almost tearing it in half. The elemental stumbled, then paused, head inclined as the rock flowed to seal the gap. Goodman cursed and fell back.

The SOC bird descended toward them. The Pyromancer, a blazing human torch, balanced on one skid. The other SOC assaulter stood on the opposite side of the helicopter, sheltering from the magical flames in the cool night air. Britton could see him trying to sight the girl, but the running fight between assaulter and elemental obscured his target.

I can do this, Britton thought. *She's not a girl, she's a monster.*

But when Britton rolled out around the helicopter's nose, leading with his pistol, all he could see was a teenager, tears tracking through her makeup. Even as she concentrated on sustaining her magic, she looked terrified.

The SOC assaulter lay dead in his melted armor. The boy sat against the metal door, he thrashed, spouting random gouts of flame. His chest and gut were a ragged collection of entry wounds. The girl stood beside him, sobbing.

Britton knelt, sighting down his pistol, blowing out his breath and taking his time.

You can do this, he told himself. *You have to do this.*

He fired by the book, easing the trigger backward, not anticipating the recoil, letting the gun go off.

But he couldn't. He pulled his shot at the last minute. The bullet broke low and left, clipping the girl's side, sending her spinning in a circle.

He felt a hammerblow to his shoulder and pitched forward, skinning his nose. He rolled over onto his back, firing two more shots into another rock elemental that had one fist raised. The bullets sparked as they ricocheted off the thing's chest. Britton tried to roll to one side, knowing it wouldn't matter, waiting for the crushing impact of the blow that would smash his skull.

But the blow never came. When Britton opened his eyes, the elemental had collapsed into a pile of gravel, cascading over his boots. He kicked out from under it and got to his feet in time to see the remaining assaulters blinking in amazement as the elemental onslaught suddenly broke off.

Then the screaming reached them.

Dawes, burning brightly, clawed the air. His carbine was a melted mass. Young doused him with foam, cursed, and dragged him by one boot toward a puddle of rainwater. Britton ran to his Kiowa for the medkit. He was intercepted by Cheatham, who had freed himself from his restraints and carried it. In a moment, the fire was out, and Britton and Cheatham were kneeling beside Dawes, spreading burn gel over his wounds.

Harlequin, recovered from his battle with the air elemental, returned to the roof and landed beside them. He reached out toward the boy, and the flames vanished as the Pyromancer's magic rolled back.

Britton stared at Dawes. He was wounded, but he would make it.

'What happened to the girl?' Britton called to Young. The master sergeant pointed at the bullet-riddled metal door leading into the school.

Maybe she's still alive, he thought. *I've got to get to her before Harlequin does*.

'Come with me,' Britton said, racing to the door. 'The rest of you get Dawes stabilized.'

'Wait,' Harlequin said. 'I can't help you while I'm Suppressing this little shit. Let me get this secure, and I'll smoke her out.'

No way, Britton thought. *I'm not letting you kill her*.

'She took a round in her gut, sir. Her elemental army has disbanded,' Britton said, moving to the door opposite Young. 'If she's not dead already, she's in no shape to fight us.' If they had any hope of bringing her out alive, they had to move quickly. 'Go with a flash-bang,' he said to Young, 'just in case.'

Young nodded. Britton tried the door handle. The knob turned easily, still cool. Young yanked the flash-bang from his vest and threw it through the door. It thumped and clattered down the stairwell as both men turned away from the blinding flash that followed.

'Go! Go! Go!' Britton shouted, kicking open the door and covering with his pistol as Young rolled around the door frame, leading with his carbine.

Blood, turning tacky on the concrete, trailed down the stairwell. The girl sprawled against the white cinder-block wall, panting. She clutched her hip where the bullet had bitten a sizeable chunk out of her. Her black skirt adhered wetly to her thigh. Britton had never seen so much blood in his life.

'Cover her,' Britton said as he went to her. She moaned weakly, half-conscious. 'Dan!' he shouted into the commlink. 'She's hurt bad. I'm bringing her out. I'm going to need a trauma bandage and a ton of gauze. Clotting powder if you've got it.'

The SOC bird landed as he burst onto the roof, setting the girl down. Goodman and Cheatham went to her as Britton raced to Dawes. The SOC assaulter ran to the helo and returned with an emergency blanket. Young helped Britton to lift Dawes as gently as they could. 'It's going to be all right, man,' Britton said. 'You're going to be fine.' Dawes whined from the clear side of his mouth. The other half of his face was a melted ruin.

The teenaged Pyromancer had expired from his wounds. His eyes stared sightlessly from his pale face.

Britton swallowed hard and helped to lay Dawes in the Kiowa. He turned back to the wounded Elementalist. 'Dan, how's she do—'

A gunshot cut him off.

By the time he had turned, the assaulter had already thrown the blanket over her, covering her face. Harlequin's pistol smoked.

'You son of a bitch!' Britton screamed, hurling himself at Harlequin. The SOC assaulter leapt between them, pushing him back.

'ROE are clear, Lieutenant,' Harlequin said. 'She's a Probe. She attacked a government agent. She's dead. End of story. We can discuss your attempted assault of a superior officer later.'

'You bastard!' Britton screamed. 'She was wounded! She wasn't a threat!'

'She's a Probe,' Harlequin repeated, 'and now she's a dead Probe. Calm the hell down, Lieutenant, your men are watching.'

Britton whirled, taking in his team. All were covered in burns and cuts. Goodman looked sick. Young was pale. 'Sir,' Cheatham said, putting a hand on his shoulder, 'Dawes needs help now. We've got to get him out of here.'

Britton nodded. The girl was dead, Dawes was alive. First things first.

'TOC,' Harlequin spoke into his microphone. 'This is Aero-1. Element has brought order to chaos. Two enemy KIA. I'm leaving one for mop-up. The other was a confirmed Probe, and SOC will take custody of the remains.'

'Negative, Harlequin. We're going to need all the bodies for our after-action,' came the commander's voice.

'I'm sorry, sir,' Harlequin said, not sounding sorry at all. 'Regs are clear. We're to take custody of any Probe remains. If you have any objections, feel free to take it up the chain. For now, I have my orders.'

There was a pause. 'Roger that,' the commander finally replied, sounding furious. 'Element status?'

'SOC Element has one KIA,' Harlequin said. 'Support Element has one WIA, and one busted chopper. You also might want to get the fire department up here before what's left of your Kiowa gets cooked. They might still be able to save the school.'

Harlequin looked around at the rising flames. The fight had been finished quickly, but the flames were spreading in spite of the fire retardant soaking the roof. 'Not to worry, sir,' he said, reaching for the girl, 'the SOC bird will exfiltrate full element and get the wounded to the cash right away.'

Harlequin gathered the girl's shrouded body in his arms. 'I'll meet you on the ground.' He leapt skyward.

They squeezed ten into a helicopter meant for six, stacking themselves in the open bay, Dawes resting on top. Britton shuddered at the cooked-meat stench. *He was under my command. It's my responsibility. Harlequin warned us to stay away.* Why had he even bothered to come? He hadn't been able to save either kid. It had been useless.

The Kiowa lumbered under the extra weight, circling the burning building and descending toward the Combat Support Hospital among the trailers.

'Fucking Elementalist,' the Pyromancer said. His uniform was perfect, not a strand of his jet-black hair out of place. There was no sign of the blaze that had raged over his body beyond a faint smell of smoke. 'Fucking Probe.'

'She was just a kid,' Britton said.

'Then she should have turned herself in. She ran. She went Selfer.'

Britton shuddered as he recalled the sound of that single gunshot. 'Yeah, I just saw how you treat Probes when they're subdued. Would it have been any different if she'd turned herself in?'

The Pyromancer looked at Britton as if noticing a bug. 'With all due respect, *sir*.' He spit out the word. 'Selfers like her hurt a hell of a lot more kids than we just did. She knew the law. She had a choice. She deserved what she got. She killed one of ours and hurt one of yours.'

'The boy hurt my man, not her. Jesus. Anyone can come up Latent at any time. It's not like she chose this. But Harlequin still shot her in the head while she was lying helpless on the ground. What the hell is wrong with you people?'

The Pyromancer shrugged. 'Rules of engagement. That's lifeblood in this business. Maybe you should memorize them, seeing how it's your job to carry them out.'

Britton didn't want him to have the last word. 'Still, those kids did pretty good, considering they haven't had a day of training, and you do this for a living.'

He shrugged. 'It's easy to display great magical power when you've got no control, sir. But theatrics don't win battles. Skill beats will, every time.'

The Combat Surgical Hospital, or 'cash', as the soldiers called it, was assembled in a trailer beside the high school. The firelight danced on its sheer white surface, washed red by the flashing sirens of the South Burlington Fire Department.

A crowd of protestors chanted outside the police cordon, too far for Britton to determine if it was anarchists, Christian conservatives, or environmentalists this time. He could see signs over the police cruisers. MAGIC = SATAN! PRESIDENT WALSH AND ZIONISTS TRAIN TROOPS IN FORBIDDEN SCHOOLS! CLOSE THE SECRET BASE! GOBLINS ARE REAL! WHY WON'T THE GOVERNMENT TELL THE TRUTH ABOUT MAGIC CREATURES?

An army nurse arrived from the Combat Surgical Hospital trailer with a gurney. Britton and Young hefted Dawes onto it, cringing as he cried out.

'What happened?' asked the nurse.

'Selfer Pyromancer cooked him,' Britton answered.

'It's his lucky day,' the nurse said. 'We've got SOC burn-trauma with us.' He motioned to a SOC captain emerging from the trailer. The captain ran his hands over Dawes's wounds. Water droplets formed around him, misting the burned skin. The angry red color began to subside.

Dawes's eyes opened, fixing on the Hydromancer's lapel pin. 'No!' he shrieked. 'Don't let him hurt me, sir!' he struggled against Young and Britton. 'Don't let him cast no spells on me, sir! I want a real doctor!'

The Hydromancer's jaw tightened, but he continued to work. Puffs of steam carried the smell of cooked flesh into the air. 'That's all I can do without a Physiomancer, and we don't have one detailed here. You have to take him inside.'

An orderly helped the nurse lift the gurney and race up the trailer steps, slamming through the door.

The Hydromancer turned to follow, but Britton caught his sleeve. 'How's he doing?'

He looked at Britton with the same contempt the Pyromancer had shown inside the helicopter. 'Please, sir,' Britton said. 'I can't lose him.' *I lost two kids already tonight.*

The Hydromancer's eyes softened. 'The burns dried him dangerously. I moisturized the affected areas and was able to drop the temperature of the burned flesh a few layers down. That should give him a head start. But he's still going to have to heal normally, and I don't need to tell you how hard burns are to treat.'

He turned to go, but Britton held his sleeve. 'Thanks, sir.'

The Hydromancer nodded and shook his arm free. 'Let me

get back in there, Lieutenant. Might be there's more I can do for him after all.'

Britton turned back to his team, but Harlequin, back from dropping off the girl's corpse, strode in front of them, blocking his view.

'How's your boy?' the Aeromancer asked.

'He'll be okay, sir.' Britton bit off the words, not trusting himself to speak.

'He'll be better than okay, Lieutenant. He's got a SOC burn-trauma expert on the case. He's very lucky. Just like you were very lucky to have an Aeromancer between you and that elemental back there.'

Britton felt his temper rise, but his men were watching; it wouldn't do any good to teach them to be proud. Harlequin was arrogant, but he was also right. The issue of the murder would be for a court-martial to decide.

'Yes, sir,' he said, trying not to sound bitter. 'It's much appreciated.'

'You can show your appreciation by writing the after-action report,' Harlequin said, handing him a packet of papers. 'I've got to get with public affairs to deal with the press.'

It was too much. 'Where do I fill in the information about you killing a helpless captive?'

Harlequin's smile went vulpine. 'Anywhere you damn well please. I can counter with a report of a Probe dealt with according to authorized ROE. I can also put you down for assaulting a superior officer and conduct unbecoming.'

Britton took a step forward, his chest touching Harlequin's. 'Go right ahead. Nothing will make me happier than to tell a court-martial the truth. You better put the rest of my men down while you're at it, because they saw everything, too.'

'Not too bright, are you? You'll get your day in court. But there isn't one in all five armed services who is going to rule against a SOC officer for killing a Probe. You might as well campaign for cockroach rights, you damned idiot. She resisted. If she'd turned herself in, she'd still be alive.'

'As a Probe?'

Harlequin sighed and slammed the paperwork into Britton's chest. 'Just don't forget; two Selfers employing Black

Magic during a lawful SOC assault. They were given ample opportunity to surrender.'

'They were given thirty seconds. And I saw one Elementalist and one Pyromancer. Heck, you just told the TOC that only one was a confirmed Probe, and you only took one corpse.'

'It's all Black Magic when they run, Lieutenant. You write that report any way you want, but I guarantee you that public affairs will have a different perspective.'

'I'll make copies. People will know what happened up there.'

'Yes, Lieutenant, they will. They also won't give a damn. That's because they, unlike you, know who the good guys are.'

Britton watched Harlequin's departing back, biting back a retort. He turned to his team. 'Dan, take the guys in there and get everyone checked out. I'll report to the TOC and get started on this damned report. I'm going to write it as I saw it, no matter what that asshole says. I want to get everyone's signature. No pressure, you only sign it if you agree.'

Cheatham nodded. 'He's right, sir. It won't mean a damn thing, you know that.'

Britton shut his eyes and gritted his teeth. 'Yes, Dan. I know that.'

'Dawes'll be okay,' Cheatham said. 'Hightide is the best burn-trauma specialist I've ever seen. He was out at our field cash in Baghdad before the pullout.'

'We both know Hightide's only here in case one of their own gets zapped.'

Cheatham shrugged. 'Same difference, sir.'

'If the SOC really wanted to help, they'd send a Physiomancer to fix his face. That's going to be tough on him.'

'No doubt, but Physiomancers are a rare breed, sir. I haven't seen a Healer on detail to the 158th in a dog's age.'

'I'll put in for him to get Physiomantic treatment later.'

Cheatham shook his head. 'That's a long line to wait on, sir.'

Britton knew Cheatham wasn't kidding. Physiomancy was a rare talent. Britton shook his head, adrenaline giving way to helpless exhaustion. *A girl's murdered, and the world just keeps on turning*, Britton thought. Dawes's plight added to the load.

'I know you did your best up there, sir,' Cheatham said. 'I've run with a lot of officers in my day, and even the best lose men sometimes. Dawes signed up for air assault, same as the rest of us. He knew the risks.'

Britton was silent. He knew the warrant officer was right, but it was too much just then.

'That girl, Dan,' he finally said. 'I can't believe that just happened.'

Cheatham nodded. 'I know it's rough, sir. I'm not saying it isn't. But Probes are Probes, and the ROE's clear. You know I've got your back, and I admire you for what you did and what you're doing, but she was dead the moment she pulled our Kiowa down.

'That doesn't mean he's not an ass.' Cheatham jerked his thumb at Harlequin, standing beside the Kiowa and berating his assaulter, a Rump Latency whose magic had never Manifested powerfully enough to actually use. By law he still served in the Corps, but would never make Sorcerer, and instead toiled among the SOC's cadre of gunslingers, administrators, and auxiliaries.

'Poor guy,' Britton said. 'Shame he's stuck working for a bastard like Harlequin. He's got the infantryman's job without the infantryman's badge.'

'Or the infantryman's brotherhood,' Cheatham said.

Britton nodded. 'Yeah,' he said. 'You're right, Dan.'

'Course I am, sir, that's why they assigned me to you. Somebody on the team has to know what the hell is going on.'

Britton nodded, trying to accept Cheatham's attempt to cheer him and failing. 'Well, let's go show some of that brotherhood. I'm camping out by Dawes's bed.'

Cheatham nodded. 'And that means we all are.'

Chapter Two
Loss

. . . that's crap! What choice do you really have if you don't want to join the army? Life as a Suppressed Marine is scarcely better than a prison inmate, and the civilian monitoring program at NIH spawns pariahs – broke and ostracized. A choice between bad and worse is no choice at all!

– Loretta Kiwan,
Vice President Council on Latent-American Rights
Appearing on WorldSpan Networks *Counterpoint*

Dawes stabilized enough to be moved to the proper infirmary at the 158th Fighter Wing. The entire team wanted to join Britton in his vigil beside Dawes's bed. He had to force them to stow their gear, shower, and change first. Britton skipped the shower and sat in his dirty flight suit, pistol still on his thigh, brooding, as Dawes stirred in drugged sleep.

He permitted himself the luxury of kicking off his boots as he reflected on the girl's death, too rattled to concentrate on the after-action report. A newspaper lay on the stand beside his chair, the front page reading MESCALERO INSURGENCY FLARES. TWO SOLDIERS KILLED IN SELFER AMBUSH. The article featured a picture of an Apache Selfer, his long hair whipped by a summoned storm cloud. Lightning arced from his fingers.

He looked at the headline. *They may send me there someday. How can I go after this?*

Eventually, exhaustion overcame grief, and Britton's head drooped to the windowsill. He was only dimly aware of Cheatham entering with a sleeping bag. 'Sent the rest off to bed,' the warrant officer said. 'No sense in all of us crowding in here.'

Britton mumbled thanks and drifted off to sleep.

A breeze washed over his face, and the low rumble of the salvage truck woke him. He opened his eyes, looking out the window to the flight line for his battered Kiowa, but there was no sign of the truck. His eyes swept over the digital billboard at the center of the tree-lined swath of lawn abutting the flight line. SOUTH BURLINGTON AIR NATIONAL GUARD, the sign read. 158TH FIGHTER WING. GREEN MOUNTAIN BOYS. The readout reported 0200 hours and 33 degrees Fahrenheit. A narrow concrete path led toward a set of trailers. U.S. ARMY SUPERNATURAL OPERATIONS CORPS (SOC), the sign above them read, LIAISON OFFICE.

The rumble that wasn't a truck engine and the breeze continued. Was Dawes snoring? Britton looked at the bed. Moonlight dusted through the window, outlining all in silver. Dawes slept; Cheatham was stretched in his sleeping bag on the floor.

The rumble pulsed. The gust of air hit him again, warm and foul.

Britton turned and stared into a black shape blocking the moonlight. Behind it, a vague rectangle hovered, its edges indistinct. Light wavered across its surface, dancing like television static. Through it he could see a vast plain, patchy with scrub grass.

Adrenaline bullied sleep aside. He jolted in his chair, and the black shape reared, snorting. Long horns corkscrewed toward him.

His mind recoiled, his skin going cold with shock. *This can't be real.*

An instant later, his training bulled the shock aside. *Later. Deal with thc threat. Go.*

He punched the creature hard on the snout, knuckles cracking against a plate of solid bone. The thing grunted and reeled away, stumbling into the corner. It vaguely resembled a bull, bunched shoulders hulking with muscle. Its slick hide shimmered and blended with the shadows, forcing Britton to squint to see it. Its broad snout snuffled, rumbling like the salvage truck.

He heard Cheatham shout, and called out, 'Give me a damn hand here!' as he pursued the thing, hammering it with his fists. It crouched, curling under the rain of blows. Reality shivered up his arm with each connecting punch. He wasn't dreaming.

Cheatham rushed to his side, seizing one of the horns. The thing heaved, tossing its head and sending the warrant officer sprawling across Dawes, who awoke with a yell. It stormed toward the flickering portal, which snapped shut, vanishing and plunging the room into darkness.

The creature turned, blinking in confusion. It lowed, a throaty mix of a moo and a growl. Britton drew his pistol and thumbed off the safety as it lowered its head and charged.

He twisted, avoiding the horns and catching the bony plate of the creature's forehead against his bruised ribs. They howled anew as the thing drove him to the floor. Britton couldn't see Cheatham or Dawes, and, not wanting to risk shooting them, he pounded its head with the pistol butt, jarring uselessly against the hard bone. He pivoted on his hips, unable to throw the creature off. It drew back its head, jaws opening to reveal rows of dark teeth.

Britton saw Cheatham rising beside Dawes's bed, well clear. He jammed the pistol into the thing's mouth and pulled the trigger. Its head whipped back and it fell over on its side, vomiting black blood. It lashed its tufted tail, kicked outward, and went still.

He leapt to his feet, training his pistol on it. His vision grayed out, and he awakened to a sense of drowning. An invisible tide suffocated him with its intensity. He felt his veins bulge with the force of the flow, penetrating his muscles, trilling in his nerves, saturating the pores of his skin. His legs went weak, and Cheatham gripped his elbow.

'You okay?' Cheatham asked.

Britton closed his eyes and cursed, feeling the tide pulse through him. He recalled the videos the army had made him watch, films with titles like *Basic Magical Indoctrination* and

Facing the Arcane. A drowning sensation was the first thing they stressed. Britton knew the invisible current he was feeling had a name.

Magic.

My God, he thought, *that was my gate. I brought that thing here*.

His stomach heaved. *I'm Latent. This can't be happening, not to me. Not now*.

He made for the chair. Cheatham's hand tightened on his elbow, holding him fast.

'Give me the gun, sir.' The warrant officer's voice was hard.

A gate snapped open just below the ceiling, hovered for a moment, then disappeared. Britton's shoulders spasmed as the current surged through him.

'It's you, sir, isn't it?' Cheatham asked.

Britton nodded. 'I can't control it. I feel sick . . .'

He heard shouting. People were coming.

'Just give me the gun, sir,' Cheatham said, 'and I'll help you sit down. You can rest for a minute, then we'll go get Harlequin.'

Britton recoiled. 'No, Dan! Portamancy's a prohibited school! They'll kill me!'

The door opened, and a sleepy-looking orderly in blue scrubs appeared. 'What the hell's . . .' He trailed off as he noticed the corpse that was not quite a bull, then fled.

'Jesus, sir,' Dawes said weakly from his bed, propped on his elbows. 'You're a fuckin' Probe? Warrant Officer Cheatham, you gotta—'

'Shut the hell up, Dawes,' Cheatham said. 'I've got this.'

'Let me go, Dan,' Britton said. 'You saw what they did to that girl. They'll kill me.'

'You don't know that, sir. You haven't attacked anyone with it.' Cheatham sounded lighthearted, but he held Britton's arm like a vise. He moved to block the door. 'Maybe they'll ship you off to one of those Marine Suppression Lances, or you can go into the monitoring program at NIH . . . Maybe they'll take you to that secret base and train you.'

'There is no secret base! You don't believe that conspiracy-theory crap! Probes don't get a break! They disappear!' Britton shouted. 'Christ, Dan! How long have we worked together? You've got to help me!'

Boots pounded in the hallway. Dawes sat up, wincing in pain, and shouted, 'In here! Help!'

Britton leveled the pistol at Cheatham's face. 'Let me go, Dan. Christ as my witness, I will shoot you.'

Cheatham didn't budge. 'Go ahead, sir. How far do you think you'll get? You give me the gun and turn yourself in now, and you have a chance. You run, you're already dead.'

Two Military Police officers appeared in the doorway, pistols drawn. One gasped at the sight of the creature. The other leveled his gun at Britton, 'Drop your weapon, sir! Get down on the ground! Right now!'

Another gate slid open to Britton's side. Beyond it, he could see the plain again, rough grasses rustling in the wind.

Britton's eyes flicked to the MPs, then to Cheatham. It was his chance to turn himself in, to lean on the system he'd faithfully served to protect him.

But his mind's eye was blotted out by the image of the dead girl's face. His ears rang with the sound of the single shot that cut off her life, echoing off the school's rooftop.

Cheatham grasped the pistol barrel, still pointed at his face, 'So, sir. You gonna shoot me?'

'Hell, Dan,' Britton said, 'you know I wouldn't shoot you.'

Britton let go of the pistol, slamming his knee into the warrant officer's groin, hauling Cheatham's body between himself and the MPs.

'Sorry, Dan,' Britton said, and shoved him hard into the MPs, then turned and ran for the gate.

Britton heard the sharp report of a pistol and felt a burning in his calf. He struck the gate, rippling edges breaking apart to admit him.

Oscar Britton landed hard on rough grass, pitching forward under an unfamiliar sky.

Chapter Three
The Other Side

. . . factors play into Manifestation. Sex and physique have a bearing. Calm males of larger size tend toward Terramancy. Women Manifest in Hydromancy or Physiomancy more frequently than men. Dreamers and mavericks wind up as Aeromancers. Caustic, passionate types show up as Pyromancers. The National Institute of Health continues with the famed Sierra Twenty-Six study group . . .

– Avery Whiting
Modern Arcana: Theory and Practice

Britton fell, skinning his hands.

He paused, breathing hard. All was silent and dark, a cool wind gently rippling over his back. He closed his eyes. His mind raced, trying to make sense of what had happened. The gunshot still rang in his ears, the shouts of the MPs, Cheatham's grip on his arm.

Breathe, he told himself, *just breathe*.

His heartbeat finally slowed, and he stood.

The gate was gone. The landscape was washed in bright light from a full moon, massive and close. The light mostly blotted out the weird stars, but he could make out a few, shining bigger than any he'd ever seen. He shivered as the breeze picked up. To one side, the plain ended at a line of smoothtrunked, straight evergreen trees stretching past his vision. On the other, it extended into darkness and the faint sound of rushing water. From somewhere in the forest, a bird called – a mournful sound, haunting and alien.

The magical tide still coursed through him. He could feel it bleeding into the air, mixing with the flow surrounding him, currents within currents.

Raw magic, heady and powerful.

It's all around me, he thought. *This is where it comes from*.

He sucked in air, the sweetest he'd ever tasted. It washed away his weariness. He blinked at the giant moon, marveling at its brightness. The ground glowed with vibrant color despite the dark.

One thing was clear. Wherever he was, it was not earth.

They'd talked about it in training, vague hints of the space where magic came from, but they'd also been clear that it was like the surface of the sun. No human could ever survive there, not for an instant.

But Britton was very much alive. And judging from the birdsong, so were others. What else was over here?

Enough. You've got bigger fish to fry. He inspected his injuries. The bullet had grazed his calf, digging a shallow furrow in the muscle. The wound bled slow and steady. His hands were badly abraded. His landing had shredded his socks, skinning his feet. Even pain was a newly heightened experience here; the intensity of feeling overwhelmed him.

He limped toward the sound of running water.

After a few minutes, the sound grew louder, chiming like bells. Moonlight sparkled on a rushing stream. The grass grew shorter and softer as the ground dipped to form banks dotted with smooth pebbles, shining like diamonds under the moon's glow. Fireflies darted above the water, bright with flashing patterns – purple, red, bright blue. He stared, amazed at the clarity of his vision in the strange air. After a moment, he realized that the fireflies were actually tiny birds, jeweled feathers dancing with inner light, pointed crystal beaks opening and closing silently. Their wings blurred in tiny circles, sounding faintly like clinking glasses.

Hard rocks ground into his feet as he picked his way to the streambed. The glowing birds scattered at his approach.

He thrust his hands into the cool water, the touch of the

liquid as amazing as it was painful. He sat, hypnotized by the sensation, for a full minute before he brought his hands together, washing them clean. He took a double handful of water and drank, thrilling at the sharp, metallic flavor.

He turned to the slowly bleeding wound in his calf. He washed it, the water simultaneously agonizing and thrilling the wound. He took off one tattered sock, rinsed it as best he could, then tied it tightly around the calf. The fabric went tacky with blood, but the fibers sank into the furrow, sealing it temporarily.

He stood, the wind whipping over him, his mind going over the events of the past few hours. 'I don't believe this,' he said, his words carrying on the air.

'Dun beleeve thass . . .' a high-pitched keening answered, mocking his words. Across the stream, the moonlight silhouetted a cluster of horselike shapes. Each snout terminated in a single pointed spike-shaped tooth. Long catlike tails lashed as they sniffed the air.

'Dun beleeve thass?' the creatures crooned. One bent to lap the water.

The rest jogged forward, pausing and sniffing the water's surface before splashing across.

Britton took a step backward, his calf reminding him of the wound. 'Oh, God.'

'Aw gud aw gud aw gud . . .' the things keened excitedly, advancing to a trot. The two closest lowered their long necks and put on speed.

Britton turned and ran.

He ignored his calf, running for all he was worth. The rough edges of the grass sawed at his feet. He could hear the pack behind him, gaining steadily.

He risked a look over his shoulder. They were on his heels, necks straining, wind coursing through tufts of spotted hair. Their hooves pounded the ground, nostrils flaring, wicked distortions somewhere between demon and horse. The single spike tooth on each snout jutted toward his back.

He put on a burst of speed, his calf screaming. He felt the magical tide surge with his mounting terror. The tree line remained far away. He'd never make it.

He heard a snort. Hot breath gusted against his neck.

He cried out, and the pack answered him with keening howls. His magical tide answered as well, exploding and rippling out from him through the interlocking streams all around, opening a gate a few yards to his left.

He pivoted sharply, running for it. He felt one of the spike teeth slice through the air behind him. The pack keened in frustration, sliding as they turned to follow.

The change in direction bought him a few moments. He closed the distance, shouting as he leapt through a gate for the second time that night.

Chapter Four
Homecoming

Legal Schools:	***Prohibited Schools:***
Pyromancy – Fire Magic	*Negramancy – Black Magic/ Witching*
Hydromancy – Water Magic	*Necromancy – Death Magic*
Terramancy – Earth Magic	*Portamancy – Gate Magic*
Aeromancy – Air Magic	*Sentient Elemental Conjuration*
Physiomancy – Body Magic	

Prohibited Practices (please see applicable Geneva Convention Amendments):
Terramantic Animal Control (Whispering)
Offensive Physiomancy (Rending)

– Magical School Reference Wallet Card
Publication of the Supernatural Operations Corps

Britton's feet slapped tarmac, and he jogged to a stop, wincing at scattered sharp rocks.

He recognized Route 7, snaking south between the base and his parents' home in Shelburne, a few miles down the rural Vermont road. The sky was still dark, the road empty. He ran off the road to crouch in the bushes. Sharp branches tore at his flight suit, and the early frost blasted his feet. The gate shimmered a few feet off the road. The demon-horses sniffed tentatively from the other side, moving toward it, darting away. A moment later, the portal snapped shut. It reappeared to his left, bathing the bushes in flickering light, then vanished again.

It's responding to my fear, he thought. *I have to calm myself.*

He closed his eyes, took a deep breath, and failed to relax.

Enough, he thought, *focus on what you can control. You're injured and cold. You might make it through the night, but you'll be caught in the daylight. You need shoes, and you need cover. They're on the lookout for a soldier, so you need to get out of this uniform. Go.*

He followed the road toward his parents' home. If he made good enough time, he could use the spare key and grab clothing before they woke.

He had to dive for cover twice at the sound of approaching cars. He moved quickly, to warm himself as much as to cover distance. The flight suit kept him relatively warm, but after twenty minutes, he could no longer feel his hands or feet. It was a mixed blessing; his numb feet let him move faster, no longer reporting the pain of stepping on twigs and roots.

The numbness and rhythm of his movement freed his mind to reflect on how, in just a few hours, magic had taken him from army officer to fugitive.

Stop it, he told himself. *If you think about this crap, it'll slow you down. If you slow down, they'll catch you. If they catch you, you know what they'll do.*

You're running. So run, damn you. Run.

He forced all he had lost from his mind and moved as fast as the cover allowed. By the time Route 7 arrived in Shelburne, orange streaked the sky, and he could feel the rising sun on his back.

Route 7 gave out onto an unpaved rural route, and minutes later he stood exhausted in the driveway of his family home. As the numbness abated in the warming air, his feet reminded him of hours running across frozen grass and rocks. He looked up at the cracking paint and patched screening of the house and felt the tides of magic ebb, lulled by the familiar surroundings.

Familiar, but never a real home.

The reason for that crouched before the steps leading to

the wraparound porch. Britton felt his pulse quicken, and the tide of magic surged anew.

It couldn't have been later than six, but his father was awake and gardening despite the early fall frost. Stanley Britton's pastel clothing flapped off his skinny body. Cheatham had once told him that there were two kinds of Marines: big and mean, or skinny and mean.

Old age had cemented his father in the skinny-and-mean variety. The retired colonel had a blade of a nose, sunken eyes, and a hard jaw, clenched to show that he still considered himself on duty. A small gold cross gleamed from his neck, refracting the growing sunlight.

Stanley moved away from the steps, attacking a line of withered dandelions. He brandished a spade like a weapon, knifing into the cold ground. Britton crept up the porch behind him.

Stanley stiffened. 'Jesus withers the fig tree and leaves me with all these damned weeds. Holy Christ, give me the strength to put up with this crap.'

Britton froze, then realized his father was talking to himself. Stanley continued to follow the dandelions around the porch. Britton slipped inside, ran past the kitchen, and took the worn stairs two at a time up to his old room.

His father had converted it to storage the day Britton shipped out; the floor was heaped with cardboard boxes. A yellowing army promotional poster depicting an Apache attack helicopter was the only hint that Britton had ever lived here.

He rummaged through a box at the base of his mother's wardrobe, packed with clothing intended for Goodwill that she'd never gotten around to giving up. He shrugged out of his flight suit and into a pair of jeans and paint-stained T-shirt. It was inadequate to the cold outside, but it was clean. More importantly, he was out of uniform and would attract no more attention than any black man in Vermont. He kicked the flight suit behind a pile of boxes and grabbed a pair of his father's shoes and old wool socks. The shoes were a half size too large and without tread, but he was grateful to have something covering his ragged feet.

He returned to the stairs, stumbling in the oversized shoes. He bent to take them off when he heard his mother's familiar hum.

Get moving! his mind screamed at him. *You have to get out of here!* But Britton drowned in the nostalgia evoked by the smell of baking and his mother's contented hum. His legs refused to move.

Desda appeared in the hallway and froze. He recognized her apron from his youngest days: a washed-out heart with the words KISS THE COOK! in letters so faded that he read them from memory. Her gray hair was pinned into an untidy bun, her body still strong and thin despite her years.

He composed himself and descended the rest of the steps.

'Oscar!' she cried, flinging her arms around his neck. Her nose only came up to his chest, and he grinned in spite of his misery.

'Why didn't you tell us you were coming?' she asked.

He paused, trying to fix the smell of her in his memory: perfume, sugar, and folded egg yolks.

He crushed her to him. 'I love you, Mom.'

'I know, sweetie. I love you, too. Oscar, I can't breathe.'

No time for goodbyes! his mind yelled. *Every second you stay here brings you closer to getting caught! Run, you damned fool!* But he didn't. He held his mother, even when the screen-door hinges announced Stanley's entrance.

He kept his eyes closed but felt his father's disapproving presence and the rage boiling in response.

'What's going on, Oscar?' Stanley asked, coming to stand beside his wife. He kept his voice mild, but Britton could feel the judgment just below the surface. 'You get yourself into some kind of trouble?'

'Stop it, Stanley!' she scolded.

Stanley waved his hand as if brushing away a fly. 'What are you doing here?'

'Dad, can't I just come home? Can't a son visit his family?' Oscar asked.

'That's crap. You never come home unless you want something,' Stanley replied.

'No, Dad, *that's* crap. I never come home because it's like walking into a freezer.'

'Come on, you two.' Desda intervened. 'Oscar's home for five minutes, and . . .'

But by now the familiar pattern was already playing out; both of the Britton men had their dander up.

'You've had a standing invitation!' Stanley said through gritted teeth. 'I invite you to First Baptist every Sunday, and . . .'

'Oh, that's a great idea! I can sit next to you while you pretend to be Christian.'

'What the hell is that supposed to mean?' Stanley asked, the cords on his neck standing out.

Britton held his mother close. Years and bruises had taught him that just about anything could set Stanley off. Better not to risk opening his mouth. But the events of the last few hours, and his one hope of refuge evaporating, made him careless.

'Where in the Bible does it tell you to hit your wife? Where does it tell you to hit your son?' Oscar asked.

'Oscar, please!' Desda's voice was pleading.

But the magical tide didn't care. It surged with Britton's fury and sadness. He pushed against it, but it was useless. The air in the kitchen archway shimmered, folded in on itself, and resolved into the static light of an open gate.

Stanley's eyes shot wide, but Desda continued to look at her son.

'I'm sorry, Mom,' Oscar said quickly.

'Sweet Jesus,' Stanley said, backing away.

'What's wrong?' Desda asked, turning. She froze as she saw the gate.

'Oh my God,' Stanley breathed. 'You're one of those . . . one of those damned Selfers. This is un-friggin-believable!' He invoked his single response to all unexpected events – anger, but still moved backward, bumping the front door. He fumbled for the handle.

'My God, Oscar,' Desda whispered, 'are you doing that?'

'I'm sorry, Mom,' Oscar said, his eyes wet. 'I love you.'

'I don't understand,' she whispered. 'This isn't right. I'm your mother, Oscar, I would have known.'

Stanley tore his eyes off the gate. 'For Christ's sake, Dez! Get the hell away from him!' he shouted, reaching for her but not daring to come closer.

Oscar could hear faint keening from the gate. The demon-horses were not far away.

Desda didn't move. 'No, no. This isn't right. Not right.'

'It's just a thing, like acne or chicken pox,' Oscar said with a certainty he didn't feel. 'I don't have a choice. It's going to be okay.'

She continued to shake her head.

The gate flickered, snapped shut, reopened deeper into the kitchen, then disappeared.

With the gate gone, Stanley found his fight at last.

'Get your damned hands off her!' he shouted, leaping forward and grabbing Oscar's arms, shouldering Desda out of the way and knocking her to the floor. For all the strength in Stanley's callused hands, he might as well have grabbed an oak.

Oscar ignored his father, reaching for his mother. Stanley snarled, pounding against his son's massive chest. Oscar stepped back, raising his hands. 'Stop, Dad. This is stupid.'

Desda pulled at her husband. 'No! No! No!'

'Shut up!' Stanley screamed. 'Get out of here! Leave us alone!'

Oscar tried to move to the door, but Stanley blocked his way.

Oscar backpedaled. Was Desda screaming at him or Stanley? He tried to see her face, but Stanley punched him in his mouth, rocking his head back. He took another step backward, caught his heel on the staircase, and went down hard, bruising his back. Stanley followed, punches raining down.

Desda screamed, the sound merging with the roaring blood in Oscar's ears. The magical tide drowned him. His skin began to burn. *Am I going nova?* he wondered. He had heard that Selfers, unable to control their magic, sometimes succumbed to its power, burning themselves to a crisp. A gate half opened above him and vanished. He saw through the window as it reappeared on the lawn, grew, and disappeared.

'Dad! Get off! You're hurting me!' he shouted. 'I'm trying to leave!'

'Fucker!' Spittle landed on his shaved head.

Stanley punctuated his cursing with punches. Somewhere the buzz that wasn't quite a scream droned on. The magic pulsed.

'Dad! *No!'*

Oscar lunged forward, throwing an elbow into what he hoped was his father's chest. The blow struck Stanley's nose with a sickening crunch. Blood sprayed from his father's face. Stanley's eyes crossed as he staggered backward, arms pin-wheeling.

A gate opened wide behind him.

Oscar reached for his father's wrist. 'Dad, look out!'

His fingers brushed the tips of Stanley's fingers as his father half stepped, half fell into the gate, tumbling onto the grass beyond and sliding to a halt.

Oscar watched through the portal's static sheen as his father looked around, his eyes huge. Suddenly, they shot wide and Stanley scrambled to his feet. 'Oscar . . .' he said.

Oscar could hear keening voices approaching fast. 'Uskar . . . Uskar . . .'

'Oscar!' Stanley shrieked, then the gate snapped shut, and his father was gone.

Oscar stood staring at empty air.

Desda reached one hand to her mouth. Her other hand reached out to the empty air. 'Oscar?' she whispered, 'Where did he go? Where did Stanley go?'

Britton wrestled to reopen the gate. 'Come on,' he muttered. 'Open, damn you.' He pried with his fingers at the empty air. Somewhere beyond it, his father was trapped, possibly dying.

'Open!' he shrieked. 'Open the fuck back up!'

Nothing. The tide churned within him, eddying uselessly. A gate opened beside his mother, but vanished before he could turn to face it.

'Where is he?' Desda repeated.

Britton shook his head, choking back a sob. 'I don't know, Mom.'

Her knees wobbled, and she sat down hard, her hands still not moving – one on her mouth, the other pointing. 'You have to . . . you have to bring him back,' she whispered. A tear escaped from a corner of her eye. 'Bring him back!'

'I can't.' His voice sounded flat in his own ears.

'What do you mean?' she asked, finally lowering her hands. 'Open it up and get him back!'

He shook his head, his hands making useless circles at his sides. 'I don't know how. I can't control it.'

She sat in silence for a moment. Then she made a sound between a scream and a growl.

'Mom?' he asked, kneeling and reaching for her. She blinked at the empty space where the gate had closed, her head shaking slowly, her mouth wide.

He stood and took a step toward her. 'Mom?'

Her head jerked toward him, her expression blank. Then her eyes registered shocked recognition, and she scrambled backward, kicking out at him. 'You get away from me!'

His father had vanished. Britton couldn't save him.

His mother shrieked.

The need to run overcame all else. He surrendered to it and let his legs carry him away from his mother's accusing eyes.

Chapter Five
Flight

. . . Latency presents a challenge to the American people and the world as unique and as dangerous as the atom bomb. It represents the greatest opportunity, but also the greatest threat we have faced as a nation since the first atomic weapon was tested in 1945. Like it or not – Magic is the new nuke.

– Senator Nancy Whalen
Chairman, Senate Subcommittee on the Great Reawakening

Oscar Britton's bloodied feet slid inside his father's shoes, pounding down the road toward the town where he'd grown up.

If the army had taught him one thing, it was how to run, and he did it well despite the screaming of his wounded calf. Somewhere behind him was a horrible thing, something he didn't want to think about, and if he could just keep running fast enough, maybe that thing would never catch up to him.

The tides of magic went with him. Gates snapped open, teasing him with the prospect of saving his father, never staying open long enough to admit him.

Sirens sounded, drawing nearer. He threw himself into a ditch, watching over the rise as two police cruisers swept past, heading for his parents' house. He bolted back to the street, racing onward.

And then he stopped, bathed in the glow of a convenience-store sign. He knew this parking lot. His friend Rob Dausman had introduced him to smoking dope here, hidden behind a bread truck and pretending the drug affected him more than it did.

For Britton, it had been a one-time deal, but Rob had made it a lifestyle. That lifestyle had bound him to this spot though he'd moved into the store and behind the counter. Britton could see him through the window, running a hand through his curly blond hair as he laughed with a customer. Britton felt a wave of relief at that smile. With Rob it had never mattered that Britton was black, or twice his size, or better in school. Britton realized why his footsteps had brought him here. If there was a person in the world who would not judge him, it was Rob.

He felt the blast of heated air strike him as the automatic doors slid aside. Elevator music bleated over the speakers. Fluorescent lighting reflected off rows of eyedrops, canned soup, and shampoo.

The customer, a middle-aged woman with short hair and a thick middle, was buying a pint of ice cream and laughing with Rob. Britton marveled at them; the world ticked on, blind to the tectonic shift in his life.

Britton looked up at the TV screen hanging from a corner of the ceiling. The news blared a block-lettered footer: RIOTS IN MONTMARTRE DISTRICT OF PARIS. SELFERS BATTLE CALIPHATE POLICE.

The screen cut to shots of 'Djinn Born' Selfers standing atop a burning armored police vehicle, SUPPRESSION MAGIQUE printed on the side. French police in riot gear and Islamic *Mutawaeen* religious police swarmed around it. The Djinn-Born were bared to the waist and covered in winding tattooed Arabic script. One spat fire over the police. The other froze a *Mutawaeen* officer with a touch, then kicked his crystalline form to splinters.

When Britton took his eyes off the TV, both Rob and the customer were staring at him, wide eyed.

'Dude,' Rob breathed.

The woman moved forward. Britton lifted his hands, but she only pushed past him and ran out the sliding doors, catching them with her shoulders in her haste to exit. He heard her car door slam and the engine start, and looked back to the TV as she roared out of the parking lot.

The news had been replaced by a mug shot. Britton recognized the image from his military Common Access Card. ACTION 6 NEWS ALERT! READ THE SCROLLING TEXT. $100,000 REWARD OFFERED FOR INFORMATION LEADING TO THE CAPTURE OF A SELFER FUGITIVE IN YOUR AREA. OSCAR BRITTON ESCAPED FROM MILITARY CUSTODY AND IS CURRENTLY AT LARGE. IF YOU SEE THIS INDIVIDUAL, PLEASE CONTACT THE AUTHORITIES IMMEDIATELY. THIS SELFER'S BLACK MAGIC IS NOT CONTROLLED AND HE SHOULD BE CONSIDERED EXTREMELY DANGEROUS! DO NOT ATTEMPT TO APPREHEND HIM ON YOUR OWN!

A toll-free number followed.

Britton looked back to Rob, who looked away, blushing. 'It's been running all night,' Rob said, then his eyes widened.

Britton followed Rob's gaze over his shoulder. An open gate glittered just inside the store's entrance.

'Dude,' Rob said again. 'This is not good.'

'Rob,' Britton managed, 'please.'

'You've got to call somebody. This is some serious shit right here. Man, I had no idea you were . . . I mean, holy crap.'

Britton took a step and winced as Rob stepped back in perfect synchronicity, fetching up against a shelf and initiating a small avalanche of cigarette cartons. 'Rob. It's me, man. It's Oscar.'

Rob nodded, forcing a smile. 'I know, man, I know. It's not a big deal. I'm just saying. You have to call somebody.' He pointed a trembling finger at a black pay phone below the TV.

Rob's hand darted under the counter. Britton thought he might produce the store's sawed-off, but Rob slapped two quarters on the counter. 'There you go, man,' he said eagerly. 'Call's on me. Don't sweat it.' He looked guilty. 'I don't even want the reward.'

But Britton didn't hear. *Don't waste any more time*, his mind said. *You're alone*.

Profound weariness followed. His shoulders sagged. For the first time in his life, Britton wasn't sure that he wanted to live.

He slapped the quarters up into Rob's face. Rob threw his

arms up and crouched, but Britton had already picked up the pay phone. He stared at the receiver.

Rob was right. Britton did have to make this call. Would they kill him? Probably. But maybe that's what needed to happen. His father was dead by his hand. He couldn't control what was clearly a dangerous weapon. Why was he prioritizing his own life over others? What gave him that right? That was why they called them Selfers.

He saw his father's face as the gate closed, heard his screaming over the keening of the demon-horses. He couldn't bear to face it, and instead took a deep breath and tried to rebuild his world.

Baby steps, he thought. *You're standing in a convenience store. You're staring at a pay phone*. Even that was too much, so he concentrated on smaller details. *The phone receiver smells like stale beer. Weeds grow through cracks in the parking lot outside the window.*

But reality would not be denied. *You're Latent. You're a Probe. You're not in control of your magic. The army has rejected you. You've killed your father. Your mother is terrified of you. Even Rob is scared of you. You're a fugitive. Your life has changed forever.*

And, most importantly, *you're alone*.

His knees buckled under the enormity of the realization.

There was a click, and a woman's grainy voice answered. 'Operator.'

'South Burlington ANG base,' Britton replied. 'SOC liaison office.' His voice sounded alien through the earpiece. Someone else was talking to the operator, someone far calmer than Oscar Britton – Selfer, Probe, and murderer. The thought steadied him. That someone else could handle the situation. He would just listen.

'South Burlington Air National Guard?' the operator asked. 'I have the main switchboard number here.'

'I need the Supernatural Operations Corps liaison office,' he said. 'There's been an incident. This is an emergency.'

The receiver went silent. He was about to ask if the operator was still there when she said, 'You should have called nine-one-one.'

'I didn't,' he answered. 'I called you.'

There was a click, and the sound of ring tones.

Another woman's voice answered, clearer than the last. 'SOC, Captain Nereid.'

He paused. Self-preservation cried out to hang up the phone and start running again. But fatigue cloaked him like a thick blanket.

'This is Lieutenant Britton, 158th Ops Support Flight.'

After a pause punctuated by the tapping of a keyboard, the voice answered, coldly professional. 'Lieutenant Britton, we've been very worried about you. I'm glad you called.'

Stanley Britton's screams echoed in his ears. Britton's voice broke as he answered. 'Yes.'

Sympathy crept into Nereid's voice. 'We know what's happened, Oscar. Are you all right?'

He nodded, tears flowing now, not realizing she couldn't see him.

Her voice grew urgent. 'Oscar. All you have to do is stay where you are. It's going to be all right. Can you hear me? We're coming to get you, and we're going to help you. All you have to do is not move, and you'll be fine. Do you understand me?'

'I'm sorry,' he sobbed. 'I didn't mean to hurt anybody. I'm trying to do the right thing.' He cringed at the pathetic whine in his voice.

Her voice was firm. 'I need you to calm down and stick by that phone, okay? Whatever you do, do not surrender yourself to the police. The police may not understand what you've done like we do. Should you see police vehicles, hide as best you can until we can get to you. Do you understand? Hello? Hello?'

The kernel of self-preservation blossomed. His mind conjured images of Harlequin descending, lightning crackling from his fingertips; the Probe girl on the roof lying helpless in a spreading pool of blood.

Oscar Britton might have a dangerous, uncontrolled power, but the army murdered little girls.

What the hell are you doing? His mind screamed at him. *You damned idiot! Run!*

He dropped the receiver, letting it hang.

He turned to see two police cars whip into the parking lot, screeching to a halt. Rob was gone.

Four uniformed officers exited the vehicles, guns drawn, and raced for the door.

Chapter Six
You Ran

Magic? Fuck that. I've got 5.56 millimeters of magic right here. Once I pull this trigger, no spell in the world is going to stop your brains from winding up all over the wall behind you. There's been a reawakening all right. We woke up our warrior hearts. We remembered Guadalcanal. We remembered Fallujah. We remembered what it means to be a United States Marine.

– Lance Corporal Jimmy 'Gonzo' Gonzales
Second Marine Expeditionary Force,
Thirteenth Suppression Lance

Britton dove over the counter, flipping and landing face-first on the rubber matting. He heard shouts as he crawled to his knees, brushing his nose against a code-locked safe.

Beside it was a sawed-off shotgun. The breech was open, shells loaded into both barrels. All he had to do was snap it closed, stand, and fight.

He couldn't run forever. Why had Captain Nereid warned him not to surrender to the police? So Harlequin could have the pleasure of killing him instead or hauling him before a court-martial to do the deed officially?

He glanced over the counter. The police officers advanced at a crouch. Two leveled pistols. The other two followed, with shotguns ready.

Just a few hours ago, he'd been on the same side as the

police. Crime needed a motive. All he'd ever wanted to do was the right thing. Rage and terror competed in his gut.

Rage won by a nose. The magic rose. This time he welcomed it.

Screw the gun. I don't need it.

He closed his eyes and let the tide flow. He could feel the current reaching out toward the cops. He stood, arms spread. The air behind the policemen reverberated. They spun, crying out.

He hesitated at their cries. There had to be a difference between him and what he'd always been taught Selfers were. *You didn't kill your father on purpose*, he reminded himself. *That was an accident. You don't hurt innocent people. If you forget that, you really are a Selfer.*

He struggled against the magical tide. One of the cops turned back to Britton and fired. The bullet punched a hole in the sliding door and buried itself in the counter.

Britton didn't flinch, overwhelmed by the magic coursing through him. He felt like his veins would burst, his cells pried apart. He desperately tried to shunt the tide back, but it would not be denied, howling toward the policemen.

Behind the cops, the air pulsed open into a shining gate.

Another cop leveled a black shotgun through the glass display window. 'Selfer son of a bitch! Switch it off!'

I'm trying, Britton thought, *but now it's out, and I can't stop it.* He could feel tendrils of magic slide through the gate, reaching beyond.

The shotgun boomed, turning the window into spinning fragments.

The magic found what it sought and hauled it through the gate.

The portal spasmed and pushed something tall and strange into the world. The cops turned, Britton forgotten.

The thing from the gate was at least seven feet tall, covered with feathers so dark they absorbed light, each veined and edged in bright red, glowing bloody. A spade-shaped crest of the same color crowned its head. It took a tentative step on a leathery leg with dark purple skin. One claw hovered in the air. Its head flicked left and right, black eyes regarding the policemen, swinging a dark purple beak as long and sharp as any sword.

'Christ,' one of the cops said, raising his pistol.

The giant bird flicked its head again, the narrow throat ballooning to basketball size, tiny black feathers stretched so far apart that Britton could see purple skin taut beneath.

The swollen throat let go its cargo, emitting a sound so deep that Britton felt, rather than heard it, sending visible ripples through the air. The sonic boom shattered what remained of the windows. The hedges lining the storefront were knocked flat, the doors knocked off their sliding course, dropping slowly inward. The cops were blown off their feet, ears bleeding.

Showered with shattered glass, Britton ducked behind the counter. When he rose, the tide was already building again. The cops lay moaning. The bird paced across the parking lot.

Britton's ears rang, his eyes dry from the wind gust. He turned and ran, bursting into the stockroom. Wire shelves lined the walls, piled high with cardboard boxes bulging with paper towels, canned food, and over-the-counter medicine.

He hit the back door, bursting it open and running into the warming dawn air.

And straight into Harlequin, emerging from the cargo doors of an unmarked white van.

Harlequin's digital-camouflage uniform was neatly pressed. His polished boots reflected the sun. A pale-faced Dan Cheatham stood beside him, carrying his carbine.

I was always a friend to you, Britton thought as his eyes bored into Cheatham's. *We were a team*.

Cheatham's gaze broke. 'I . . . Sir, I . . .'

'See, here's the problem,' Harlequin cut him off. 'You ran, Oscar. Warrant Officer Cheatham advised you to report to me immediately. You elected not to do that.'

Britton could feel the eddy of Harlequin's magic. The wind about the Aeromancer whipped into a funnel, swirling dust and pebbles over his head.

The tide of magic overwhelmed Britton's senses. *Help me*, he mouthed, his body burning with energy. He sank to his knees. *I can't stop it. It's killing me*.

Harlequin's brow furrowed, the dust devil collapsed.

Britton's tide rolled back, and he fell forward, gasping. He gulped air, feeling his magical flow intersected by Harlequin's, rolled back. Britton's training had taught him to expect that as well. They used it on the Marines in Suppression Lances and those civilians who enrolled in NIH's monitoring program. Magical Suppression.

Cheatham leveled his carbine and advanced a pace.

Britton stood weakly, pointing at the carbine. 'You don't need that.'

'I'm afraid we do,' Harlequin said. 'As long as my magic is tied up Suppressing yours, I have to keep you under guard.'

'No,' Britton said. 'I called. I turned myself in.'

Harlequin shook his head. 'Dan tells me you Manifested at around 0200. It's now roughly 0800, You're miles off post. You ran.'

'What the hell did you expect me to do? I'm a Probe. You're just going to kill me anyway. I needed to see to my parents.'

'Yeah, that worked out well,' Harlequin said. 'We now have another incident here, a murder. I know what you did to your father.'

'That wasn't my fault! He attacked me . . . I couldn't control it . . .'

Harlequin folded his arms over his chest. 'That's why we always follow orders. I guess that's something you big army guys never understood. Well, in the SOC, we live by our orders. Because, when we don't, people die. You decided that you knew better. As a direct result, your father is dead. This is what happens when you run, Oscar.'

'I called the SOC at South Burlington!' Britton shouted, inching backward. 'I talked to Nereid! I just tried to surrender! Ask her!'

Harlequin reached into a trouser leg pocket and produced a pair of plastic zip cuffs. 'She radioed, Oscar. I know you called. That's the only reason you're still alive. You Manifested in a prohibited school. You ran. You killed your father. Act like a soldier and man up to it.'

Britton knew he wouldn't get three steps in any direction before Cheatham put a bullet in his back. 'You're going to kill me,' he said. 'Maybe not here, but you'll do it.'

Harlequin shrugged. 'That's for a court-martial to decide. For now, you go to the stockade. Get on your knees and put your hands behind your head.'

'Freeze!' Two of the cops burst through the door, pistols leveled at Britton's back. 'Hands in the air!'

'Damn it, wave off!' Harlequin shouted. 'I'm army Supernatural Ops! I'm taking this man in!'

'He injured a police officer,' one cop said. The other lowered his pistol, confused.

Surprised, Cheatham pointed his carbine at the cops. The one with the raised pistol reacted instinctively, pointing his weapon at Cheatham.

If you go with him, you're dead, Britton thought. He spelled it out for you – you Manifested in a prohibited school, you ran, you killed your father. No court-martial in the country would let you off for that. He thought of Cheatham's grip on his elbow, his father's flailing fists, Rob slapping two shiny quarters on the counter, the girl's corpse on the roof. The army had been the only home he'd had outside the house in Shelburne. *It's all gone. Move, and quickly.*

Britton took a step back alongside the cop with the raised gun and chopped down with both hands, striking the policeman's wrists, sending the weapon spinning. Then he ducked around the corner of the building.

Harlequin cursed, conjuring up the dust devil. Britton felt the magical current surge back into him as the Suppression dropped away. Britton heard the crack of a bullet tearing into the building's corner. Britton knew that Dan was a better shot than that.

Britton raced into the front parking lot, surprising the other two cops. One was leaning over the other among the flattened azaleas, bandaging the prone man's bleeding ears.

His partner spotted Britton and shouted. The other cop turned, dropped the medical tape, and fumbled with his holstered sidearm. The magical tide responded and opened a gate between them as the cop drew and fired, the bullet passing harmlessly into the other world. From behind, the gate was a shimmering rectangle of air. Britton couldn't see the television static surface or the landscape beyond. The gates apparently had a facing – front and back.

He ran for a cruiser, lights still flashing, engine running, and passenger door open. A computer keyboard and screen covered the center console. An empty shotgun sheath stood beside it, blocking Britton's plan to throw himself across and reach the driver's seat. He turned to run around the vehicle.

A crack of thunder stopped him.

'And you told me that you turned yourself in,' Harlequin said. The captain floated above the store's russet-shingled roof. The wind whipped around him, stripping leaves from the trees. Above Harlequin's head was a black cloud, out of place in the placid sky. Light churned in its dark recesses.

A sheet of rain shot from the cloud to lash Britton's face, leaving dry ground just a foot beyond him. The cops stood below Harlequin's polished boots, looking up in awe.

'Believe me, I'd far rather bring you in,' Harlequin shouted over the gusting wind, 'but if you take one more step, I will cook your sorry Probe ass. It's over, Oscar. Get on your knees and put your hands behind your head.'

Britton backed away from the cruiser, lining up with the driver's-side door.

The cloud opened like a locket. Boiling light swept out with a deafening crack, shaking the ground. Britton shielded his eyes against the flash and spray of shattered asphalt. When he opened his eyes, the hair on his shins was smoldering. A two-foot crater had rent the parking lot. The smell of ozone lingered in the air.

'Get away from the car, or I won't miss next time,' Harlequin said. 'Knees, damn it. I'm tired of this.'

Britton measured the distance. He couldn't get to the car, open the door, and get inside in time.

He sank to his knees.

'Smartest thing you've done all damn day,' Harlequin said, descending toward him, the cloud trailing. 'Hands over your head, Oscar.'

As Britton raised his hands, he caught a flash of black and red in his peripheral vision. He stood and raced for it, clapping his hands and calling. The giant bird-thing froze, its sword beak pointing toward him.

'Damn it, Oscar!' Harlequin yelled. Britton felt the hairs all over his body stand on end as electricity arced around him. He froze, wincing, waiting for his skin to burst into flame.

But the strike never came.

Harlequin blazed in the sky, wreathed in crackling electricity. The cloud expanded, haloing him in gray. 'The thing that burns me is that you think I'm the bad guy. You're the walking time bomb who has already killed one person and now wants a chance to spread more of it around. I'm not the bad guy, Oscar. You are. And I'm not going to let you hurt anyone else.' He spread his hands, electricity shooting from the storm cloud up his arms to buzz along his fingertips.

He dove.

Britton raced toward the bird, motionless on a single purple leg. Its long neck lowered menacingly, the throat puffing out in warning.

Harlequin's shadow overtook him, the conjured cloud covering the sun. The Aeromancer shot past him, spinning in the air and touching down on the tarmac between Britton and the bird, one hand and knee on the ground, his body coiled to spring, bristling with blue lightning.

Britton stopped short, scraping his feet, flinging himself toward the cruiser. He heard the electric sizzle as Harlequin sprang airborne behind him, closing the distance like a dive-bomber.

A boom sounded. Britton felt as if a giant hand had swatted him. He turned in the air, his back slamming against the car door, shattering the window. The rippling air caught Harlequin, spiraling him into the store's roof, sending shingles flying. The storm cloud dissipated, drifting apart on a suddenly calm breeze.

The bird took a lurching step, its throat smooth once again, stabbing the air with its huge beak.

Britton scrambled to his feet, ears ringing. He fumbled for the door handle, wincing at the pain in his shoulders as he threw himself into the seat and put the car in gear. Harlequin stirred weakly on the store's roof. One of the cops helped Cheatham scramble up the air-conditioning unit to reach him. The other ran toward Britton, shouting.

He stopped short as a gate opened in front of him, closed, then reappeared a few feet to one side of the cruiser.

Britton gunned the engine, leaving patches of smoking rubber as he drove the car through the gate, the static light washing over the hood.

The convenience store, cops, and soldiers all vanished behind him as the world beyond bumped beneath his tires.

Chapter Seven

Gone to Ground

That's the thing with you leftists. You shed copious tears for the Apache. You bemoan the crushing of 'native ways' that have more to do with drinking and gambling than whatever you're imagining. You want an exemption to the McGauer-Linden Act for them, but you don't get it. I've kicked through barricades of burning tires in Mescalero. I've run and gunned against Selfers and their 'Mountain Gods' in the Chiricahua passes. You think Apache magic is all horses, scenic vistas, and flowing black hair. It's not – it's fire and blood and rending teeth. You want to preserve it, but you wouldn't last thirty seconds within a mile of it. You're like people admiring a caged tiger. You ooh and ah over a pretty thing that wants to kill you.

– Major 'Icebreaker' (call sign)
Supernatural Operations Corps Liaison Officer (LNO)
Bureau of Indian Affairs, Mescalero Reservation Task Force

Britton could hear shearing metal as the uneven ground ripped off pieces of the undercarriage. The radio hissed static. The cruiser bumped to a halt.

Dawn had come to the other side as well. The plain came alive beneath it, sawtooth grass flecked with tiny red and yellow flowers he had missed in the darkness. It rolled out for miles, ending at a line of rocky foothills. Currents of magical energy eddied all around him. He leaned out the cruiser's broken window, looking behind him. The gate still shimmered. The cop stared through it, gaping.

'You want magic?' Britton shouted at him. 'Come and get it, you bastard!'

If the cop heard, he gave no sign.

'Baztaad . . . commageddit . . . ?' keened a voice.

Three of the demon-horses sniffed toward the car. One poked at the passenger door with its single tooth, jumping back from the hard surface.

Frustration boiled into anger. 'Can I get a damned break?' Britton shouted.

The magic tide swept about him, far more powerful on his side of the gate. Before he knew what had happened, he felt the current snake through the gate to wrap around the cop, hauling him through.

The gate's light washed over him as he came stumbling, eyes big as dinner plates. The pack streamed around the cruiser toward the easier target.

'Oh, dear God. No,' Britton whispered.

The cop screamed, hauling out his pistol and firing madly, in no danger of hitting anything.

'Hang on!' Britton shouted. 'I'm coming!'

He slammed on the accelerator, pulling the steering wheel to run down one of the demon-horses. The thing turned, keening a rumbling imitation of the motor before the grill caught it, its ribs cracking as it slid up the hood to shatter the windshield. Its horselike head lolled toward him, eyeless, the spike tooth leaking blood. Britton punched it hard, jarring it enough to send it back over the hood. The car shuddered as the wheels crunched over it.

The other two demon-horses leapt aside as he guided the cruiser toward the cop. He threw the driver's-side door open. 'Get in!'

The cop backpedaled, his face a mask of terror. He changed magazines mechanically, then raised the pistol.

Britton ducked as a bullet whined through the space where the windshield had been, thudding against the bulletproof divider behind him.

'Damn it, you idiot! I'm trying to help you!'

The cop answered him with another round, slamming into the engine block.

The demon-horses flowed around the car toward the cop. Britton spun the steering wheel and drove away. Another bullet whined off the cruiser's roof before the cop noticed the pack and turned the gun on them.

Britton spun the wheel again, turning the car back, but another bullet hissed past as the policeman fired blindly at the monsters. Britton heard a coughing bark, the best impression of the gunshot that five more demon-horses, coming at a run, could muster.

You're no good to him with a bullet in your head, Britton told himself. *Get out of here.*

He swore and floored the accelerator, bumping the car over the plain until the cop and the demon-horses vanished behind him. Assuming the cop had a seventeen-round magazine, he'd already expended at least ten of them. There was no way he could take out the whole pack, shooting like he was.

He's as dead as your father.

Another gate opened. Through it, he could see deep forest alongside an overgrown trail.

The devil you know is better than the one you don't. He drove through.

The cruiser rumbled onto an old logging trail. The car bottomed out over roots and rocks, making it a few feet before the front tires blew out, sending his scraped nose into a half-deployed air bag. He sat with his head against it, numb and exhausted.

He raised his head as the wind wafted steam from the radiator through the shattered windshield. Another gate hovered four feet off the ground. It had opened into an underwater portion of the other world. Shafts of weak sunlight penetrated green depths that stirred with the languid movements of huge bodies. Not a drop spilled through the gate.

'What do you want from me?' he shrieked, pounding the steering wheel. He sank back in the seat, weeping. 'I don't want you . . . I just want . . .' *I just want to go home.*

And where exactly would that be now? his mind asked.

'Stop,' he said. 'Just stop. Pull yourself together.'

He searched the interior of the car. He found an unlocked gun case under the passenger seat, but it was empty, as were the backseats. The glove compartment contained a plastic first-aid kit, three chem-lights, a pocketknife, and a pack of tissues.

He took them all, stuffed the lot into the gun case, and exited the car in time to watch the gate close on the watery depths and vanish.

What exactly was he planning to do? He'd managed to keep a half step ahead of his pursuers, but that couldn't last long. And even if he could stay ahead of them, what then?

You'll just have to figure it out, he answered himself. *Maybe you can make your way to New Mexico, join up with the Apache insurgency. Maybe you can find one of those Selfer street crews hiding out in New York City.*

And fight the government I've served?

The government that murdered a confused girl. The government that's trying to kill you. Live or die, Oscar, make your choice.

You didn't want to kill anyone. They'll never believe that, but you know it. Britton hung on to that thought, repeating it to himself over and over again. *It's the reason you're not a Selfer, not like they use the word.*

So, he thought again, *make your choice.* What do you deserve?

Britton choked back tears of relief as he realized that he did not deserve to die. His choice was made. He would run.

Step one, find a place to lie low, get your bearings. Step two, find someone who can help you get control of your magic. The Green Mountain National Forest was miles from here, but it was big enough to get lost in. Big enough to go to ground while he figured out a way to head south without being spotted. It was a paper-thin plan, ridiculous in the face of what was sure to be a manhunt conducted by the most powerful military in the world.

But it was life. And, for the moment, it was all he had.

'Got to hide this car,' he said. The police probably had some way to track their vehicles. He wasn't certain where he was but figured that distance on the other side approximated distance in this world. He couldn't be too far from where he'd stolen the car. A thick carpet of ochre pine needles blanketed the ground, but that wouldn't cover the cruiser.

The magical tide rose with his frustration. Another gate flashed open, cutting through the car's front quarter panel. It shimmered there, then vanished, severing the wheel, bumper, and headlight. Water pooled beneath the sliced radiator. He stared, thinking what a gate would do if it appeared in the middle of a person, and shuddered.

'All right,' he said. 'You want to help? Fine, you can help.'

'Magic,' he asked, feeling ridiculous, 'you listening? I need you to open up and suck in this car.' He made a pincer motion, sweeping his arms up over his head.

A light breeze gusted over his back, drying his sweat and reminding him of the cold.

'Come on,' he said. 'Do it. I command you, swallow the car.'

He motioned again. Nothing. He sighed, looking around at the trees swaying gently in the breeze. Somewhere in their branches, a squirrel chattered.

He threw back his head and laughed. 'Oh, God! I have no idea what the hell I'm doing.' He laughed again, the sound strange in his ears. But he felt a little better as he moved into the woods.

Once he was out of sight of the trail, he treated his wounds with what he found in the first-aid kit, using up its entire contents. Nearly every inch of him was covered in gauze, Band-Aids, and antibiotic ointment. He had no water to wash his wounds and used the bottle of peroxide instead, wiping with gauze and a miraculously clean corner of his ragged T-shirt.

His ears rang, but the drums felt intact. He looked at his reflection in the plastic case and saw no blood leaking from them. His calf throbbed. The sock had sealed the wound though blood still oozed through the black crust that had formed on the fabric. His shoulders ached from the impact with the car.

Treating his injuries restored a measure of humanity but reminded him of his surroundings and lack of supplies. He shivered in the chill air, hungry, thirsty, and exhausted. The blanket of fallen needles was soft enough, but he couldn't eat them and doubted they'd keep him very warm.

The relative peace calmed him, and the tide of magic receded. He shut his eyes and found it hard to open them again. Exhaustion beat hunger, and he burrowed deeply into the soft pine needles. The trees blocked most of the wind, keeping them from blowing off.

Before he knew it, he was fast asleep.

He awoke in the deep of night, filthy, starving, and freezing.

The night air stung him, and his teeth chattered. *Got to get moving, only way to keep warm*. He broke one of the chem-lights and shook it, wreathing the woods in its neon green glow. He lurched to his feet, wincing, and trudged off into the dark.

He stumbled along in the darkness for hours. When the chem-light eventually failed, he didn't bother to light another one, moving by touch along tree trunks and kicking over rocks he could no longer feel through frozen feet. The moon was a sliver. What little starlight penetrated the tree cover was inadequate to navigate by. He groped along, conscious that he might be going in circles and long past caring. All that mattered was staying warm.

A sharp burning pulled taut across his chest, bringing him to his senses.

A half-crumbled line of fence posts stretched before him. Strung across the top of two of them was a rusty length of barbed wire, hopelessly tangled in the rags of his T-shirt. Beyond it, the trees gave way to an overgrown, star-dappled field.

A low, wooden tobacco barn dominated the field. The peaked roof was supported by hinged slats, gray-brown with creosote, louvered open to admit the air. A small house with dark windows and a beat-up blue pickup parked outside stood farther off.

He blinked, seeing shelter and possibly food and water. He disentangled himself from the barbed wire and trotted toward the barn.

The barn's massive doors were unlocked. He winced as they groaned on their hinges, but there was nothing for it. It was there or the woods, and he wasn't sure he would last another night without at least something to drink. A dog began to bark from the vicinity of the house. He ignored it, praying the owner would think it alerted by some animal.

The barn interior wasn't much warmer, but it kept the wind off better than the trees. The strong smell of tobacco nearly overwhelmed him. He took out another chem-light, cracked and shook it, sending horror-movie shadows dancing. The weird light couldn't penetrate the shadows in the rafters, but he could barely make out a loft above him. The ground was neatly brushed with straw. Long clutches of drying tobacco hung in orderly rows, marching away from him down the barn's length. To his right was a tractor, smelling of oil.

He turned to his left and nearly cried out. A wooden barrel bound by rusty hoops and brimming with water stood under a rotted portion of the roof.

He seized the barrel's sides and thrust his head in, drinking deeply. The water was rank, but he couldn't stop. He finally tore himself away, feeling the chilly fluid pour down his torso, stinging his wounds. His vision grayed momentarily, and he sank to his knees, resting his cheek on the barrel's rim.

A fat black Labrador retriever sat before him, head cocked to one side, tongue lolling happily. A frayed collar suspended a bunch of silver tags. The thirst surged again, followed by powerful nausea.

'Nice doggie,' he mumbled. He batted at the dog, trying to scratch its head and missing. Then he was doubled over, vomiting before collapsing facedown in the contents of his stomach.

He lay, dimly aware of the dog licking the back of his head.

'Thank . . . you. Thanks,' he mumbled.

'On Jake's behalf, you're welcome,' a man said in a thick New England accent. 'When you've recovered, I'll need you to stand up and keep your hands where I can see 'em.'

Britton slowly got to his feet, then checked himself as he heard the familiar clack-clack racking of a shotgun's pump action.

Chapter Eight
Trespasser

There is absolutely no substance to the rumors of a secret government base. I want to put paid to this crazy notion once and for all. Unauthorized magic users, in particular those practicing prohibited schools of magic, are dealt with according to the provisions clearly laid out in the McGauer-Linden Act, the Geneva Convention, and the Uniform Code of Military Justice. We do not cart them off, we do not train them, and there is not, nor has there ever been, a 'Shadow Coven'.

– Lieutenant General Alexander Gatanas
Commandant, Supernatural Operations Corps
Press conference responding to an article allegedly exposing a hidden SOC program trafficking in prohibited magic

Jake nuzzled Britton's elbow as he leaned against the big animal's neck, balancing between barrel and dog.

A sixtyish man stood in the entrance, wearing bedroom slippers, dirty denim overalls, and a faded cap. He was paunchy, with a wide, jowly face, small eyes, and a slightly upturned nose. He kept the shotgun leveled at Britton's chest.

'Come on over here, Jake,' the man called. 'You get away from him.'

Jake turned toward his owner, panting. He nosed Britton's hand, his bulk upsetting the barrel, dark water slopping out. The man rolled his eyes. 'Useless goddamn dog,' he muttered.

Jake backed away from Britton, bristling as the magic rose

in reaction to the gun, opening a gate between them, the back of it to Britton. He couldn't see the landscape facing the man, but he could hear the keening of the demon-horses clustered beyond.

The man took a lateral step and raised the shotgun, sighting down the barrel at Britton's face. 'You just put it away, now,' he said. 'Whatever it is you're planning to do, I promise you I can pull this trigger before you can do it.'

Britton struggled against the magic but he still felt its tendrils push into the gate, reaching for the pack beyond. Their keening became frenzied as they resisted, terrified of the flickering portal.

'Come on, you damned fool,' the man said. 'Don't do this. You don't want to do this.' His finger tensed on the trigger.

'I can't control it,' Britton rasped. 'It's worse when I'm stressed. I'm hurt and I'm hungry and you're pointing that damned gun at my face.'

The man looked down at his dog, then up at Britton. Slowly, he lowered the gun. 'Okay, son. Gun's down,' he said. 'You get a lid on this, and I'll get you fed and put some Band-Aids on you. Scout's honor.'

Britton desperately tired to reel in the magic, but how could he pull on something he couldn't see or touch? The keening grew louder. The gate wavered as one of the demon-horses began to come through.

The man's eyes widened. He pointed the gun at the gate. 'Come on, son. I'm not going to hurt you. You've gotta trust me. I know it's hard, but you can do it.'

Britton felt the magic recede slightly at the kind words. He concentrated on the calmness of his surroundings – the roof over his head, Jake's well-meaning slobber on the back of his neck, the man's voice.

Jake lowered his hackles and woofed softly as the gate shimmered and closed, sending them back into semidarkness.

The man sighed and wiped the back of his neck with a pudgy, callused hand. 'Well, that's a goddamned relief,' he said.

'I'm Oscar,' Britton said. 'My name's Oscar.'

The man tugged the brim of his cap. 'You can call me Nelson.'

They stood for an awkward moment, the silence broken only by the sound of Jake's panting as he nudged under Britton's hand again.

'Well, let it never be said I'm not a man of my word,' Nelson said. 'You sit tight, and I'll be back with some food and my first-aid kit.' He looked uncomfortably at his feet and turned to go. Britton's mind screamed at him to run, but he ignored it. There was nowhere for him to run and nothing else to do. He had to eat, to rest. He had to trust Nelson. The man could have easily shot him and hadn't. That would have to be enough.

The old farmer made it a few steps, then turned, not meeting Britton's eyes, and whistled for Jake. The big dog thumped his tail happily and didn't budge. Nelson called him again, then sighed. 'Most goddamn useless guard dog in history.'

Britton sagged to the floor, exhaustion mingling with relief to swamp what little strength remained. Jake licked him enthusiastically, and he batted ineffectually at the dog, scratching its ears and trying to duck its darting tongue.

He was so engrossed in the dog's affections that he barely noticed Nelson swing the barn doors shut.

Britton started as a light thud from the opposite side indicated that a crossbar had been put in place.

'Nelson?' Britton called, getting slowly to his feet and pushing Jake behind him.

Silence. Sudden panic bullied exhaustion aside. He raced to the doors and pushed.

They gave a few inches, then held fast.

Britton banged on the doors, the grayed wood rattled under his fists. 'Damn it, Nelson! You said you'd help me!'

Even through the barn's walls, the farmer's voice sounded sheepish. 'You just sit tight now, Oscar. I've called the SOC, and they're on their way.'

Britton looked frantically over his shoulder, scanning the barn's interior in the pale glare of his chem-light. Jake sat, panting patiently, where Britton had left him. Shadows swam across clapboard walls that showed no other exit.

'You fucking lied to me!' Britton shouted. 'Let me out of here!'

'Well, I'm no fan of lyin',' Nelson's voice came back, 'but I reckon I got a wife and a home and a life here. And if a bit of lyin' is what's gonna keep it all from burnin' up, well, the Lord'll forgive me my trespasses. Now I got a bead on this door here, Oscar. Don't do nothin' stupid, or I'll punch you full of holes.'

Britton turned and raced around the barn's interior, running his fingertips over the boards, desperately looking for an exit. In his mind, he could already hear the squealing of the white van's tires, Harlequin crouching inside. Jake padded along behind him, barking enthusiastically.

'I've got your fucking dog!' Britton cried. Nelson didn't respond. Britton looked back down at Jake, who sat and emitted a long stream of barks that almost ran together into a howl. What was he going to do, hurt the animal? He shook his head. 'Sorry, buddy,' he muttered to the dog, trying to master his panic.

He looked up in the loft and saw no exit that way either, and the panic surged, bringing his magic with it. Jake backed away from him, growling low in his throat, hair bristling and ears flat against the ridge of his skull. A gate flashed open just before the dog, sending him whining and running for the wall. It rolled shut and reopened in the middle of the tractor, slicing the machine neatly in half, collapsing it in a cascade of grinding metal.

'Damn it, Oscar!' Nelson bellowed from outside. 'I told you to just sit tight! Don't do nothin' stupid!'

The gate flashed away from the tractor and appeared lodged diagonally in the barn wall.

When it vanished, it left a clean, angled slash in the wood, the splintered edges clipped as neatly as if they'd been burned by a laser. Through it, Britton could see the light of the stars and feel the cold blast of the air. Without thinking, he launched himself at the rent.

The impact knocked the breath out of him, his shoulder singing out in pain. His head whipped backward, and, for a moment, he thought he had just made the dumbest move of his life. But then the weakened wall exploded, the jagged edges of wood ripping into his skin and sending him spinning into the darkness, feeling as if he had been set alight as the chill air trilled in the rents in his skin.

He staggered, fell to one knee, skidding across the frost-kissed grass of the field, arms pinwheeling for balance. He could hear Jake barking in the background and Nelson panting as he ran from the front of the barn to the side. The lights were on in the house by then, and a small figure, probably a woman, stood on the front porch, a cell phone clutched in her hand.

'Now you just get down, Oscar!' the farmer shouted. 'Get right down and keep your hands where I can see them!'

Britton staggered, got to his feet, met the farmer's eyes levelly.

Nelson leveled the shotgun at Britton's chest. 'You just stop right there. Don't be a damned fool.'

But the magic had other ideas. It flowed through Britton, borne on his sense of betrayal and desperation.

A gate snapped open in front of Nelson. The farmer stepped around it and thrust the gun's muzzle forward. 'Damn it, son, I warned you.'

The shotgun boomed, and Britton's chest erupted in agony, followed quickly by merciful darkness.

Contractor

Manifestation, done right, isn't a curse. You give up your place in the old social order and take up your position in the mechanism that stands ready to defend it. Life in the Corps isn't easy, nobody is claiming it is. But a gift so powerful makes you suddenly part of something so much bigger than yourself. Army Sorcerers recognize it and accept it fully. It is their greatest pride and their greatest burden. That's what makes the Selfer so despicable. You're giving the middle finger to the whole world. You're saying that your interests trump the interests of every community you come in contact with. Do I feel bad when I take a Selfer down? Only for the wear and tear on my equipment.

– Major 'Rockslide' (call sign), SOC Fire Team Whiskey
Law Enforcement Support Element
New York City, New York

Chapter Nine

You're Hired

Willingness to use magic in the private sector is perhaps the single biggest economic advantage the Chinese have over us. It's ironic that this Communist giant trusts its populace to make use of a power forbidden to the general public in our so-called 'free' country. Yes, it's tightly controlled, but look at the advantage Terramantic engineering has bestowed on their heavy-equipment sector alone. We have to put in a request that the Army Corps of Engineers never gets around to handling, while they have major public works completed in a week. It's commercial suicide.

– Lee Thomson, host of WQXR Radio's *Friday Night Fights*

Britton jarred awake, his back thudding on metal runners. He blinked his eyes, trying to clear the darkness from them, but blackness clung to him. He tensed his muscles until he was sure by feel that his lids were open, then he felt his breath, sour and close, reflected by cloth against his face. He was hooded. He tried to raise a hand to lift the hood and felt the sharp bite of plastic zip cuffs against his wrists. His chest still throbbed as if a hammer had struck it, and his breathing felt wet and shallow. But a curious warmth was spreading through him, moving across his chest. It dampened the pain, radiating outward, soothing his strained muscles. He felt the surface of his skin tingling, the delicious heat erasing the irritating burn of the field of abrasions there. The feeling spread to his calf, calming the pain there as well.

Even through the hood, Britton could make out familiar smells – lubricating oil, old boots, dried mud. He heard people clambering around him, doors slamming. The runners pitched beneath him as a motor revved somewhere under him.

'Whatha . . .' Britton tried his voice. His lips felt thick. He turned his head, trying to shake the hood loose, but it was useless.

'I'm sure you know this next part, Oscar,' came Harlequin's voice. 'Just like in the movies.'

A hand wrenched his sleeve roughly up, followed by the stab of a needle. Inside the hood, Britton's vision began to shift from black to white. Then all went black again, his thoughts dissolving into spinning stars.

When he opened his eyes, the hood was off and he was sitting upright. He blinked, his vision blurry and his head aching. Apart from the headache, he felt no pain at all. He was breathing normally, and the sore muscles and scratched skin no longer troubled him.

A larger motor hummed, the throaty growl of a bus or big rig. He sat on a bench that ran the length of the vehicle, up to metal bars through which he could see a driver in army camouflage. Just before the gate stood a bank of computers with a young SOC sergeant first class seated before it, her hair in a neat blond bun. Another bench stood across from him, lined with lockers – each faced with a wire-mesh door that screened an armory that would make a gun collector drool. He recognized the vehicle as a mobile command center.

He shook his head, groggy, working his tongue against the roof of a mouth that felt stuffed with dirt. Harlequin sat on the bench across from him, beside an Asian man in a charcoal gray suit, his buzz-cut hair graying at the temples, his face stern and lined. A small black woman sat beside him, her head shaved as bald as Britton's. Her eyes were large and sympathetic. Captain's bars were stitched in black thread across the center of her digital camouflage blouse. Her lapel bore the stylized cross-within-a-heart that marked SOC

Physiomancers. The remainder of the bench was taken up by enlisted men, all wary. Submachine guns rested in their laps, barrels pointing at Britton.

'How are you feeling?' Harlequin asked, handing him a water bottle. 'Sorry about the dry mouth. Unfortunate side effect.'

Britton reached out for the magical current instinctively, already knowing the result – blocked by another flow. He slewed his head drunkenly to the left and saw a SOC Suppressor, his lapel pin featuring their badge of the armored fist clutching a cluster of lightning bolts. The man waved and smiled.

Britton tried to drink, coughing and dribbling water down his chin.

'Go easy,' Harlequin said. 'Your head will clear, but it takes a little time.'

He was already feeling a little more clearheaded, but the words still came through a fog. He raised a hand and found he wasn't cuffed. He was wearing a one-piece orange jumpsuit, his feet chilly in white tube socks. His skin was pristine, as if the events of the previous days had never occurred. He rolled his shoulders experimentally. The joints slid seamlessly against one another. There was no pain at all. Apart from the fog and the dull throb in his head, he was whole.

'Where are you taking me?' he croaked.

'That depends on you,' Harlequin said. 'You have some choices to make, and you have to make them right now.'

Britton leaned back, closed his eyes, and gulped more water until the spinning eased. When he opened them again, the Physiomancer regarded him evenly. Her shaved head and square jaw spoiled what otherwise would have been a very pretty face.

'You fix me up?' he asked her.

'You're lucky that gun was loaded with shot,' the woman said, her voice low and sweet. 'If he'd loaded slugs, you'd probably have died before I got to you. I'm sure it hurt plenty, but it would have taken you a long time to bleed out. You're young, and your flesh responded well to magic. You're good as new.'

'A Physiomancer,' Britton said to Harlequin. 'For me? I must be more important than I thought.'

Harlequin smiled and leaned forward, holding up a small metal cylinder, scarcely bigger than an eraser's head. A light pulsed within. 'Captain Bloodbreaker did more than heal you, Oscar. She inserted this device right next to the pulmonary valve of your heart. It's an ATTD – Asset Tracking and Termination Device. It tells us where you are. It also doubles as a bomb. We'll always be able to find you. We can always take you out on either side of a gate. The captain here is one of our best Physiomancers, but even with her skill, the procedure would have been extremely painful, far beyond what your actual wounds were causing you. Much better for you to be out during the process.'

Britton could almost feel the tiny metal ball embedded in his heart. His mind reeled, working backward over the successive explosions of the past few hours, dispersing the remaining effects of the drug.

'Why did you save me?' Britton asked. 'I ran. I'm a Probe. I've attacked government agents. Per ROE, I should be dead. That's what you do, isn't it? You kill Probes.'

Harlequin shrugged. 'Sometimes. I've killed a lot of people, Oscar. I sleep like a baby. Do you know why?'

Britton didn't answer.

'I sleep at night because, unlike you, every life I take is authorized,' Harlequin continued. 'There are some people who weren't killed to protect anyone. Their deaths weren't justified by any ordinance, civil or military. Those people include your father and a Shelburne sheriff's deputy. You know what crime that deputy committed, Oscar? He did his job. Your father was just trying to protect his wife.'

'I'm not going to explain myself to you,' Britton rasped. 'You use stupid and arbitrary rules as an excuse to kill people. You may sleep easy at night, but it's not because what you do is right. Charlie Manson slept well at night. So did Hitler. Right and wrong aren't about laws.'

Harlequin grinned. 'That may work for you smart guys. Now, me? I'm just a dumb-ass public servant. I'm like Adam before he bit the apple. I don't know right from wrong. Left to my own devices, I might do some very bad things. But God in his wisdom gave us the Constitution and qualified men and women who we elect to interpret it. To this he added the Uniform Code of Military Justice and the New Testament. Between those, I'm able to muddle by without making too much of a mess of things. But I must say, Oscar, I envy you the brilliance that allows a man to make those calls for himself.'

Britton read the surety on Harlequin's face. 'Get me my JAG. I don't want to talk to you anymore.'

Harlequin shook his head, chuckling. 'Those aren't the rules, Oscar! You don't get a damned lawyer! You sure as hell don't get a trial.' He raised a hand, ticking off on his fingers. 'You Manifested in a prohibited school. You ran. You employed your illicit power to bring about the death or wounding of at least one civilian and two police officers. Rare and valuable school or no, I have the authority to execute you right here and now.'

'So?' Britton said. 'Shoot me like you shot that Probe girl on the roof of that school. ROE is clear, you said. Probes who attack government agents are dog food.'

'Well, that's the rub, isn't it,' the Aeromancer said, leaning back and folding his arms across his chest. 'What you don't realize is that I don't enjoy killing people, Oscar. Despite this bad turn, you used to be a good soldier. Your team spoke highly of you. Your warrant officer practically begged me not to hurt you. He said you loved being in the military.'

'I did,' Britton said. 'The army was my home.'

He thought of the house with the poorly mended screening. *Homes don't last long for you, do they?*

'Well, there's good news and bad news about that,' Harlequin went on. 'First, the bad news.'

He handed Britton discharge papers.

'You were court-martialed in absentia,' Harlequin said. 'It's a shame you weren't there to make the same speech about the difference between laws and morals that you just made to me. Perhaps you could have swayed the presiding authority. But this came down from the president himself. Your commission has been rescinded. The court-martial also found you guilty of unauthorized magical use, gross insubordination, and murder. You've been sentenced to death.'

'And yet here I am, alive,' Britton said.

'And kicking!' Harlequin agreed. 'That's because the SOC commandant agrees with my assessment of your past record.'

'Which is where I come in, Oscar,' said the Asian man, moving to Britton's side. He placed a leather briefcase across his knees, popping open the brass catches. 'I'm Howard Kwan, with the Office of General Counsel.

'The president is inclined to agree with the SOC commandant. He doesn't want to see an ability as precious as yours lost to lethal injection. He's authorized me to give you this.'

He handed Britton another document. Gold-embossed letters read GRANTING CONDITIONAL PARDON TO OSCAR BRITTON – BY THE PRESIDENT OF THE UNITED STATES OF AMERICA. A PROCLAMATION, across the top.

'Conditional?' Britton asked. 'These things come with conditions?'

The Asian man nodded. 'In rare instances, yes.'

'Let me guess,' Britton said. 'My condition is that I join the SOC.'

Harlequin recoiled. 'Hell no, Oscar! You've been dismissed by the president and convicted by court-martial! You can never serve in the armed forces again. You can't even hold a position of public trust, which means you can't be hired as a government civilian.'

'So . . . what do you expect me to do?' Britton asked.

Kwan smiled and produced a glossy-faced white folder from his briefcase, stuffed with papers. 'I've discussed your case with one of our top vendors. The Entertech Corporation has been one of our leading providers of technology and manpower solutions for over twenty-five years. You'll find a conditional offer of employment in the packet.'

Britton almost burst out laughing. 'You want me to become a government contractor?'

Kwan's face was completely serious. 'That's right, Oscar. Your acceptance of Entertech's offer and the associated conditions satisfies the terms of your pardon. Your sentence will be commuted. You will be permitted to return to the service of your country and repay the debt to society that your crimes have incurred. It's a win-win solution for everyone.'

'Conditional pardon, conditional job offer. Everything comes with a catch,' Britton said.

'Naturally.' Kwan smiled. 'The catch in this case is just a simple nondisclosure agreement. Of course, since you're a criminal, even one with a commuted sentence, you can't hold a security clearance. However, Entertech is going to share proprietary information with you that's confidential to their business enterprise.'

'Meaning,' Britton said, 'I don't talk about whatever I see.'

'Exactly,' Kwan agreed. 'If you do, you negate the pardon, and your sentence is reinstated.' Kwan passed Britton yet another document.

'This is binding for ninety-nine years!' Britton exclaimed. 'What if I refuse?'

'Then I have the authority to pop that cork in your chest right now,' Harlequin said. 'We'll turn your body over to our medical research facility to see if they can learn anything from your tissues. Either way, you help us.'

'Bull,' Britton said. 'You're not going to kill me. The commandant himself just told you that my ability is too rare and precious to lose. You put expensive hardware in my chest to keep me in line. You got one of your best Healers out here to fix me up. You don't invest that heavily in someone you're intending to fry.'

Harlequin leaned in, his face hard. 'Try me. I'm begging you, Oscar. I follow the regs, but that doesn't mean I won't take some personal satisfaction in zapping a guy who killed his own dad. Please, try me.'

He waved to the blonde behind the computer bank. She nodded, flipped a plastic cover off a switch, and looked at Harlequin, her finger hovering over it.

Britton tried to fathom the depth of the bluff. The Aeromancer's eyes were blue ice. Britton looked down at the sheaf of papers.

'How much do I make?' Britton asked, trying to buy time to think.

'The company is offering you eighty-five dollars an hour,' Kwan answered, 'to be garnished one hundred percent toward the fine of $250 million levied against you at your sentencing.'

'What happens if they fire me?' Britton asked.

'Boom.' Harlequin smiled.

'So, I'm a slave,' Britton said.

'You're alive, Oscar,' Kwan said. 'Slaves don't get choices.'

'I wouldn't call do-this-or-die a choice,' Britton said.

Kwan only shrugged.

Britton's mind spun. The trailer's air-conditioned interior felt thick and close. Did he really have anything to live for? His home in the 158th was as lost to him as his home in Shelburne.

Why go on? Because he did not deserve to die. Britton reminded himself of the internal conversation he'd had beside the stolen police car. *Just because they have power and authority, doesn't mean they're right. They don't get to kill you. Not without your fighting them every inch of the way.*

He could run anytime he wanted. Dying on his feet would beat the hell out of having his heart burst in the back of a stuffy truck.

'Anybody got a pen?' Britton asked.

Kwan produced a slim gold pen from his coat pocket. Britton took the pen, swallowed, and signed.

And signed.

And signed.

By the time he had signed all the documents in all the places that Kwan indicated, his wrist was cramping.

Kwan shook Britton's hand. 'On behalf of Entertech, welcome aboard.'

Britton turned back to Harlequin. 'What happens to Mom?'

'Desda Britton will be well cared for,' Harlequin answered. 'We have some questions for her about her son's proclivities and upbringing, but I'm sure she'll be more than cooperative once she's recovered from the nasty shock you gave her.'

'You fucker. If you do anything to her . . .'

Harlequin dismissed him with a wave. 'Whatever, Oscar. You stormed into her house and killed her husband.

Something tells me that you're probably not the best advocate for her interests just now. She'll come to no harm. I've seen more than enough folks suffer over you.'

'What are you going to do to her?' Britton asked.

'Nothing,' Harlequin said. 'We'll just keep an eye on her. Should anything go south with the deal you've just struck with ol' uncle sugar, we might need to call her in for additional questioning, and perhaps for her own safety. You with me?'

Harlequin let the threat hang in the air. *Oh, I'm with you*, Britton thought, *but only so long as I have to be and not one second longer*.

Chapter Ten

Pack Out

Zazen is critical to training. Only when you center yourself and place your spirit in balance, will you be able to call the elements to your hand. The Kensei told us that the way is in training. This is as true for the Shukenja as it is for the Senshi.

– Japanese Self-Defense Forces Instruction Manual 4.677
Shukenja Corps Policy and Procedure

The vehicle shuddered to a stop amid the hiss of the air brakes. The doors slid open, and two soldiers lowered a collapsible stair. Kwan hefted his briefcase and exited without another word.

'Time to start your new career,' said Harlequin, motioning Britton to the exit.

Thousands of brilliant stars winked at him from the cold night sky, outlining the tops of pine trees and a stretch of gravel road. Farther on, a Little Bird helicopter stood, rotors spinning up.

Britton accompanied Harlequin, the Suppressor, and one assaulter onto the bird. Kwan was already on board. They strapped in, and Harlequin held out the hood again. 'Last time you'll have to wear it. I promise.'

Britton shrugged and slipped it on himself as the helicopter lifted off.

He had no way to track how long they flew, but it felt like hours. Only the roar of the engine and the occasional unintelligible burst of static talk from the radio broke the quiet. The air intakes mere feet from his head drowned the pilots' replies.

At long last, he felt the helicopter descend. Harlequin removed the hood, ushering Britton outside.

The rotors washed dust over him as the helo pulled skyward the instant its passengers had off-loaded. The dust gradually cleared, and Britton was able to make out a clearing.

The stars outlined a ring of tall trees enclosing three odd-looking tobacco barns. He thought of Nelson's farm and gritted his teeth.

Apart from two run-down pickups, the space was bare. Two rifle-toting men leaned against the back of one of them. They were dressed to match the stereotype of New England farmers – denim overalls and flannel shirts, worn baseball caps with frayed brims; but their eyes were alert, veteran. They roved – lighting on Britton and moving on, searching for threats. Their guns were pointing at the ground in military fashion instead of slung over their shoulders. The huge scopes and black plastic stocks didn't look like any hunting weapons he'd ever seen. A vigilant-looking German shepherd stood beside them, growling softly in the back of its throat.

Starlight bleached the area of color, cloaking all in gray shadow, but Britton could still make out the rough surface of the louvered clapboard slats, pulled shut against the cold night. It took him a moment to realize what was odd about the barns. The peaked roofs reared up past the treetops. Their length stretched out past his vision. He was no farm boy, but he'd been in rural Vermont long enough to know that no barn should be that big.

Harlequin led him to the first barn as a diamond-tipped breeze drilled between his shoulder blades. The Aeromancer flipped open a panel, produced a badge from his breast pocket, and swiped it, punching numbers into a keypad. A beep was followed by a click and a hiss of air.

The barn doors silently swung inward, then shut behind them, leaving them in darkness before harsh fluorescent lights flickered on. They stood in a featureless white room. Twin gray metal doors stood before them. Harlequin placed his hand on the knob, waiting a moment before another click sounded, and the doors swung open.

They entered a cavernous room humming with activity, lit by fluorescent globes suspended from the ceiling. The far end was taken up by rows of bunks and lockers and had an enclosed shower. A small kitchenette stood beside a lounge, dominated by a flat-screen TV. Soldiers relaxed on couches before it, playing video games and napping.

Two giant flags hung from the ceiling – The Stars and Stripes and the SOC arms, fringed in gold thread. Stitched across the Stars and Stripes were the words PORTCULLIS – US ARMY LOGISTICAL STAGING AREA. A desk stood beside the door, covered by computers and manned by a soldier who could have been the twin of the blonde Britton had seen in the vehicle in which he'd awoken.

'Hi, sir,' she said.

'Specialist,' Harlequin replied crisply. 'Would you mind buzzing Don over here, please? We've got to get our guest here prepped and moved on.'

'Sir,' she said, picking up a black handheld radio from the desk and pushing the button on the side.

A moment later, a door at the far side of the structure opened and a smiling young man carrying a clipboard jogged over to them. He wore khaki cargo pants bloused into combat boots with a military web belt. A black compression shirt sported the Entertech logo with the words LOGISTICS OFFICER beneath.

'Oscar Britton, right?' he said, extending a hand and putting on one of the most corporately insincere smiles Britton had ever seen. 'I'm Don, the logs officer here at LSA Portcullis. I'm also the admin officer for any Entertech internal matters. But I assume human resources has taken good care of you, and you're ready to go, right?'

He clapped Britton on the shoulder, grinning. Britton looked back at him in silence.

'Don, if you'd dispense with the formalities, I'd appreciate it,' Harlequin said. 'I need him to make a written statement, then the brass wants him suited up and off the Home Plane ASAP.'

The young man glanced at his watch and turned to the Suppressor standing behind Britton. 'Sheesh, Plug. You're about due for a break.'

Plug grinned and ran a finger around the collar of his uniform. 'Hell, you know me, Don. I joined the army for that sweet overtime pay.'

Don chuckled. 'Rampart! Would you please be so kind as to relieve your counterpart here before he drops dead?'

Engrossed in their video game, nobody on the couch moved. Yellow cars sprinted over a digital rise, accompanied by tinny rock music.

'Damn it, Lieutenant!' Harlequin shouted.

A broad-shouldered man with close-cropped brown hair stiffened and stood, letting his game controller fall to the couch. He turned, his rugged face sullen. He was clothed to match Don, save that his pants were digital camouflage. His T-shirt bore the SOC arms instead of the Entertech logo. The caption beneath read SUPPRESSOR above the armored fist clenching lightning bolts. A star above the badge marked him as senior in his school.

Rampart walked over and nodded to Plug. Britton felt the slightest flicker in the interdiction of his magic, his own tide surging at the momentary freedom, only to be blocked again.

'Got it,' Rampart said, folding his arms and moving behind Britton.

''Bout damned time,' Plug responded, tugging at his uniform blouse and heading for the showers.

Harlequin nodded. 'Let's move it along and get him out of here.'

Don led Britton, Rampart, and Harlequin through a door at the far side of the room and down a short hallway to another massive room. The far end of the room contained a small firing range. One wall had been kitted out as an armory. Britton could see weapons lockers crammed with guns, ammunition, scopes, tripods, and other tactical gear. A soldier was cleaning a carbine at a small bench. ARMORER was written below the SOC arms over his breast. His enormous head looked mounted directly to massive shoulders. He worked with the bored efficiency Britton had come to associate with senior enlisted men.

Another set of double doors, painted white with diagonal red stripes, occupied the far wall. A yellow rotating light, dark for now, was mounted above them. A sign above read: RESTRICTED AREA – VISUAL INSPECTION OF CREDENTIALS REQUIRED – 21-FOOT APPROACH ZONE RIGOROUSLY OBSERVED. DEADLY FORCE IS AUTHORIZED. YOU ARE RESPONSIBLE FOR YOUR OWN SAFETY AND COMPLIANCE!

Two SOC Pyromancers stood in front of the portal, eyes alert, slung submachine guns across their breasts. Their body armor read – STATIC ELEMENT – PYRO above stylized flame bursts. Britton arched his eyebrows at the tremendous expenditure of firepower to guard a single door.

The armorer glanced up with little interest before returning to his work. 'Hey, James,' Don said, smiling, 'would you mind kitting our newest hire here for immediate pack out?'

'Where's he headed?' James asked, sounding bored.

'Load him for bear,' Harlequin cut in gruffly. 'I need him to hit the ground ready to shoot.'

James looked up with one eyebrow arched, then picked up the newly assembled carbine. He checked the magazine well and the chamber before sliding the bolt home. 'He already qualified?'

'Our friend here is a former soldier of no mean accomplishment.' Harlequin smiled. 'He's qualled. Pistol, long gun, and grenades. No history of domestic violence. I'll get the paperwork sent over from his unit.'

'This ought to fit him,' James said, handing the carbine to Britton. 'Grab yourself a sidearm from the locker over there and a vest. The magazines are already full. Should be six mags for your long gun, two for the pistol. Two clips for grenades. Grab one smoke, one frag. Go bag should already be loaded and on your vest.'

While Britton selected his gear, the armorer fussed over the clothing rack, muttering about guys who were too damned big for their own good. His surly tone reminded Britton of his father and of Nelson, which in turn reminded him of Jake. He shook his head. The only way now was forward. He could feel the tiny ball resting in his heart, holding him fast on course.

Britton was soon decked out in khaki cargo pants and a black Entertech T-shirt. A ball cap with a subdued American flag topped the ensemble, reinforced sunglasses perched on the brim. Britton slung his body armor on over it all. He could tell by its weight that it was the heaviest rating, designed to stop even armor-piercing bullets. The tac vest fit over it, dripping with ordnance and medical supplies. Both legs were strapped with drop holsters – one for the pistol, the other for documents and tools. Britton had been trained as a pilot, not a ground operator, and felt off-balance in all the gear.

It took him almost an hour to zero his weapon. When at last his groupings of three shots plugged dead center every time, Britton slung the rifle and turned to face Harlequin and Don, chatting in low tones behind him.

'You ready?' Harlequin asked.

'I'm ready for a nap, a shower, and to get this gear off.'

Harlequin grinned. 'Gripes just like a real soldier. Very nice. You can shower and rack out at your new post.'

'And where is that?' Britton asked.

Don stepped forward with his clipboard and passed it to Britton along with a pen. 'First, I'll need you to sign this non-disclosure agreement. What you're about to witness are proprietary processes and . . .'

Britton waved a hand at him and signed. Nowhere to go but forward.

Don handed Britton a plastic badge. 'Hold your thumb against this please.' Britton did, feeling the space beneath it grow warm. Don took the badge from him and placed it in a slot on the front of Britton's vest. It bore Britton's old military mug shot above an imprint of his thumb, still glowing softly in the plastic. LSA PORTCULLIS – GATE ACCESS read the words beneath.

They approached the door.

One of the Pyromancers came forward and indicated a black pad on the wall. 'Place your right thumb here, please.' Britton complied, and a spray of red light shot from the pad, streaming over his chest and neck. The thumbprint on the badge glowed, and a beep sounded. Both Pyromancers leaned in, visually inspecting the badge, then nodded to one another.

There was a click, and the striped doors slid slowly apart.

Beyond was another warehouse-sized room, pitch-black save for the opposite wall, where a single fluorescent bulb provided a disc of harsh light.

In the center of the disc stood a metal chair occupied by a man in a light blue hospital gown. Vacant blue eyes stared into the distance from deep-sunk sockets. Patchy, thinning black hair was plastered to his sweaty forehead. A day's growth of stubble covered his weak chin. His head twisted back and forth, mouth working silently. Pink, fuzzy slippers covered his feet. Medical leads sprouted wires trailing from his forehead, chest, arms, and thighs. Several more snaked from under his gown, trailing off into darkness.

Black letters were stenciled on the front of the gown: PROPERTY OF THE UNITED STATES ARMY.

An older woman in a floral print housedress stood behind him. Her gray hair was cut short, and thick-lensed glasses in cat's-eye frames hung around her neck. She gave them a genuine smile.

'Hello, boys,' she said, 'you here to see my Billy?'

Harlequin clicked his heels and bowed slightly, smiling. 'How are you doing, Miss Cartwright?'

'Tolerably well,' she answered in a thick Southern drawl. 'Billy's fine, too. Thanks for asking.'

Harlequin chuckled. 'This is why I love talking with you, ma'am. You never cease to improve my manners.'

'I am overjoyed to serve my country in any way I can, sir.' She massaged Billy's shoulders. 'Billy's been a good boy, Captain. I don't think it's too much to ask for his bear back?'

'That's not up to me, ma'am.' Harlequin sighed. 'The CO said three days. But you know you can count on me to put in a good word.'

'So, what can my son do for his country today?' Miss Cartwright asked.

'A comms portal first, if you please. Just a quick status check,' Harlequin said.

Miss Cartwright leaned low, her soft chin grazing her son's ear. 'Sweetheart, are you ready to do your nice thing for Momma? Just the little hole, please. Thanks, baby. Momma loves you.'

Billy's mouth moved, making tiny sounds. His mother seemed to understand. 'No, sweetie. Momma's right here, there's nothing to be scared of. Just the little hole, then you get a treat, okay?'

The pallid figure in the chair whipped his head side to side, whining, straining the leads connected to his head. His mother dug her fingertips into his shoulders and waited. A moment later, a tiny pinpoint of static light opened in the air before them.

Harlequin lost no time. 'Comms line to LSA Barbican. I need Landing Zone status for entry.'

'Roger that,' a voice came from the darkness. Radio static was followed by a muttered voice. A moment later, the voice called out again. 'Barbican confirms. LZ is hot.'

'How long till they have it clear?' Harlequin asked.

'No estimate,' the voice came back. 'LZ Logs says it could be an hour, could be a week.'

Harlequin swore. 'Damn it. We don't have time for that. I need an escort, please, on the hop. Do they have assets ready for cover?'

'Roger that, sir,' the voice replied. 'They're ready for you. Platoon sergeant says be ready to come out shooting.'

'Damn it,' Rampart muttered under his breath.

'Will you secure that crap?' Harlequin said to him. 'Or did you join the army for the free clothes?'

'Sir,' Rampart said through gritted teeth, 'if we're going into a firefight, I need to be able to lay off him in case we get hit by indig sorcerers. You sure he won't go nova?'

Harlequin swore again, tapping his chin. 'You're right, we can't risk it. I was going to wait until we arrived.'

'Your call, sir,' Rampart said. 'He fries himself, I don't want it on my conscience.'

'You mean you don't want it on your record,' Harlequin said. 'You got Dampener?'

Rampart shook his head, but Don nodded and produced a

syringe filled with a clear yellow fluid that looked disturbingly like urine. A white label read – SOC DISPENSARY – 6A. SOC USE ONLY AS ORDERED. ALL OTHERS RETURN TO CO IMMEDIATELY.

Harlequin handed Britton the syringe. 'Inject all of the fluid into either thigh. Go right through your trousers. Be sure to use it all.'

Britton looked dubiously at the needle and hesitated.

'Are you kidding me?' Harlequin yelled. 'We got you, you idiot. Do as you're fucking told.'

Harlequin's words struck home. Britton stuck the needle in, depressing the plunger.

In seconds, he felt calmer. The anger at Harlequin, the sadness at losing his family, the fear over his uncertain future, all shifted. The emotions shunted off, compartmented, available at his wish. He rifled through them, calling up his nervousness, feeling the magic rolling along with it as much as the Suppression would allow, then pushing both away. His mouth went uncomfortably dry, his tongue quickly feeling thick and clumsy in his mouth. He looked up at Harlequin, feeling the serenity on his face. 'Got any water?'

The Aeromancer laughed. 'Cottonmouth's a bitch, eh? That's the worst part of the Limbic Dampener. It helps control your emotions. It'll make calling magic slightly more difficult and impair the power a bit. Well worth it, though. Your control will greatly increase, and there's no danger of your going nova. The injection will last anywhere up to three weeks depending on your metabolism, and on a big guy like you, I'd imagine it's pretty slow.'

'And pricey,' Rampart added. 'You just injected roughly the cost of an Abrams tank into your leg, my friend. We don't just hand that stuff out.'

Britton's eyes went wide.

'We save it for special cases,' Harlequin said. 'People with serious control problems, or' – he paused for dramatic effect, one corner of his mouth rising– 'particularly valuable magical assets.'

An engine revved in the darkness. A massive eight-wheeled Stryker armored vehicle rolled into view, headlights blinding.

A soldier sat behind the fifty-caliber machine gun, still buckling on his helmet.

Miss Cartwright pressed a piece of candy into Billy's hand. She kissed his cheeks and whispered into his ear. He shook, the leads trembling.

The gunner gave Harlequin the thumbs-up sign, and the hatch in the back of the vehicle hissed down. Four soldiers sat on metal benches inside, each as battle-ready as Britton and Rampart, still adjusting straps and slamming magazines into their weapons.

The blackness rolled back. A giant gate – easily twice the size of anything Britton had conjured, opened in front of the vehicle. Billy yelped and grinned, drooling. His mother had thrown her arms around his neck, her mouth still moving against his ear.

'He's a Portamancer,' Britton said.

'Just like you,' Harlequin said. 'Or just like you will be if you don't do as you're told. Get in the Stryker, Oscar. We're moving.'

Britton's mouth went dry, but not from the Dampener. The thought of being killed frightened him, but the thought of spending the rest of his life as a drooling idiot shook his bones. Only the Dampener kept him from being paralyzed with fear.

Beyond the gate, Britton could make out a cratered track. The Stryker's massive wheels would make short work of it. A soldier raced across his field of view, weapon blazing. In the distance, a ball of fire bloomed.

'Sir,' called one of the soldiers inside the vehicle. 'Seat's warm for you.'

They got in. The hatch shut, leaving them in the cramped half-light of the vehicle cabin. Claustrophobia, fear, and excitement all rose in Britton's gut. Controlled by the Dampener, the emotions barely impacted his tide at all. His face remained calm.

'You're not going to gear up, sir?' one of the soldiers asked Harlequin.

Harlequin balled his fists as the vehicle lurched forward, the bench vibrating. Electricity blazed between his knuckles.

'Just keep your geared-up ass out of my way, and you might learn something.'

Britton felt the sudden change in magical flow as they pierced the gate. Rampart's Suppressing field intensified, then softened as he adjusted for the increased current on the gate's far side.

'Welcome to the Source,' Harlequin said, grinning fiercely.

Overhead, the gunner cursed as he opened up with the fifty-cal, blazing lead at some unknown foe.

Chapter Eleven

Hot LZ

Yes, I know what Dawa means. It's Arabic for . . . what? Conversion? Preaching? When Islam first took hold here, we had plenty of that, I can tell you. But Dawa is an older word for us. It was our way – our medicine of the old gods. When the world awoke the Dawa came back to us. Some of us, very few and very old, remembered what to do with it. But we taught the young and it gave them the strength to fight. The many old gods against the new one.

– Hihhu Okonkwo, Kisii Tribe, Bantu Nation

The Stryker rocked on the uneven track. Britton could hear the dull booming of explosions and the staccato rhythm of the machine gun despite the armored hull. And something more – the rush of wind and the crack of lightning striking, far louder and closer than any lightning should have been. He heard banging on the hull and a muttered conversation as the gunner ceased firing. A moment later, he called down into the squad bay. 'They cut the road, sir. Rotary wing's the only way to the Forward Operating Base. Blackhawk is spinning up on the pad right now.'

Harlequin cursed and jerked a thumb at Britton. 'Close detail on our guest here. Anything happens to him between here and the helo, you'll wish it had happened to you. Rampart! If you don't run Suppression, I have to, so keep yourself out of the fight. Dampener or no Dampener, I'm not taking any chances. You keep his flow blocked. Oscar, keep your head down and go where I damn well tell you! On deck!'

The hatch dropped, and the dawn flooded over them. Even the half-light was dazzling, the rough ground glittering with bits of crushed rock. The air had the same intense, alive smell, tainted with other odors, all strengthened by the Source's heightened sense of things: gasoline, cordite, ozone, and blood.

A Blackhawk helicopter stood thirty feet across from them, rotors spinning. A gunner stood in the open door behind the whirling barrels of a minigun, its blurred muzzles blazing, spitting a stream of rounds into the distance. The scream of the motor and the clatter of casings on the cracked concrete pad were loud enough to hear over the beating rotors, swirling up enough dust that Britton jerked his sunglasses over his eyes as the escort lowered the goggles on their helmets.

They stumbled down the ramp. Harlequin leapt out of the hatch, rocketing airborne. The dust whipped up by the Blackhawk's rotors whirled around him, his magic gathering it into a funnel. The sunglasses were too dark in the early light, so Britton slipped them back onto the cap brim, taking advantage of Harlequin's drawing off the dust.

He caught his breath.

Over Harlequin's shoulder, Britton could see a massive bird banking toward them. Its brown feathers were flecked with gold, black beak opened wide enough to swallow a car. A mottled bird's nest of ropes was strapped between its wings.

'Move, damn it!' Rampart said, shoving him hard. The escort pushed across the perennial saw-edged grass, withered and burned in patches, making for the helo. A long line of concrete blast barriers formed a wall that stretched past Britton's field of vision.

The helo gunner stopped firing, motioning them onward. The escort stopped short as a long, metal javelin thudded into the earth before them, quivering. It was quickly followed by the popping sound and dancing earth that indicated rounds impacting. Britton threw himself backward, knocking Rampart into the soldier behind him. The three went stumbling.

The soldiers in front of him scattered, firing their carbines skyward. The gunner in the helo worked the ammunition feed to his minigun with panicked speed.

The bird circled above them, the basket on its back writhing. Britton's eyes widened as he saw it was crammed with small, brown-skinned humanoids. Huge heads topped gnarled bodies and large, pointed ears jutted, pinned back by the wind of the giant bird's descent. Garish paint adorned their faces – ragged stripes, handprints, streaking stars. One of them, painted completely white, clung flat to the bird's neck, just behind its head. Most of the creatures in the basket brandished bright metal javelins in their long, thin hands, but at least one held a carbine.

One of the creatures hefted a grenade launcher meant to be attached to the underside of a rifle. It shouted something Britton could not hear and fired, the recoil knocking it back into the basket. The grenade detonated way off mark, but succeeded in spraying the group with spinning fragments of dirt and rock. One of the escorting soldiers cursed and collapsed, dropping his carbine and grabbing his ankle.

Britton spun away, shielding his eyes from the scattering dirt. He looked back at the bird. Red holes blossomed in its wings as bullets tore into it, but it didn't seem to notice. It opened its giant beak in a piercing cry and dove lower. Britton raised his carbine and sighted down it. Rampart slapped the barrel down. 'What the hell are you doing? Get your ass in the helo!'

Britton hesitated. The men around him were his captors and enemies, but his instincts rebelled against leaving fellow soldiers in the midst of a fight, his muscles responding to the sight of the uniforms and the sound of gunfire, rooting his legs to the spot.

A cluster of javelins burst from the basket. One of the escorts fell gurgling, impaled through the neck. Bullets plucked two of the squat, brown-skinned creatures shrieking out of the basket. More rounds tore into the bird.

It just kept coming. Britton could feel the wind swept toward them by its massive wings.

Rampart threw his shoulder into Britton, setting his legs moving again as the two ran for the helo.

A funnel of wind drilled horizontally through the air, focusing all the gathered dust into a gritty corkscrew. The tornado slammed into the bird's back, rolling it over and sending it tumbling across the track until it slammed against the concrete barrier wall. Gold-flecked feathers, each as long as a sword, exploded from the impact and showered down around them. The small creatures tumbled from the basket, pitching across the ground. A few stirred. Blasts of sizzling electricity turned them into piles of smoking meat before they could rise.

Harlequin swooped low over them, the remains of the dust devil swirling about his fists. 'Damn it, Rampart! How hard is it to get him in a damned helo?' He kicked off in the air and shot skyward, making for two more of the birds, distant but closing fast.

Rampart cursed and hurled Britton forward. The helo gunner had reloaded his minigun but checked his fire as Harlequin swerved in front of the spinning muzzles.

A hammerblow threw Britton on his back, his body armor digging a trough in the rough ground, his nose filled with a burning stink.

He blinked, struggling to rise onto his elbows, weighed down by his gear. His carbine was gone. His magazine pouches smoldered in his vest. The magazines inside must have absorbed the blast. They were melted, the bullets fused with their containers.

One of the brown creatures rose some fifty feet over the concrete barrier wall, its body wreathed in blue electricity. Its eyes were long and yellow, catlike. Its long nose hooked over a snarling mouth, showing tiny pointed teeth. Its skin was crusted with thick white paint.

'Christ!' Rampart said. 'Don't you run!' Britton felt the magic tide return as the Suppression fell away. The flow came gently, controlled by the Dampener in his blood. Rampart dropped his carbine to dangle from its sling and raced forward, hands outstretched.

The creature flew forward, the halo of electricity pulsing for another strike. Britton scrambled backward on his hands, palms scraping the shattered earth.

And then the electricity winked out, the tendrils flickering off with tiny popping sounds and puffs of black smoke. The creature hung in the air for a moment, eyes wide, then plummeted, shrieking, to the ground. It struck hard and bounced, its huge head flopping on a scrawny neck, the white-painted surface turning red. It lay, stirring weakly.

Rampart hauled Britton to his feet and propelled him the last few feet to the helo. The gunner left his weapon and helped them into the bay. A crew chief, head invisible in his flight helmet, knelt over him, clipped a carabiner to Britton's belt and secured the other end to a metal ring in the center of the Blackhawk's floor.

'He's in!' the chief called to the pilots. 'Let's go!'

The escorts were left to scramble back to the Stryker's relative safety as the Blackhawk lurched skyward. The Suppression took hold again as Rampart settled himself beside the crew chief. Only then did Britton realize that he hadn't even thought to use his magic to escape when he had that brief chance. Even if he had thought of it, how could he have made it work? The Dampener protected him from the overwhelming power of the current, but he still lacked the control to call it to his will. He cursed himself, his heart pounding. He still imagined he could feel the tight pressure of the bomb within it.

Britton gripped the metal ring as the Blackhawk banked, watching out the open door past the gunner's hip. Harlequin arced through the air toward one of the giant birds. The creatures on its back fired guns at him, the bullets flying wide.

That far above the ground, Britton could see the land outside the concrete barrier wall that ringed the LZ. It was dotted with small groups of the brown, squat humanoids, each surrounding one of the white-painted ones that had nearly fried him a moment ago. One of the white-painted creatures burst into a fireball, which shot upward, missing Harlequin by several feet. Britton recalled the words of the SOC Pyromancer who'd assaulted the school. *Theatrics don't win battles. Skill beats will, every time.*

That adage was being proved on the ground. Britton could make out army fire teams, moving and covering in perfect order. The troops poured fire and took cover behind the broken fragments of concrete barriers and the few Strykers that rolled with them, working with the near-perfect efficiency that had always made him so proud to be a soldier, man as machine. The creatures took the worst of it, falling back.

A piercing shriek dragged Britton's gaze to Harlequin, who had conjured a thick gray cloud. It draped one of the birds. Britton could see its wingtip as it struggled to stay aloft, the feathers sopping from the cloud's innards. The Aeromancer somersaulted upward, allowing the bird to pass beneath him and alongside the Blackhawk, waving to the gunner as he went. The bird shrieked again, shaking free of the cloud – bursting out broadside of the helo.

The gunner grinned as he opened up with the minigun. The barrels spun hot as the weapon pumped one thousand rounds each second into the passing bird and its crew. Britton looked away, but not before he saw much of it dissolve in red mist, screaming as it hurtled earthward.

Harlequin turned to the second bird as it banked away from him. He shook his head and flew to the helo, matching its speed.

The bird shrieked as something impacted with its shoulder, exploding in a cloud of burning feathers. It rolled onto its side, flapping uselessly with the remaining wing. The massive talons flexed, grasping empty air as it fell.

Over its back roared two Apache attack helicopters. They buzzed along, vicious horned insects, metal thoraxes gleaming with armament – twenty-millimeter cannons, laser-guided Hellfire missiles, Hydra rocket pods. They spiraled over the fallen birds before taking up escort positions behind the Blackhawk. Britton's throat tightened. He'd hoped to pilot one of those agile gunships long ago, before magic had carried him far from such dreams.

The fighting raged beneath them, but the creatures were falling back, helpless without air support. Erupting balls of fire and brief flashes of lightning spoke of magic on the ground, but it came less and less frequently, and, at last, they swept beyond it.

'What the hell are they?' Britton asked.

He could imagine the crew chief's eyebrows arching behind his tinted visor. 'Really big birds, sir.'

'No, I mean the things on their backs,' Britton said.

The chief shrugged. 'Goblins.'

'Goblins? Is that what they really are?' Britton asked Rampart.

'Nobody knows what they are,' Rampart answered. 'They're the indigenous around here. Until somebody comes up with something better – they're Goblins.'

Britton's mind reeled. Goblins. Real, live Goblins. The storybook legends come to life. Were other creatures from fantasy stories living here? Dragons? Unicorns? The Limbic Dampener kept his emotions from overwhelming him.

'They have guns?' Britton asked, his voice cracking with wonder.

'Every once in a while, they get lucky and take out a supply truck' – Rampart shrugged– 'or one of the indig workers at the FOB smuggles one out. I'm not worried, though. They don't know how to zero them, and their bodies are too small to handle the recoil. Half of them don't bother to use the sights. It's not stolen weapons you need to worry about with these bastards, it's the magic. They live in the Source all their lives and come up Latent at around twice the rate we do.'

'Indig,' Britton breathed.

Rampart nodded. 'A lot like the Mujahidin back in the old War on Terror. Bunch of broken-up tribes fighting themselves. The only thing they hate more than each other is us. They lay off somewhat in the winter, but they go on the warpath something fierce once the weather gets warm.'

Britton shook his head and rubbed his temples. Why not Goblins? They didn't fit the description he'd come to know from his days of role-playing games and fantasy books. But the birds did – massive creatures with black beaks and talons, large enough to threaten a ship at sea? Britton had read of them in Persian mythology and comic books. They were Rocs.

The battle below him surged around a creature he couldn't identify. A towering black figure, vaguely man-shaped, swept among the Goblin ranks, darting out toward the soldiers. It moved, lightning quick and oily smooth – one moment in one location and the next several feet forward. It gibbered, huge mouth slavering, flashing giant teeth in a horned head that reared ten feet above the multitude.

'Jesus,' Britton breathed. 'What the hell is that?'

'What?' Rampart asked, but the helo had banked sharply and moved on, leaving the battle behind.

Britton looked out the open doors again as the Blackhawk banked, shedding altitude. Past the gunner's boot, a much wider line of concrete blast barricades formed a massive wall. Behind it, makeshift wooden buildings stretched under corrugated-metal roofs. The spaces between were alive with people and vehicles.

'Where the hell are we?' Britton asked.

'Forward Operating Base Frontier,' the Suppressor answered. 'Hope you like it, because you're going to be spending an awful lot of time here. The FOB's the one place in any world where Probes like you are permitted to exist.'

The helicopters descended toward a helo pad along a flight line long enough to support strike fighters and fixed-wing support aircraft. It was well maintained, with armored control towers and fueling facilities in good repair. A ground crewman waved them into position with lit wands. A Humvee drove out to meet them. The Apaches wheeled off and regained altitude, heading back to the fight.

Britton shook his head as he remembered yelling at Cheatham beside Dawes's hospital bed.

Maybe they'll take you to that secret base and train you!

There is no secret base! You don't believe that conspiracy-theory crap!

The Blackhawk's wheels touched down on the tarmac, the Humvee pulled up to receive him, and Oscar Britton realized it wasn't crap after all.

Chapter Twelve
Shadow Coven

What are you? Keach. Lost. You abandoned the flow that bore you. You wandered far. What can you expect? Take the blood from Heptahad, and they die. That's what you are – walking dead. We are not killing you. We are merely reminding you of that death. We are forcing you to lie down and accept what happened to you long ago.

– Captured Sorrahhad 'defender' Goblin warrior
(Custodial debriefing transcript translated to English)

The Humvee turned onto a dirt road that snaked its way between shipping containers converted into windowless housing. Each was surrounded by piled sandbags, gabions rigged from wire fencing and packed earth, or the occasional concrete blast barrier. Water tanks stood atop showers built from blue tarps stretched across plywood frames. Longer trailers and enormous military tents indicated all the patchwork efforts of a forward-deployed center – a Band-Aid of a dining facility, a smudge of a gym and Morale, Welfare and Recreation building. Britton had called them the DFAC and MWR. He missed the membership those old acronyms implied.

The Humvee bumped past a busy Combat Surgical Hospital. Ankle-deep mud sucked at the tires. Britton felt naked without his weapons and armor, which an armorer along the flight line had forced him to check in, trading him a camouflage parka inadequate to the harsh cold.

The Forward Operating Base was a joint operation. Air force airmen in digital tiger stripes, navy sailors in work dungarees, marched alongside SOC soldiers. Britton saw Marine Suppression Lance grunts in surly rows, their magic kept under wraps by their Suppressing officer, anchoring the line. His eyes grew huge at the number of full-fledged SOC Sorcerers simply walking around. He saw a Pyromancer helping a work crew by heating a piece of metal. Terramancers raised firm paths out of the mud. Aeromancers in flight suits streaked overhead.

More incredible were the Goblins. He saw them everywhere, wearing blue jumpsuits like prison uniforms save for the Entertech patches on the shoulder and chest. They clustered in groups, spreading gravel over the mud, tending tiny beds of grass, running the septic truck as it pumped out the latrines. As they passed the cash, Britton saw at least one of the things in blue scrubs carrying out a barrel marked as biological waste. Each group had at least two soldiers in full battle gear standing watchfully by. The other humans ignored them.

Harlequin followed Britton's gaze to the Goblins and smiled. 'You're not the only Entertech employee we've got working out here. The indig are decent workers, when they're not stealing supplies or spotting targets for their brethren outside the wire.'

The Humvee passed through a checkpoint, then rattled to a stop outside a forty-foot shipping container, gray paint rusting off its ridged metal sides. P-4 was stenciled on the door. The flat roof was piled high with sandbags; more were stacked haphazardly around the sides. A small wooden staircase, stained dark with moisture, leaned precipitously away from the doorway before drowning in mud. Beside it stood a giant concrete staple, piled high with sandbags. A red-and-white sign reading BUNKER hung from the top. Several more identical converted containers stretched away in a row.

'Home, sweet home,' Harlequin said. 'Chow hall's up

the road about a hundred yards. Latrine and showers are the other way just as far. DFAC is twenty-four/seven for sandwiches and cereal, standard mealtimes if you want indig serving you freshly grilled cats and dogs. Your supervisor will be meeting you outside the MWR tomorrow morning – 0630 sharp. I recommend you get cleaned up, fed, and rested. Entertech's a demanding company. They're going to expect you to hit the ground running.'

Britton stepped out and nearly lost his boot to the thick mud. He turned to look up the track and froze. Three men were crossing the lane, military uniforms faced with red edging and gold buttons, the Indian flag stitched onto the shoulder. Their heads were wrapped in white turbans. Neatly trimmed beards hugged their chins.

Britton blinked at what glided along beside them. It towered over the makeshift structures, huge shoulders surmounting a chest as broad as a coffee table with biceps the size of footballs on at least a dozen pairs of arms. The torso terminated in a snake's tail, as thick as an oil drum and trailing off out of Britton's view. The vaguely humanoid collar sprouted into a bevy of snake's heads on spear-length necks. The creature was covered in gleaming, jewel-like scales, shading from purple-green at the heads to jasmine-pink along the tail. An arsenal of swords, axes, and bladed discs were thrust haphazardly into a red silk sash around its waist.

A few of the heads swung his way, tasting the air with varicolored tongues as the party passed.

Harlequin tapped Britton's shoulder. 'I forgot to mention. FOB Frontier is a combined operation. The Sahir Corps are just one of the foreign attachés we've got here. You're not to have any contact with them unless specifically authorized.'

The SOC Captain turned to Rampart and nodded. Britton felt the magical tide flow back into him, strictly controlled by the Dampener. Harlequin leaned forward and tapped his chest. 'No more Suppression,' he said. 'Just remember, we've got our eye on you. The FOB's roughly thirty square miles. Your ATTD pops anywhere outside that zone, even for a minute and . . .' He grinned.

'Boom,' Britton finished for him.

'The Dampener should cover you for the next couple of days at a minimum. If, God forbid, you feel like you're being overwhelmed anyway, just get down in the mud and shout 'Suppress, Suppress, Suppress!' with all you've got. I assure you that you will never be out of earshot of someone with significant Suppression capabilities anywhere on this FOB, day or night.'

'Sounds more like a warning,' Britton said.

'Take it however you like,' Harlequin said. 'Good luck in your new career. I have to say I'm very pleased that you elected to cooperate with us. You were a talented soldier, and I have every confidence that you'll be just as good in your new role. Just remember what I've been telling you. Stick to the regs, and everything will be fine. The rules are in place to protect you. Don't mess with them.

'Remember, outside the MWR tomorrow. Don't be late.'

The Humvee rolled off, spraying mud that covered Britton from the thigh down. The sky stretched above him, nearly cloudless. The Source's curious sensory intensity magnified everything. The smells of overcrowded latrines and mechanical-grade grease assaulted his nose, strangely beautiful in their magnitude. Soldiers griped, and vehicles rumbled in musical concentration. The sun shone as uncomfortably big and brilliant as the moon.

The inside of his container was carpeted in mud-stained blue and occupied by a particle-board desk, closet and dresser. A metal-framed army cot occupied one wall under the light of a single, long, fluorescent bulb. An army duffel rested on the bed, packed with rough linens, towels, and a toilet kit. The duffel also contained a dark gray ball cap with the Entertech company logo and two identical sets of clothing – khaki cargo pants rife with ammunition pouches and clip-points for carabiners, and skintight black shirts. The shirts were blazoned on the right shoulder with a subdued American flag, white on black. The left shoulder was stamped with the SOC arms. Over the right pectoral, a ghosted star emerged from behind a crescent moon. Over the left pectoral was another symbol he knew was unique to him – the outline of an arched doorway.

Britton rolled his eyes. *That's hardly keeping my ability a secret.*

Beside the duffel lay a massive binder, as thick as a telephone book, crammed with papers. PERSONNEL MANUAL – SPECIAL REGULATIONS FOR ENTERTECH PERSONNEL SERVING IN FORWARD AORS. Britton leafed through it, then tossed it aside. It would take him a week just to read a quarter of it.

He trudged through the mud toward the shower, looking for exits. They were letting him walk around unsupervised. There had to be a way to escape. He felt the flow of the magic still surging through him, kept in check by the Dampener. He could try to open a gate. Heck, he probably didn't even need to. He'd been on enough military installations to know how poorly guarded they could be. He could probably just walk off base. But then what? He'd be in unfamiliar country already proved hostile, and they could set off the ATTD the moment he appeared outside their designated perimeter.

He racked his brain for an answer and kept returning to the same thing – a hard steel transmitter packed with explosives deep inside his heart. There was no escape. *That's bullshit*, he thought, *there's a way, and you will stay on the throttle until you figure out what it is*.

He crowded in with a dozen soldiers, shivering under cold water that poured from black bags insufficiently warmed by the sun, cringing with each breeze blowing through the gaps in the tarp walls. They griped enthusiastically, whining about chow and the lack of women. If not for the magical tides flowing around him, there was no way to know he wasn't in a regular army FOB.

Just as Britton finished washing, a SOC Hydromancer joined them, warming the water with a gesture to collective cheers. By the time he'd dressed and taken a few steps, Britton was filthy again, the bits of gravel and scrap wood laid across the track failing to stop the mud from spurting with every step, sticking to clothes as if it possessed a will of its own.

Britton shook his head and headed toward his container, when suddenly his feet steadied. He looked down to see the mud firm up into a proper road. The dirt leapt from his boots and trousers, spraying into a cloud of dry dust.

A stocky SOC lieutenant brushed past him, grinning. His huge size and oak-tree pin marked him as a Terramancer. Britton nodded thanks. *At least they're not all like Harlequin out here.*

He flopped onto the thin mattress without bothering to set the sheets. He tried to figure a way to defeat the ATTD, but fatigue overwhelmed him, and in moments, he was swamped in dreamless sleep.

He woke in blackness, shivering in air gone frigid. He changed into the only clean clothing available – the odd uniform he'd found in the duffel. Still groggy, he pulled on his coat and stumbled down the muddy steps.

The night was alive with stars, the massive moon bright enough to read by. Britton stumbled backward, his reaction dulled by grogginess, as two soldiers on off-road motorcycles sped past.

'Cold, huh?' came a high, nasal voice. Britton turned to face a young man in glasses so thick that his brown eyes looked huge, swimming in fishbowls. He was tiny, his brown hair only coming up to Britton's chest, his skin so pale that it practically glowed in the moonlight. His uniform, identical to Britton's, flapped off his scrawny frame. A stylized skull grinned from his left pectoral.

'Uh, yeah,' Britton said, pulling his coat more tightly around him. 'You work for Entertech, too?'

The man's reply was cut off by a whooshing sound followed by an explosion. Britton saw a fireball bloom off in the distance. A siren began to wail, followed by a woman's calm voice over a loudspeaker. 'All FOB personnel, all FOB personnel. Take cover. I say again, take cover. FOB Reaction Force, action stations. I say again, action stations.' Another whoosh. Another explosion. Britton turned for the bunker.

'I wouldn't bother,' the man said, putting on a brave voice, but clearly rattled. 'The Goblin Pyromancers conjure flame strikes from the sky or just outside the walls. If you get tagged, a bunker isn't going to help. Might as well enjoy the night as best you can. If it's your time, it's your time, right? Just don't go anywhere. The MPs get annoyed if they catch you walking around during an attack.'

Britton started as another explosion bloomed a bright fireball skyward, much closer that time but still well distant. He heard the grinding of rotors as a pair of Apaches streaked over the barricade wall, searchlights flashing beneath them. The sirens stopped, and there was a curious silence, broken only by a distant shriek and muttered cursing. An electric cart whined down the lane, forcing Britton and the young man to retreat up the steps. The cart was piled with Goblins in jumpsuits, shouldering shovels and hammers. An improvised flatbed held a mound of tools and extension cords, as well as two human guards – feet dangling off the back. It raced down the lane and turned onto a side street. A platoon of MPs coming from the opposite direction turned to run behind it.

The young man shrugged, pushing his glasses up on his nose. 'Happens most nights, sometimes a few times a night. You get used to it.' He extended a hand. 'Simon Truelove.'

Britton's grip enveloped Truelove's tiny hand. 'Oscar Britton, nice to meet you.'

'Welcome to Contractor Row,' Truelove said, indicating the row of converted trailers, 'or you can call it P block, if you're so inclined.'

'All the contractors live here?' Britton asked.

'All the magic-using ones, yeah. Right now, that's just four of us, including you. The rest of the P pods are occupied by regular SOC Sorcerers. Fitzy is on the end closest to the DFAC.'

'Fitzy? Pea pods?'

Truelove smiled nervously. 'You're half-asleep, aren't you?'

Britton nodded, rubbing his head. 'I guess my sleep patterns haven't been consistent, lately.'

Truelove let out a honk of a laugh. 'I was heading down to the Officers' Club for a drink. We meet up there most nights. Why don't you come along? You can meet the rest of the Coven and we can explain everything to you.'

Britton followed him down to the road in the direction of the chow hall. The mud track ran several hundred yards, punctuated on either side by identical trailers converted to living quarters, each with the letter P stenciled on the doors, along with ascending numbers.

'P pods,' Britton said.

Truelove nodded. 'The O pods are just outside our checkpoint. There are some joint service troops and big army types, but you're in the middle of SOC territory here. We don't go out to the rest of the FOB, and they don't come here.'

Twice they passed burned pods. A Goblin crew worked on one under the watchful eye of their minders, clearing debris and spraying flame-retardant foam from a tank on the back of their electric cart. The female voice broadcast again. 'All clear, all clear, all clear.'

The lane was unlit, and when a wandering MP challenged them with 'ID, please, sir,' Britton recoiled in surprise. Truelove flashed a badge for the MP's flashlight, which was covered in colored gel to preserve his night vision. After Britton tapped his empty pockets in a vain search, the MP, a mere silhouette in the moonlight, reached out for the badge around his neck and nodded, satisfied. 'Thanks, sir. Mid-rats ended an hour ago, but you can still grab a sandwich.'

'Midnight rations,' Truelove explained.

'So we're in the same . . . Coven?' Britton asked. 'I noticed the uniform.'

Truelove nodded. 'Coven Four, that's us. We're the contractor unit. Covens are like squads in the SOC. We catch some crap for it. You know, bloodsucking contractors, but you get used to it. For one thing, we're not under the Uniform Code of Military Justice.'

'. . . and we can drink,' Britton said.

Truelove honked laughter again. 'All the officers drink here. SOC isn't under General Order One out here in the Source.'

Truelove's voice trembled. At first, Britton thought it was the cold, but the edge in his next comment revealed it as excitement. 'Man, Oscar, I'm really glad that you're here.'

'Why's that?'

'Your timing is perfect. The two of us have been stood up for a month, just going over basics. They'll put you and Downer in the SASS, teach you the basics, and we can get started right away.'

Britton opened his mouth to ask another question as the track gave out into the wide dirt square where the chow hall stood, well lit by bright sodium arc lights. Other vast tents bordered the square – what Britton guessed was the Morale, Welfare, and Recreation building, the Post Exchange, and the gym. Britton scanned the square once more before realizing what was missing – the Army Post Office that was standard on all military installations.

Even at that late hour, a line snaked out of the chow hall's main entrance. They wore an assortment of uniforms, gym gear, civilian jeans under light coats. Goblins scuttled in and out of a side entrance, carrying pots and crates bulging with food. A few of those on line noticed Britton and Truelove and tapped buddies on the shoulders, whispering. In moments, the tail section of the line was doing its best not to obviously gape at them and failing miserably. A few junior Seabees, navy construction-battalion workers in hard hats, pointed before being abruptly silenced by their chiefs.

Truelove shook his head at the line. 'Sorry, Oscar. You get used to it.'

'It's the uniforms, isn't it?'

'Yeah, they kind of freak people out.'

'Why?'

Truelove looked at him before shrugging an apology. 'They didn't tell you? We're the Probe Coven. That's why it's all contractors.'

Britton stared for a moment. 'I had an inkling when they didn't kill me. I've seen them kill Probes, especially when they fight.'

Truelove nodded sheepishly. 'The SOC bends the rules sometimes. I guess they think that so long as we don't work for the government, that's okay. I didn't run or anything. Not like you did.' He looked at his feet, embarrassed. '. . . I don't judge you or anything. It's all fine with me. I just called the SOC hotline as soon as I Manifested.'

'But you're a Probe. Didn't you think they'd kill you?'

Truelove shrugged. 'I didn't think about it, honestly. What choice did I have? You can't run from the SOC.' Britton didn't know how to respond, so he turned to the Officers' Club, marked by a stencil-painted wooden board – cobbled together from plywood sheets to form what looked like a giant one-room schoolhouse. The roof was scraps of corrugated plastic sprayed irregularly with fire-retardant foam.

Beside the door, some enterprising navy Seabees had built a small plywood pedestal, to which they'd affixed their emblem, a worker bee wielding a tommy gun and construction tools in its six legs. A cigar protruded from the grim mouth. CAN DO SINCE 1942! the logo read. A silver statue of a huge boar topped the pedestal. Its giant ridged back glinted in the hard light, the metallic bristles sharp as needles, so fine they swayed gently with the breeze. The long tusks curled between snarling teeth to sharp, brass-tipped points. Its silver eyes seemed to be glass.

'It's real,' Truelove said. 'I know it looks like a sculpture, but I saw them take it down in the woods between the LZ and here. We're mostly confined to the FOB, but you get out once in a while. The Source is an amazing place.'

The wind picked up, and Truelove tugged him inside.

Interior and exterior were equally ramshackle. Pressboard tables and chairs had been slapped together around the mud-spattered floor. One wall was covered in license plates from various states in varying degrees of rust consumption. A tall bar, also made from license-plate-encrusted plywood, stood before a giant mirror draped with the flags of the five uniformed military services. An American flag hung beside a corkboard covered with photographs. An old Wurlitzer-style jukebox blared country music from the corner.

The Officers' Club was crowded, some in and some out of uniform – looking every bit as tired and disheveled as those on line for the chow hall. A few of the barstools stood empty. A coast guard ensign in rumpled blue utilities stood to grab another drink from the bar, his eyes falling across Britton and Truelove.

He froze, staring.

A moment later, an army captain followed his gaze. He shifted in his chair, tapping a buddy on the shoulder, and gesturing. Within moments, all talk, clinking of glasses, and stubbing of cigarettes had stopped. The only sound in the

Officers' Club was the upbeat two-step belting from the Wurlitzer – the singer reminding the audience never to forget the old dirt road in their heart of hearts.

Truelove self-consciously made his way to the bar, muttering apologies as the room began to empty until only a few die-hard marine officers sullenly occupied a table near the door.

Britton joined Truelove at the bar but kept the marines in his peripheral vision. The bartender, a pale-faced, ginger-haired Entertech contractor, glared at them, muttering into his beard. Truelove looked embarrassed but didn't dare ask for a drink.

Britton followed Truelove's lead before deciding it was ridiculous. He opened his mouth to order a drink when the door banged open, and three more figures entered.

The first was a Goblin, small even for its race. It wore blue surgical scrubs, its broad, three-toed feet bare. Its bald brown skull was covered with a small blue surgical hat and a face mask that hung from a large, pointed ear. Tiny white dots covered its forehead and cheeks.

Behind the Goblin stood a young girl in a Coven Four uniform – the left pectoral showing the four elements surrounding a central eye. She was in the prime of adolescence, slightly chubby. Her head had been recently shaved.

Recognition hit him as she approached, smiling at Truelove.

He'd last seen that face slicked with sweat, panting in a stairwell, where a nine-millimeter round had taken a bite out of her side.

Harlequin entered behind her, seeing the recognition on Britton's face and smiling ruefully.

The marine officers muttered at the new arrivals, glaring hard at the Goblin. '. . . that Coven. Hang out with those freaks. You believe that?'

The girl looked at them, and the marines suddenly found the depths of their drinks fascinating. Her eyes returned to him, and Britton felt himself swamped, unable to speak. Alive? She was alive? He started to stand, reach out for her, then thought better of it and sat down.

'You must be the new arrival,' the girl said.

Britton ignored her, holding Harlequin's eyes. When he could finally speak, he said, 'But you killed her.'

'This is your basic problem,' Harlequin said, 'which I thought I made clear on the ride out to Portcullis. You think you're so much smarter than everyone else.'

The girl looked askance at Harlequin, who smiled. 'This is one of the assaulters who took you down. Turned out to be a Probe himself.'

The girl turned back to Britton, her eyes widened. She swallowed but said nothing.

'I'm . . .' What could he say? 'I'm sorry.' The words came out in a rush. 'I didn't want to . . . I had to.'

The girl opened her mouth to say something, then closed it. She looked at her feet.

'I don't believe this,' Britton said.

'Believe it,' Harlequin said. 'While you're at it, believe that you wasted a lot of time and effort and hurt a lot of people unnecessarily by running. If you'd just done the right thing, we'd have taken care of you. But you decided that you knew better. Did you honestly think we kill Probes, particularly Portamancers? Christ, Oscar, it's possibly the rarest and most powerful school of magic. We're not just going to chuck that in the trash.'

'You faked her death,' Britton said. 'You kidnapped her. That's slimy even for you. How'd you manage it?'

Harlequin shook his head. 'A good magician never reveals his secrets, Oscar. And considering that the law would have given her death, we figured taking her into custody was a step up.'

'It's all right,' the girl said in a voice that didn't sound like it was all right at all. She pulled up a vacated stool. 'It's better than running. They train you and have your back. We'll be real Sorcerers now.' Her words were rote, wooden.

'How many times did you make her repeat that?' Britton asked Harlequin.

Harlequin shook his head. 'So much smarter than everyone else.'

Britton framed a retort but was cut off by the girl's quavering voice. 'Sarah Downer,' she said, extending a hand.

The gesture took all the fight out of him. *So brave. She's been ripped from her moorings, same as you. And she's so much younger. Yet here she is, swallowing her fear and offering her hand to the man she knows shot her.*

Shamed by her bravery, it took him a moment to take her hand. 'Oscar Britton,' he said, overwhelmed.

Harlequin chuckled at Britton's stunned expression. 'Take a lesson from young Downer here. She seems to have figured out some things you'd do well to imitate.'

Downer lit up at the compliment, her pale cheeks blushing as she studiously avoided looking at him.

Britton stared at his lap, speechless. Was it possible that Harlequin was right? The SOC hadn't killed her. Was there a method to their madness? Could they be the good guys after all? He shook the thought away, his anger returning at the sight of her reaction to Harlequin's compliment. 'She's just a kid,' he said. 'You scared the crap out of her. You've probably been interrogating her nonstop since I ran. Are you surprised she's supposedly "come around"?'

Harlequin shrugged. Downer blanched, and Britton's anger immediately gave way to shame again.

'You know, for a so-called kid, she's a hell of a lot smarter than you, Oscar,' Harlequin said as he leaned down to help the Goblin onto the stool beside Truelove. Downer rushed to help, her eyes fixed firmly on the Aeromancer. Truelove grinned, clapping it lightly on the back and turning to the bartender.

'You know I ain't gonna serve him,' the bartender said, gesturing at the Goblin.

Truelove looked studiously at his lap, but Harlequin folded his arms over his chest. 'And you know I'm not going to ask you twice, Chris.'

The bartender bristled, but Britton could see the fear in his eyes. 'I'll leave. You can serve him your damn self.'

'I think we can manage opening a couple of beer bottles. If you'd care to take your useless ass off to bed, I'd be delighted to oblige,' Harlequin said.

Chris threw down his bar cloth and strode around the bar. He thrust an angry finger at the Goblin, who sat passively on his stool, ignoring him. 'You know he's a damned spotter. Hell, he's probably running weapons out to the tribes. I can't believe they let him work in the cash. Who knows how many people he's poisoned?'

'Entertech and the army seem to feel differently,' Harlequin said. 'Now get lost before Simon brings your great-grandma out here to lecture you on the pitfalls of bigotry.'

Chris turned purple but shuddered at Harlequin's words. He stormed out, the last of the marines on his heels.

Harlequin groaned and shook his head. Truelove slid off his stool and went behind the bar. He rummaged around, producing two long-necked bottles of cold beer and a cup, which he set in front of the Goblin.

'You've got to cut Chris some slack,' Truelove said haltingly, clearly uncomfortable from the confrontation. 'The tribes don't take kindly to our presence here. Most folks at the FOB have a tough time distinguishing between the Goblins that work for us and the ones trying to kill us.'

Britton grimaced as Truelove found a container of sugar and filled the cup halfway, following it with water until the cup brimmed – a soupy white mess. The Goblin reached forward, grinning like a child, and grabbed it in his wrinkled, three-fingered hands.

'Okay, Sarah,' Harlequin said. 'I've got to get to the flight line before I miss my helo out. You all set?'

'Yes, sir,' Downer replied. 'I'm good, thanks.' She didn't sound good at all.

'Don't stay up too late.' Harlequin winked. 'You've got to be up bright and early tomorrow now that you're all here.'

'I won't, I promise,' she said, sounding so young that Britton felt like his heart would break.

Britton marveled at her girlish obedience. This was the Selfer who'd taken on an entire assault force? Who'd almost killed him? He looked over Harlequin's smart uniform, pressed and polished to perfection despite the mud that spattered them all. Britton could only see the man who'd hounded him, but he guessed that man would do for a confused teenaged girl. Nothing could make a kid turn her coat like puppy love.

'Jesus, Harlequin, she's just a kid,' Britton said, instantly regretting it as Downer's face curled into a frown.

'She's a kid who can teach you a thing or two,' Harlequin said. 'Magic forces us to grow up faster than normal. If I were you, I'd stop thinking I was so damned smart and start paying attention to how things are done in this brave new world. Otherwise, you're in for a rough adjustment.'

He went out into the night, leaving the OC to Truelove, Downer, Britton, and the Goblin. They sat in silence before Truelove shrugged and tapped Britton's knee.

'Welcome to Shadow Coven,' he said. 'The new Shadow Coven, anyway. We've just been reconstituted.'

'Reconstituted?' Britton asked, scarcely able to take his eyes off Downer, to believe she was alive. She sat silently, looking lost. Britton wanted to talk to her but didn't know what to say, and was grateful for Truelove's nattering, which kept the shocked silence at bay.

'The last outfit apparently deployed to a bad end. They won't give us the details,' Truelove said, smiling grimly. 'We're still short, unfortunately. You're looking at all of us. Well, there's Richards, but he's passed out right now.'

'Him, too?' Britton asked, indicating the Goblin, who snorted busily at his cup of wet sugar.

Truelove smiled indulgently at the creature. 'Nah, Marty's just a friend.'

'Marty . . . ?' Britton asked.

'His real name is tough to pronounce,' Truelove said. 'Nearest I can figure it's Mardak Het-Parda. Everybody calls him Marty.'

Marty snorted again, looking up at the sound of his name. 'Umans no talk me,' he said. 'Only you and Doctor Captain.' His voice hissed from his nose, harsh and nasal.

'I'm Oscar,' Britton said, unsure if he should shake hands. 'Nice to meet you.'

'Uskar . . .' the Goblin said, sounding so much like the demon-horses that Britton started.

'You speak English pretty well,' Britton said to the Goblin, who smiled, wiggling his long ears.

'Better than any other Goblin we've got,' Truelove said,

beaming with pride. 'They use him sometimes to do 'terp work, you know, interpreting, with detainees and tribal delegations. But most of the time he works in the cash. He's really good with the local flora, and I swear I feel a slight current off him. I think he's got a touch of Physiomancer in him.'

Britton concentrated, but felt no current coming from the Goblin. Perhaps it was overwhelmed by Downer's and Truelove's strong magical tides.

'Of course, they don't call themselves Goblins,' Truelove said, embarrassed. 'I really shouldn't, it's not nice. But you start to fall into it since everyone around you does.'

'No angry,' Marty hiss-whispered. 'Goblin okay.'

'What do they call themselves?' Britton asked.

'Water baby!' Marty said.

'Like that,' Truelove said. 'Near as I can tell, he means children of the stream. I think it means they came from magic.'

Marty nodded, slurping the last of the solution in his cup. Britton frowned.

Truelove smiled at his reaction. 'They didn't have sugar before we came here. They absolutely love it. We keep them clear of alcohol, they can't process it. Even one sip makes them falling-down drunk. A full glass can kill them.'

Britton shook his head. He looked down at his beer, then cracked it open. 'Nothing for you?' he asked Downer, trying to break the silence between them.

She shook her head. 'I'm not old enough to drink.'

'I'm not going to tell anyone.' He looked a question at Truelove, but the smaller man only looked down at the bar.

'It's against regs,' Downer said, frowning. 'Harlequin says we've got to stick to the regs from now on.' Again that wooden voice.

'Harlequin's not here,' Britton replied. 'When I last saw you, the regs didn't mean a lot to you.'

He meant it good-naturedly, hoping to coax a smile from her, but Downer flushed. 'That was a long time ago.'

'That was a day ago,' Britton said, 'maybe two.'

'Harlequin said you might talk like this,' Downer retorted.

'Sticking to the regs is what makes us different from Selfers.'

Britton knew better than to argue with the patronizing certainty in her voice. What teenagers didn't think they knew everything? *Cut her some slack. She's been through hell, and is less equipped to deal with it than you are. You put the damned bullet in her. You owe her for that.*

Unable to think of a way to recover from the rising tension, he took a swallow of his beer and turned to Truelove instead. 'So, Shadow Coven?'

The small man nodded. 'Each Coven gets a name and number. We're Shadow Coven. Entertech contractors, all. Welcome to the company. We're the one Probe Coven in the whole SOC.'

Prohibited schools. Britton suddenly realized the significance of Harlequin's comment about Chris's grandmother. 'You're a Necromancer,' he said to Truelove.

Downer brightened, grateful for the change of subject. She pointed to the floor beside the bar. 'Come on, Simon, show him.'

Truelove's pale cheeks went crimson. He looked uncomfortably at Downer from beneath his narrow brow, and Britton thought he caught of glimpse of the same smitten look Downer had showed to Harlequin.

Pushing the thoughts away, Britton followed Downer's finger to the floor. A largish roach lay there, crushed flat by an uncompromising combat boot.

Truelove shrugged again and stared at it. Britton felt his tide ratchet up. The broken, flat insect peeled itself away from the ground and stood, one broken leg remaining in the dirt and another dangling by a thread of chitin. It bowed to Britton, shedding the broken leg in the process, then turned a graceful pirouette on the bottom of its abdomen before flopping over on its back.

'Impressive,' Britton said.

'It's just Physiomancy in reverse,' Truelove said. 'They do live flesh. I do the dead stuff.'

'How about you?' Britton asked Downer, trying again. 'You're an Elementalist.'

She didn't give him a chance. 'How about you?'

Britton barked a nervous laugh. 'Portamancy.'

Downer worked to keep from looking impressed and failed. 'Fitzy said as much,' she said. 'We didn't believe him.'

'Fitzy?' Britton said.

'You'll meet him tomorrow,' Truelove said. 'Don't mess with him. He's not a nice man.'

'Fitzy is asshole!' Marty chirped proudly. Downer and Britton laughed, but Truelove looked embarrassed. 'I've been trying to stop him from doing that . . . It just makes things harder on him.'

'Is he an asshole?' Britton asked.

Truelove shrugged uncomfortably. 'He's a good instructor, he'll help you get a handle on your magic.' His eyes brightened behind his thick glasses.

'Gate magic,' Truelove said. 'That's amazing.'

Britton sighed. 'Believe me, I'd rather be flying helicopters. That's what I joined the army to do.'

Truelove's eyes widened farther. 'You were a helo pilot? That's awesome! What'd you fly?'

'They had me in Kiowas. I wanted Apaches, but I didn't have enough time in. I Manifested before I could get reassigned.'

As Truelove interrogated Britton about flying, Downer eyed him intensely. Britton did his best to pretend he didn't notice and focused on answering Truelove's enthusiastic questions – covering everything from training to flight mechanics – but the line of conversation frustrated him. He wanted to talk about magic and the Coven and was grateful when Downer cut in.

'You can't control it, can you?' she asked.

'No,' Britton admitted, 'not yet.'

'We go to the SASS tomorrow. Fitzy says we'll learn there.'

'Suitability assessment,' Truelove offered. 'They test your loyalty and teach you to get control of your magic. They enrolled me when I first got here. Since you're a contractor, you don't have to raise the flag.'

'Raise the flag? What the hell are you talking . . . ?' Britton asked.

A crackle sounded outside, followed by a boom that shook the flimsy plywood walls, resulting in a minor avalanche of license plates.

'Medic!' a voice screamed from outside. 'Medic!'

By the time they raced outside, two more booms had sounded, each farther away than the last.

The line out of the chow hall was gone. The front of the tent smoldered gently, melted canvas and plastic sending up wisps of foul-smelling smoke. Dark clouds drifted apart above them, far lower than any cloud should have been. The ground was rent and smoking, a deep, charred groove that ran the length of where the line had been.

Two twisted, man-sized masses lay in the trench, burning brightly. Just beyond them lay a young soldier. Two of his comrades were already stripping off his smoldering camouflage trousers. The bottoms of his boots had been blown off. The soles of his feet were burned an angry red dotted with black.

Marty let out a high-pitched squeak and ran to the man's side. He muttered to himself in his own language, his long fingers moving over the wounds. The men kneeling at the wounded man's side paused in shock before the larger one – a navy Seabee with hulking shoulders, reached out and belted Marty across the face, sending the Goblin sprawling.

'Get the hell away from him!' he shrieked. 'You trying to finish him off?'

The other soldier cursed and returned to the wounded man's side. He continued stripping off the burning trousers, revealing the charred and bubbling flesh that had once been a pelvis. 'Medic!' he cried again. 'Somebody get a fucking medic!'

'He is a damned medic,' Britton said, helping the Goblin to his feet and pushing him forward. 'He works in the cash, for chrissakes.'

The kneeling soldier ignored him, but the Seabee took a step forward. Britton saw the anchor pinned on his white hard hat – marking him as a chief, senior enlisted, and not to be trifled with. 'He's a fucking Goblin, and he's going to kill him! Hell, he probably called the strike!'

Britton stabbed a finger into the man's chest, pushing him backward and sending his hard hat tumbling. 'He's not even fucking Latent, you jackass.'

The Seabee surged forward, fist cocked. Britton stepped into the punch, letting it collide with his shoulder and catching the smaller man by the throat. The magic surged along the current of his rage. It came to him wildly, pulsing and erratic. Instinctively, Britton reached for it.

Truelove stumbled backward as a gate snapped opened inches from his face.

'I, on the other hand, am Latent,' Britton seethed. 'And I don't have time to compare dicks with you. This man is dying, and that Goblin can help him. You're going to let him help or you and I are going to enter into a rather dynamic disagreement.'

The man reached up to wrench at Britton's wrist, then saw Downer and Truelove standing at his side. His eyes flicked to the ghosted star and moon over their chests, to the shimmering gate, and back. He ceased struggling.

Britton released him and let the Dampener take control. The gate rolled shut, and Truelove exhaled loudly.

Marty scrambled back to the wounded man's side. He reached beneath his hospital scrubs and produced a worn leather pouch, divided into several pockets. He grumbled to himself, poking his fingers into its depths and sniffing them before he settled on a fine green powder, which he poured out into his palm. He spat in his palm and rolled the liquid in the powder until it formed a vile paste that stank so badly Britton wrinkled his nose. He leaned forward, and the Seabee jerked his chin toward Marty's hand. 'What the hell is that shit?'

Britton looked doubtfully at Truelove, but the Necromancer nodded. 'Trust him. Marty's very good at his work.' The Seabee looked daggers at Marty but let the Goblin apply the paste around the wounded man's nostrils. He writhed, swatting weakly at the air, and moaning.

'He not die now, soon,' Marty said. 'Go cash fast.'

Sirens wailed in the distance, and Britton could see a plume of fire rising farther out, but still inside the barricade wall of the FOB. Britton and Downer lifted the wounded soldier as gently as they could. He moaned softly, half-conscious, as they carried him behind Marty, who scampered down the muddy track toward the Combat Surgical Hospital. Truelove jogged alongside. The Seabee and the other soldier trailed a few paces back, whispering to one another.

The hospital was overwhelmed. The massive tent literally jumped with activity, the flaps opening and closing so fast to admit new wounded that wind vibrated through the entire structure. Army doctors, navy hospital corpsmen and SOC burn-trauma officers ran to and fro, fussing over a mounting flow of stretchers.

'That was amazing,' Downer breathed.

'That *was* amazing,' Truelove agreed. 'But you're not supposed to use your magic until you've been enrolled in the SASS. You could get in deep shit for that.'

'I'm just amazed I could do it at all,' Britton said, the reality hitting him. He had called magic entirely on his own, and it had worked. 'The Dampener is incredible. Why the hell don't they just hand the stuff out?'

Downer sounded peevish. 'Against regs,' she muttered.

'And expensive as hell,' Truelove added. 'Most in the SOC don't get it if they can control their magic okay on their own. But everyone in Shadow Coven gets an unlimited supply.'

A SOC Hydromancer appeared at the entrance and recognized Marty, moving toward him.

'Doctor Captain,' Marty said, jerking his hand at Britton, Downer and their weakly stirring cargo. 'Specialist Lenko has thunder burn. I give him . . . bad smell herbs. He needs . . .'

Britton remembered Dawes's care and breathed a bit easier. The Hydromancer moved forward and motioned for two orderlies bearing a stretcher. They loaded the wounded soldier onto the stretcher, and he vanished into the hospital, the Hydromancer following close behind.

Marty went after them, then paused, turning to Britton. 'Thank you,' he said, his brows arching until the white dots on his forehead were reduced to thin lines. He bowed slightly, tapping his closed eyelids.

Britton realized the Goblin had called the wounded soldier by name. 'You knew him?'

Marty nodded. 'Specialist Lenko is wise. He dies, I eat his eyes.'

The Hydromancer reappeared in the hospital-entry flaps and motioned brusquely. 'Marty! Come on! We need every hand we can get!' The Goblin turned and ran after him, leaving Britton with Truelove and Downer and the steady flow of wounded. The Seabee and the other soldier had vanished. They made their way back toward the P pods in silence.

'Thanks for sticking up for Marty,' Truelove finally said.

'How'd you two get to be such buds?' Britton asked.

'I've got some stomach problems,' Truelove said, casting an embarrassed look at Downer, who didn't appear to notice. 'The docs at the cash didn't really know what to do about it, and the one Physiomancer they've got is so overworked, he doesn't have time for something that isn't life-threatening. Marty gave me some herbal remedy. It doesn't fix it totally, but it really helps.'

Britton nodded. 'He seems like a good . . . guy.' In fact, the Goblin's kindness deeply impressed him. If he'd let that navy chief have his way, Lenko would probably have died while those idiots sat around shouting for a medic.

Downer laughed. 'He's all right. We keep him in sugar, he keeps Truelove from crapping his drawers.' Truelove turned crimson at the remark, but Downer missed it, punching him in the shoulder.

'Did he actually say he'd eat that guy's eyes?' Britton said, trying to change the subject.

Truelove nodded. 'It's a custom. They do it to honor their dead. They believe that if you eat the eyes of a dead man, you ingest everything he's ever seen, the sum of his life experience. That way he lives on forever through you. It's a high compliment. Of course, try telling that to our forward squads who come across Goblins actually doing it. There's not a lot of patience for the practice around here.'

Britton shook his head and suddenly realized how cold he was. Smoke still billowed in distant columns, flickering red-orange inside. The late-fall chill was intense, the flame-whipped winds piercing. 'Christ,' Britton said, 'what the heck is the army doing out here?'

'You haven't figured it out?' Downer asked. 'FOB Frontier is a bridgehead in the Source. You're in occupied territory.

'We're conquering the magic kingdom.'

Chapter Thirteen

Fitzy

Magical Suppression occurs when a Latent individual crosses his own current with that of another Latent individual, effectively interdicting the magical flow. It is a concentrated effort. If the Suppressor's Latency is weaker than the individual's he is acting against, a breakthrough may occur, resulting in ineffective Suppression. Some interviewees have described this sensation as painful or exhausting. Skill and training can compensate for this to some degree, but in the end, it is a matchup of strength. Some SOC Sorcerers devote their entire careers to Suppression. These 'Master Suppressors' rarely find a current they are unable to lock down.

– Avery Whiting
Modern Arcana: Theory and Practice

Britton didn't bother trying to sleep. He lay on his cot, staring at the corrugated-metal ceiling and remembering his mother. His mind returned to her eyes, staring at him in horror and realization.

The 158th. His mother. Dawes. He had lost them all. He gripped the coarse blanket, balling it in his fists.

Was this it? Was this his life from here on? *It can't be. You've got to get out of here.*

His mind returned to the ATTD, holding him as surely as if he were surrounded by bars.

Find a way. You have to find a way to get that thing out.

As the first streamers of dawn filtered underneath the door, Britton heard the triple succession of booms that marked another attack. The sirens sounded far away, and he didn't even budge at the tremors, surprised at how quickly he had become inured.

The next morning, he found the inside of the chow hall was much as he'd come to know from other bases. Long tables backed up to a line of metal trays piled high with steaming slop that could scarcely be called food. The line was manned mostly by Goblins in paper hats who endured the sullen looks of their customers with resignation. Britton got himself a foam tray piled high with a yellow slurry that roughly approximated eggs and some sausage patties as chewy as old spare tires, then sat at a bench that quickly cleared of other occupants as soon as they saw his uniform. A moment later, Truelove appeared and sat across from him.

'Good morning,' the Necromancer said. 'You fill out your time sheet?'

Britton paused, eggs steaming on his fork. 'Time sheet?'

'You're not a soldier anymore,' Downer said, plopping down beside him. 'Contractors get their time sheets audited daily.'

'Make sure you fill yours out like clockwork, or Fitzy'll have your ass,' Truelove said. 'Apparently there's a new admin colonel here. He's a real hard-ass about accounting, and he comes down hard on Fitzy when things slip. Fitzy always makes sure it rolls downhill to us.'

'When do I meet this famous Fitzy?' Britton asked.

Truelove examined his watch. 'It's 0615, which gives you fifteen minutes. There's a terminal in the MWR where you can do it electronically. Just put in your social security number and eight hours for yesterday. Make sure you do it before bed from now on.'

Britton stared at him, expecting a joke. Truelove didn't laugh.

Britton sat at the terminal in the Morale, Welfare, and Recreation tent, struggling with the irony of filling out a time sheet in the middle of a war zone. He was still laughing to himself as he stepped out of the tent and nearly bumped into a man who more than made up for his lack of height in sheer muscle. His head was shaved as bald as Britton's, gleaming in the rising sun as if it had been oiled. A tight moustache was parked on a stern upper lip. Dark, deep-set eyes stared into Britton's, showing a hint of amusement. The hard line of a mouth was all business. The man wore a Shadow Coven uniform, the Entertech logo noticeably absent. Instead, the striped bar of a chief warrant officer adorned the peaked ball cap. Britton could feel a slight magical current off him. The Suppressor's armored fist, gripping its clutch of lightning bolts, marked the left of his shirt. A star crowned the fist, a laurel wreath spanning beneath.

'Morning, Novice,' the man said. 'I'm Chief Warrant Officer Fitzsimmons. You can call me God, or sir, whichever is easier. Got your time sheet filled out?'

Britton towered over the man by nearly a foot. 'Yes, si . . .' He stopped himself before completing the honorific. He had been an officer before and was presently a civilian contractor. Thus he was unsure if the man deserved the honorific.

'Sir,' the man finished for him. 'You'd better get used to it. You'll be saying it a lot. Did you fill in the proper task number and authorization account for each day worked?'

'Sir?' Britton asked.

'I take your charming but clueless expression to mean that you have no idea what I'm talking about,' Fitzsimmons said.

'I saw those fields on the time sheet, sir,' Britton answered, 'but I didn't know what codes to put in.'

'And why the hell not, Novice?' Fitzsimmons asked. 'Surely you've read sections nine A and B in the manual that I left on the rack in your hooch. Had you bothered to perform the requisite reading required by your job, which, might I remind you, your conditional pardon depends on, you would have found those sections entitled "timekeeping" in twenty-four-point font.'

'Sir,' Britton explained, 'that manual was enormous, I didn't have a chance to . . .'

'Is that a fixed or rotary wing whine I'm hearing, Novice?' Fitzsimmons asked. 'Do you honestly think I give a rat's ass for whatever bullshit excuses you care to mine at this particular moment? Ooooh, I was really tired, sir. That manual was just too big, sir. Like I give a fuck about any of that.'

Britton swallowed his anger and nodded. Such treatment might work in boot camp, but he was a former officer and pilot and not even in the army anymore. 'Yes, sir,' he said. 'I'll go check the codes in the manual right now.' He turned his back on the man and moved toward the P pods. He'd barely taken a step when the chief warrant officer slapped him in the back of the head so hard that he stumbled forward. Britton whirled, the Dampener easing the magic that flowed along the current of his anger.

'I was warned that you weren't very smart,' Fitzsimmons said, moving so close that the brim of his cap touched Britton's chin. 'I also heard that you assaulted a chief petty officer last night in an effort to assist a damned Goblin. You also used your magic under unauthorized circumstances before we'd had a chance to enroll you in the SASS. Not off to a very good start, Novice. So, no. You don't get to go check the manual now. Instead, you get to do fifty push-ups, and I'd like to hear you say "sir" at the end of each count off. On my deck, right now.'

Britton looked down at the thick mud – wet, chilly, and at least four inches deep. For a moment, his composure failed him. 'You've got to be fucking kidding me.'

Fitzy grabbed Britton's balls, squeezing hard. Britton howled, pushing him backward, and letting the surge of magic flow through the Dampener's wall. The man smiled, and Britton felt his magical current roll back as the Suppression took hold.

Fitzy kicked Britton hard in the knee. As Britton doubled over, he grabbed his neck and slammed a knee into his stomach. Britton fell face-first in the mud and struggled to rise out of the choking thickness. He could feel Fitzy's boot on his back.

'Count off, Novice!' the chief warrant officer roared. 'I don't have all damned day!'

'Fuck you!' Britton struggled, but Fitzy's boot held him down with surprising strength. He leaned down and pressed a fingertip into the base of Britton's neck. Pain blossomed into numbness. Britton's face dropped into the mud, and Fitzy held it there. Just when he felt he would choke, Fitzy let him lift it a few inches. He gulped air, swallowing mud in the process. He sputtered, choking.

'Count off!'

Britton tried to speak but couldn't find the breath. His face went down in the mud again until his universe shrank to a pinhole filled entirely by the need for air. His throat burned. His lungs swelled. When he thought they might burst, Fitzy let him raise his head.

'Count off.' Fitzy's voice was calmer.

Britton got his arms underneath him, but his veins felt full of lead. He managed one agonizing push-up. 'One.'

'One what, Novice?'

'One, sir.'

'That's better. The agreed number was fifty.'

Britton thought of air and how badly he wanted it. His peripheral vision filled with onlookers, but he swallowed his pride and channeled his rage and humiliation into his arms. He collapsed at thirty-two, his chest a flaming wreck. Fitzy took his boot off his back and Britton rolled over, coughing.

'You still owe me eighteen, but I'll collect later, Novice. On your feet.'

Chastened, Britton rose, gasping. He remembered his time as a butter-bar lieutenant straight out of his commissioning. He'd been dressed down and humiliated in front of a crowd before. He stared straight ahead, ignoring the eyes around him. He knew when he was beaten.

'We have an understanding?' Fitzy asked.

'Absolutely, sir.'

'Outstanding, Novice.' He gestured past the chow hall. 'About half a klick down that way you'll find a checkpoint. The guard there will let you in. There's a muster field just beyond it. You've already met Downer and Truelove. Form up with them when you arrive. Any questions?'

'No, sir.'

'Much better, Novice. That mud looks fantastic on you. It's an outstanding reminder of the fact that I am your government customer and a very demanding one at that. I'm going to expect top-notch customer service from you, and you wouldn't want me to have to let your project manager know that I'm dissatisfied with your performance, would you?' He tapped Britton's chest meaningfully. Britton felt the ATTD nestled in his heart beneath his sternum.

'No, sir.'

'Make tracks, Novice. I'll meet you there shortly.'

Britton trudged through the ankle-deep mud down the track beyond. It wasn't the beating that angered him most though he felt his magic surge at the thought. It was the comment about defending Marty. Britton already had an inkling of the status Goblins held at the FOB, and it felt far too close to the way Selfers were treated in his own world. So far, Marty appeared far more decent than most of the humans he'd met on the FOB.

At the end of the track, a small plywood booth held a single SOC guard, shivering in his mud-spattered parka. The area beyond was screened by two corrugated-metal doors on wheels, topped with barbed wire and protruding from ad hoc walls of concrete blast barriers and piles of sandbags. A huge yellow sign hung from one of them, bearing the SOC arms. RESTRICTED AREA: APPROPRIATELY BADGED SOC PERSONNEL AND CONTRACTORS ONLY. ABSOLUTELY NO FOREIGN NATIONALS OR SOURCE-INDIGENOUS CONTRACTORS PERMITTED WITHOUT ESCORT.

Britton cleared the mud off his badge, but the guard was already opening the gate at the sight of his uniform. Britton stepped past and into a broad field, nearly stumbling as his feet touched hard ground. Beyond the gate, the earth was dry and smooth as a hardwood floor. Goblin contractors toiled in small teams along the edges of the square, keeping their eyes scrupulously on their work, their minders watching them closely.

The area before him looked like a holiday campsite, with ten low, star-shaped buildings clad in cheap vinyl siding abutting a parade ground. Each entrance was marked by a swinging brown sign. Britton scanned them; one read COVEN 6. CAMELOPARDALIS. Below that, in smaller script – NOTHING IS BEYOND OUR REACH! Beneath the writing was a stylized image of a giraffe stretching its long neck toward an apple on a branch. Coven Five bore the image of a belching furnace with the words FORNAX. HELL HATH NO FURY! Coven Seven fielded the image of a swan, beneath which was written: CYGNUS. GRACE UNDER FIRE. Here was an arrow in flight. There a peacock with feathers spread in a glorious sunburst.

The Covens had begun to assemble, each clustering around a yellow pennant stapled to a wooden pole. Each bore the image of the Coven assigned to them. Behind each Coven stood a Suppressor, the fist-lightning symbol on a black band around his upper arm.

Britton spotted Truelove, shouldering the only black pennant in the field, fluttering the ghosted star behind the moon. COVEN 4 – UMBRA, it read, THE MAGIC BEHIND THE MAGIC.

Downer stood at attention beside Truelove. A third man, tall, broad shouldered, with close-cropped ginger hair, stood behind them. Shadow Coven alone wore Entertech uniforms. The rest of the Covens were in standard digital camouflage, their SOC shoulder patches and magical-school lapel pins the only indicators they were not regular soldiers.

The soldiers to either side of Shadow Coven whispered, moving away reflexively. Britton jogged over and fell in beside the redheaded man. He had a wide, doughy face, spotted with freckles. His mouth was lined, wrinkled into a permanent smile. Beside the Coven symbol on his chest was a stylized image of a man calling, three wolves howling in answer. He winked at Britton, and two sparrows landed on the guy's head, twittering and hopping. He paid them no mind, the corners of his eyes smiling.

Truelove turned, took in Britton and the mud drying all over him, and mouthed, *What happened to you?* Britton shook his head and stared straight ahead. One of the Novices of Carina Coven stared frankly at the birds, his eyes platter wide. Britton noted a Terramancer's lapel pin.

'Just what the hell are you looking at, Novice?' Fitzy yelled, arriving on Britton's heels and turning to the Novice from Carina.

'Nothing, sir.' The man's voice cracked.

'Sure didn't look like nothing, Novice,' Fitzy seethed. 'Looked like you were staring at one of our erstwhile contractors here, who, I might remind you, are none of your damned concern.'

'It's just birds, sir,' the Novice quaked.

'Birds?' Fitzy asked. 'What goddamned birds are you talking about, son?'

The sparrows chirped triumphantly, dancing and flapping their wings atop the redhead's ball cap. His shoulders shook with suppressed laughter.

'Uh, sir . . . I guess . . .' the Novice stuttered.

'You guess nothing, Novice,' Fitzy said. 'You're a god-damn earthmoving, rock-crushing combat Terramancer of the Supernatural Operations Corps. You are not some kind of pansy-assed Selfer Druid who chats with bunny rabbits and cuddly puppies. If, in its wisdom, the Corps elects to examine certain practices via its contractual staff, that is no affair of yours and is certainly covered by the nondisclosure agreement inherent in your security clearance which, if I remember correctly, you agreed to abide by. Do I make myself perfectly clear?'

'Perfectly, sir,' the Novice said.

'Now tell me again what the hell you were looking at?' Fitzy demanded.

'Nothing, sir,' the Novice said, recovering his composure. 'I am not aware of what you are referring to, sir.'

'Outstanding,' Fitzy said, then spun on the redhead. 'Get rid of 'em, Richards, or, God as my witness, I will have your ass.' Richards's smile vanished, and the birds took wing.

Britton marveled at the disciplined rows, awash in the mixed currents of so much channeled magic. He had never seen so many Sorcerers in one place.

Fitzsimmons took his place in front of the Coven pennant as a stern-looking SOC lieutenant colonel strode out in front of the assembly, the flame pattern on his lapel pin marking him as Pyromancer.

'Morning, campers!' he said. 'I apologize for the repeat here, but we have a newly constituted Coven joining us.' He nodded toward Fitzy's group. 'So, I'm going to ask for your patience while I go over the indoc brief one more time.' He turned to Coven Four and went on. 'My name is Lieutenant Colonel Allen, but you may refer to me by my call sign of Crucible. I want you to know that I live up to my name, and you are going to have to pass through me before you can graduate here. "Here" is the SOC's Sorcerer's Apprentice/ Officer Leadership Combined Course or SAOLCC. This is our Source campus, and it is a rare honor for all of you to be here. I need not remind you that the existence of this campus, or FOB Frontier in general, is classified at the secret level, and you are forbidden to discuss anything you do or see here with any persons who do not have a strict need to know.

'You will live, work, and train with your Covens for the rest of your tenure here. You will notice that our new Coven is contractually provided.' He gestured to Coven Four. 'Umbra Coven is a private entity that will work on the fringes of this school. You will assist them as required, but they are outside the realm of your concern, and I do not want to hear anyone in this assemblage discussing them beyond what is specifically required of you in training exercises. Am I making myself perfectly clear?'

'Yes, sir!' the assembled Novices responded in a single voice.

'Outstanding,' he said. 'I will insist on military discipline here at all times. At the head of each pennant, you will see your Coven Commander. I fully expect each of you to adhere to his word as if it were my own, the very word of God Himself. That said, we're not the regular army, and it is essential that you feel free to ask questions. This is just like high school, folks. Raise a hand and wait to be called on. Everyone clear?'

'Yes, sir!' the Novices chorused.

'Very well,' Crucible said. 'Any questions before we get started?'

Silence. Britton looked uneasily at Fitzy's broad shoulders, Crucible's words sinking in. Obey his orders like the word of God. He felt his magic surge.

'All right, you will follow me to the practice field on

the other side of your quarters. Coven Four, please follow Chief Warrant Officer Fitzsimmons to enroll in Suitability Assessment. Fall out in Coven order!'

Crucible led the way past the star-shaped buildings to a corridor of firm ground that snaked off through a tiny opening in the blast barricades across from them. A massive concrete dome rose off in the distance, the surface pitted and showing rusted rebar supports.

Signs were mounted to the barricade wall pointing in either direction: TERRAMANTIC ENGINEERING RANGE, WEATHER CONTROL RANGE, FLIGHT EXERCISE ACTIVITY, FIRE CONTROL RANGE, and SUITABILITY ASSESSMENT. Noise sounded in the background, obscured by the maze of concrete walls. Britton heard booms, sizzling, tortured groans of metal.

The group moved through the gap to a football-field-sized parade ground surrounded by high sandbag walls. The ground had been left to mud – blasted in places, burned in others. The mud rose into weird shapes, vaguely resembling sculpture. Here and there were bits of rock walls. A few dark patches looked suspiciously like blood. Fitzy gestured to Shadow Coven, walking them in the opposite direction, through a separate gap in the blast barricades.

Beyond it, a chain-link fence rose some thirty feet in the air, topped by razor wire. Wooden guard towers broke its length into sections, covered by peaked roofs. The railings sported spotlights and light machine guns fixed by hard points to the metal railings. Magic Suppressors patrolled the catwalks intersecting them, black body armor displaying the armored fist with its perennial clutch of lightning bolts.

Through the fence line, Britton could make out a row of low-domed Quonset huts, their corrugated-metal roofs patched with rust and stenciled with numbers. People lounged outside them, smoking, sitting, sullenly talking. They contrasted sharply with the crisp uniforms of everyone else Britton had seen on the FOB thus far. Most wore a patchwork of civilian clothes; cheap hiking jackets and blue jeans. They were a mix of men and women, and here and there Britton spotted people wearing the one-piece orange jumpsuits he had found himself in when he'd first woken from the shotgun blast. The biggest shock was their hair, a variety of lengths and shades, defying the military orderliness present everywhere else.

A long row of blast barricades separated the line of Quonset huts from a flat, muddy field, where groups of people in civilian clothes or cast-off military uniforms stood in orderly rows facing two SOC officers. As Britton approached the fence line, he watched the officers extend their hands, pillars of flame rising from the earth before them. A moment later, the rows of civilians followed suit with mixed results. Some of the pillars sputtered and collapsed, some teetered wildly, some failed to manifest at all.

Across from the Quonset huts stood a small replica of the plaza Britton had seen outside the P pods; a chow hall, a morale facility, rows of schoolhouses. It was a base unto itself, all packed tightly within the confines of the razor-wire-topped fencing and guard towers.

Britton, Downer, Truelove, and Richards silently followed Fitzy toward a gap in the fence line, overlooked by two large guard towers. There, the fence was wheeled at the bottom to form giant sliding panels that rolled aside as they approached. Guards scurried out to drag wooden barriers wrapped in razor wire out of the way.

A long sign spanned the length between the two guard towers. FORWARD OPERATING BASE FRONTIER, it read. SUITABILITY ASSESSMENT AND MAGIC INDOCTRINATION SECTION.

Just inside the gate, a short walk from the entrance to the Quonset huts, a waist-high bit of telephone pole had been erected in the mud. A thinner pole reached from it roughly ten feet skyward. Lowered about the base was a rigid plastic American flag, colored reflective orange, the stars and stripes in subdued black. *They want to be sure everyone can see it clearly when it goes up*, Britton thought.

Just beyond it, tucked into a corner of the compound, was a flat-topped cinder-block pillbox, scarcely seven feet high and fitted with a single, rusty metal door stenciled with the words: INTENSIVE ROOM. The door was handleless, its chipped surface marked only by a sliding panel at eye level. Two Suppressors stood vigilantly just outside it, their belts replete with the full scope of law-enforcement panoply – collapsing baton, pepper spray, Taser, zip cuffs.

The guards snapped crisp salutes, which Fitzy returned as they entered. The knot of indolent-looking civilians rose to their feet, extinguishing cigarettes and looking toward the group, whispering among themselves.

A small cluster of them stood apart from the rest, casting surly glances toward Fitzy and his Coven. They surrounded a tall man, pale and sickly thin, his black hair plastered to his forehead. His face was narrow and arrogant, with a hooked blade of a nose and small, dark eyes. His mouth was set in a look of dramatic disapproval. Noting Britton's gaze, the pale man crossed his arms over his chest and cocked an eyebrow. Belts of lightning sprang from his shoulders to crisscross his chest before one of the Suppressors on the catwalk above him rolled his magic back. The Suppressor yelled something and was met by the man's middle finger. But his eyes never left Britton. The group gave a wide berth to a long-haired boy not much older than Downer, his clothing soaked, skin beaded with moisture. The water coursing through his hair made it look grayish, slick as seaweed. The boy's wet skin and clothing made him shiver in the chilly air, and one of the soldiers guarding them offered him a parka in military camouflage. The boy looked sheepishly like he might take it, then shook his head angrily at a glare from the black haired man. The rest of the group nodded their approval of the refusal. The boy stood shaking, looking miserable.

'What's that all about?' Britton asked.

'That's the No-No Crew,' Fitzy replied, 'and the piece of crap they have elected to lead them. They'd rather have that kid freeze to death than take a coat from one of us. You want to learn how to be worthless, there's your best bet. I catch you hanging with them, and I'll know you're well and truly lost. The upside of that will be that you'll have outlived your usefulness, and I can pound you into oblivion with a clear conscience.'

He turned and grinned at Britton, his sunglasses preventing Britton from telling if his eyes were smiling or not.

'The No-No Crew?' Downer asked. 'Why do they call them that?'

'I suspect you'll find out shortly,' Fitzy answered.

A SOC major, whip-thin and with a shock of flaming red hair, strode forward to meet them. The pale sun flashed off the Pyromancer's pin secured to his lapel. He returned Fitzy's salute, then shook his hand with genuine affection. 'Chief Warrant Officer Fitzsimmons.' He nodded to Richards and Truelove. 'Good to see you two again as well. Colonel Taylor told me to expect you. So these are the new enrollees?'

'Yes, sir,' Fitzy replied. 'Just these two' – he indicated Downer and Britton – 'I'll be collecting them just before chow. Colonel Taylor just wants the control quals met, and we'll take it from there.'

The major chuckled. 'You sure you don't want them spending the night? We just had four enrollees raise the flag this morning. Got a few empty bunks in the squad bay.'

Fitzy didn't appear to appreciate the humor. 'Thank you for the offer, sir, but Colonel Taylor's orders are clear. They'll be bunking in the P pods.'

'What's the matter?' the pale man called. 'Afraid we might be a bad influence? Teach them how to think for themselves?'

'Ah, our dear Swift,' the major said. He nodded confidentially to Britton and Downer. 'You'd best steer clear of that one. He won't be happy until no one is. All righty then, we'd best get you started. I'm Major Salamander, and I run our little corner of paradise here.'

'You obey the major's commands as if they were my own,' Fitzy growled, 'with a sense of deference and urgency.'

'All right, Chief Warrant Officer, I'll take it from here,' Salamander said indulgently. He returned Fitzy's salute as the chief warrant officer led Richards and Truelove back out through the gate, then steered Downer and Britton toward the line of Quonset huts. Swift moved to intercept them, his group coming with him, but a SOC Aeromancer leapt from one of the guard towers and hovered over them, conjuring a gust of wind that knocked them all backward, checking them hard against the hut wall.

'Sorry about that,' Salamander said. 'Some folks are bigger

fans of how we do things around here than others, but I'm pleased to say that we get through to pretty much everybody sooner or later.

'So, on behalf of the Supernatural Operations Corps and the Camp Commandant, welcome to FOB Frontier's Suitability Assessment Section, or as most folks call it, the SASS. This is where we put our captured Selfers until we can be certain that they can be trusted with a SOC commission. We aim to please, and I know you're going to enjoy your time here.'

Over Salamander's shoulder, Britton could see the far end of the compound, lined by another length of high chain-link, razor-wire-topped fence. Through it, he could see the rolling plain of land outside the camp. The SASS was located right up against the edge of the FOB, with only a few bits of chain link between the inmates and whatever roamed outside.

Britton thought of the fighting he'd seen coming from the LZ to the FOB, and shuddered. The wind picked up, turning it into a full-blown shiver, and he felt Downer jockey against his shoulder instinctively.

Behind them, the gates rattled shut with a click, and he could hear the scuffling of boots as the bladed barriers were drawn back into place.

Chapter Fourteen
Suitability Assessment

Remember! Safe and controlled magic use is everyone's responsibility. Accidental magical discharges (AMDs) can disrupt the mission, harm your teammates, and even be fatal. Since the magical current is tied so closely to your emotional state, it is critical you use your Limbic Dampener as directed and contact medical immediately if you are feeling unduly stressed. During psychological profiles, be sure to be fully open and honest. Remember, you can only conceal a problem for so long, and no adverse action will occur so long as you report quickly and fully. Failure to do so is punishable under the UCMJ.

– *Magical Operational Readiness and Security,*
A Sorcerer's Guide, Pamphlet 01-13
Supernatural Operations Corps Media Services

Major Salamander led them opposite the pillbox to a low building: plain, unadorned, and constructed of plywood and corrugated metal. A screen door swung on rusted spring hinges, shutting out clouds of tiny, weird, varicolored bugs.

Inside, a uniformed SOC sergeant sat behind a plastic desk typing at a laptop. He took Britton's and Downer's names, checked their badges, and tapped away. He handed each of them a laminated piece of poorly mimeographed paper that listed bulleted rules of conduct for the SASS and explained what was required for enrollees to be deemed 'suitable'.

'Just remember,' the sergeant said, his voice monotone from long practice, 'our watchwords here are "safe and controlled". Don't rumble with the other enrollees, follow the orders of your instructors, and, above all, no unauthorized magic use. We've got Suppressors but prefer not to engage them. Every time your magic is forcibly Suppressed, you will be assigned a score of plus one. These points are deducted over time. A score of zero is preferred for suitable SOC candidates and contractors.'

'I can't control my magic,' Downer said, her voice anxious.

'Don't worry about that, Novice,' Salamander answered, steering them both back outside. 'We're going to start teaching you to get a handle on it as of today.

'The rules here are simple,' he said, glancing at Britton, his voice taking on a harder edge. 'Just remember what the sergeant showed you and . . . ah, perfect timing. Take a look.'

One of the SASS enrollees, a young man with his hair in a ponytail, shivering in cast-off bits of military uniforms, had broken away from the group practicing their Pyromancy and made his way toward the main gate. None of the guards moved to stop him, but Swift and the group around him erupted, shrieking and calling after him.

'Don't do it!' Swift cried, running after him. Three soldiers emerged from the base of one of the guard towers and advanced, weapons pointed at him and his small gang, who began to back up.

'Stand down, Swift!' Major Salamander shouted to him, smiling. 'Looks like you lost another one. You just watch and enjoy.'

The long-haired man shot a sheepish glance toward Swift, who called out to him. 'Don't! Don't be their dog!'

He looked at his feet and marched on toward the pole with the plastic US flag.

One of the soldiers switched his carbine from single shot to three-round-burst with an audible click. He pointed it at Swift's face. 'With all due respect, sir, shut up.'

The long-haired man reached the flag and hauled on the thin white cord that anchored it to the pole, raising it to the top in a few moments. The soldiers clapped in unison.

Applause echoed from the fence line, guard towers, and gate.

'If I could trouble you to just wait one moment, please,' Major Salamander said to Downer and Britton as he stepped forward.

He stood at the position of attention in front of the young man and raised his right hand. The young man imitated him with the earnest awkwardness Britton had seen in new recruits since he first joined the army.

'Do you swear to use magic only in service to the duly authorized government of the United States of America, abiding by the tenets of the McGauer-Linden Act?' Salamander asked.

'No!' chorused Swift and his group, pumping their fists in the air.

'I d . . . I do,' the young man said, his eyes locked straight forward.

'Do you agree to obey the orders of the superiors appointed over you?'

'No!' Swift's group shouted again. The soldiers pressed forward, muzzles leveled.

'I do,' the man said.

Major Salamander shook his hand and clapped him on the shoulder. 'Welcome to the SOC, son. I'm proud of you, and the army is lucky to have you. Sergeant Perelli!'

'Sir?' One of the soldiers peeled away from covering Swift's group, trotted over, and saluted.

'If you'd be so kind as to take young master . . .' He looked a question at the man.

'Ruiz, sir. Everybody called me Rock Monkey,' the long-haired man said.

'Ruiz! Right! The Terramancer. I remember,' Salamander said. He turned back to the sergeant. 'Please take young master Ruiz here for outprocessing and assignment to an SAOLCC Coven.'

'My great pleasure, sir,' Sergeant Perelli said, leading the man toward the same low building where Britton and Downer had signed in.

Major Salamander turned to face Britton and narrowed his eyes. 'Two simple questions, with two simple answers. That's all we ask of our enrollees here. Once they're on the Dampener and under our expert instruction, most master the basics of keeping their magic under control in fairly short order. But their loyalty to their country and their suitability to handle magic in its service remains an open question. Takes a little time for some folks. There are always holdouts, like Swift and his No-No Crew over there, but, eventually, they always come around.'

'What happens if they don't?' Britton asked.

Salamander only stared at him, his expression severe. 'It doesn't come to that.'

Major Salamander turned to Downer, and his face returned to its former open friendliness. 'I doubt we're going to have trouble with you, young lady, are we?'

'No, sir,' she answered enthusiastically.

'Outstanding,' Salamander said. 'You two are already assigned to a Coven, so you're not truly mine, but Chief Warrant Officer Fitzsimmons has entrusted you to my care to ensure you learn to control your magic and to purge any fool ideas out of your head. Can't do the job if you're not on board with the mission, right? This way, please.' He began to walk toward one of the schoolhouses, motioning to the soldiers who had drawn down on the No-No Crew as he went. The soldiers motioned with the muzzles of their carbines, herding the small group along. Swift walked proudly at their head. He genuflected in the direction of the pillbox as he passed, the rest of the group following suit. The Suppressor standing outside looked nervously over his shoulder at the rusty door.

Britton jerked his thumb at the cinder-block pillbox. 'What's that, sir?'

Salamander looked uncomfortable. 'That, my good man, is the end of the road. The final consequence of recalcitrance. You don't want to go there, and you sure as hell don't want to have anything to do with what's in there.'

Salamander turned away from the pillbox and led them into the schoolhouse. The interior was marked with the same temporary military utility as the exterior in classic Seabee style. The plain plywood walls were covered with posters straight out of a high-school civics class. One diagramed the meaning of the American flag, another explained the Constitution, three or four depicted the dangers of unrestrained magic use. A huge photograph of the rubble of the Lincoln Memorial dominated the room, THE BLOCH INCIDENT written in red letters beneath.

Major Salamander poured himself a cup of coffee from a stained decanter on a folding table. Beside it, a Goblin contractor was hooking up a computer monitor. Salamander motioned Britton and Downer to the chairs, just as the No-No Crew shuffled in, sullenly taking their seats with a resignation born of long practice. The soldiers who had ushered them in took up positions on either side of the door. After a moment, a few more civilians straggled in, filling up the remaining chairs. The long-haired boy with the seaweed-slick skin sat a good distance away from the rest of them, puddling water around his feet that tracked on the concrete flooring to pour out the seams between floor and wall. He looked embarrassed, his eyes on his feet, but Britton could occasionally catch him casting glances toward them. Britton could feel his magical current – pulsing, wild, barely under control.

Swift slumped down in his chair beside Britton and stared at him, tapping a bitten fingernail against the corner of his mouth. Britton stared straight ahead for as long as he could stand it, then finally turned to face him.

'Nice outfit,' Swift said. 'What are you doing here if you're already in a Coven?'

'I have no idea,' Britton answered.

Downer shifted in her chair, leaning forward and putting her elbows on her knees. 'You're lucky they didn't shoot you.'

'Oh, I'm worth way too much for them to shoot me,' Swift said. 'And I suppose even fucktards like the good major here have some sense of obligation to free citizens of the United States.'

Salamander smiled, his back to him, pouring nondairy creamer into his foam cup. 'Running's a felony, Swift, you know that,' he said. 'Per the McGauer-Linden Act, you don't have a whole lot of rights anymore.

'Besides,' he said, turning to face them and stirring his coffee, 'as far as folks back on the Home Plane know, you're all dead anyway.'

'Trust me, little girl,' Swift said, his eyes hardening at Downer. 'You'll curb your enthusiasm fairly rapidly. Within a month, you'll be wishing these fuckers had shot you.'

Britton looked at his lap. *I'm the fucker that shot her.*

Downer didn't look at him; instead, she bridled, standing up and lifting her shirt to show a patch of smooth, pink flesh that slightly contrasted with the skin around it, the mark of rushed magical healing. 'They did shoot me, here. They had to, but I get it now.'

'Your hip, huh?' Swift said, turning to a scrawny, pale adolescent, only barely a man, with spiky blond hair, wearing black denim jeans and a gray hooded sweatshirt. His upper lip was studded with patches of peach fuzz that Britton guessed would never become a true moustache. 'Looks more like they shot genius here in her head, eh, Pyre?'

'Brain's still addled,' Pyre agreed. 'She'll get it eventually.'

'I already get it!' Downer stood, her adolescent fury showing in spite of the Dampener. 'You don't get it! Why would you want to be a fucking Selfer?'

'Selfer is a badge of honor,' Swift said. 'Someday, hopefully, you'll come to understand that. Now, sit down, little girl, and mind your elders.'

Pyre flicked Downer his middle finger, which burst into flame.

'Unauthorized,' Salamander gestured at him, his current reaching out to Suppress the Pyromancy, 'and that's yet another point added to your record. What does that put you at now? One million? Two?'

'Fuck you,' Pyre said. 'And maybe fuck you, too,' he said to Downer. 'Jury's still out on that so far.'

Britton stood between them. 'She's just a kid. Leave her alone.' The Dampener kept his emotions in check, but he could feel the eddying magical currents intensifying around Swift and Pyre.

'Now, now,' Salamander said, waggling a finger. 'Swift? Pyre? Do you want to join your mommy in the hole?'

The currents died, and Swift slumped in his chair, chastened. *No*, Britton thought, *he's terrified*.

'She's going to get out, someday,' Swift said, 'and when she does, we're free, and you're screwed.'

Salamander chuckled. 'For your sake, I sincerely hope that day never comes to pass. Because we both know nobody is going to be free. Everybody, including you, will be dead.'

Swift sat silent in his chair, his fear palpable.

'All bark and no bite.' Salamander smiled. 'Swift, Novices Britton and Downer are contractors from Umbra Coven. They're only here to go through basic indoc and control. They're already spoken for. You're wasting your time.'

'Maybe,' he said. 'But it sure is fun . . .'

The door hinges squealed again, and another woman entered. Britton caught his breath. He rifled through his mental index and quickly came to the conclusion that she was the most beautiful woman he had ever seen. She wore faded blue jeans that hugged slender thighs and rode low on gently curving hips. Her shirt blazed an image of a beatific Christ, dispensing benediction from a metallic burst of golden fire that accented her breasts. Almond-shaped eyes dominated her face. Black hair fell to her back, thick and shining.

'Ah,' Swift said. 'Our lady of perpetual, nagging guilt. Nice of you to join us.'

'Hi, Ted,' the woman said, ignoring Swift and addressing the soaking boy in the corner, smiling warmly. He mumbled a greeting, shooting a fearful glance at Swift, who stared daggers at him.

'Don't talk to her, Wavesign,' he said. 'She's so keen to raise the flag, you can feel it. That crap's contagious.'

'Shut the hell up, Swift,' another woman said. She was pale and raven haired, lean like Swift but with a gentler look. 'He can do what he wants.'

'Aren't we all here for instruction, Tsunami?' Swift said to her, cocking an eyebrow. 'I'm instructing.' He turned back to the new arrival, unfazed by her beauty. 'Besides,' he said, 'somebody's got to counter the bullshit this one can't seem to stop spewing.'

The beautiful woman ignored him, smiling at Britton.

'Welcome, Therese,' Salamander said. 'Better late than never, please take a seat.' Therese pulled up a chair behind Britton, who was facing forward but could feel her presence behind him, like a heat on his shoulders.

If Swift's attitude cowed her, Therese didn't show it. 'Hey, man.' She engaged Wavesign again. 'What's going on?'

Swift growled, but Wavesign only glanced uncomfortably at him for a moment before turning back to her. 'Steak night.' He chuckled.

Therese chuckled with him. 'Everybody loves steak night.'

Swift and Pyre scowled at the conversation, but Wavesign seemed to be taking courage from Therese's presence and pretended not to see.

Britton seized the opportunity and leaned into them. 'What's steak night?'

'We get second round off the main chow hall's supply. They have steak night on Tuesday, we get it on Wednesday,' Wavesign explained.

'What's wrong with that?' Britton asked. 'Steak doesn't go bad in a day.'

'This steak was never good,' Wavesign said. 'Therese found one of the flattened boxes in the Dumpster before they carted it off.'

'Grade B: for military or prison consumption only,' she said.

Britton smiled. 'That's no surprise. You learn to get used to that when you're in the military. It may be new to you folks, but I've been eating that crap since I signed up.'

'You were army?' Swift asked, taken aback.

Britton nodded.

Swift was silent at that, brooding, but Pyre laughed out loud. 'Man! That sucks. You're in the army, and your punishment for coming up Latent is that you have to join the army!'

A few of the No-No Crew chuckled at this.

'That is truly special,' Tsunami said.

'All right, all right,' Salamander said. 'If we're all done getting to know one another, let's get started. As you can see, we have two new enrollees here, Oscar Britton and Sarah Downer from Umbra Coven. They are already assigned and billeted elsewhere. I certainly hope you'll give them a genuine SASS welcome and be extra nice. The rest of you are here either because you're new to the SASS or we feel that your loyalty to the United States is questionable.

'But you all have one thing in common. You all ran from the SOC and violated the McGauer-Linden Act. We had to track you down. We had to bring you to justice. You are publicly dead. You belong to us. You may not be grateful for the gift of your lives, but that doesn't change the fact that it's a gift your government has graciously given you.

'The SASS is a second chance for all of you. The smart ones will realize that, like it or not, your Latency has changed your place in the world. You have the option of trying futilely to buck a system that, for all its flaws, was established for everyone's improvement and safety' – he gestured to Swift and the No-No Crew – 'or you can do the smart thing and realize that the only way to use your magic productively and rejoin society is attached to that flagpole out there. There are two questions, and I'm sure you know them by heart now. The only acceptable answer to both is "yes". You must mean it, and you must adhere to that oath for the rest of your lives.

'The essential challenge that we're trying to overcome' – Salamander paused to sip at his coffee – 'is that some of you still harbor dumb-ass notions of who the bad guys are. The video you're about to see should put paid to that notion. In case it doesn't, you'll be pleased to know it's the first in a series that will continue throughout your training.

'You hear a lot about the Mescalero insurgency. Most of what you hear is filtered through sympathetic media outlets. The poor Indians are having their culture squashed. Magic is their birthright. It's the big, bad white man oppressing them all over again. What you don't see is what these bastards do to their own.'

The screen flickered to life, showing a clip of Apache Selfers, stripped to the waist and brightly painted, gathering a string of other Apaches, mostly old men, into a line. Their mouths moved silently, screaming. The men were forced to their knees, their hands bound. Britton could make out a few women among them.

'You can guess what's going to happen,' Salamander said. 'You should know that the crime these people committed was "collaborating with the enemy". That's us. That's the United States government, it's every American.'

One of the Selfers stepped forward sweeping his hands upward. Scorpions boiled out of the sandy earth around the prisoners, enveloping half the line. They covered the prisoners until no flesh could be seen, only a surging mass of the stinging arthropods. They scattered at a gesture from the Selfer, leaving a pile of discolored, swollen bodies, some still twitching in their death throes.

Britton's stomach heaved. Downer gasped in horror. Therese shifted behind them both. The No-No Crew's faces were deadpan. Swift rolled his eyes.

'Oh, it gets better,' Salamander said, indicating the prisoners that remained.

One of the Selfers gestured to something offscreen.

The screen flickered as something black leapt into view, vaguely man shaped and impossibly fast. It gibbered, slavering among the remaining prisoners, who leapt to their feet and tried to flee. One of the Selfers conjured a wind that blew them back into the black creature's path. Britton saw flying gore. He imagined the screams in his ears despite the film's silence.

The thing spun long enough for Britton to make out teeth as long as daggers before the video cut out.

Britton shivered. He remembered a very similar creature dancing through the Goblin ranks as he'd flown in a helicopter toward FOB Frontier when he'd first arrived in the Source. If that thing was an ally of the Goblins, then what the hell was it doing among the Mescalero?

'The Mescalero call them their "Mountain Gods". We call them monsters,' Salamander said into the appalled silence. 'We're pretty sure they come from here, and we're still trying to work out how the Apache got hold of them. Eventually, that's what you're going to be fighting. That's the alternative to what you are. Remember that.'

'It's all bullshit,' Swift said to Britton, as they headed outside toward the flat expanse on the other side of the blast barricades from the Quonset huts where the SASS enrollees made their homes. 'That's only one side of the story. Who knows what they're not showing us?'

Therese walked beside them, talking in low tones with Ted, the young man wrapped in his vapor cloud, whom Swift had called Wavesign. He spoke with her in quiet tones, keeping his eyes down, clearly terrified that Swift would notice.

'Yeah, right,' Downer said. 'You saw what they did.'

'Tapes can be faked,' Swift said. 'I don't understand what your sudden loyalty to the SOC is about. Presumably you were a Selfer at some point yourself, or else you wouldn't be here.'

'I changed my mind,' Downer fumed. 'I can do that.'

'She's young,' Britton offered by way of explanation.

'Shut up!' Downer yelled. 'I'm old enough to know right from wrong.'

'Most folks far older than you don't know that.' Swift laughed.

'What kind of a name is Swift anyway?' Britton asked.

'His name is Andrew.' Therese spoke up for the first time. 'Everybody in the No-No Crew makes up their own names. It's ridiculous.'

'Our real names died when they kidnapped us,' Pyre said. 'The SOC gives themselves call signs; so do we.'

Therese shook her head. 'You're still who you are. Why would you want to be more like them anyway? It doesn't make any sense.'

'My, my, Mother Teresa,' Swift said. 'Is your Christian charity waning?'

'My name is Therese Del Aqua,' she answered.

Britton could certainly understand Swift's anger, but he didn't like him directing it at Therese. 'Andrew, huh?' he asked. Swift grimaced at the sound, and though Britton felt foolish for taking pleasure in it, he was pleased to see Swift's surly veneer momentarily crack. 'That's a nice name.'

'Fuck you,' Swift growled. 'If you and your teenaged girlfriend here are happy being lapdogs for the SOC, that's your call, but you're not going to get any slack from me.'

'Who the hell said I'm happy working for them?' Britton stopped walking and put his hands on his hips.

'You're wearing the uniform,' Swift put in.

Britton gaped in silence before mustering a response. 'As if I had a fucking choice!'

Swift stepped forward, his expression utterly submerged in smoking rage. 'You always have a choice. If they didn't drag you in here, kicking and screaming, then you're fucking cooperating.'

'Easy,' Pyre said, put off by his friend's rage. 'Salamander's watching.'

'Seriously,' Tsunami added. 'Calm the fuck down, dude.'

'Don't waste your time,' Therese said to Britton. 'He's totally sold on the futility angle. The only thing to do now is pray for him.'

'Listen you little . . .' Swift began to walk around Britton, reaching for Therese. Britton stepped sideways to intercept him. Swift's eyes flickered to him momentarily, seeing him only as an obstacle. Britton read the anger there and knew the man was not in control. That was fine; out of control meant no real threat. Britton's anger was cold and disciplined. Skill beat will, every time. Pyre backpedaled as Swift punched at Britton, but Britton was ready and dodged. Swift reversed his hand midstrike, nails raking across Britton's cheek before Major Salamander drove in between them, pinning Swift's arms behind him and dragging him backward. The No-No Crew surged to Swift's defense, then retreated just as quickly as the soldiers advanced, carbines leveled. Though Pyre had tried to stay out of the fight, he was rounded up with the rest, hands raised. Only Wavesign, who had been on the other side of Therese, was left unmolested.

'Now, that's not very welcoming to our new friends, is it?' Salamander said. 'And I guess you need some time in the hole to teach you manners.'

'Come on, man!' Swift shouted. 'I didn't even hurt him! It was just a little scuffle. You don't need to put me in there with her!'

'What's wrong?' Salamander asked, dragging Swift backward. 'She's Suppressed, and I thought you were all on the same side.'

Swift struggled briefly in Salamander's grip before relaxing. 'You know what she's like. Please.'

Salamander pushed Swift toward a pair of soldiers who had approached as the fight broke out. 'Sorry, no sale. Maybe some quality time with the fair lady will cure you of your bullshit. Enjoy.'

Swift's eyes returned to Britton's. Britton took a step backward, checked by the depth of the senseless, animal hate that smoldered there.

A pair of burly soldiers took custody of Swift and began walking him slowly toward the pillbox. Britton felt wetness trickling down his cheek and raised his hand to dab at the wounds, which had begun to smart as the shock of the exchange faded.

'You're bleeding,' Downer said.

'You are,' said Therese, reaching out a hand and cupping his cheek. Where Swift's eyes had held unmitigated hatred, Therese's were pools of concern. 'You have to forgive him,' she said. 'Nobody knows exactly what happened to him, but some say the SOC killed his girlfriend bringing him in.'

'I heard his wife,' Pyre added. 'He doesn't talk about it. Nice going.' He glared at Britton.

But Britton ignored him, overcome by the kind words. *Careful, that damned farmer said nice things to you, too. Then he shot you*. But Britton was momentarily swamped by Therese's beauty, the touch of her hand on his cheek. Without thinking, he raised his own hand to hers. Warmth flooded his face, the same tingling he'd felt in his chest when he'd lain in the Humvee with the hood over his head. The pain of the scratches vanished, and he could feel the skin on his cheek knitting underneath her touch.

'You're a Healer,' he said.

'A Healer using her magic in unauthorized conditions.' Salamander stepped forward. 'Come on, Therese, you know better. That's a point for you.'

'Suppress me,' Therese said. 'Throw me in the hole with Scylla. I don't care.'

Salamander raised a hand, but Therese's work was done. She stepped away from Britton, leaving him rubbing his smooth cheek and longing for the warmth of her hand again.

Salamander shook his head and motioned them starkly toward the open ground, where most of the SASS enrollees were lining up in front of a female SOC captain, her long black hair in a businesslike bun on the back of her head. Five SOC Suppressors milled loosely behind her, submachine guns slung across their chests.

Behind them, Britton could hear the steel door in the cinder-block bunkhouse slam shut behind Swift. He thought he heard a woman's voice, dark and sonorous, welcoming him. Something in its syrupy tones made him shiver.

'You don't have to do that,' Britton said to Salamander. 'It was just a scratch.'

'It's for his own good,' Salamander said. 'Swift's got a history here, Novice. Escape attempts, violence against guards and fellow SASS enrollees. If we don't break that spirit of his, command might decide he's not worth the trouble.'

'And then what?' Britton asked. 'Would they kill him?'

Salamander frowned. 'It won't come to that. They always cooperate in the end.'

Britton thought of Billy, his head covered in electrical leads, his mother crooning in his ear. Had he always been like that? Had the SOC made him that way? Harlequin's words came floating back to him . . . *just like you will be if you don't do as you're told*. Britton shuddered.

'What's going to happen to him in there?' Britton asked, motioning to the pillbox.

Salamander motioned Britton to get into position with the rest of the group. 'You ask a lot of questions, Novice, and I've been very patient with you thus far. Swift is being rehabilitated. Now, my patience is beginning to wear thin, and you need to stop talking and start listening.

'All right, listen up!' Salamander bellowed to everyone. 'It's been an interesting morning that's put me out of the mood in which I patiently tolerate your bullshit. This is your morning magical-control class. Some of you have some notion of control. The rest of you are only prevented from having dangerous magical discharges by virtue of the Dampener running in your veins. We're going to fix that issue.

Dampener and the regimented nature of SOC training will impair the raw emotional outpouring and check your power. But it has been the SOC's experience that cold discipline is ever the master of wild emotion. It is our mantra, and one you will take to heart – "safe and controlled". Selfers may make great displays of powerful magic, but the reason they cannot stand against us is because they don't know the meaning of those two words. It is the same reason why the Goblins lack the ability to truly affect this outpost. Given the choice between power and control, a SOC Sorcerer chooses control. Remember, skill beats will, every time.'

Britton thought of the last time he'd heard those words, hovering in a Kiowa beside a burning school.

'We're going to talk about the two fundamentals of safe, controlled magic use. These are Drawing and Binding. Before we talk about these, I want to reiterate what I just said. Safe and controlled, remember it, learn it, live it. First question, how do we stay safe and controlled?'

There was a pause as he waited for an answer from the audience.

'Anybody?' goaded Salamander, starting to smile. He turned to the female SOC captain beside him. 'Captain Stormspinner?'

'Come on, people,' growled Stormspinner, her voice deep and mannish. She crossed her arms impatiently. 'In case you didn't notice, that's a giant fucking fence all around you. It's not like you can go anywhere. We own you for the nonce, and the only way out of here is attached to that flagpole. Demonstrating control of your magical abilities is the first step to making it there.'

Finally, one of the Novices shot his hand up. 'By obeying orders?' he asked.

'That's right,' Stormspinner said. 'You have to stick to the rules. They may seem constraining at first. Magic is a wild and tempting thing, but it can only be manipulated to effective use under safe and controlled conditions. The rules have been laid down by more experienced soldiers who have gone before you. Respect them and respect this power you are lucky enough to possess. Okay?'

'Yes, ma'am!'

'An overachiever, but I like your enthusiasm. Good. All right, here we go. Drawing and Binding. There are two things that every sorcerer must be able to do to manipulate magic. The first is to Draw it.

'Magic is little more than an elemental force here in the Source. I'd say it's like air over here, but the truth is that nobody knows what it is. You may notice that magic is much stronger in the Source than it is back in the Home Plane. Keep that in mind as you work with it. When you are going to work magic, you first have to gather the fuel for it. You have to *Draw* the fuel supply from the magical current around you. Everybody with me?'

'Okay, good,' Salamander took over. 'Drawing from your current is easier than you think. Remember, you all Drew from it either knowingly or accidentally when you first Manifested. I'd bet a lot of you already know how to Draw. After we've discussed this, we're going to teach you some meditative exercises to help you learn how to Draw at will, but as you get better, you'll find you can do it without even thinking. For most of you, it'll be that easy by the time you go back to the schoolhouse to do your studying.'

He turned to Stormspinner. 'Captain, would you mind demonstrating?'

There was no look of concentration, no mumbling of incantations. She merely extended her hand, and a bright, blue ball of ice hovered in her open palm.

'Now, this isn't Drawing alone,' Stormspinner said. 'I have to Bind the magic to make it visible. There isn't a way to make the Drawing process itself visible, but what you're looking at is Hydromancy at its rawest. This is the material that I use to build a spell.'

With that, she tossed the ball up in the air. It came down as a quantity of water, splashing a few of the Novices, who laughed and covered their heads.

She smiled. 'Now that was a spell.'

'Okay, settle down people,' Salamander called to some of the enrollees who were laughing and flicking water at one another. 'We've got a lot of ground to cover today.

'Here's where your first safety tip comes in. When you Draw from the Source, you're offering your being up as a magnet to pull it out. It's like fishing, and the bait is you.

'Raw magic is extremely powerful. If you aren't safe and controlled, and by this I mean knowing how to cut off the flow and how to Bind the magic safely away from you, you risk becoming what's called "a magic sink". Magical energy is like water; as soon as it spots an opening, it puts its full weight behind flowing through it. You are that opening. If you're not careful, the weight of the current can overwhelm you. Believe me when I tell you that you don't want that. The Dampener should suffice in this case, but if one of you should begin to go nova, we've got plenty of Suppressors here to take the edge off.'

Major Salamander gestured to the body of enrollees. 'Our usual practice is to have the more experienced Novices assist their newer peers with their training.' Both he and Stormspinner began to gesture to members of the crowd, who stepped forward to talk to their counterparts.

Therese stood forward and faced Britton and Downer. 'I'm still fairly new, but I've got the basics pretty well down.' Downer smiled shyly at the pretty older woman, and Britton nodded thanks.

The No-No Crew stepped backward, folding their arms across their chests. Wavesign went to join them, but Therese grabbed his upper arm, ignoring how it soaked her to the elbow. 'Come on, Ted, you need the training.'

'Not him,' Salamander said, pointing to Britton. He pointed to a small square of four blast barricades twenty yards across the muddy expanse, far away from the rest of group. 'He sits in there.'

'Why?' Therese asked.

Salamander paused, stunned. 'Young lady, did I not just tell you that I am no longer in the mood for your bullshit right now?'

Therese was unfazed, but Britton answered. 'Because I'm a Portamancer. The gates can open up anywhere, including in the middle of this crowd.' He turned to Salamander. 'With all due respect, sir, I don't think those T-walls are going to help.

I've seen my gates slice a car and a tractor in half. I don't think the concrete will make much difference.'

Salamander sighed. 'I appreciate your respectful tones, Novice, but you are rapidly becoming a fucking burr under my saddle. Now get your ass in the middle of those barricades and await instruction.'

Therese moved to follow. 'What the hell are you doing?' Salamander called after her.

'I'm helping,' she replied. 'If those barriers can protect us, then I'll be fine. He needs somebody to talk him through the beginning part, and he'll do better if it's someone nice to him.'

'Damn it, Therese!' Salamander called after her.

'Throw me in the hole!' she answered. 'Throw us all in the hole. Or you can shoot me.'

Salamander cursed and turned his back on them, saying something to Downer and Wavesign, as Therese and Britton walked off.

'That was brave of you. Thanks,' Britton said to her.

'It's no big deal,' she said. 'Salamander's a sweetheart, actually. He's probably the one guy in this whole nasty organization who actually wants to help Latent people. He puts on a show to keep things under control, but in the end, he's on your side.'

'Therese, he wasn't kidding. The gates can open anywhere, and they cut through anything.'

She nodded. 'I trust you.'

'Why?'

'I don't know. You seem like a good sort. Maybe it's because you stand up to both Swift and Salamander. Maybe it's because you tried to protect me back there. Maybe it's because God tells me so. I'm just going with my gut.'

'Call me Oscar.'

She smiled. 'I'm Therese.'

He stepped through the space between the barricades into an enclosed patch of mud roughly five feet square. 'What about Swift and the No-No Crew? What does God tell you about them?'

He saw her shrug through the gap between the barriers.

'They're all good, Oscar. Swift's just trying to cope with his loss, I guess. Pyre's just a kid. He follows along. The anger is just so . . . useless is all. I know it's a bad situation, and I know that none of us want to be here, but . . . fighting everything, everybody, all the time. Swift isn't happy just taking his own stand; he wants everyone else to take it with him. The guy's the definition of bad influence.'

Britton nodded as Therese moved out of his field of vision. 'I can understand where he's coming from. I was already in the army, and they didn't give me a chance once I came up Latent.'

'Well, here's your second chance,' Therese said. 'If you believe Salamander.'

Britton didn't answer, unsure if he did or didn't. *You promised yourself you'd find a way out of here. A couple of kind words, and you're going to forget that?*

'You ready to get started? Can you hear me okay?' she called from the other side of the barricade.

'Let's do this.'

'Have you ever Drawn magic before . . . ?' Therese asked.

Britton thought for a moment. 'It comes from feelings . . . emotions. I know it responded to stress when I ran. It picks up when I'm angry or sad.'

'That's right. Your emotions are the motor, but your brain is the steering wheel.'

'So how do we steer?'

'You just do,' Therese answered. 'You have to feel it. Visualization helps. I picture the body whole, and the magic bends that way. Sometimes, I have to push hard, but it works. And you also . . . talk to the body. Tell it to knit. I don't how to explain it. You can always try a prayer, Oscar. God never fails me when I reach out for Him.'

Britton frowned, unsettled by her words, thinking of his father's violent religiosity. But she seemed so different from his father, beautiful where Stanley was ugly, kind where Stanley was cruel. *Judge not*, he thought, then laughed inwardly at the biblical turn of phrase.

'You're real religious?' Britton asked.

She nodded.

'I don't want to go after you about it, but I don't understand how. The church has been the biggest persecutor of us . . . oh, my God, I just referred to Latent people as "us".'

Therese laughed. 'It makes sense, I guess.'

'I hope I'm not offending you . . .'

'You're not, Oscar,' she said. 'A lot of people lose religion when they find magic, and I guess that makes sense. I know the church hasn't been a big supporter. But I mean, hell, it's not the first time that the church has been turned to work against God's intentions. You've got the Inquisition, the Crusades, clinic bombings, what have you. This is no different. God knows what's right, and so do those who really follow Him.'

'But doesn't the very existence of magic turn some of that on its head?' Britton asked.

'Not really,' she said. 'But to be honest, I don't really think about it. I would never have gotten this far without my faith, Oscar, I think I would have given up a long time ago. It keeps me going. When you have something that important to you, sometimes it helps not to ask a lot of questions. Make sense?'

Britton was silent for a moment. It did make sense, but he didn't like it. He knew it wouldn't help to say that. 'Sure it does,' he said instead. 'So, how do we start?'

'You're going to . . . get emotional. Recall something significant from your past – an exciting event in your life, something tragic or momentous. You're going to do your best to channel it. You know how to reach past the Dampener? Activate your emotions?'

Britton thought of his unauthorized use of a gate from just the night before. 'Yeah.'

'The Dampener should keep it tight and give you the ability to shunt it back, but if you feel yourself overwhelmed, give a yell and one of the Suppressors on the wall will roll it back for you. Ready?'

'Here goes nothing,' Britton said. He reflected on a sad memory to help trigger the magical flow, picturing his old house. The memory intensified under the influence of his heightened senses on that side of the gate, the image of his former home as vivid as if he were standing on the sunken porch steps. He could smell his mother's baking from the kitchen window. He could feel the tide roar into him, building along with the emotion behind the Dampener's barrier. He reached for it as he had outside the DFAC, and it flooded him with such intensity that for a moment he feared he would be unable to control it. But in the end the Dampener kept it regulated, and the gate snapped opened mere inches from his face. It flashed closed again, reopening so close that he took a step backward. He focused on the air a few feet before him and pictured the gate opening there. His muscles cramped at his effort to stem the flow, channel it, shape it to his will. *Come on, you bastard*, he thought, *you're mine. Obey me*.

The gate rolled open right where he had wanted it to.

Britton blinked. The shimmering portal had opened on his parents' house. Startled, he gave the Dampener rein and let his emotions slide back into the compartment. The gate vanished, leaving him breathing heavily.

'You okay?' Therese's voice came from the other side of the barrier. 'How'd it go?'

'It worked,' Britton answered. 'Just not like I expected.'

He cursed inwardly. That was it? It was as simple as mastering your emotions? If only he'd known when his father had crouched over him, fists pounding his chest. If only he'd had the Dampener then! It made it so easy. The thought that the SOC had it, could have just given it to him, to Downer, to anyone who was struggling with Latency, enraged him.

He focused his mind, conjuring up fresh in his mind the rooftop where he'd shot Downer. He focused on the air a few inches in front of his face, where he wanted the gate to appear. The gate opened about a foot back from that spot, but its television-static surface showed the charred remains of the school's roof, the battered remnants of the helo still on its side.

'Holy shit,' he breathed.

'Oscar, what's going on?' Therese asked.

'I think I know,' Britton said. 'Let me try one more thing.'

He focused and thrust out his hands again. That time the gate opened on his barracks room in South Burlington. It stood empty, every drawer open, every item removed. The door had been taken off its hinges. Yellow tape reading CRIME SCENE: KEEP OUT stretched across the doorway.

Britton shut the gate and blew out his breath. 'Holy crap. I can go anywhere I want with this. All I have to do is picture the place.'

He heard Therese suck in her breath and turned to look. She had come around from the safety of the barricade and stood in the gaps between them, watching him. 'Oh my God, Oscar. That's amazing. What's on the other side?'

'Anywhere.' Britton grinned through the effort of keeping the gate open. 'Anywhere I want.'

Therese put her hands on her hips and cocked her head at him. 'So, what are you still doing here?'

Britton instinctively jerked a hand to his chest and didn't answer.

Chapter Fifteen

Practice

Stormcraft is the keystone of the Aeromantic arsenal. To properly harness it, the Sorcerer must understand the electrostatic relationship between colliding ice particles and be sensitive to the electric fields they generate in moist air. A number of elements – temperature, moisture level, particle size, and wind strength – all must be manipulated in perfect synchronicity to harness lightning to combat-effective levels. This sounds complicated, and it is, but by the time you graduate from this course, you will be able to do it while airborne, tracking multiple targets and without a second thought.

– From the introduction to *Stormcraft I:*
Offensive Aeromantic Maneuver
Publication of the Supernatural Operations Corps

Once he was sure of his control, Britton experimented on his own; he opened a gate on the logging trail where he'd abandoned the police car, stretched it twenty feet high, then shrank it to a one-inch box. He focused on a tiny pebble. When he opened the next gate, it split the rock precisely in half. The flow was weaker, but not by much.

Once Salamander was satisfied with Britton's control, he was permitted to rejoin the rest of the group. Downer was animating tiny fire elementals from a lit Zippo that one of the other enrollees was holding. She grinned as the marble-sized flames danced around her feet, boiling the mud in little patches.

She smiled at Britton and Therese as they approached. 'It's amazing!' she said. 'I could have practiced on my own forever and it would never have come so quickly! The Dampener makes all the difference in the world!'

Britton couldn't help but smile at her enthusiasm, but his stomach twisted in anger. *If they'd just made that drug available, publicly, there wouldn't be any reason for anyone ever to go Selfer.*

Wavesign stood against the line of barricades along with the rest of the No-No Crew, his arms folded across his chest. He looked ridiculous to Britton, trying so earnestly to fit in with a group who wouldn't even stand next to him for fear of getting soaked.

Tsunami approached him. Britton guessed she was a Hydromancer, as the moisture wicked away from her as soon as it touched her. She spoke to Wavesign in low tones, but he pointedly ignored her, doing his best to look aloof for the No-No Crew. Eventually, she shrugged and walked off.

'What's his deal?' Britton asked Therese, gesturing at Wavesign.

'Severe control issues,' she said. 'Salamander says it happens sometimes. Even with the Dampener, that's the best he can do. I feel bad for him, but he makes it worse for himself by hanging with that crowd.'

'Ted!' she called to the young Hydromancer. 'Come on! You need this training more than anyone. The only way out is through. Come on and work with me.'

Wavesign first tried to ignore her, then when she called him again, looked askance at the rest of the No-No Crew, who ignored him. Finally, he shook his head and walked over.

'Therese, just stop. Leave me alone, okay?' he said.

'Ted, you keep hanging around with that crowd, and you're never going to get a handle on this.'

'As soon as I do, they'll just jump on me to raise the flag,' he said, deliberately pitching his voice loudly enough for the crew behind him to overhear.

'Nobody can make you do that,' she said. 'Being in control

of your magic is one step closer to being in control of your life. Let me help you.'

'It's not that hard,' Britton offered. 'If I can figure it out, anybody can.' He opened a gate in front of them, expanded it, shrank it, then closed it again.

Wavesign's face set, and he looked at his feet again. Britton swore internally at his mistake. This kid had been in the SASS for God knows how long and still hadn't mastered basic control of his magic. Britton had figured it out in a couple of hours. 'I'll help, too,' he said, trying to recover, but the damage was already done. The vapor cloud surrounding the boy intensified.

Over his shoulder, the No-No Crew whispered to one another, pointing.

Therese pointed at a small patch of wet mud. 'Dry it out.'

Wavesign shrugged and gestured. The mud splattered everywhere, as if it had been kicked.

'Come on,' Therese said. 'You're not even trying. Don't show off for their sake.'

Pyre opened his mouth to shout something, but Salamander shook his head, and the young Pyromancer kept quiet.

'Therese, this doesn't work for me,' Wavesign said. 'We've been through this.'

'Then let's go through it again.

'Here, look,' she said, taking his hand. 'Can you feel my current? It always starts off intense. I used to try to haul the magic back, but now I realize that all I have to do is let it go.' She let out a deep breath for emphasis. 'Can you feel my current change? That's the Dampener at work. You just let the tension go. Remember, it's emotions you're dealing with, so try to center yourself.'

Britton marveled at the clarity of the explanation. It was exactly how he'd been managing the magic, but he'd never put words to it before.

'I can't,' Wavesign said. 'I don't know how to explain it . . .'

'Is something bugging you?' Britton asked.

Wavesign jerked to look at him, glowering in silence. 'I'm just saying' – Britton patted the air with his palms – 'it's emotions that cause the problem here, so if you've got something on your mind, that could be the root of the issue.'

'Whatever,' Wavesign said, folding his arms and returning to the No-No Crew. 'This is stupid.'

'You're wasting your time,' Tsunami said, trotting over. 'It's nice of you, but I've tried with him before. He's completely committed to throwing his lot in with those idiots. I thought, because we were both Water Sorcerers, that I could get through to him, but he's young. He'd rather be cool than competent.'

'I don't know about that,' Britton said, cocking an eyebrow. 'Kids can go either way. He just needs a nudge in the right direction.'

Tsunami snorted. 'Like Swift? That a-hole has been nudged every which way since I got here. If Wavesign's anything like him, it's a lost cause.' She gestured at the squeaking of a metal door.

Over Wavesign's shoulder, Swift was already being hauled out of the pillbox. He was even paler than before, shaking. He slumped in the guards' arms, pliant and passive. A soldier gestured back toward the group, and he nodded, offering no resistance as he made his way back toward the rest of the enrollees, his head down, meeting no one's eyes.

Britton suddenly felt sympathy for the man, despite the injury to his cheek. 'Jesus, what happened to him?' he asked Therese.

She shrugged. 'Scylla's extra creepy. You'll see her eventually, when they exercise her around the yard. She gives me chills.'

'Who is she? Why is she in there?'

But before Therese could answer, Fitzy's voice barked from the SASS gate, motioning Britton over. 'Playtime's over, Novice! Get your ass in gear. School starts for real now.'

Britton knew better than to argue after the drubbing Fitzy had given him that morning and headed over to him. He had already forgotten Therese's words as his mind focused on the new challenge of dealing with Fitzy's ire, but as he moved past the pillbox, he heard the panel in the doorway slide open.

'Such pretty doorways, Oscar Britton.' The voice that drifted through the panel was liquid amber, rich and haunting. 'Oh, they are beautiful.'

Britton turned to answer, but the Suppressor guarding the door kicked it hard, then again, and finally the panel shut. For all his show of force, the man looked terrified as he turned away.

Britton had jogged the rest of the way toward Fitzy before he realized that chills had run up his spine.

Truelove and Richards met them outside the P pods, where another converted trailer bore the Shadow Coven logo of the ghosted star behind the moon.

'It was awesome!' Downer gushed, but her voice trailed off as she saw Truelove and Richards standing in silence. Britton followed their gazes to where a huge man walked, hands thrust in his pockets, shoulders hunched. His nearly shaved head sported ginger-colored hair to rival Richards's own. His cold blue eyes took in Shadow Coven as he pushed past them, his camouflage-pattern parka not matching anything Britton had ever seen before. As the man passed, Britton caught the flag sewn onto his shoulder even as the man's magical current hit him hard enough to make him grimace. Whoever the stranger was, he was highly Latent.

Their eyes followed him, staring unabashedly as he moved along until he was gone from sight behind one of the concrete blast barricades.

'Who was that?' Richards asked.

Britton shook his head. 'Russian army, I think. At least, that was the flag sewn on his jacket.'

'Didn't know they had a SOC.'

Britton thought of the giant snake creature he'd seen when he'd first arrived on the FOB. 'Everybody does. Harlequin said we're not to talk to them unless authorized.'

Downer opened her mouth to say something, then shut it. An awkward silence followed.

Richards broke it, grinning. 'I thought you might like it,' he said, clapping Downer on the shoulder.

'Like what?'

'The training. The SASS. The Dampener. All of it.'

'SASS isn't so bad,' said Truelove. 'The videos are pretty annoying, but once you get your magic down, it's actually a lot of fun. Did you meet Swift?'

'That guy was a piece of work,' Britton said.

'Yeah,' Truelove said. 'If the guy would let the Dampener scale back his anger, he'd be set, but he just can't stop fighting. He rode me pretty hard when I went through.'

'The Dampener is incredible,' Britton said. 'Skill really does beat will.'

'Yeah, it is pretty incredible . . .' Truelove said.

'What's incredible, needledick,' Fitzy cut him off as he tromped toward them, 'is your unrivaled ability to state the obvious. Perhaps if you had Manifested in the magical ability to shut the hell up, you'd say less stupid stuff. Now, if you'd be so kind as to refrain from teaching our new arrival how to be a moron, maybe I won't have to break another nail administering a repeat ass-kicking to him.'

Truelove stood at attention, his eyes focused on the middle distance, but not before Britton caught him casting an embarrassed glance at Downer, who didn't appear to notice.

Fitzy warmed to his task, stepping closer to Truelove. 'You put on a brave face, little man, but we both know that if it weren't for this "incredible" Dampener you keep going on about, you'd be crying all four of your eyes out right now.'

Thanks for reminding me that I've got to get out of here, Britton thought. *For a minute there, I was starting to enjoy myself.*

'All right, I suppose some congratulations are in order,' Fitzy said. 'Not that learning a little basic control is much of an accomplishment. The Novices in the SASS are raw meat. If you hadn't mastered the basics so quickly, I'd have been disappointed. Well' – he looked back to Truelove – 'more disappointed than I already am, anyhow.

'You all just remember one thing: you are Coven Four, Shadow Coven, the magic behind the magic. You are this Corps' secret weapon against all that is unknown and terrible in the world. When the army can't cut it, they call the SOC, when the SOC can't cut it, they call us. Like it or not, that's your role, and I expect you all to act like it. Almighty God must have a particular sense of humor to have Manifested such rare and precious abilities in a pack of imbeciles like you, but we will all simply have to cowboy up and go to war with the army we have.

'And that, folks, is exactly what we intend to do. We're going to get started right now.'

He led the Coven back into the converted trailer, stomping up a small flight of wooden steps, the Coven following, pushing past a cluster of Goblins hauling bags of trash out of the room.

Inside was a simple classroom that was a near-exact copy of the SASS schoolhouse, complete with whiteboard and plastic folding chairs. The Coven sat while Fitzy stood in front of the board.

'Among the many functions you will have as Shadow Coven, first and foremost is to not embarrass me. You have all Manifested in prohibited schools, or in Richards's case, perfected a practice that has been outlawed under an amendment to the Geneva Convention. By all rights, you should be rotting in jail or strapped to a lethal injection table, and, with a little work, you might still get there. However, for the time being, the president of the United States himself is giving you a free pass so long as you put your skills to work in the service of this country. What I expect from each and every one of you is to earn that amnesty, and to make certain that your customers do not regret their decision to take a chance on you. I can assure you that I will take any failure to meet that standard as a personal affront and deal with you accordingly.

'First off, we are arranging the Coven so that each of you performs roles in proportion to your Manifested ability. These are as follows.' He turned to write on the board.

'Downer, you will provide force protection, under the call sign "Prometheus". Truelove, you will provide combat overmatch capabilities, under the call sign "Rictus". Richards, you will provide reserve capability as required, under the call sign "Whisper". Britton, you will provide logistical support under the call sign "Keystone". These capabilities do not absolve you of your duties as agents of the United States

Army. The primary mission of this organization is to kill people and destroy property. You will ensure that, whatever the designation I have just given you, you are properly trained to put warheads on foreheads when called to do so. Is that perfectly clear?'

'Yes, sir,' the Coven said in unison.

'The great thing about Probe schools is that they're all pretty much force multipliers,' Fitzy went on. 'The constitution of this particular Coven, now with instantaneous transport' – he gestured to Britton – 'enables you to deliver a hammerblow whenever and wherever the SOC needs it. In short, the four of you can show up in an enemy's backyard and have an army there inside of a minute. We are going to train to do just that.

'First things first; some ground rules. You will not use your magical abilities except in the line of duty when specifically authorized. You will not speak to or associate with the indig unless specifically authorized. You will obey all my orders as if they were the word of the Almighty Himself. Also clear?'

'Sir.'

'Outstanding,' Fitzy said. 'This is trailer B-6. We will meet here every afternoon, after you complete your SASS morning indoc and basic control training. By then I expect you to have completed your time sheet and eaten a proper breakfast. Big-boy rules, people. Nobody will wake you up and ensure you get anywhere on time, but I will personally kick your ass if you are even slightly tardy. Instructions will be written on this whiteboard or delivered in person. Because your abilities are unique, much of your training and some of your assignments will be performed independently. As unit cohesion is a goal, I will try to keep you together as much as humanly possible, but it won't always be. For now, you will follow me to the adjacent trailer.'

The adjacent trailer was empty and covered with soft matting. A short-haired, kind-voiced older woman dressed in a white jumpsuit greeted them and bade them sit Indian style on the mats. The next two hours were spent in meditation exercises. The woman led them first through stretches, then chants, and finally silence, attempting to rid their minds of conscious thought. Britton heard Truelove begin snoring faintly during the last of the exercises, but the Necromancer was brought around by Fitzy's boot in his ribs. Richards smirked but choked back his laughter before Fitzy could provide similar discipline.

'Try to take this seriously,' the instructor admonished. 'Disciplining your emotions is the key to magical control. Even the Dampener isn't as effective as a person who has attained true self-mastery. Meditation is an important part of that.'

The other soldiers in the evening chow hall avoided them, stepping out of line as the Coven approached. The few humans working the food lines slopped the food onto their trays in a hurry, thrusting them at the Coven as if trying to ward them off. The Goblins murmured among themselves in their own language. A few bowed to Britton as he passed, tapping their closed eyelids as Marty had done.

Marty appeared among a cluster of humans and Goblins from the cash, all in blue medical scrubs. He waved to the Coven, and Truelove waved back. 'How's it going?'

'You just secure that crap, Rictus,' Fitzy snarled. 'You want to buttfuck your fairy-tale boyfriend in the privacy of your own hooch, then I guess everyone is entitled to blow off a little steam, no matter how nasty that particular mental image may be. But God as my witness, you will not fraternize on my watch!'

Marty looked at his feet and moved on.

They ate without speaking. Fitzy munched away beside them, eyes fixed straight ahead.

Back at the trailer, they were split up.

Britton followed Fitzy down another track to a huge canvas tent that enclosed a bare patch of ground some hundred feet square. Foam mats lay scattered about. Ropes hung from metal brackets attached to the tent's canopy. Their breath steamed in the cold air. Fitzy strolled to the center of the tent and faced Britton.

'You get the pleasure of spending more time with me than any of the other Novices in the Coven, Keystone. This is because while all of Coven Four must develop hand-to-hand combat skills, your training plan calls for particular expertise in the Modern Army Combative system, which we will now refer to as MAC. It just so happens that before I Manifested, I had the pleasure of serving as a MAC instructor in the Eleventh Infantry. Before being assigned to lead Shadow Coven, I taught MAC to the SOC. I don't think I've ever taught fewer than ten men in a class. But you get one-on-one training, which perhaps makes you the luckiest man on this whole damned FOB.

'The end goal will be to develop a concept coined by my predecessor, with the only other Portamancer we had the pleasure to work with – Gate-Integrated MAC or GIMAC. I affectionately term this as "gate-fu". But if I ever hear you call it by that name, I will hand you your ass more than I am about to. GIMAC integrates all the MAC moves with conjured gates, used as a cutting weapon. You will also use your magic to position yourself more advantageously against your opponent.'

'You're going to teach me hand-to-hand combat?' Britton asked.

'For the nonce,' Fitzy replied, 'I will forgive you for asking a question out of turn. I will even tell you that, once you have learned how to integrate your Gate Sorcery with MAC, you will be deadlier than an entire rifle company. You'll use your gates like an extra fist. No, like a cleaver, only one that can cut through absolutely anything. You'll be able to appear in the enemy's backfield and take out fifty of him before he knows you showed up. But there's a long, long way to go before you can do that, and we have to crawl before we can walk. So, MAC first, GIMAC when you're ready. Now, let's begin.'

Fitzy advanced. Britton retreated, hands extended. 'Sir, I've done some MAC before, but I'm not ready to . . .'

Fitzy snapped a kick at Britton's knee. Britton jerked his leg back, slapping the boot down, but Fitzy landed on it and brought the other foot up, crashing into Britton's head and sending him sprawling. Even under the influence of the Dampener, the magic threatened to surface, and Britton concentrated on shunting it back.

'Get up,' Fitzy said.

Britton propped himself up on his elbows, hesitating.

'Learning to take a hit is the first step to being able to deliver one, Novice. Now get the hell up, or I'll just pound you while you're down.'

Britton jumped to his feet, and Fitzy snapped a jab at his face. Britton dodged, trying to remember what little MAC he'd had before. As an aviator, it had hardly been stressed, and he regretted his refusal to 'roll' with the rest of his team when they practiced between sorties. He hooked Fitzy's arm in his own, whipping his elbow toward the chief warrant officer's face. Fitzy jerked his head back and out of the way, flexing his hooked arm. The man was impossibly strong. Despite being half his size, he yanked Britton toward him, using his own momentum against him. Fitzy's fist pounded Britton's gut so hard that he lost his dinner, forcing the Master Suppressor to leap backward to avoid being spattered.

Britton collapsed in his own vomit, gasping.

'Jesus, Keystone,' Fitzy said. 'That's disgusting. Now, get up, and let's give this another round.'

Chapter Sixteen

Scylla

MAC? Yeah, it's pretty cool. Mixed martial arts, more Brazilian Jiujitsu than anything. SOC operators put all their eggs in that basket. In any magical school, there's little need to carry more than a sidearm, but if someone gets the drop on you, or you're off the Dampener and can't get your mojo going – sometimes a good old-fashioned can of ass-whoopin' is called for. My bootheel on your spine is every bit as effective as a fireball in your face.

– Lieutenant 'Sunspot' (call sign),
SOC Liaison Officer (LNO)/ Pyromantic Assault Team Leader,
101st Airborne Division

Despite the drubbing Fitzy had given him, Britton was in a celebratory mood. He played with the Dampener as he sat in the OC, chatting with the rest of Shadow Coven, calling the current, then shunting it back, thrilled to feel some semblance of control, no matter how slight.

Downer's enthusiasm was infectious. Britton's early irritation at her flip-flopping allegiance was replaced by genuine joy at seeing someone so happy. Richards shook his mug of beer, and Downer animated the foam across the top. Sudsy elementals lined the bartop, boxing with a weird, multitailed rat that Richards had Whispered to his command. She giggled as the rat made short work of one elemental, rolling in the foam, then licking the suds off its fur while the remaining creature flailed at it ineffectually.

Truelove and Marty cheered uproariously, the little Goblin wiggling its fingertips and making deep-throated barking noises that Britton assumed were supportive.

'Outstanding.' Britton chuckled, patting Downer on the back. A piece of him rebelled against the comfort. *Don't get settled. You can't stay here. You have to find a way to escape. But you're not Swift. You don't have to rebel for rebellion's sake. Why not stay here? What better life is waiting for you if you break free?*

Britton pushed the thought away as Downer turned at his patting. 'What about you?'

'What about me?' he responded.

Britton looked at her. Truelove paused in midsentence.

'A gate, silly,' she said. 'Open one.'

Britton looked around the empty room. '. . . I don't think I'm supposed to. What about your precious regs? You're not even supposed to be making those beer monsters.'

Downer looked down at her lap and shrugged, suddenly looking very young. Truelove said nothing, but his eyes lit up. Marty set his cup of sugar water down on the counter and blinked.

'Okay,' Britton said, thinking of places he'd visited. 'It only works for places I've been before. What do you want? Statue of Liberty? Grand Canyon?'

Downer said nothing, cheeks still burning over Britton's rebuke. 'Ever been to Mount Rushmore?' Truelove asked. 'I've been telling Marty about it.'

Britton had, once, on a road trip with his father as a high-school freshman. The forced attempt at bonding had been a cold, drawn-out week that Britton couldn't wait to end.

'Not sure if this'll work,' he said, concentrating. 'It was a long time ago.' He closed his eyes, trying to recall the wonder he'd felt as the massive stone faces had appeared over the guardrail along the side of the road, eclipsing Stanley Britton's brooding presence with a sense of posterity, permanence, and majesty.

The gate sliced through the middle of the guardrail. Four stone presidents fixed stately gazes from the distant mountain. There was a squeal of tires as a passing car swerved away from the gate. Britton saw it slew right and left, nearly careening into the far guardrail before righting itself and speeding away. He closed the gate.

'Christ,' he said. 'Don't tell anybody about that.'

He rubbed his head. Calling the current had exacerbated his headache, still hurting from the pummeling Fitzy had given him.

'You okay?' Richards asked.

'Yeah, the MAC practice is a little rough,' Britton responded as Marty clucked in his throat and began rooting through his leather bag.

'You need a Healer,' Downer said. 'Fix you right up.'

Britton thought briefly of Therese, the warmth of her hand on his face. He stopped, momentarily stunned. *A Physiomancer put this bomb in your chest. A Physiomancer could get it out.*

The next morning continued along the same lines. Britton woke himself just in time to bolt down breakfast and make his way back to the SASS.

Downer had beaten him there. She stood with Therese, Swift, and the rest of the enrollees gathering outside the schoolhouse as he passed through the gate. The enrollees stood stiffly, staring at something, cigarettes held forgotten in their hands. He made his way toward Therese as the guards dragged the barriers back into place but stopped short.

The door to the pillbox stood open, its interior shrouded with shadow. Goblin contractors worked inside it with brooms and hoses.

Britton followed the gazes of the enrollees and saw two Suppressor guards following a few paces behind a woman. Her skin had the unhealthy pallor of one denied sunlight, the blue tracery of veins clearly visible. Her jet-black hair was cut in a severe bob, the points almost sharp where they passed the line of her jaw. She was thin, tall, and clad in a one-piece orange jumpsuit similar to the one Britton had worn when he was first captured. Her hands were cuffed before her.

She made her way slowly around the compound, stretching her legs and working kinks out of her neck. The Suppressors gave her a wide berth, their fingers braced along the trigger guards of their guns, eyes never leaving her rolling shoulders.

She turned a face dominated by large eyes with jet-black pupils and smiled at the No-No Crew. Many of them genuflected at her, save Swift, who only nodded briefly. Her grin was all teeth, huge and vulpine. And yet there was no denying her beauty, an older, experienced brand, sensual and wise. Britton felt his pulse quicken at the sight of her.

'That's her,' Pyre said. 'That's the queen of Selfers right there. One of these days, she's going to bust out of there and make these fuckers in the SOC pay for what they've done to us. One of these days, she's going to set us free.'

Britton only nodded. For a man talking about his savior, Pyre sounded terrified.

The woman rounded the corner of one of the Quonset huts and met his gaze evenly, the smile never faltering. 'Oscar Britton,' she said as she approached. 'You're even prettier in the sunlight.'

'Ma'am,' he said instinctively, responding to the authority she projected.

'Oh, there's no need for that. You can call me Scylla.'

'That's not your real name.'

'I'm beyond names. So are you. That's why they're terrified of us.'

'Shut up and keep moving, ma'am,' one of the guards said from behind her.

'See?' Scylla said to Britton, not even acknowledging the guard. 'Can you hear the terror in the human's voice? This little gulag is all to buy them a little more time before they're forced to face reality.'

'What reality is that?' Britton asked.

The guard inched forward, as if to touch her, appeared to think better of it, and looked askance at his partner, who likewise refused to move.

'The reality we all see around us but refuse to acknowledge, human and Latent alike. That we are a new race, better adapted to our environment than the old. The humans can imprison us for a time, but, sooner or later, we will rule them as surely as they rule dogs and cows.'

'That's . . . crazy,' Britton stammered. *Is it?*

'That's the way it is,' she went on. 'You know it as surely as I do. Think on it, Oscar Britton. You possess the ability to move between the fabric of dimensions under your own power, and yet you are hounded and ruled by those who cannot even fly through the air without the aid of a machine. How does that make sense?'

Britton struggled to find a way to refute her, but the fact was that it didn't make sense.

'Welcome to the new apartheid, Oscar Britton,' Scylla said. 'It will fare no better than the old one.'

'Get moving,' one of the guards said, finally mustering his courage and pushing her from behind. Scylla stumbled forward a step and slowly looked over her shoulder, her smile fading as she met the guard's eyes.

'CWO-2 Blankenship. Three good conduct medals. Recently treated for gallstones. Your boards are coming in a month, and while your dog tags mark you as a Christian, you don't really believe it.'

Blankenship's mouth worked, his eyes wide and terrified. 'It can't be magic,' his partner said. 'I've got her Suppressed.'

Scylla smiled. 'Do you know why I was put in the hole?'

'Everybody knows,' Blankenship said, instinctively leveling his weapon at her.

'It might not earn your respect, but it should at least earn your fear. So. Don't. Ever. Push. Me.'

Both guards took a step back, mouths open. One jerked his weapon at her. 'Let's go. You get an hour of exercise. Use it or lose it.'

Scylla turned back to Britton. 'See? Terrified. Never forget that, Oscar. These people may limit your movements for now, but deep down? You own them.'

She moved past him, her elbow brushing his stomach and sending chills through him, the guards dogging behind, squared shoulders and long strides obvious efforts to mask their fear.

Britton made his way to the knot of SASS enrollees entering the schoolhouse.

'What was that all about?' Therese asked him.

'I'm not really sure,' he said. 'You weren't kidding about her being creepy, though. How'd she wind up in the hole in the first place? She said everybody knows.'

'She got one of her Suppressors to drop her for a moment. That was all it took. By the time she was done, she'd unleashed hell.'

'Hell?'

'Twenty, maybe thirty dead.'

'How? She some kind of super Pyromancer?'

'Scylla's a Witch,' Wavesign said. 'Negramancy. It's supposedly nasty, nasty stuff. Black magic and all that.' His vapor field intensified, Britton guessed as a reaction to his fear.

'But how does it work?' Britton asked. 'Does she turn people into toads?'

Therese shuddered, and Wavesign looked at his feet. 'It's nasty,' he said eventually. Britton noted his discomfort and didn't press the matter.

'How'd she get the Suppressor to drop her?' he asked instead. 'She whack him over the head?'

Therese looked even more uncomfortable, and Wavesign kept his eyes on his feet.

'She, you know,' Swift said, trailing off.

'Oh,' Britton said. Scylla wasn't an unattractive woman, for all her wicked charisma. She'd used the only tool she'd had to hand.

'How's it going, Wavesign?' Britton asked, trying to change the subject, extending his hand.

'Don't do that,' the young Hydromancer responded. 'I'll just get you wet.'

'I don't mind if you do,' Britton responded, shaking his hand. His grip was slippery, like trying to run kelp through one's palms. Britton suppressed an instinct to grimace. The kid already had problems without further damage to his ego. The boy nodded shyly, then cast a glance up at Pyre and Swift, as if seeking their permission.

Inside the schoolhouse, Salamander cued up another video, this one showing Aeromancers working weather control for the coast guard, rescuing shipwrecked fishermen.

Swift sidled over to Britton and whispered, 'Sorry about yesterday,' when Salamander stepped out to use the latrine. 'Let's start over.'

'Wow,' Britton murmured back. 'Scylla really put the fear in you, didn't she?'

'It's not that.'

'Then what is it, Swift? Cut to the damned chase.' He could almost feel his cheek, still stinging from Swift's nails. 'I'm no fool. I don't believe you suddenly want to be friends.'

Swift sighed and looked at his lap. Both Therese and Wavesign were looking over at them. Pyre leaned his chair against the wall, arms folded, pretending to sleep, but Britton could tell he was listening. Every so often he would open one eye and glance over at Downer to make sure she wasn't eavesdropping, but the young Elementalist was sitting at the front of the class as usual, and if she overheard, she gave no sign. Tsunami stared intently at them but was too far away to hear anything. Wavesign glanced nervously at the door every so often. 'It's the gate magic. You're a Portamancer.'

Britton tried to meet Swift's eyes, but the pale man looked steadily at his lap. 'What about it?'

'You can get us out of here. Why haven't you escaped already?'

'Maybe I don't want to escape.' *Is that true?* Britton asked himself. *Are you enjoying finally being in control, no longer having to run?* His stomach turned over at the thought.

Swift looked amazed and horrified.

'Anyway,' Britton said, his voice sounding apologetic in his own ears. 'It won't work. They tagged me with some kind of tracking device that can detonate. I run, I die.'

Swift finally looked up, his eyes dancing. 'There has to be a way to get it out.'

There is a way, Britton thought looking over at Therese. *But can I ask her? Will she rat me out?* He didn't think she would, but how could he know?

They proceeded along the same lines for the next week. Mornings were spent in the SASS, watching propaganda videos and working on basic magical control. Then Britton and Downer reported back to Fitzy for classroom instruction, meditation, and another propaganda video, chased with basic group-magic exercises. Richards summoned battalions of rats and spiders, while Downer and Truelove practiced their animations, with Britton sometimes dispatching their creations, slicing them in half with the flickering edge of a gate. He always opened them on the black recesses of an area off LSA Portcullis's loading bay that Fitzy had designated as his staging area. 'Gate here at will,' Fitzy said. 'You show up anywhere else? You'll have cost the army a good bit of money.' Britton's one attempt to open a gate on Harlequin's office had earned him a Suppressing and boot to the back of his knee from Fitzy.

'Pinpoint gating,' Fitzy observed the first time he'd noticed that Britton was actually opening his gates on the same location. 'You picked that up quickly.' He made a note on a pad thrust into his belt and moved ahead with training.

For all his talk, Britton found Salamander surprisingly lenient, at times like a kindly old father, even giving them the day off control practice to play pickup football in the SASS yard. Britton sat with Therese and watched Swift weave through the other enrollees, the ball tucked under his arm.

'Guy's got talent,' Britton said.

Therese nodded. 'He does. Pyre says he was a receiver in high school. But he cheats a lot, too.'

'Cheats?' Britton asked.

'Watch.' She grinned.

A squat woman with broad shoulders and short hair, whom Britton recognized from the No-No Crew, raced to intercept Swift. 'That's Peapod,' Therese said. 'She never told me her real name. Woman's rugby star at U of New Hampshire.' She ducked her head and angled toward him, lowering her shoulders and pushing from her thighs. She moved directly across Swift's path, there was no way Britton could see for him to avoid her.

Britton smiled as Peapod's thick thigh muscles propelled her on, steady as a freight train. 'Oh, man,' he said. 'This is going to hurt.'

Swift grinned, stuck out an arm.

His fingertips lightly brushed Peapod's forehead as he vaulted over her, corkscrewing through the air and landing behind her, not missing a step.

'He's an Aeromancer,' Britton said, swiveling to look at Salamander, who stood with his arms crossed, chuckling.

Therese nodded.

'Isn't he going to get in trouble?' Britton asked.

'I told you, Salamander's a good guy. He lets it slide when it's harmless like this. I personally think he likes it.'

'Because it demonstrates control.'

Therese nodded. 'Yeah. And I think it does his heart good to see people playing with magic. It can get kind of serious in the SOC, you know?'

Britton nodded. 'Do I ever. I think that's what bugs me the most about magic.'

'What?' Therese asked.

'You know. When you're a kid, you read stories about it, and you're told that magic is this wild, kick-ass, amazing thing. It's unicorns and flying carpets and adventure. But then you actually come face-to-face with magic, and it—'

'It's deadly,' she finished for him.

'More than that,' he added. 'It's boring. It's hyperregulated and bound up in red tape. It's every bit as controlled and locked down as a missile arsenal. There's nothing adventurous about it. Or, at least, not the kind of adventure anyone would want to have.'

Peapod continued after Swift, who danced lightly out of reach, floating through the air. She lunged, slid on her forearms in the hardened mud, cursed, and rolled over on her back. She gestured toward Swift, and a small lip of earth rose in front of his foot, tripping him. He went down hard, the ball spiraling out of his grasp. Downer caught it, pushing hard in the other direction. Her face was ferocious, the concentration intense.

'Go go go!' Britton cheered, clapping.

He laughed, and Therese laughed with him, putting her head on his shoulder. *God, it feels so good to laugh, almost normal.* He put his arm around Therese, savoring the smell of her hair, feeling for all the world like a regular guy watching a game of pickup ball with his girl under his arm. *Except she's not my girlfriend, and I'm on a secret military base in a magical parallel world, and I have a radio transmitter packed with explosives implanted in my heart.* There was nothing regular guy about that at all.

Pyre charged Downer, and Peapod blocked him with equal ferocity, upending him and sending him over her shoulder. Downer crossed into the end zone with a shout and spiked the ball, dancing for a moment before Peapod vaulted her onto her shoulders, carrying her above the shouts of her teammates. Downer's face was a study in adolescent joy.

Salamander was doubled over with laughter. Swift got to his feet, grinning and dusting himself off. 'All right! All right!' he shouted. 'Huddle!' He stripped off his shirt and jogged toward Pyre, sweating freely despite the cold air. His chest was dominated by a broad tattoo of a scissor-tailed bird, pointed wings spread, black beak pointing skyward.

Wavesign sulked on the sidelines, squatting on his haunches. Tsunami jogged past him on the way to the field, motioning him to join. He ignored her, and she shrugged, charging out on to the grass. He scowled for a moment, then looked up at Britton, and they held one another's eyes. Britton jerked his head toward the game and nodded. *Get in there*, he mouthed.

Wavesign looked away, pretending he hadn't seen. Britton reached down and picked up a small chunk of earth, hardened by the cold. He chucked it at Wavesign, striking his shoulder.

The young Hydromancer looked back at him and frowned, then broke into a smile when Britton made a face at him.

'Come on, what's wrong with you?' Britton asked. 'You never played football?'

Wavesign looked at the ground and shrugged. 'Pretty decent hands, actually. But I was too small to block.'

'So? Get in there! I can't understand why you extricate yourself from everything.'

'Come on, Wavesign!' Tsunami shouted.

'You think those guys are a bad influence anyway,' Wavesign said to Britton.

'Only sometimes. What are they going to do now? Influence

you to be better at football? Besides, Tsunami's not one of the jackass crew.'

Wavesign looked annoyed. 'You don't get it.'

'Maybe you don't get it,' Britton said. 'You had decent hands. That doesn't change.'

Wavesign snorted, holding up his hands, so slick with moisture that they looked greasy. 'I don't know if you noticed, but they're not exactly sticky fingers anymore.'

Britton paused, then jerked his head at Wavesign's hands. 'Kind of makes you tough to tackle, though, doesn't it?'

Now it was Wavesign's turn to pause. After a moment, he shrugged and joined the game.

Swift made a face, but after a failed pass to Pyre, he handed the ball off to Wavesign, who ran hard for the end zone, showing surprising agility. Downer and Peapod both ran to block him with all the single-mindedness of runaway trains. Wavesign paused, ducked, then pushed left. Downer threw herself at him and fell short, giving Peapod the chance to make the tackle as Wavesign backpedaled. The Hydromancer spun as Peapod tried to grapple him, her arms sliding on the greasy seaweed surface of his skin. She slid in the dirt again, and Wavesign gave a victory cry as he hurtled toward the improvised end zone.

'Not fair, you slippery fuck!' Peapod groused.

'What do you want?' Wavesign called back. 'I've got control issues!'

Salamander chuckled, and Britton smirked. It was good to see Wavesign make light of his issues for even a brief moment.

Pyre jogged over to Britton and Therese. 'Come on, big man. Might as well get out here and give us a chance to pound on you.'

Britton grinned. 'You sure you want to take that on? It's your funeral.'

Pyre gestured to Therese. 'Unless you think you can do a better job. Now that I think about it, she might be a better linebacker than you.'

'You calling me fat?' Therese groused.

'Heck no,' Pyre said archly. 'Just calling you tougher than Mr Candypants here.'

Britton laughed and Therese grinned.

A shot rang out from the fence line, and they all crouched instinctively. Britton stared through the line of chain link that separated them from the Source beyond the FOB. Two small black dots had surfaced in the waving surface of the saw-toothed grasses and were moving quickly.

'Goblin spotters,' Pyre said. 'They're always out there watching the FOB.'

'FOs.' Britton nodded. Another shot sounded from one of the SASS guard towers, and one of the dots disappeared into the grass.

'FOs?' Pyre asked.

'Sorry, I keep thinking everybody is in the army out here. Forward observers. They call in fire. You know, for artillery.'

'Oh, right. Well, yeah. We call them spotters. They sight in for the magical attacks,' Pyre said.

Another shot, the second dot vanished.

'Looks like they got them both,' Therese said.

'There'll be more,' Pyre said. 'There always are.'

The group stood in silence, the jovial mood suddenly turned sober. *That's war. You kill, then you try to pretend that everything's as it was.* After a moment, the football players returned to their huddle, the chatter breaking the tension.

'So?' Pyre said. 'Coming?'

'I should get in there,' Britton said, trying to shrug off the sound of the gunshots, the drifting odor of cordite. 'I can be anywhere on the field that I want.' He stood, dusting himself off.

Salamander abruptly stopped laughing and shook his head. 'Not you,' he said.

'But . . .'

'I didn't stutter, did I?' the major said. Noting Britton's crestfallen look, his voice softened. 'I'm sorry, Novice. You want to get out there, fine, but no magic.'

'That's bullshit,' Britton began.

'No, it's common sense, something you apparently lack. If Swift is momentarily indiscreet, then maybe there's an unfair touchdown. If you leave the FOB in an effort to get around a blocker, then I've got a huge mess on my hands and the SOC is down one Portamancer. They're not fucking around about the ATTD, Oscar. Don't you risk it. Not ever.'

Britton knew Salamander was right, but the surly anger wouldn't leave him. He turned to Pyre, 'I guess that's an order,' and sat back down.

'Not an order,' Salamander said, 'just friendly advice.

'Of course, it just so happens if you elect not to follow it, you die.'

'Fine,' Britton said, standing and rubbing his hands together. 'No magic, I get it. But you can't stop me from playing.'

'I can do whatever the hell I want with you,' Salamander said. 'But so long as you don't use magic, I wouldn't dream of interfering with your getting embarrassed out on the field.' Britton cocked an eyebrow at Pyre. 'So? Candypants, huh?'

Pyre shrugged. 'We'll see.'

'Oh,' said Britton, jogging out to the field. 'I do believe you will.'

Chapter Seventeen
Research

The Qu'ran is very clear on this. It says, 'And they followed what the devils gave out falsely of magic of the reign of Solomon; for Solomon did not disbelieve, but the devils disbelieved, teaching men magic and such things that came down at Babylon . . .' There is no argument among any of the schools on this matter. For once, all from Maliki to Hanafi are united. Even the Shi'a forbid magic. All praises to Allah the merciful, the compassionate, who has shown us the Djinn in our midst, that we may drive them out.

– Shaykh Abu Hassan al-Masri
Interviewed for Public Television series
Islam and the Great Reawakening

Mornings at the SASS were followed by afternoon MAC practice, one-on-one, under the giant tent. Britton improved slowly. At times, he managed to turn some of the blows, disengage the mount, or control the battlespace for a moment, but Fitzy had years on him. The smaller man always won out in the end, and Britton spent his evenings in the OC under Marty's care. The little Goblin never hesitated to take care of him, and Britton felt a growing sense of camaraderie. The bruises faded to mottled patches by morning most times, and the swelling had gone, though Britton still went about looking like he'd just been hit by a car most days. He counted himself lucky that he hadn't lost a tooth.

Until he did.

Fitzy's boot split his lip and sent one of his lower canines spinning, lost in the mud. The blood was too much, and Fitzy had gotten tired of being spattered every time he closed. At last, he'd sent Britton to the hospital in disgust. 'Get that hole plugged up and get your ass back here.'

'Sir, there's a Physiomancer in the SASS. Let me see her.'

'Negative, Novice. Your authorized hours in the SASS are over for the day, and I don't need to be breaking protocol just to preserve your good looks. The United States government is interested in your performance, not your charisma. You will go directly to the cash, then immediately report back here, and if I find out you went anywhere else in between, there will be hell to pay.'

Britton had spun on his heel and jogged away. He had no intention of returning, no matter how long it took to get seen.

Colored canvas partitions, suspended by strong lines snaking through steel grommets, divided the massive hospital tent. Shadows played off the fabric, giving a fun-house cast to the rows of steel cots, medical electronics, and shelving. Navy corpsmen bustled back and forth between white-coated army doctors. Britton moved down a double row of makeshift beds where the more badly wounded drowsed in drug-induced slumber. Shadows writhed amid groans from behind a partition under a sign reading TRAUMA.

Other signs hung throughout the tent. BURN UNIT, SURGERY, RADIOLOGY. Britton searched until he found one that read DENTAL UNIT. He followed it out of the main cash tent and down a short track toward another one. The signs took him through the phlebotomy section, where blue-scrubbed orderlies took blood from a dozen pale-looking men. The other side of the hallway was occupied with a row of makeshift stalls rigged behind ribbons of canvas under a sign reading URINALYSIS.

The orderlies collecting the yellow vials from the occupants of the stalls were entirely Goblin contractors. Blue cloth masks designed for human faces contended with giant pointed noses and ears. A few of the Goblins had gone so far as to cut holes in them for their noses to poke through.

The sign to the dental unit directed him straight through, but Britton stopped short. Marty stood near the tent exit, a steel test-tube tray, brimming with stoppered tubes half-filled with yellow-green urine, in both hands. The two stared at one another before Marty turned to one of the other Goblin orderlies and chattered in their own language, passing him the tray. The Goblins surrounding Marty bowed in unison, deeply, backing slightly away, muttering softly in their guttural hissing tongue.

Marty reached out and touched Britton's face, his rough hands surprisingly gentle. 'Come,' he said, taking Britton's hand and leading him the way he had come. They pushed back into the main hospital tent and out a side entrance over a makeshift wooden boardwalk that kept them out of the mud and into another tent with a sign reading RESEARCH/SPECIAL PROJECTS.

A wave of cold hit Britton as they pushed through the tent's clear-plastic flaps. Beyond was an entry room with a beat-up but comfortable-looking couch in front of a battered desk, atop which sat a television playing a kung fu video. A doughy, fortyish captain sprawled on the couch, his fingers bright orange from a bag of Cheese Puffs. He paused at the intrusion, scowling as he wiped his hands on his rumpled uniform and stood. His name tape, stained with food, read HAYES.

His lapel pin showed the Physiomancer's heart and cross.

'What the hell are you doing in here?' he fumed at Marty, then stopped short at the sight of Britton's Shadow Coven uniform.

'You fix him,' Marty said evenly, tapping Britton's elbow. Britton's heart sank as he realized that Marty was referring to his tooth, not his heart.

'If he needs attention, he can go back to the check-in desk and put his name on the list. He's hardly sustained a life-threatening injury,' Hayes said, glancing nervously at Britton. 'Indig aren't supposed to be in here! You get the hell out of here right now before I call the MPs! I'm in the middle of important work!'

He followed Britton's gaze to the kung fu flick and rolled his eyes. 'I was taking a break!'

'Fix him,' Marty repeated, not moving.

'I told you to get the hell . . .' the Healer said, advancing on Marty, reaching out a hand.

Britton grabbed the captain's forearm. 'Don't,' he said as well as he could through his split lip.

Hayes jerked out of Britton's grasp with such force that he upset the TV.

'Fix him,' Marty said again, 'or Goblins stop work again.'

Hayes steadied the TV and glared at Marty. 'We'll fire you and throw you out! You can try your luck with the Defender tribes! They'll kill you for working for us.'

Marty pursed his lips and wiggled his ears in what Britton assumed was the equivalent of a human shrug. 'You get more Goblins for work. Easy, yes?'

The captain paused, fat cheeks quivering, before rolling his eyes again, reaching forward and placing a thick hand on Britton's face. The man's skin stank of sweat and Cheese Puffs. Britton had to force himself to keep from pulling away as the magic did its work. The Healer only kept his hand there for an instant before pulling it away, but the pain was still intense. Britton touched his face. His fingertips told him the lip had been healed only partially, he could feel a notch in the flesh as it slid over the stub of a re-formed tooth.

The captain was already turning and moving behind the partition, throwing it aside as he went. 'Now get the hell out of there before I call the MPs!'

He drew the partition shut, but not before Britton saw the room behind it. The cold emanated from a small industrial chiller, cooling the space enough to make the captain's breath mist. Stretched out before him were more rows of metal hospital cots, covered with Goblin corpses in various states of dissection. A few held other creatures; Britton saw several he couldn't recognize, but spotted two demon-horses, one missing its hooves and tail. Across from it was a smaller version of the bird he'd gated into the convenience-store lot, nailed upright to some kind of frame. Its throat was tacked open, an empty gray hole. Two tables had been pushed together to support a giant gray snake, a large portion of the scales sliced out of its back, leaving a black patch beneath. The partition fell, cutting off his vision.

He took a step, but Marty gripped his elbow with surprising strength and led him out of the tent. His face was set, but Britton could see the grief there, mingled with resignation. 'No anger,' Marty said.

'Christ,' Britton breathed. 'What the hell are they doing in there?'

Marty made his Goblin shrug again. 'Srreach,' he said. It was a moment before Britton realized he had tried to say 'research'.

On Goblins? On the indigenous population? He looked again at Marty, noting his drawn brows, his half-lidded eyes. He looked exhausted. And sadly resigned, Britton thought. *How the hell can he work for an army that does this to his own people?*

The silence grated at him. 'He didn't even finish my lip,' Britton finally said, touching the newly uneven surface.

'Fixed okay,' Marty said. 'No more trouble.' His narrow shoulders were thrown back, making him look taller, regal. He shrugged the sad look away.

They reentered the phlebotomy and urinalysis tent, and Marty collected his sample tray from one of the orderlies and turned back to Britton. He fixed his mask back over his face with his free hand, small and meek as ever.

'Fixed okay,' he repeated. 'Fitzy is asshole. Sorry.'

Now that he had seen the deference with which the other Goblins treated Marty, he could no longer miss it. In tiny ways – the distance they kept from him, how they inclined their heads as they passed, he noted the difference in rank.

'You're an important guy, aren't you?' he asked, leaning close.

The surgical mask rose as Marty smiled, then the ear-wiggling shrug yet again.

'So,' he said. 'We no work if I say.'

Britton nodded, then placed a hand on the creature's shoulder. The other Goblin orderlies stiffened at the gesture, but when Marty put his hand on Britton's, they relaxed.

'Thank you,' Britton said. 'You've been better to me than any of my own people since I got here, Marty. That means a lot to me.'

'Same,' Marty hiss-whispered. 'All water baby. You, me. Doctor Captain. Fitzy.'

'Fitzy is asshole.' Britton chuckled.

'Yes,' Marty said, 'but water baby, too.'

Britton nodded reluctantly.

The Goblin smiled. 'Follow. I show you.'

Britton followed him out of the urinalysis section toward the entrance, where they turned down another narrow aisle to a smaller attached tent under the sign reading BURN UNIT.

The room was more crowded than the rest of the hospital, with nurses and orderlies squeezing between beds pushed so tightly together that there was little room for the tables piled with equipment. Marty made his way to a bed where a young man lay asleep under a thin blanket, his vital signs pinging faintly on a monitor.

'That's . . . Lenko, right?' Britton asked. 'The guy who got tagged by indirect the first night we met . . .'

Marty nodded. 'You save him.'

'No, Marty. Come on. You saved him.'

'Soldiers anger. Not want me. You save him.' He pulled back the blanket to show the specialist's legs and hips, covered with hairless skin, pink and shiny under the light.

'Healer fix burn. But Lenko now sick underneath. Healer not help that.'

'An infection?' Britton thought of Dawes as Lenko moaned in his sleep, twitching.

Marty wiggled his ears. 'Sick. Maybe he live. I see every day.'

Britton looked back to Lenko, watching his face, seeming even younger in sleep.

'Marty, you're the fucking man, you know that? You're amazing.'

'You fixed. I work. Bye-bye,' Marty said, smiling.

He turned away, one gnarled brown figure among many, carrying his specimen tray out of the tent, around a corner, and out of sight.

Chapter Eighteen
Worm

'Whispering' is as deceptive a term as I've ever heard. 'Hammering' is more like it. How about 'will crushing' or better yet 'mind control'. Let's call this thing what it really is. You are taking a creature, stripping of it of its free will, and overriding it with your own. You are making it a slave. We outlawed that among humans. It's high time we did it with animals too.

– Arnold Dishart, Vice President
People for the Moral Treatment of Animals (PMTA)

Swift avoided Britton the next morning, but Britton caught him casting furtive glances his way. Swift's smoking anger still lurked below the surface, but Britton felt it cowed for the moment. *Because now he feels that he needs me. Because now he knows I could be a potential way out of here. Seems like just about everybody's got a use for me.*

Wavesign continued to work on his magic with no appreciable results. Britton took it upon himself to join Therese, trying to talk him down from the emotional surges that were too strong for even the Dampener to manage properly. Only Britton and Therese were willing to withstand the soakings anyone working with him had to endure when his magic went wrong. While working with Britton, Wavesign lost control of his vapor cloud and generated a small river, which flowed around him, soaking Therese, Britton, Swift, and Pyre to the ankles. Britton chuckled, and Swift kept silent; but

Pyre cursed and slapped Wavesign on the back of his head. 'Fucking A, man! It's cold enough out here already!'

Wavesign looked horrified and humiliated, and Britton paused. *Are you going to take that?* He waited another moment, and realized that, yes, Wavesign was going to take that. Just as Therese opened her mouth to say something, Britton stepped forward and cuffed Pyre on the ear, sending him staggering backward. 'You touch him again, and wet feet are going to be the least of your problems.'

Pyre looked up at Britton, stunned, his mouth dropping open. 'Maybe all this babying him doesn't help, you ever think of that? Maybe what he needs is a firm hand.'

Britton snorted. 'Look around you, genius. He's in a prison. A military prison. That a firm enough hand for you?'

Salamander jogged over. 'Problem, gentlemen?'

Britton shook his head.

'No problem,' Pyre said, cupping his ear and walking away, making an exaggerated showing of shaking off his soaking feet. Salamander nodded and returned to the rest of the group.

'Why do you put up with that?' Britton asked.

'Whatever,' Wavesign said. 'It's not . . . it's . . . just. I can understand where he's coming from. It's annoying.'

'Sure, but that doesn't mean you deserve to be treated like that,' Britton said. 'You've got to stand up for yourself.'

'Are you okay?' Therese fussed over him, but Wavesign pushed her hands away.

'It's fine,' he said.

'We've been at this for a while,' Britton said. 'What do you think is holding you back?'

'It's like I'm in a circle,' the boy confessed. 'The magic comes to my feelings, you know? It comes when I'm sad. So what do you do when you're sad all the time?'

Britton looked over at Therese. 'I guess you have to think about what's making you sad and try to make peace with it.'

'I appreciate your help, you know,' Wavesign said, barely a whisper.

'You're helping me, too,' Britton said. 'In a lot of ways, I'm lucky. I Manifested as an adult, and a trained soldier at that.

I have a lot of advantages you don't. Watching you deal with all that teaches me how it's really done.'

Wavesign was quiet. Therese punched him in the shoulder. 'Talk to us, Ted. What makes you sad?'

The boy rolled his eyes and pitched his voice low, looking up at where Swift and Pyre stood talking with the rest of the No-No Crew. Peapod spoke to Pyre, her voice low and admonishing as she gestured at Wavesign. 'When I came up Latent,' Wavesign said, 'my brother hauled me into the woods and kicked me around pretty bad. Told me not to come home. Cops picked me up walking along the road. I like it here, honestly. It's better than what I had. But . . . still . . .' He cuffed at his face, so constantly beaded with water that it was impossible to tell if he was crying.

'It's not a family, is it?' Britton asked.

Wavesign nodded. 'My folks weren't nice. My mom died when I was too young to remember, and my dad took a strap to me most times. My brother was just doing what he knew they always wanted.'

'He got rid of you,' Therese said.

Wavesign nodded.

'What he didn't do was lock you in your room and call the SOC,' Britton added.

'So?' Wavesign asked.

'So, maybe, deep down somewhere, he wanted to protect you,' Britton said.

Wavesign shrugged.

'Even with everything your family did to you,' Therese said, 'it's okay to miss them.'

'Not them,' Wavesign said bitterly. 'My grandma and my cousins. My friends at school.'

Britton thought of Cheatham and Dawes, Rob Dausman, even the snarling Stanley Britton. He thought of movie theaters and shopping malls, Monday night football in the squadron break room, burgers grilling outside. All that was beyond him, all the smiling faces he'd felt sure would be an e-mail or phone call away for the rest of his life.

When he looked up, Peapod stood there. She worked to find words, her excruciating discomfort apparent in her shifting stance. 'Pyre's sorry,' she said. 'You're a good guy, and you didn't deserve that.' She looked over her shoulder at Pyre, who made eye contact with Wavesign and nodded curtly.

'You're still part of the crew,' she added.

That's the problem, Britton thought. But now wasn't the time to say anything about it.

'Ready for another try?' he asked.

Later, as Britton and Therese took a break, leaning against the front of one of the Quonset huts, Britton decided to take the plunge.

'So, Therese. Do you remember asking me earlier why I didn't try to use my gates to escape?'

'Because you have a bomb in your chest,' she said without hesitating.

'How the hell did you know that?'

'Swift isn't exactly reticent,' she said, laughing. 'Everybody knows. He already asked me if I could get it out.'

It took Britton a moment before he could speak, but Therese shook her head. 'I'm sorry, Oscar. I'm getting there, but there's a big difference between closing a bullet hole and moving something out of a heart ventricle while keeping the thing beating. I'd probably kill you at this point. I need time to get better. I need practice.'

Britton sighed. 'How much time do you think?'

'Healing gashes or knitting veins isn't too tough, but the complicated organs – the heart, the brain, they're tricky. If your muscle doesn't function for a moment, or if a vein has a bulge in it, that's not the end of the world. Not so with your heart.'

'So it could be a while.'

'A long while. I'm sorry. I don't get a lot of practice in here.'

'They've got a cash, Therese. I'm sure they could use your help in there.'

'I'd have to raise the flag, Oscar,' she said, her eyes narrowing.

She'd have to be willing to be the SOC's instrument. She's not.

Are you?

They both stood in silence while Britton grappled with the surge of emotions the conversation had brought. Perhaps it was the effect of the Dampener, but did he actually feel relief? *Are you actually glad that running might not be an option? Deep down, do you really want to stay?*

Therese caught her breath, and Britton looked up to see Scylla making her exercise round again. She paced toward him confidently, her guards towing behind, giving her a wide berth.

'Good morning,' she said. Her voice was serene.

'What do you want?' Therese asked.

'That's unkind,' Scylla replied. 'I've just wished you joy of the day, and you treat me as someone who would do you harm.'

'You're a murderer,' Therese replied. 'Everybody knows what you did.'

Scylla laughed. 'Am I?' She gestured at the guards lining the wall, the soldiers patrolling the SASS grounds. 'These men have slaughtered Goblins by the score, tracked down so-called Selfers for the crime of being born with an ability they didn't ask for. I killed my mortal enemies, who deprive me of freedom and dignity. Can I help it that the weapons I have at hand are more powerful than theirs? How can you murder soldiers? They're paid to kill their enemies and to be killed by them.'

Britton shook his head. 'What do you know about soldiering?'

She turned to Britton, held his eyes. 'I didn't ask the SOC to chase me down and capture me. I didn't write the unjust laws, and I had no say in their implementation. I defended my rights and my freedom, as Americans have done since this nation's founding. Who can blame me for that? I'm not dropping bombs on schoolyards and hospitals, like your army did in the old War on Terror. I kill my enemies, same as you do.'

She turned back to Therese. 'You're a gifted Physiomancer. Perhaps knitting flesh has made you averse to tearing it. I understand that, and it speaks well of you. I only hope you will consider that sometimes, in war, bloodshed is justified. I take no joy in killing, Therese. Try, if you can, to think better of me.'

And then she was gone, the guards goading her along, leaving Britton to marvel at her words.

Coven Four sat in the OC. Britton cradled a head that felt the size of a bowling ball and weighed twice as much. He clutched a bag of ice over his left eye, swollen shut by one of Fitzy's expert strokes. Britton tried to contain his disappointment. There was no way Captain Hayes would ever help him. The fat, self-interested Healer didn't appear to be anyone's friend but his own. To even ask him would be too great a risk. Therese was his only hope if he was to have any chance of escape, and who knew how long it would take until she could help him?

And what about Swift, Wavesign, Peapod, and the rest of the SASS enrollees? What about Truelove and Downer? If he could get out of there, would he take them with him? Would they want to go?

More importantly, did he? The truth was that he was getting better. Would life on the run, even free life on the run, be an improvement?

The officers were beginning to accept the idea of a newly reconstituted Shadow Coven's frequenting the establishment. While they gave the group a wide berth, they didn't evacuate the premises. Richards had summoned one of the abundant rats on the FOB to perch on his shoulder, where it worked diligently, building an impressive cowlick out of his curly red hair.

'It'll be okay,' Truelove said, looking Britton over anxiously. 'Marty'll get off in a few and meet us here. He'll fix you up.'

'Dear God,' Britton muttered. 'It feels like somebody put a spike in my eye.'

Richards laughed. 'Stop being such a baby. You're Shadow Coven now, baddest of the bad and all that, right? Have a drink and suck it up.' He motioned to Chris, who poured him a tumbler of something that Britton downed too quickly to taste. It burned his throat and belly, but he felt better.

'Aren't we not supposed to hang out with Marty?' Britton asked. The thought made him uneasy. He'd come to rely on the Goblin's kindness, a rare ray of sunshine in the otherwise bleak landscape of the FOB.

'I guess,' Truelove said. 'But I've never seen Fitzy come in here. It's not our fault if Marty decides to come in on his own, right?'

'Regs are regs,' Downer said.

'Regs are guidelines,' Britton said. 'People bend them all the time. I don't think I ever drove a car a day in my life without speeding, and that's probably true for ninety percent of the drivers out there.'

'I never did,' Downer said.

'That's because you aren't old enough to drive,' Britton growled. 'Besides, you saw Harlequin stick up for him before. Harlequin outranks Fitzy.'

Downer blushed at the mention of Harlequin. 'I am so old enough to drive.'

Britton's head throbbed. 'Fitzy is a real piece of work,' he said. 'I better get this MAC down fast, or I swear he's going to kill me.'

'MAC? Damn. My training is just a lot of boring chemistry,' she said. 'It's kicking my ass, but not in the same way as you, it seems.'

'How does that work for Sentient Elemental Conjuration?' Britton asked, glad to get past the tension. Downer's mindless devotion to SOC doctrine burned him.

She nodded. 'I guess they want me to be able to make elemental fuel quickly. Most of what they're teaching me is pyro . . . pyro . . .'

'Pyrotechnics,' Truelove finished for her.

'Yeah, how to make fire out of nothing.' She pursed her lips, looking so young that Britton's heart went out to her. His stomach twisted with guilt. It seemed like just yesterday he'd shot her on top of a burning school.

'That's better than what they've got me doing,' Richards chimed in. 'I'm Whispering worms.'

Britton cocked an eyebrow.

'Big, fat purple things,' Richards continued, slurring

slightly. 'Like maggots on steroids, except that they prefer live flesh. They're native here. They burrow into you, eat muscle, and lay eggs in the fibers. Well, they'll do it anywhere, but they prefer muscle tissue. Apparently, we've lost a soldier or two to them.' He shuddered.

'But under Whispering,' he went on, 'they're the most effective surgeons we have. They prefer unhealthy but still-living tissue apparently. They love tumors. You just have to keep them from laying their eggs and setting up house, and you're good to go.'

'That ain't right,' Downer said.

'What ain't right is your being here,' Britton said. 'I mean, I know you have to be, and I know you want to be. But it sucks that we live in a world where a teenaged girl spends her adolescence in the army instead of getting drunk and running up her dad's phone bill.'

'I ran,' she said. 'That's what happens when you run. You had to take me down.'

'Did you think I liked that?' Britton asked. 'Did you think any of my team did? Hell, half of us were ready to turn around and pack it in. You're just a kid, Sarah. You deserve better than this.'

'I'm not just a kid!' she fumed, standing. 'That's what everyone says, and it's just BS you pull to try to make yourself feel smarter. I'm a Sorcerer!'

'Okay, okay. You're right, Sarah. I'm sorry,' he said. He looked down at his empty tumbler. The army tore people down and built them back up with the goal of making their self-worth dependent on their success in the organization. Downer had bought that lock, stock, and barrel.

Downer plopped back onto her stool and stared moodily at her soda. 'I've probably done just as much fighting as you have,' she muttered. Britton doubted it but let the matter drop.

'Richards isn't even a true Probe,' Truelove stammered as he tried to break the tense silence. 'He taught himself to Whisper while serving in the SOC as a Terramantic Engineer.'

'What did you expect?' Richards asked. 'I spent all my time building berms and ditches. If I had to shore up one more foundation, I think I would have shot myself. Chatting with the wildlife saved my sanity.' The rat sat up and squeaked triumphantly, pumping its fist in the air.

'You told me you didn't run, right?' Britton asked Truelove.

'I called the SOC the second I realized what was going on,' the Necromancer answered.

'And I got caught in the act and was given an offer I couldn't refuse,' Richards finished. 'Looks like you two are our runners.'

But only one of us has a bomb ticking away inside his chest.

A moment later, Marty entered to a surge of muttering from the OC patrons. A look from Britton silenced the worst of it, but a few of the officers stood to go, grumbling. Britton turned to Chris. 'You going to yield the bar again?'

Chris grumbled under his breath. 'Gotta serve the other customers.' But he slammed a large mug and a container of sugar down on the bar. Truelove smiled and set about preparing Marty's drink.

The Goblin ignored the mug, making soft noises as he climbed on an empty barstool to run his fingers over Britton's face. The rough pads of his fingers felt cool, soothing.

'Fitzy is asshole,' the creature muttered, reaching into his scrubs and producing the worn leather pouch. He took out a pair of broad leaves, licked their backs, and, despite Britton's groans of protest, stuck them over the largest swellings, clucking admonition when Britton tried to pull away. The bruises began to feel better the moment the plant touched his face. Even his headache subsided slightly. 'Damn, Marty,' he said, smiling in spite of himself. 'Why do all of your remedies involve spit?'

The Goblin didn't reply, gently pressing the leaves down to make sure they stuck.

'We're really not supposed to be hanging out with him,' Downer groused, still moody over their confrontation.

Britton's anger sparked. The Dampener shunted it to the side, but he gave it rein. After all Marty had done for him, after all the patient kindness he had never hesitated to show in spite of how the humans there treated him, he deserved better. Zealots, especially the newly converted, sometimes gave way when you applied a little pressure.

'You know, these people don't love you,' he said. 'Why do you think we're contractors? If we're the good guys, why doesn't the army acknowledge us?'

'Because we're Probes . . .' she said.

Take it easy, Oscar, he told himself, *she's just a kid*.

'And they're willing to destroy our lives because of it,' he went on. 'We're the same, Sarah.'

'No, we're not the same,' she said. 'I know that I did something wrong. I want to make it right. I want to serve my country.'

'What did you do wrong?' Britton asked. 'You woke up one morning with a power you didn't ask for. You decided that you might want to take a second to play with it before someone else stepped in and told you how to run your life. That's your big crime?'

Scylla's words echoed in his mind. *We are a new race, better adapted to our environment than the old. The humans can imprison us for a time, but, sooner or later, we will rule them as surely as they rule dogs and cows*. Her words were crude, but he couldn't deny the truth in them. The thought of them being accused of crimes at all burned him.

'I killed people! I damaged property!' Downer shouted, and the OC began to empty again.

'That's Harlequin talking,' Britton said. 'I might as well gate over to his office and have him lecture me.'

'You leave him alone!' she yelled. 'He took care of me. He gave me a second chance!'

'Oh, come off it. Your magic gave you a second chance,' Britton said. 'You're here for the same reason I am; the SOC wants your magic. If either of us had gone Selfer in a more common school, we'd probably be dead. Now we get to be government slaves instead.'

'I'm not a slave! I'm a Sorcerer!' Downer's face was red.

Truelove let out a nervous, honking laugh and stepped between them. 'It's okay, it's okay,' he said. 'We're all in the same Coven.'

Downer ignored him and held Britton's eyes. *The SOC can force me to work for them, he thought, but they can't stop me from making her grow up*.

But not tonight. He had nothing left to give. 'I'm going to hit the rack. Lots of studying to do for tomorrow.'

He stepped out into the chill air and looked up at the night sky. The huge stars winked back at him. *Therese can't help. Who knows when she'll be able to? You're out of choices, Oscar*, they seemed to say. *They've got you.*

He shook his head and started toward P block. A hand touched his elbow. He looked down into Marty's black eyes, surrounded with painted dots. Britton reached out to touch the creature's head, then jerked back his hand. Would Marty take it as patronizing? What was it he had seen them do? Britton closed his eyes and bowed, tapping the lids. Marty smiled broadly, then repeated the gesture, murmuring in his own language.

'You important,' Marty said, sketching a doorway in the air with his fingers. 'Special.'

Britton sighed. 'Yeah, people keep telling me that. It's not helping any.'

Marty looked at him, uncomprehending. Britton sighed. 'God, what a fucked-up life this has turned out to . . .' He paused, then looked back down at the creature. His eyes widening.

'Holy shit,' he breathed.

Because he suddenly realized that there might be a way out of this after all.

Marty stared back at him, the blue surgical mask dangling from one ear, flapping in the wind.

Britton knelt to Marty's height. 'Have you ever heard of a flesh-eating worm?'

Marty turned pensive. '. . . wurm?'

'It's a worm from here. It eats muscle.' Britton thumped his chest.

Recognition dawned across Marty's face. He corkscrewed one finger over his sternum. 'Worm! I know! I know! Worm very . . . few. Very . . . important. Some in srreach room. Cold room with Doctor Captain, remember?' The research tent where they'd met Captain Hayes. Britton remembered.

He sagged with relief, sitting on the ground.

'Why?' Marty asked.

'Marty, there's a bomb in my heart. You understand a bomb?'

Marty nodded gravely. 'You' – he searched for the word – 'captured.'

Britton nodded.

'Worm very . . . hurt you. Kill you.'

'Not with magic, Marty. Not with someone to Whisper it. Maybe it can break the bomb.' More than likely it would set the ATTD off, but that was a chance Britton was willing to take. He remembered Rampart's words to him in the helo as they left the LZ. *They live in the Source all their lives and come up Latent at around twice the rate we do.*

'Do you have a Goblin buddy who can Whisper, Marty? Please tell me you do.'

Marty grinned. 'I know. I important. I bring friend with magic for worm. Talk worm no kill you. Eat bomb.'

Britton grinned in spite of himself, nodding so hard his neck hurt.

'Can you help me?'

Marty was silent for a moment, then looked back up to Britton and nodded. 'Secret.'

Britton grinned. 'Can you get a worm? Do you have someone to Whisper it?'

Marty's face went serious. 'Difficult.'

Britton considered what he was asking. The little Goblin was not well liked on the FOB as it was. If he were caught stealing from a SOC facility . . . he batted it away. He had to try. He couldn't stay there. It couldn't be his life.

'Can you get one for me?'

Marty was silent for a moment before nodding. 'You important.'

Britton smiled, then tapped his lids again. Marty repeated the gesture, then pointed to the leaves plastered to his face. 'Keep on. When you no feel, take off. Keep on to sleep is okay.' He waved and trotted back inside the OC.

Chapter Nineteen
In the Hole

The potential of combat Necromancy is staggering. Your buddy goes down next to you, then five seconds later, you're fighting his corpse. But you know what? Blinding lasers also provide combat overmatch. So do bioweapons. Just because a system provides a force multiplier doesn't mean we ignore the ethical ramifications of employing that system. We're the good guys. The second we forget that, we cease to be a nation we can be proud to fight for.

– LTG Amelia Dernwood,
Deputy Commanding General US Army Materiel Command,
Fifth Annual Conference on Magic and Military Ethics,
Geneva, Switzerland

Therese was missing from the knot of SASS enrollees gathered around the schoolhouse as Britton entered the next morning. He strolled toward them, noting the pillbox's closed door and Scylla's absence from the yard. They exercised her at random intervals, different times each day, and while Britton couldn't be sure why, he guessed it was as a security measure. The group of enrollees stood easier, though even the No-No Crew cast nervous glances toward the pillbox door and its patina of rust.

'Where's Therese?' Britton asked Downer as he joined them. As with every morning, she was at the SASS long before he arrived. She shrugged her shoulders, and Britton turned to Wavesign. 'Did she raise the flag?'

Wavesign shook his head. 'A couple of soldiers came and got her this morning. No idea where she went, and Salamander won't tell us.'

Britton's stomach turned over. He was surprised at how deeply her absence affected him, how it worried him. He looked up at Swift as they were being ushered into the school-house, and the pale man shook his head.

Britton couldn't concentrate on the morning's video, a longish civics lesson extolling the virtues of the US Constitution. He thought of Therese's kindness to both him and Wave-sign. Where had they taken her? Had she done something wrong? His stomach suddenly tightened into a ball. Had someone somehow overheard their conversation about the ATTD? Was that why they'd taken her? Why would they punish her and not him? As soon as the video ended, and they turned to head outside, he approached Salamander.

'Sir, where's Therese?'

'You're about the tenth person to ask me that question today, Novice. She's an awfully popular gal around here. I recommend that you attend to your training and think a little less about dating. You can always chat with Scylla the next time she does her rounds of the exercise yard. I've noticed you two like to chew the fat.'

'Sir, I'm . . . concerned. Therese is a friend,' Britton said, his powerlessness making him clench his teeth and forcing him to lean on the Dampener to shunt the magic back.

'Are you, now?' Salamander asked. 'Are you concerned? Well isn't that just touching. I suppose now I'll just tell you whatever you want to know in an effort to allay your concerns about your friend?'

'Sir, please,' Britton stammered, knowing where this was going.

'Novice, military decorum isn't going to save you from an ass chewing if you continually overstep your bounds. Now, I take my position as administrator of this facility with a large grain of salt. That is to say, I don't act the jailer any more than I absolutely have to. My goal here is to convince you all of the value of raising the flag out there and to ensure that you have a modicum of control over your abilities by the time you do.

Other than that, I try to give you a free hand. But it has to go both ways. If you start trying to ride me about every decision the army makes, you may jog my memory that I am a fucking jailer, and that might just remind me that I have the authority to have you clapped in fucking restraints if I so choose. Am I being perfectly clear here, Novice?'

Britton had been dressed down before. He had felt helpless in the hands of authority many times since he'd joined the army. But this was the first time he'd felt it over someone who mattered to him. Since he'd come up Latent, she was the first person other than Marty to show him an ounce of kindness. And something had happened to her, but there was nothing he could do about it. The tide of his anger gathered, building behind the wall of Dampener.

'Crystal clear, sir,' Britton answered through clenched teeth.

They gathered, heading toward the magical-control range. The panel on the pillbox door slid aside as he passed. 'Pretty Oscar,' Scylla crooned from behind the door. 'They took your lady away. Why do you let them?'

'Shut up!' one of the Suppressors on guard said, punching the door. Scylla muttered something low through the panel, and the guard blanched, taking a step back.

'Why do you let them?' Scylla repeated. 'Why, Oscar? They're roaches. They're not holding you. You're holding them. You're sparing them.'

I have a fucking bomb in my chest! Britton's anger addled mind howled. He didn't need her manipulative bullshit. Not now. Not when he was so worried and angry. He took a step toward the door. The guard was terrified of Scylla, but not of him and stepped forward to intercept, one hand on his pepper-spray canister. Britton halted, and growled, 'You talk pretty tough, Scylla, for a girl in a box.'

'Silly boy,' Scylla replied. 'This box is the only thing that keeps them safe.'

'Shut up!' the guard said, this time mustering enough courage to slide the panel shut. 'You best be moving, sir,' he said to Britton, tapping the canister of pepper spray. 'This stuff cuts something awful.'

The fury beat against the Dampener, scarcely contained.

For a moment, he thought he understood what Wavesign was facing. 'Yeah?' Britton asked, letting a gate roll open over his shoulder. 'Well, so does this stuff.'

The guard blanched for a second time, taking a step backward, his mouth working silently. Britton closed the gate, turned, and stormed off toward the rest of the enrollees, shame and a sense of power mingling in his gut. For a moment, he understood what Scylla meant. The guard, for all his Suppressive ability, for all his kit and belonging to the institutional power of the army, had been terrified. But at the same time, Britton was glad that the Witch hadn't seen him. He wasn't a murderer, and people weren't cattle. He didn't want to be the SOC's toy, but whatever it was that Scylla had let her magic make her, he didn't want to be that either.

Britton tromped back into the line of enrollees just as Salamander was starting to break up the groups into their practice pairs. If Salamander had seen Britton open the gate, he wasn't mentioning it. He didn't doubt that the guard would file a report of unauthorized magic use, but he couldn't worry about it. Therese was gone, and Wavesign milled around uncertainly on his own. The No-No Crew was back against the wall of the Quonset hut, refusing to help as usual. Britton nodded to Downer, but the young girl was already busy with another enrollee, who stood in the mud, kicking up clods of dirt that she animated. Wavesign's misery was palpable. The boy wasn't raising the flag and joining the SOC, which suited Britton fine; but sticking with the No-No Crew was simply aggravating the boy's lack of control, and by extension, his misery. Britton couldn't just stand by and watch that happen. He sighed and stepped forward.

'Come on, Wavesign. Let's work together. I've got the basics down now.'

Wavesign looked up, embarrassed and a little frightened. Britton realized too late how much of the anger he'd let manifest in his voice. 'I'm fine, Wavesign, really. I'm just worried about Therese. Let me help you.'

Wavesign shrugged, sidestepping closer to the No-No Crew, who stepped away at the touch of his vapor cloud. 'It's fine. I'm good.'

Britton's anger doubled. It was so senseless. 'You're not fine, and you're not good, and anyone with eyes can see it. You need this training more than anyone. Just because you get control doesn't mean you have to raise the flag.'

'I said I'm fine.'

'Then what's this?' Britton asked, reaching into the mist cloud and shaking the droplets off his hand.

'That's none of your business,' Swift said, and stepped forward. 'He doesn't want to be a soldier boy. Unlike you, he's showing some fucking balls.'

'Are you fucking kidding me?' Britton asked. His next words came out in a rush. 'He's a kid who wants to belong to something. Unfortunately, he's chosen your rancid company, as opposed to the army, which would at least help him come to some productive use.' He shocked himself with his own words. Was he actually defending the SOC? Advocating for Wavesign to serve it? *What's happening to me?*

'Doing what?' Pyre asked, his face reddening. 'Running down and murdering his own people?'

'No, he's better off with your crew, engaging in civil disobedience for . . . well, for no reason really. You're not Gandhi, chucklehead. You don't have a TV audience. You're not changing anyone's minds but your own. And, meanwhile, you're convincing this poor kid to live under a rain cloud when the people who could help him get out from under it are standing three feet away.'

'Fuck you!' Swift seethed. 'Bomb in your chest, my ass. You work for those fuckers, and everybody knows it. You could get yourself and everyone out of here tomorrow if you chose, but you won't. You don't want to.' Peapod nodded agreement, her thick arms folded across her chest.

'What? You dumb fuck. Even if that were the case, which it's not, that would be my choice. Being free means being free, Swift. It means belonging to myself. Not to the SOC or to you. You're not interested in freedom, just replacing one tyranny with another. You're a fucking wannabe despot.'

'Better that than a killer,' Peapod said.

'Yeah, he's really into nonviolence,' Britton fumed, the

concern and anger coalescing on Swift. 'Therese isn't here for you to hit. You want to take a shot at me again?'

'Stand down!' Salamander shouted, as the crowd started to back away from the two of them. Wavesign's vapor cloud coalesced into solid rain as he moved with them.

Swift took a step forward, cocking his fist. The magic surged along the tide of Britton's adrenaline, and, angered past caring, he let it come. The gate snapped open between them, facing Swift. The flow was heady and strong, and Britton rode on the sense of immortality that the singing current imbued in him. God, but Scylla was right. He was powerful, and it felt so good to be that way. The tendrils of magic snaked back to the Home Plane, seeking something to protect him from the threat of Swift, ignoring the fact that he was backpedaling, using his own magic to leap into the air, to fly to safety.

Salamander was shouting, running forward, but the anger released, freed from the confines of the Dampener, felt far too good to let go. Britton rode it for another moment, knowing that he would have to shunt it back in a moment and face Salamander's wrath.

Another moment was all it took.

The magic found aid and hauled it through the gate, rolling shut as its work was done.

The biggest black bear Britton had ever seen, its prehibernation coat thick and shaggy, reared to its full height, howling in rage and terror. Britton guessed it weighed over five hundred pounds.

Britton felt his magic roll back as Salamander Suppressed him, but the Suppression broke a moment later as the huge animal turned and swatted Salamander across the chest with a massive paw, sending the Pyromancer sprawling in the mud. A bullet thudded in the dirt, inches from Wavesign's foot, as one of the guards took aim at the bear, which flailed among the packed enrollees, just beginning to scatter. Swift soared skyward. Two Aeromancer guards hurtled after him, leaping from one of the guard towers. 'Down!' they shouted. 'Fucking down right now, or we will fucking fry you!'

Wavesign gritted his teeth and pointed at the animal, his rainstorm lashing forward in a wild spray of ice. The ice shards hammered the bear's flank, whipping its hindquarters around, freezing one leg solid. The bear scrambled on its free leg, dragging itself toward Salamander. Britton almost applauded Wavesign's rare burst of focused magic, but there was no time for that.

'Hold your fire,' Salamander wheezed to the guards as he tried to struggle to his feet. 'You'll hit somebody.'

The bear wheeled on its good leg, sniffing the air where Swift had escaped, and turned toward the next threat.

Salamander stumbled again, raising his head just as the bear growled and padded toward him, raising a giant paw, claws extended.

He pointed, a firebolt leaping from his hand and clipping the side of the animal's head. Much of its skull vaporized. Streaks of flame arced down its neck. Britton could see the seared surface of its brain, just visible through the charred fur. But the bear didn't go down. It roared, staggered back a step, and sniffed the air. It shook its head with rage, determining the smell was itself, and charged forward again.

Enrollees sprawled in the mud on either side of Salamander. The guards milled on the catwalks and around the gate, carbines leveled. Most cursed, unable to shoot through the crowd of enrollees. One squeezed off a round, thudding into the bear's flank, making it angrier. Another bullet tore into its shoulder.

Britton focused and opened a gate. The tide of anger and panic threw him off. Without the Dampener controlling the flow, the portal opened a few feet behind the creature. The drug in his system kept the flow from overwhelming his senses, from burning his flesh as it had outside the convenience store, but he was off, and he knew it. He tried to close the gate, and it vanished momentarily, only to flicker back open closer to the creature.

The bear cuffed Salamander again, throwing the Pyromancer down in the mud. It reared up over him, roaring, its pelt burning brightly, patches slick with sizzling blood.

Salamander rolled over on his side, trying to drag himself out of the way.

Britton pushed the magical tide, extending the surge

forward and letting the gate flicker shut and open again. It inched closer, appearing to slide along the ground, stutter-starting toward the creature as its huge limbs came down on Salamander's head.

The gate cleaved through the bear, sliding onward as it did, slicing it neatly in half. The creature gave a grunt that turned into a gurgle and was cut abruptly short. Britton gave in to the Dampener, terrified that the gate would cut Salamander as well, shunting the magic away as quickly as he could.

The bear collapsed in halves, the spray of blood clearing to show Salamander, curled in the fetal position and soaked by the creature's innards but otherwise unharmed. Britton rose shakily to one knee, trembling with relief.

In the distance, he saw Swift returning to the ground, his arms gripped by two SOC Aeromancers. 'Are you okay?' he called to Salamander, 'I'm sorry, I j . . .' He was silenced by a boot in his ribs. He felt Suppression take hold, and his hands were roughly forced behind him and cuffed.

Salamander rose to his feet and made his way toward Britton. He was so covered in gore that it was impossible to tell if he was actually injured or not. 'Don't say a fucking word,' he said, trembling with rage.

'What should we do with him, sir?' one of the men holding Britton asked.

'What the fuck do you think you do with him?' Salamander rasped. 'Throw this piece of shit in the hole until I can look at him without wanting to shoot him in the face.'

The inside of the pillbox smelled like sweat, musk, and old paint. Another odor rode just below the others, something high and chemical. The only light filtered in from the cracks around the door panel, illuminating an interior bare of anything except a metal bench with a bedroll resting on it and a stainless-steel toilet bolted to one wall.

Scylla had not bothered to graffiti the walls; she had made no scratched tick marks to count the days. She sat in a corner beside the bed, arms on her knees, eyes bright and smiling as if there were nowhere else she'd rather be.

'Well now,' she said. 'I suppose you must have done something particularly naughty to join me here today. I thought I heard a ruckus outside my door.'

Britton felt his back fetch up against the inside of the door. *She's just a woman*, he thought. *She has powerful magic, and she's done awful things, but the rest is just stage presence. She's Suppressed. In a stand-up fight, you'd easily overpower her. There's nothing to be afraid of.*

Then why was he so terrified?

Britton slid to the floor with his back to the door, crossing his arms in front of him.

'Oh, you don't have to sit so far away,' Scylla said, moving to the bed and patting the surface beside her. 'I may be a miscreant and ne'er-do-well, but I do so enjoy a man's touch.'

'Is that what you did with Swift when he was in here?'

She laughed, her eyes dancing. 'Oh, I'm sure he wishes. No. Swift is nowhere near as pretty as you.'

'He's a fucking fool, and so are you.'

'Am I? And here I was thinking I was the only person in this whole mad place who makes any kind of sense.'

'You killed twenty people.'

'Oh, far more than that, actually. It's been a while since I did the full tally. You, my little rumor mill tells me, killed one. You might have killed more if the SOC hadn't taken you down when they did. So, really, what's the difference?'

'There's a big difference. I wasn't in control.'

'Really? What about now? What about that nastiness out there? Were you in control then?'

Britton didn't answer.

'Why'd you do it, Oscar? Why'd you let it go, knowing in your heart of hearts the destruction and havoc it could wreak?'

Britton thought for a moment. 'A lot of reasons. Because I was angry. Because I was tired of being pushed around. Because I liked how it felt to just let go for a minute, to be myself.'

Scylla nodded thoughtfully. 'That's right, Oscar. That's why I did it. Because, frankly, I cannot imagine a life lived under someone else's thumb just to keep him from having to be afraid. I cannot imagine having to never truly be myself again.'

'You're always under someone's thumb, Scylla. That's life. You always have a boss.'

Scylla shook her head. 'You're wrong, Oscar. That's the change magic has wrought in the world. We didn't ask for this power, but it's finally put us beyond the system that we've been yoked to since the dawn of civilization. There are no more bosses, Oscar. Not for us. Not anymore. It's a chance for us to live as we like. It's real freedom, the kind of freedom that only power can grant. It doesn't have to be used for evil, but some evil may have to be wrought to take possession of it. Is it unfair that it came to us and not others? Sure. I don't have an answer for that, but that doesn't mean that I need to ignore it just because it makes the likes of Senator Whalen and her precious Reawakening Committee nervous. This is mine, Oscar. Mine and no other's. I want the freedom that it promises me.'

Britton was silent. Scylla patted the bed beside her again. He shook his head.

She smiled, beautiful in the dark. 'Oh, Oscar. Don't you want to be free?'

'Of course I do.'

'Then why not open a gate and walk away? They don't have you Suppressed half the time.'

'Because they put a bomb in my chest, Scylla. They can track my movements and tear out my heart anytime they like. Or didn't your rumor mill tell you that?'

She smiled again, resting her tiny chin in her hands. 'Well, of course it did. But are you going to let a little thing like a machine stop you? You are a being of magic, Oscar Britton. You are beyond human technology.'

'That's a very grand statement with nothing behind it. I can be beyond whatever I like. I'll still be just as dead the moment I walk though that gate.'

'No, Oscar. You won't. Not if you deactivate it. Not if you take it out.'

Britton swallowed. 'How the hell do you propose that I do that?'

'Oh, Oscar. Don't you know how magic works?'

'Enlighten me.'

'It's elemental. It draws on each element as its fuel, permits the Sorcerer to manipulate it. Fire for Pyromancers, earth for Terramancers, the fabric between dimensions for you.'

'That doesn't help me.'

'But it does, Oscar. Do you know what element Negramancers manipulate?'

Britton shook his head.

'Decay, Oscar Britton. Witches are queens of rot.'

Britton's head spun. 'And?'

'And that means we can decay human flesh, or stones. We can rot the bolts out of a tank and make it fall into its component parts. We can collapse buildings into blowing piles of desiccated mortar.

'We can rot machines, Oscar. We can cause wires to fizzle, metal to break down into ore, explosive chemicals into inert elements. I can break the ATTD, Oscar. I can rot it into sludge that will filter out of your system in a few hours.

'Get me out from under this Suppression for five minutes, and I can free us both.'

Chapter Twenty
Small Victory

We're not exactly certain how the 'Mountain Gods' got onto the reservation, sir, but it's apparent there's some kind of affinity. They're clearly cooperating with the insurgency. If the Selfers have a Portamancer, we don't have any reporting on it. The intel staff at FOB Frontier is currently working on the possibility that they may be Source indig entities who breezed through some kind of 'thin spot' in the interplanar fabric. If that is the case, it's a serious threat, and one we're definitely going to have to spend some resources on researching.

– Unidentified briefer to the Chairman of the Joint Chiefs of Staff

They let him out of the hole just as the sun was beginning to set. Salamander looked resigned, refusing to make eye contact. Two guards dragged him to the gate, where they flung him at Fitzy, who caught him in midstride, looking him over.

'You okay?'

It was the nicest thing Fitzy had ever said to him. The shock crippled his answer, and it was a long while before he could nod dumbly. 'How's everyone else?'

'They're fine.' Fitzy looked over his shoulder and made eye contact with Salamander. 'Thanks for your compliance, sir. You'll have no more trouble from this one.'

Salamander grimaced. 'Just get him the fuck out of here.'

Fitzy saluted. Salamander paused for a long while before returning it.

Fitzy's fingertips dug into the meaty portion of Britton's upper arm as he steered him away.

'What the hell is going on?' Britton asked. 'What happened back there?'

Fitzy stopped him midstride and spun on him, chests touching. 'You are fucking done asking questions, Novice. You are also done picking fights with anyone, anytime, ever. I have no idea how long that little stunt you pulled just fucked up things between SAOLCC and the SASS for, but I assure you that it won't be over quickly. You are lucky as hell that you're needed; otherwise, I would have been happy to let you rot in there with that fucking hag. Next time, I may have no choice. Is that perfectly clear?'

'Yes, sir.'

'Did you ever stop and think that you represent a Coven here? That what you do reflects on how Downer will be treated in there?'

Britton's stomach sank. 'No, sir. I . . . I didn't.'

'You're goddamn right you didn't. Now, do you have any other questions for me?'

'No, sir. No questions, sir.'

'Good. Now, you were so anxious to practice gating aid in combat, you're going to get some hard practice at it.' Fitzy spun Britton and marched him back toward the P pods.

Britton went meekly, his mind overwhelmed with the thought of Scylla's offer. Could she really get the ATTD out? She probably could. But how could he get her out of Suppression? And even if he could, what would he be unleashing on the world? She'd killed twenty people. Probably more, she claimed. She viewed her captors as cattle.

With the sun beginning to set behind the barricade walls, Fitzy took Britton to the MAC practice tent to find a SOC K-9 handler. He instructed Britton to open a gate onto the Portcullis loading bay. The dark vastness had been filled with three chain-link pens, each housing five mean-looking German shepherds.

'So you first tried Portamantic Summoning back in Shelburne,' Fitzy said. 'Took a recovery team about six hours to clean up that particular mess. Now you've successfully screwed up whatever goodwill I had with Major Salamander thanks to your little stunt today. What you did by accident before, I now want you to do on purpose. Let's try bringing these pooches through the gate and into the MAC tent one at a time.'

It was surprisingly simple. Britton recalled the sensation of the tendrils of magic snaking through the gate, driven by the sense of dire threat, grasping for something to assist him. He opened a gate inside one of the pens and recalled the feeling, giving the magic free rein to do its work. The shepherd popped through without complaint and crouched in the mud of the tent floor, ready to spring.

'Outstanding,' Fitzy said. 'Now do it again.'

So Britton did it again and again. When the kennels had been emptied, and the dogs all stood to their hocks in the mud, Britton gated into Portcullis and practiced bringing them back. He thought of the worm, digging into his chest, hauling out the ATTD. *I would trade my gates for Whispering if I could*. It seemed a far lesser power, but Whispering could save him, Portamancy kept him chained there. Scylla's offer hovered at the edges of his mind, tempting him. The worm plan had too many moving parts, hers was simple. Get her out from under Suppression for just a few minutes, and freedom.

But freedom to do what? There was nowhere in the world he could hide from the SOC. It would be freedom to run, forever a fugitive. And what had the SOC really done to him? They had captured him, they controlled him, but they were training him. He was beginning to master his ability. He had dispatched that bear as easily as he'd gated him in. If he ran, if he escaped, all that training would be lost to him, forever. But did that make them worth serving? They lied about so many things. They had faked Downer's death, hidden the truth about the Source, kept Limbic Dampener away from the public. They were so obsessed with controlling magic that they failed to do real good with it. Britton could never serve such masters. He had to find a way out. There were

Selfers out there who evaded capture. There were entire Indian reservations that boiled in active insurgency. If they could do it, then so could he.

At night, Britton sat on the steps to his hooch and looked up at the sky, trying to make sense of the spray of stars that gleamed so much brighter than back in the world he had simply begun thinking of as 'home'.

The attacks continued nightly. He became so used to the pattern of arcing flames or low-sweeping clouds that dispensed columns of lightning that he no longer flinched as the sirens wailed or the Apaches leapt airborne, droning over the barricades like angry hornets in search of an assailant already long since melted into the darkness. Once or twice, Britton could make out shadows in the sky and recognized the broad wingspan of Rocs. Other nights, he thought he saw leathern wings of smaller shapes and heard shrill cries he couldn't identify, but it wouldn't be long before the antiair systems would open up, funneling twenty-millimeter rounds in a shining white pillar, until the things flew off or were cut to a shrieking mist.

A shape jogged by in the darkness as Britton sat on the steps. He strained his eyes as the shape materialized into Richards.

'Hey,' Britton said nervously. 'Where you headed?'

Richards jumped, startled. 'Heading to the latrine,'

Britton felt a fool. The man had to piss, so it was not a good time to bother him. But his stomach was in knots. Scylla's offer had given the idea of the worm added immediacy. If there was another way, he had to use it. Richards could Whisper, Britton had to know if he could help him.

He started to speak, then said nothing.

Richards shifted from one foot to the other.

'Forget it,' Britton said. 'It's nothing. Go drain the vein.'

'Well, now I can't,' Richards said. 'It'll crawl back up because I'll be wondering what you were going to say.'

Britton chuckled, grateful for the humor. 'I just . . . we don't talk much at the OC. I can't sleep, and I wanted to shoot the breeze. I wanted to know if you're happy here.' *Clumsy*, he thought. *Don't be so damned obvious*.

Richards's voice went hard. 'I'm very happy here, Keystone. You should be, too.'

Britton was silent. Damn it. *You knew he wouldn't help you. Why did you even risk asking him? You'll be lucky if he doesn't tell Fitzy.*

Richards's voice was more sympathetic as he said, 'I know the girl pisses you off, and she can be a little overbearing, but she's young. Cut her some slack. She's right about one thing, you'll come around, eventually. This won't suck like this forever.'

That's what I'm afraid of. 'Yeah,' Britton replied. 'You're right.'

Richards laughed. 'I feel like we've both grown from this conversation. If you'll excuse me, I'm going to break this romantic moment before I wet myself.'

He jogged on to the latrine while Britton mounted the steps to his hooch, cursing his stupidity. He dozed with cries and explosions of FOB Frontier's night in his ears, drifting into half sleep. There had been so many explosions, so much screaming in the past months. Such sounds had come to define his life, and Britton didn't realize how at home he'd come to feel among them.

Therese didn't come back to the SASS. Salamander didn't mention the incident with the bear and gave Britton a wide berth. Swift avoided him as well, catching a sharp look from Salamander whenever he appeared as if he would talk to Britton. Britton continued to work closely with Wavesign, his only link to the memory of Therese, but the boy made little improvement even when Britton could convince him to practice his magic. The glimmer of control Wavesign had exhibited during the bear attack didn't repeat itself, and the young Hydromancer's magic remained as wild and unpredictable as ever. 'Guess it was a one-time thing,' he said, shrugging when Britton complimented him.

Things progressed with Shadow Coven. Pistol shooting was added to the mix, with the Novices firing at targets on the run, employing magic in the process. Targets were mounted on stands in Portcullis's loading bay, and Britton practiced opening gates, plugging away at them and shutting them in three-second intervals under Fitzy's critical gaze.

At last they were moved to a practice yard, where they worked in tandem. Britton opened gates on the penned attack dogs at Portcullis that Richards Whispered out from their staging areas, sending them after cloth dummies on wooden posts around the open field.

He improved. He fought Fitzy to a standstill more than once. His control over the gates reached the point where he wondered if he needed the Dampener anymore. If SOC operators had even a fraction of his level of control, then no Selfer could hope to stand against them.

The daily meditation calmed Britton, left him centered. The regular exercise worked out much of his angst over his capture, the losses of the past month. At times he even permitted himself to feel the slightest bit self-satisfied, at home in the Source, feeling his abilities come to fruition, his relationship with Marty and the rest of the Coven deepening. Such times made him angry with himself.

Do not get comfortable, he told himself. *This is not your home. If you become a tool of the SOC, then you have made the wrong call. You still have to find a way out of here. You still have to find a way to do good with what you have.*

And then one day, as magical control practice was winding down, Therese appeared.

She wandered through the gate with no guards escorting her. She looked pale, her eyes shadowed, her cheeks streaked with tears. She wore blue hospital scrubs, still smeared with a dull rust that could only be dried blood.

Britton ran for her. He heard Salamander start to call to him, then the Pyromancer shut his mouth and let him go.

Britton ran to her and took her elbows as Therese sank into his grip, resting her head on his chest, crying freely.

'What's wrong? Therese? What did they do to you?'

'Oh, those bastards,' she sobbed. 'Those fucking bastards.'

'What? What? Are you hurt?'

She shook her head. 'They got me, Oscar. They fucking got me.'

'What do you mean? How did they get you?'

'Where do you think I've been these past days? They put

me in the cash, Oscar. They've had me healing the wounded there. The victims of the Goblin attacks, accidents on the base, the sick. They come in every day.'

Britton was swamped with relief, but paused, unable to understand. 'Why is that bad?'

'Because now I have to help them, Oscar. It's as sure an anchor as the bomb in your heart. They know me. They know I can't leave those people. They know I have to work for them now.' She rocked against his chest, crying afresh.

Britton held her, patting her back, trying desperately to think of something to say. He had no words. Her argument was so persuasive, so plain. *Isn't this what you're beginning to feel?* he wondered. *This sense of purpose? Of control? How could you deny that to her?*

'Therese, I . . .'

'Don't,' she said, pushing away from him. She dried her eyes and smoothed her filthy hospital scrubs. She looked at the knot of enrollees, all staring at her in openmouthed silence. Wavesign's cloud had coalesced into rain again.

She nodded firmly to Salamander and marched purposefully toward the flagpole. Before Britton realized what she was doing, she hauled it to the top and stood at the position of attention.

Salamander jogged over to stand before her, raised his right hand, and began to speak.

'Yes, yes. I swear, and I will,' she said. 'Now get me the hell out of here before I change my mind.'

Salamander nodded and motioned toward the sign-in building. Therese shot Oscar a final look before heading off in that direction.

From all along the fence line to the SASS gate, the applause rang out as the guards expressed their approval for the newest member of their ranks.

Britton's gut churned as he watched her go. He struggled with the emotion before nailing it down.

Jealousy.

Why? he asked himself. *Why would you be jealous of her? She's with them now. She caved. She joined the other side.*

The answer came quickly. *Because she's using her magic*

for good. Because, no matter who she works for, she's helping people. Therese's magic heals.

And you, Oscar? What are you doing?

The question hung in his mind, unanswered.

The next morning, Britton left his hooch to head to the SASS, only to find Fitzy waiting for him in the muddy track outside.

'Morning, Novice,' the chief warrant officer said, smiling.

'Good morning, sir,' Britton answered slowly.

'How'd you like a day off from the SASS? Your control has made big strides recently, and I was figuring you'd appreciate a break from the daily brainwashing flicks.'

'I'm fine to go, sir.'

'Actually, Novice, I'm not asking. You've stirred up a serious fucking hornet's nest over there, and I figured it would be smart to let it blow over. Also, both you and Prometheus have been making strides in terms of your control, and I'd like to start putting that to the test. That okay by you?' Fitzy leaned in, his grim expression showing it was a rhetorical question.

Shadow Coven assembled in the yard to find it spread with the usual cloth dummies, a disabled Humvee at the far end. More dummies sat inside, a dummy gunner slumped in the ball turret behind the rusted machine-gun mount.

'You've done well in your individual exercises. It's high time you got serious about working as a team. Shadow Coven is the ultimate force multiplier,' Fitzy said. 'You will enter the field as four operators and build your own army. Everything on the field is fuel. Every bug, every spark of flame, every enemy you take down.' As Fitzy spoke, Goblin corpses were unloaded from a flatbed electric car, soldiers placing them directly behind each of the target dummies. 'Rictus, you see a dummy with a bullet hole in it, you may consider it dead, and the corpse behind it is game on.'

He distributed pistols and magazines. 'These are loaded with forty-five-caliber incendiary ammunition. It lacks the tungsten carbide penetrator you are accustomed to hearing about in its larger-caliber cousins but still contains the zirconium powder. The result is a slightly weaker round. But they are pretty much guaranteed to catch anything they hit on fire. Normally, I wouldn't be too thrilled about a battlefield roaring in flames, but when you've got an Elementalist in your ranks, that sort of thing comes in handy.' He shot Downer a wry smile and mounted a small wooden crate that gave him a better view of the field.

'Stage at Portcullis, gate in, and work your way left to right across the target range. By the time you reach the Humvee, I expect you to have the force necessary to destroy it. You have forty-five seconds from jump. Do not draw your sidearms until you are clear of the gate.'

They paused, waiting for further instruction.

'You ladies waiting for Christmas?' Fitzy asked. 'Get moving!'

Britton opened the gate on the darkness of Portcullis's loading bay and closed it once the Coven was safely through. He inhaled the stale air, thick with the smell of motor oil. Somewhere on the other side of the wall, Billy sat drooling, his mother's pale, elephantine arms draped around his neck. The chain link of the dog pens stood off to the side, empty of animals for now. He gave himself a moment for his eyes to adjust, then met the gazes of each Novice in turn. Truelove's glasses reflected what little light filtered through the warehouse from the glowing exit signs. He looked terrified. Britton put out a hand. 'Magic behind the magic,' he said, smiling foolishly.

Downer and Richards smiled, placing their hands on his. Truelove shrugged and put his on top. 'Magic behind the magic,' he said, not sounding convinced at all.

'Is there any way in hell we can do this in forty-five seconds?' Richards asked.

'Absolutely not,' Downer answered, smiling.

Truelove sighed. 'Fitzy is asshole,' he drawled.

They loosened their pistols in the holsters and checked the safeties. 'Okay,' Britton said, his officer's instinct for command kicking in. 'Stay on my six and watch my lead. I don't know what Fitzy's got planned for us, but I'm sure it won't be nice. I'll be first through the gate. Put your hands on your weapons and come out shooting.'

Truelove looked grateful, Downer sullen. 'I'm fine,' she said. He didn't argue.

The gate sprang open on the yard, and the Coven charged through just as Fitzy tossed a flash-bang in their midst. Britton shielded his eyes and looked away. 'Close your eyes!' he shouted as the low boom erupted, throwing Truelove off his feet and sending Downer and Richards scattering. Fitzy doubled over with laughter as Britton aimed his pistol and squeezed off a round, taking the first dummy in the chest and sending a puff of white flame that crawled across the cloth surface, spiraling upward and growing.

Richards turned back, his eyes streaming, and fired three rounds before one found its mark, tearing through the dummy's neck and starting its own small fire. With his free hand he gestured, and the ground before them boiled. Fitzy grinned and pulled the pin on another flash-bang, tossing it toward Britton. Britton fired again, taking a dummy between the eyes and opening a small gate in midair. The flash-bang passed through and thumped along the logging trail where he'd abandoned the police car before detonating. The gate shut, cutting the boom short.

The boiling ground vomited a throng of black insects, pouring forward on hundreds of tiny legs. They swarmed the next dummy, the white cloth gone black and chitinous beneath their squirming mass, shreds flying.

Downer recovered and swept her arms upward. The flames about the dummies danced, grew and solidified into three man-sized bodies of fire, leaping from their source and racing to the next dummy. They wreathed it in withering fire. Five more elementals jumped from it, making for the Humvee.

'Damn it, Rictus!' Britton shouted. 'Get in the game!'

Truelove staggered forward, blinking. He fired a few shots, wild, as Richards and Britton drilled the last remaining dummies and Downer's elementals set one more aflame to bring the number of elementals to eight. 'They're all dead, damn it!' Britton yelled.

Truelove stretched out his hands. The Goblin corpses behind the posts lurched upright. 'The Humvee! Go for the Humvee!' Britton called, advancing on the vehicle.

Richards's insects swarmed it, sliding their tiny bodies through the seams in the doors. Inside, the dummies began to jerk beneath hundreds of tiny mandibles. The elementals leapt onto the ball turret, incinerating the gunner and pressing fiery limbs against the turret hatch. Britton could see white sparks as the metal ignited under the intense heat. Truelove's walking corpses shambled with surprising speed to the vehicle's side, throwing gray shoulders against one quarter panel. They heaved, and the Humvee trembled. Britton saw legs crack and shoulders hang limp as the joints tore loose, but the zombies pushed, faces blank. One looked at him and stuck out a swollen gray tongue. Truelove smiled as the Humvee jerked upward and toppled onto its side, burning brightly, its occupants rent to ribbons.

Britton sent a gate sideways through it, slicing the Humvee down the middle in a *coup de grâce*. The wreck collapsed in a heap as the Coven turned to Fitzy, who stopped his watch with a beep.

'Minute thirty,' he said. 'You fail. Keep up like this in a real combat situation, and you'll be dead before you get to do any stupid show-off moves. Rictus, what the hell was that? You lose a goddamn contact back there?'

Truelove looked at his feet, shrugging. Fitzy boiled in response. 'What the hell would you have done if that had been a real grenade? Christ, you're pathetic.'

Despite Fitzy's words, Britton flushed with pride. In less than two minutes, they had wiped out a small platoon of enemy and disabled a crew-served vehicle. They had done exactly what Fitzy had instructed – entering alone and finishing with an army.

Fitzy ranted, and Britton turned away. They had done brilliantly. He wasn't going to listen to any crap.

'Where the hell do you think you're going?' Fitzy called after him. 'You still owe me MAC practice.'

Britton turned back to him, face hard. He holstered his pistol. 'MAC, sure. No time like the present.'

Fitzy jumped down off the crate and advanced. 'You want a public whooping? That's fine. You've certainly earned it.'

He jabbed at Britton's nose, and the larger man skipped

back lightly, slapping the hand down. Fitzy followed with a sharp kick at Britton's knee, but Britton was ready and spread his legs apart, letting Fitzy's boot pass harmlessly between them. He threw a jab of his own. Fitzy jerked his head out of the way, catching Britton's wrist and twisting it around, bringing his boot up toward Britton's exposed crotch. Britton took a step, stomping on Fitzy's ankle, earning a grunt of pain. He wrenched his arm free and pushed hard on the chief warrant officer's chest, sending him staggering back.

Fitzy paused, his eyes narrowing. He spit, his eyes flicking across the rest of the Coven, standing agape. He looked back at Britton, concentrating. 'If that's the way you want it.' He rushed forward.

Britton caught his right cross in midair and pivoted, swinging Fitzy forward. He opened a gate in front of him, and Fitzy went sprawling into the darkness of Portcullis's loading bay.

Britton closed the gate and opened another one directly behind Fitzy. He jumped through and spun on one heel as Fitzy turned to face him. He opened another gate behind the chief warrant officer as his boot connected hard with Fitzy's face, sending him sprawling back through into the practice yard, blood spraying from his mouth.

Britton stepped through after him, assuming his guard. 'Yes, sir. That's the way I want it.'

Fitzy spit blood and cursed. 'GIMAC. You're getting a little ahead of yourself, don't you think?'

'Just trying to impress you, sir,' Britton said.

'Oh, I'm impressed,' Fitzy replied, raising a hand. Britton felt his magic roll back. 'Now, let's see how you do with no tricks up your sleeve.'

He advanced again, no feinting jabs this time. Britton tried one of his own and Fitzy slapped it down, using the momentum to pivot on his boot, bringing an elbow crashing into Britton's ear so sharply that he staggered, seeing stars, his head ringing.

Fitzy paused in front of him, hands on his hips. 'Harder when you've got to fight fair,' he said, then brought the steel toe of his boot up into Britton's balls. Britton collapsed in the mud, retching, unable to breathe.

'Delusions of adequacy,' he heard Fitzy say through the ringing in his ears.

Oscar Britton lay facedown in the mud, feeling the ATTD like a stone in his heart. The thought of taking Scylla up on her offer chilled his soul. And there was no word from Marty about the worm, and without it, no way out.

Chapter Twenty-One

No Way Out

This attack was just a taste of what's to come. The word of the Lord is clear – 'I will come near to you for judgment. I will be quick to testify against sorcerers.' When this government of Satan heeds the word of Almighty God and ends the tolerance of the devil's magic, we will lay down our arms and negotiate.

– Recorded message – Church of Christ, Militant

'We did good today,' Truelove ventured, as they sat in the OC. Britton nodded, groaning inwardly. Truelove probably thought he was comforting him after the beating he'd taken, but he couldn't have cared less about that. Marty hadn't mentioned the worm since Britton had first asked, and Scylla's offer hovered like a vulture on the fringes of his mind.

'Hell, we did great,' Downer said, smiling. 'No matter what Fitzy says. That was a damned sweep.'

Richards snorted, knocking back a tumbler. He slapped the empty glass down on the counter for Chris to fill. 'Pour one out for the toughest act in the United States armed forces!'

'Make that two,' Downer added to everyone's surprise. 'He knows what he's got now. It can't be long before they start running us on real missions.'

'Against whom?' Britton asked.

Downer shrugged. 'Against whomever. The bad guys.'

'The bad guys will probably be a pack of confused kids like

you used to be, or maybe Marty's kindred. You like that idea?' Britton asked.

Truelove moved to intervene. 'He needs another dose of Dampener,' he said, but Downer silenced him with a look. Her hair had grown in a bit, the stubble beginning to give way to short hair. Her cheeks were gaunter, the chubbiness fading fast. At that rate, she'd be downright lean in another couple of weeks.

'What the hell is wrong with you?' she asked. 'You've been given a clean slate. They're making you into a superhero, and you don't even care! Look what your magic is doing! You saw what I did today!'

'Have you seen this place?' Britton asked. 'It's a damned fortress. Look at the locals! Look how they treat Marty and the rest!'

Silence settled over the OC as the crowd stopped their drinking to take in the confrontation.

'They're fucking Goblins, Oscar!' she yelled. 'They attack our base every damned night!'

'And why do you think they do that?' he growled back. 'Maybe it has something to do with the fact that we set up a military outpost in the middle of their land?'

'We give them jobs! They work here!' Bright spots of color rose in her cheeks.

'For what? I don't even know what they're being paid. Surely they're not using US dollars out there in the open country.' He turned to Truelove. 'How does Entertech pay them?'

Truelove swallowed hard. 'With coupons for the PX,' he finally said. 'They use them mostly for stuff they don't make themselves, plastic containers, synthetic clothing. But mostly processed sugar. They love it.'

Britton looked back to Downer. 'And for that they're treated like indentured servants. They're carved up like high-school lab experiments!'

Richards coughed. 'What the hell are you talking about?'

'Go to the damned cash,' Britton yelled. 'They're dissecting them there. Christ, Truelove, you use their dead as practice dummies! You want to tell me that's okay in their culture? They don't honor their dead the way we do?'

Truelove blanched, and Richards stammered, but Downer met Britton's gaze evenly. 'So? We study them. Big deal! We dissected frogs in biology class all the time!'

'They're not frogs, damn it!' Britton pounded his fist on the bar.

Downer ignored him. 'For all you know, they're honored to give us their dead.'

Britton recalled Marty's look of resignation as the Physiomancer let the curtain fall. 'I doubt it.'

'Guys, it's okay, it's okay,' Truelove said. Richards ignored them.

Downer took a breath. 'Look, I'm trying here.'

'So am I,' Britton retorted, 'and that doesn't mean doing whatever the hell some murderous idiot tells me.'

'What's so wrong with that?' she asked. 'Why is it so bad to fight for your country?'

'Nothing, so long as you choose to take that fight on. Didn't you take civics class? Don't you know what this country was founded on?' he went on. 'Freedom, Sarah. Freedom to choose sides. We're a democracy, damn it. Or, at least we were before the Reawakening Commission and the McGauer-Linden Act. Christ. Do you even know why I'm really here?'

Downer didn't blink. 'Because they tagged you. You've got an ATTD implant.'

Britton nodded. Fitzy or Harlequin must have told them. Hell, Therese had said half the SASS knew.

'So run, then.' She shrugged. 'If it's so bad, take a hike. Those things work fast. You won't feel a thing.'

Britton opened his mouth, then closed it. It was not as if he hadn't considered the option.

'I know why you don't,' Downer said. 'Because you used to be army, and now you almost are again. You're protecting your country, and you know it. Harlequin said we'll probably wind up fighting narcoterrorists in South America, or keeping the Chinese out of Taiwan, or catching pirates in the Straits of Mal . . . Malacca, or whatever it's called. Once we're doing that, you're going to be happy again because you'll be helping people.'

You're wrong, Britton thought. *I'm holding on because*

there's a chance, however remote, that I can defuse this damned thing.

'She's got a point,' Richards said, tipping back another tumbler. 'But you know the real reason you stay?'

'*Et tu Brute?*' Britton asked.

'Curiosity,' he went on. 'There's a whole world out here and like it or not, you've got the keys to the kingdom. You want to see what's up just as much as the rest of us do.'

Britton searched his head for a rebuttal and found none.

But Scylla's words haunted him. *I cannot imagine a life lived under someone else's thumb just to keep him from having to be afraid. I cannot imagine having to never truly be myself again.* The SOC might train him, give him a chance to do something with his magic, but it would always be by their leave and for their ends. There had to be a better way, to neither run nor fight. Serving the SOC wasn't it.

'No anger,' Marty said, coming up behind them. He touched Downer's wrist, and the girl instinctively jerked away. 'No anger us. Plenty anger others.'

The rest of the patrons of the OC muttered at his entrance but gave him and the rest of the Coven a wide berth.

'Tell her, Marty,' Britton said. 'Hell, tell me. Why are you even here? Why do you work for Entertech? I see how they treat you. Why aren't you fighting with the rest?'

'Other tribes,' Marty said calmly. 'Not Mattab On Sorrah.'

'Mattab On what?' Britton asked.

'It's the name of his tribe,' Truelove offered.

'Why doesn't your tribe fight?' Britton asked.

'All water babies,' Marty said.

'What the hell does that even mean?' Britton fumed, unable to contain his frustration.

'He means we all come from the magic,' Truelove explained.

'I get that,' Britton said. 'But that's not even true. Marty, we came from another world.'

'Came back,' Marty said. 'You tribe . . .' He paused, searching for the word. 'Lost.'

'What?' Britton asked. 'You mean we're from the Source originally?'

Marty spread his hands, uncomprehending. He smiled

broadly. 'Mattab On Sorrah no fight. All water baby. Mattab On Sorrah help. Marty help. Long time. We wait. Everything okay.'

'How can you let them do this to you?' Britton asked, Marty's patience building his frustration to a pitch that surged his magic. 'That's not helping, that's suicide.'

Marty shook his head. 'Help, always help. Wait.' Britton was rocked once again by Marty's patient kindness. He was a leader among his own, but the military on the FOB treated him like a servant, an animal. Still, he stood by them.

'See?' Downer said. 'He doesn't mind. Why can't you just be happy where you are?'

'We're slaves,' Britton said, 'slaves that kill.'

'You killed my boyfriend,' Downer said. 'You almost killed me. I killed people, too. Harlequin says that's all behind us now. It's a fresh start. That comes from the president. All we have to do is forget it and start over. I can do that. Why can't you?'

Britton knew she was right. The truth was that Britton was beginning to revel in his newfound control, that the rest of Shadow Coven were becoming colleagues if not friends. He had lost his home and was beginning to build a new one on the razed foundation. Was it better to pout and scream like Swift? To stew in the hole like Scylla? Even Therese had raised the flag and joined up once she'd realized that her magic would be put to some use.

And yet.

'The hell with this,' was all he said as he stood and left. For the second time, Marty followed him out, stopping him with a hand on his elbow.

'Okay,' Marty said. 'No anger.'

'It's not okay,' Britton growled. 'You might be some kind of a saint, but I'm not. You're one of the best . . . people I know, and I'm angry on your behalf.'

Marty did his ear-wiggling shrug, not appearing to understand.

Britton squatted in front of the Goblin, putting his hands on Marty's narrow shoulders. Worry made his voice hard. 'Marty, I need that worm. I really need it.'

Marty frowned. 'Srreach room is . . . hard. Many people.'

Britton cursed and looked at the ground. He knew what he was asking of the creature, but he couldn't stand the thought of another day here. 'Maybe I could help?' He thought briefly of gating back to his world, then into the cash from there, but the ATTD would alert whoever watched it.

Marty's frown deepened. 'So important?'

Britton gritted his teeth. He thought of the half-dissected corpses he'd seen in the cash and shuddered. Who knew what punishment the SOC would levy on a Goblin contractor caught stealing from there?

But Downer's zealotry moved him. Scylla's offer made him shudder. He couldn't make that place his home. He just couldn't.

It was different for Therese. She was helping people. Britton was training to be a walking meat cleaver to be used against God knew whom.

'Yeah,' Britton sighed. 'It is.'

Marty looked at him, folding his arms across his chest. His massive head bobbed on its scrawny neck over narrow shoulders, but Britton couldn't miss the regal look in his pointed chin and broad brow. Marty sucked in air and clucked, deep in his throat, a hitching sound that Britton had never heard a human make. He realized it was Goblin pensiveness.

Marty nodded again. 'Important,' he said.

'Important,' Britton repeated.

Chapter Twenty-Two

Do Some Good

The tongues of blazing fire,
The ice storm's savage trill,
The gale and steadfast mountain,
All serve our nation's will.

– Excerpt from the SOC anthem 'Phaleratus Ministro'

Therese's absence from the SASS set off a war of emotions in Britton. Betrayal competed against worry that eroded into simple loneliness. Britton slumped his way through the morning video, wondering vaguely if the rest of the enrollees felt her absence as keenly as he did. They all seemed down to a greater extent. Swift sagged in his chair, pale and harrowed-looking. Pyre and Peapod bickered quietly beside him. Wavesign's control seemed to have regressed, and he rained steadily in a corner.

One of the enrollees had raised the flag during control class that morning, which set Swift into his usual fit of impotent screaming that a resigned Salamander didn't bother to check. He administered a perfunctory oath at the base of the flagpole before jogging back to the group to resume instruction.

Britton went through the exercises, not really paying attention. He realized that he no longer needed them. His basic control was fluid, solid. He could call and shunt away the magic at his will. There was nothing more for him to learn there. He looked at Swift and shook his head. It was becoming impossible to sympathize with him. The man's impotent posturing trapped him in that tiny space, his world become the whole of the little muddy compound. And for what? Pride? Some obscure ethical point that nobody apart from him even cared about?

How are you any different? Britton asked himself. *You're both resisting. How are you any better?*

I am better. I'm looking for a way out. Swift is sulking. I don't know what the hell he thinks he'll accomplish by spinning his wheels here. At least I've got a plan.

Really? And what plan is that? Get the worm that is never arriving? Get Scylla out of her cage?

Face the music, pal. Your plans stink. You and Swift are closer than you think.

Scylla paced the yard, her guards quaking behind her. All her power, Britton thought, and all she'd managed to do was intimidate two soldiers who locked her up anyway. She was nothing more than a bully. When she paced past him, she nodded greeting. Was that madness he saw in her wide-eyed grin? 'Have you forgotten me, Oscar?' she asked. 'Won't you let me help you?'

Britton looked at his feet until she passed, the guards moving sheepishly behind her, doing their best to look as if they were hurrying her along.

But he could feel her presence, her feet crunching on the frozen mud, the guards standing uneasily behind her. Why had she stopped? Weren't they supposed to keep her moving? 'Scylla, I . . .' he said, looking up.

Scylla had moved twenty yards down, along with her guards. It was Fitzy who stood before him. The chief warrant officer's condescending look was gone, replaced instead with an earnest concern. 'Morning, Novice, you ready to do some good?'

Britton looked around him at Wavesign's childish lack of control, Swift's pouty impotence, Scylla's half-mad, half-reasoned hostility. He was surprised to find himself actually glad to see Fitzy. Hope blossomed in his chest. *Is he serious?* 'You bet I am, sir.'

'Good, let's go.'

Downner looked wistfully after them, but Fitzy waved her away. Salamander only nodded as Fitzy turned on his heel and took off without saluting. He set a good pace, walking so fast that Britton had to jog to keep up, even though his legs were much longer.

'We in a hurry, sir?' Britton winced as soon as the words were out, waiting for the string of invective that Fitzy usually reserved for those who asked foolish questions.

But Fitzy only nodded. 'Got a problem that you're uniquely suited to solve, Keystone. About time you earned your wings, so to speak.' The seed of hope in Britton began to flower.

They moved up the muddy track and through the checkpoint out of the SOC enclosure and down another wider road that led toward the FOB's central plaza. Britton realized a moment later that they were heading toward the cash. Therese. His heart leapt.

He opened his mouth to ask another question, and Fitzy silenced him with a wave. 'I'll give you the full rundown in exactly two mikes. Just shut up and haul ass for now.' The chief warrant officer broke into a run.

They dashed through the cash's front flaps, pushing past the signs marking the trauma ward, and headed through a side flap that led to a covered walkway that looked recently erected judging by the shiny new tent poles and fresh gravel. Britton looked around for Marty, but they were nowhere near the urinalysis section, and, while he saw many Goblin orderlies helping out in the bustle of the trauma floor, he couldn't spot Marty's dotted-paint pattern, his kindly eyes, his wide, splayfooted stance. *When I first got here, I couldn't tell one Goblin from another,* Britton mused.

At the end of the covered walkway, a miniature trauma center had been set up under a new tent on a freshly laid gravel bed. Two sentries stood at the entrance, carbines ready. They nodded at a glance from Fitzy and stood aside to let him and Britton pass. The center's interior was kitted out for emergency care, with two gurneys and mobile medical pallets piled with equipment. Britton could make out surgical tools, a defibrillator, and a heart monitor. A doctor stood ready, two Goblin orderlies at his sides, already scrubbed up and ready to work. Beside them stood Therese, also in scrubs, a Physiomancer's lapel pin prominently displayed, as well as a polished and worried-looking army colonel. His name tape read TAYLOR.

Britton nodded to Therese, and she smiled back behind her surgical mask. He started forward to embrace her, but Fitzy's hand on his shoulder stopped him, rotated him to face the likely reason all this medical might was on standby.

Three combat operators stood in the tent's other half, geared for dynamic entry in all the tactical gear Britton's own men had worn on the high-school roof. Tabs arced across the Velcro patches on their shoulders: SPECIAL FORCES. Beside them, a SOC Hydromancer stood. He was likewise rigged for war but carried no weapon other than his holstered pistol, not that he would need one. BREACHER, read the subdued gray lettering across his chest, just below a thin stylized gray wave.

A burly Entertech contractor nearly knocked Britton over, fitting body armor and a tactical vest over Britton's head, strapping a pistol and go bag to his legs, stuffing the pouches with magazines.

'This him?' said one of the SF operators, a grizzled sergeant first class, his face half invisible under the brim of his helmet and the fittings for his night optical device. His name tape read SHARP.

Fitzy nodded. 'Just give me a sec to get him briefed up, and, hopefully, we can make this work.'

'We don't have a lot of time. They could be moved, or worse,' Sharp said.

'You can't rush this,' the colonel said. 'Let Chief Warrant Officer Fitzsimmons do his job.'

The SOF operators stared at the colonel with open contempt, completely unimpressed by his rank.

Fitzy faced Britton squarely and placed his hands on his shoulders. 'All right, Keystone. I need you to listen carefully and to focus completely. We don't have time to go through this twice. You with me?'

'Locked on, sir,' Britton said.

'Good.' Fitzy nodded. 'You've been kind of cut off from the news out here, so you aren't tracking on the fact that we've got two kidnapped marines out of the Second Marine Expeditionary Force running support for the Bureau of Indian Affairs on the Mescalero reservation. The res is gigantic. We have no idea where the hell they are, and to be frank, we were starting to lose hope that we'd ever get 'em back. But just about two hours ago, the kidnappers posted a video to the Internet showing proof of life. The video also shows the room.'

Britton nodded. 'You want me to gate there.'

Fitzy pointed to a computer monitor mounted to a wheeled cart behind the SF operators. 'The video has a pretty good pan of the entire room, hopefully enough for you to get a fix on the location. We had one of our information operations bubbas work up a scratch-and-sniff kit for you, so you can get a sense of what the place smells like. Mission is simple. You gate the team in, keep to the rear, and get the team out when the hostages are secured. Bring everybody home so the medical crew here can work on them. Sergeant Sharp runs the show, for you and even for Captain TrueZero here. The Apache husband their magic users carefully, and we're not expecting a ton of sorcery on this run, but TrueZero can Suppress well enough if it comes to that.'

'You stay on our six and out of the fight,' Sergeant Sharp added. 'I can't afford to be worrying about you once we hit the target.'

'Don't worry about me,' Britton said, trying not to bristle. 'I was doing assault-team insertions for years before I came up Latent. I know the drill.'

Sharp looked unimpressed, and Fitzy jerked his head toward the computer monitor. 'Let's give this a shot.'

Britton nodded, a lump of fear and excitement working its way from his stomach up to his throat. *I'm finally going to put it to use. I'm finally going to do something.*

The video was grainy, but clear enough for Britton to make out a wide brick-walled space. A dirty gray concrete floor, a drop-tiled ceiling with water stains. Rusted machinery parts were jumbled in one corner. A flag hung on the rear wall over a green-painted door, depicting crossed fists, each clenching a rifle, positioned behind what looked like a winged wheel. A narrow black shape, vaguely manlike, rose from the wheel's center. A wide, knife-toothed grin stretched across it, narrow hands flexing dark claws. Britton thought the shape looked familiar, and a chill ran across his back. Crowning the display was a giant bird skull, striped red and orange. Four hooded men stood behind the two marines, seated Indian style in their uniforms, their faces bruised past recognition.

But they were alive. *Don't worry about that. Focus on the room. Your job is to get the guys in to do the job.*

But something about the scene nagged at him. 'Sir?' He said to Fitzy, 'That bird skull's awful big. How the heck would the Apache get their hands on a Ro . . .'

'Focus, Keystone!' Fitzy silenced him. 'Intel's not your job here.'

Britton bit his lip and concentrated.

As he looked at the video, he felt a movement beside him, and one of the Goblin contractors began to wave a small plastic canister under his nose. The fumes rose, carrying foreign scents – spent diesel fuel, animal manure, dust, and mold. 'Close your eyes,' Fitzy said. 'Get a real good sense of the place.'

Britton did his best to focus on the smells and the room in the video, trying to ignore the heady silence around him, the stares of the SF operators, Fitzy, Therese, and the medical crew, Colonel Taylor. The pressure made him nervous, and he leaned on the Dampener to shunt the emotion aside. *Focus, focus.*

After a moment, Sharp coughed. Fitzy stirred at Britton's side. 'What do you think?'

'I've got it,' Britton said.

'Are you sure?'

'No, but it'll have to do, won't it?'

Fitzy nodded grimly. 'I guess it will. All right, I want a pinhole, Keystone, open for no more than five seconds. I want a quick recon of the room and ID any threats. Can you do that?'

'I think so, sir.'

'Remember, no bigger than a pinhole. We alert the enemy to our entry, and this whole thing is going to go south.'

Britton nodded and cleared his mind. He tried to push all other thoughts from his mind's eye, focusing on the image of the room, repeating it in his head, centering on the details of the filthy brick, the hung banner, the pile of soiled machine parts. He recalled the smells, the dull cordite tinge burning his nostrils. Then he leaned on the Dampener, letting his nervousness, his desire not to disappoint the crowd staring at him, fuel the magic. The gate materialized perfectly, barely the size of a dime, shedding a tiny pinprick of light. He looked through it, then leaned back, shutting it and nodding.

'Room's empty, sir. No light source or obstructions. No threats visible. Looks like they abandoned it after making the video.' Britton kept his voice even, but inside he was exulting. *I did it. I watched a video for a minute and sniffed a canister and I can take us right there*. The control, the sense of accomplishment was almost overwhelming. Fitzy grinned at him, and Britton grinned back, grateful in spite of himself. Bastard gave me this chance.

'All right,' Sharp said. 'I wish we had more time to prep, but we need to go now. Keystone, Captain TrueZero, on our six, and do not engage unless called upon. In and out, quick as we can. Normally we'd have weeks to drill for an op like this. But . . . but things are different.'

You bet things are different. Now the army's got a guy who can get you there in an instant. You probably wouldn't have even attempted this mission before. Don't worry, I won't let it go to my head.

'I've got it,' the SOC Hydromancer groused.

'With all due respect, sir,' Sharp said, 'I need you to secure the attitude. I cannot afford to be worrying about either of you.' He nodded to his men, slipping the night-vision device into position over his eyes.

'You might want to hold off, Sergeant,' Britton said. 'The gate makes a lot of light. Better wait until you're through, and it's closed, before you go to the night optical devices. Otherwise, you might be running this op blind.'

TrueZero smirked, and Sharp nodded, slipping up his NODs and making a *you-got-me* face.

Britton nodded to Fitzy and widened his stance. 'Folks might want to step back a bit.'

As the group complied, he heard Therese whisper behind him, 'Good luck, Oscar.'

'Yes,' added the colonel, almost as an afterthought. 'Godspeed.'

'Don't fuck it up, Keystone,' Fitzy added, 'or it's your ass.'

Britton grinned and slid the gate open, wide enough to admit the operators abreast. The SOF soldiers hesitated a moment, staring at the portal. Sharp motioned them forward, and they went, following their carbine muzzles as if they were dragged by them, walking evenly, calm, perfectly stable firing platforms. Sharp made a zipping motion across his lips to Britton and TrueZero before moving through. Britton and TrueZero drew their pistols and followed behind. They entered into the darkness, and Britton shut the gate, an array of smells hitting his nose. The IO guys had gotten it almost exactly right. The air was thick, close, and freezing.

He heard the low clicks of the SF operators snapping their NODs into place, and Britton followed suit, the world transforming from black into pale green and white. He'd operated on NODs before and paused to adjust to how they flattened the world, robbing him of depth perception and color, plunging him into a weird ghost world, mechanical and unforgiving. But it was well worth it. The benefit of seeing in the dark far outweighed any minor adjustments that had to be made to do it. Britton looked left and right, able to take in the rest of the room that the camera's aperture had cut off. Two metal doors stood at the far end. The SOF operators were already stacking up alongside it, Sharp anchoring the three men. Britton and TrueZero took up position on the door's far side, shoulders pressed against the wall, pistols pointed at the floor, out of the line of fire as instructed.

Sharp nodded, and the operator across from him knelt, sliding what looked like a dental mirror under the door. He looked at it briefly, then nodded back to Sharp and made a fist, thumb up. *Clear*. He then stood and tried the door handle, his touch surprisingly gentle and silent. The handle didn't budge. He sliced his hand flat through the air. *Locked*. Britton looked up at the hinges, rusted nearly solid. There would be no way to open it without making a lot of noise.

Sharp signaled TrueZero, and the SOC Hydromancer moved to the door. Britton felt his magical current surge as he placed his hands against the rusted surface, and within moments it paled, sparkling with frost and turning a faint, glowing blue that softly illuminated the darkness. The cold was so intense that Britton could feel it from his position feet away.

TrueZero stood back and kicked the door. It shattered, the metal pieces flying apart with no more sound than a broken window. The SF operators dashed through, their infrared sights casting pencil-thin beams down the hallway, invisible to all but those wearing night-vision optics.

A short hallway stretched out before them, the floor cast from the same dirty, chipped concrete, and the walls made of the same moldering brick. Graffiti covered most of it. A dog corpse sprawled to Britton's left, stretched out among piled garbage. Two doors were set in the hallway's left side and one in the right. Sharp signaled one of the operators to cover the two doors, while he and his remaining man knelt and checked through the garbage. Sharp flicked out his pocketknife with a soft click and slit the animal carcass, spreading it wide and peering inside the cavity with a small flashlight, checking for hidden explosives. The odor nearly made Britton gag, and he had to grit his teeth and press his forehead against the wall to keep from vomiting. By the time the feeling passed, Sharp had made the clear sign and joined his remaining man to stack on the single door. This door was unlocked, and they rolled into the room, emerging a moment later, signaling to their remaining man. *Clear*.

One operator moved to cover one of the remaining doors while Sharp and the other operator stacked on opposite sides of the second one. The operator knelt, sliding his mirror underneath once again, then stood and shook his head, giving an exaggerated shrug of his shoulders. *Can't see*. Sharp trotted to Britton's side. 'Can you look in there?' he whispered.

Britton shook his head. 'I have to know what it looks like first.'

Sharp cursed and moved back into position. He pulled a grenade from his vest and tried the handle himself this time. Again, locked. He nodded to TrueZero, who ran to the door, placing his hands on it. The magic poured forth from his hands, chilling, then freezing the door; the soft blue glow began to radiate outward as the Hydromancer worked.

Then the door exploded.

Britton heard the sharp report of gunfire and the frozen shards exploded outward, flying in TrueZero's face. The SOC Hydromancer went flying backward, the fabric of his body armor ripping as a round caught him in the chest. He fetched up hard against the opposite wall and slid into a sitting position, senseless.

Sharp rolled around the corner to hurl the grenade, and a round caught him in the leg, spinning him off-balance. He collapsed, already lifting his carbine and firing one-handed into the darkness. The grenade, pin pulled, rolled a couple of feet down the hallway and stopped.

The other operators turned toward it, their guns dangerously out of the fight.

'I've got it!' Britton shouted, and snapped open a gate between the grenade and the team. It glimmered over a section of the berm beside Route 7 in Shelburne just as the grenade exploded. He felt the hot air of the thermal discharge engulf him, his ears ringing from the percussion. The solid rubber balls, intended to stun and incapacitate the enemy without killing the hostages, whisked harmlessly through. Britton could hear them pattering off the tarmac of the thankfully empty stretch of road.

The operators wheeled, dropping to their knees, knocking their NODs up onto their helmets and flooding the room with white light from the mounts beneath their carbine barrels. Gunfire exploded from their weapons, and Britton was momentarily blinded until he had a chance to push his own night optics away from his eyes.

'Get down!' Sergeant Sharp had begun to shout. 'Get down on the fucking ground right now!' Over his back, Britton could see ragged men, gaunt and long haired, moving in the room beyond. At least two lay on their sides on the floor before them, stirring weakly, bleeding out into the dust beneath them. Behind them, he could make out the hostages, their uniforms filthy, lying facedown with their hands bound behind them. Another round hissed by Britton's head as the Hydromancer slouched over on his side.

Sharp's face had turned gray as the pool of blood from his leg expanded, spreading out to make the floor slick. One of the operators slipped in it and went down. The enemy was pinned down in the close confines of the room, but they would make no headway. Britton knew a stalemate when he saw one. As Britton watched, a man stepped into view, one foot on the back of one of the hostages. His thick black hair tumbled from under a beaded cap, a cluster of feathers sprouting from the peak. He wore a tactical vest, the magazine pouches bulging with long rectangles covered in duct tape, wires extending from their tops to his belt.

No time for a stalemate.

Britton stepped into the doorway.

'What the hell are you doing? Get the hell out of the way!' one of the operators shouted.

Britton snapped open a gate back on the trauma tent at the FOB and leapt through. Fitzy, Therese, and Colonel Taylor gaped at the sight of him, but he ignored them as he opened another gate on the back of the room and stepped through directly behind the man in the vest. *Come on guys, hold your fire*, Britton thought. A bullet streaked past his ear close enough to make him wince, but then the rounds stopped as the operators figured out what was going on.

The man had a cell phone in his hand, a curling cord extending from it to his belt. Britton opened a small gate below his elbow and severed the cord just as he shouted something in Apache and punched a button on the phone.

Nothing happened. Stunned, the man punched the phone again, then turned, his eyes widening as Britton raised his pistol and brought the butt of it crashing into his temple. Other men in the room were turning, whirling to face him, leveling their weapons. Seeing their chance, the operators came storming into the room as Britton opened another gate and stepped backward through it into the trauma tent.

'It's okay,' he said to Fitzy, 'we've got it.' And then he was gone again, running to Sharp's side and dragging him backward through another gate to the trauma tent. The sergeant was unconscious, but the other operators were inside the room, and the shooting had stopped. Britton felt strong arms grab the sergeant from the other side and haul him through, and he raced to TrueZero's side. The Hydromancer stirred weakly. Britton fingered the bullet hole in the fabric and felt dented but solid plating behind it. No penetration. He'd probably escape with a broken rib.

Sharp gave a weak thumbs-up as Therese bent over his leg, her eyes closed and hands gently drifting over his knitting flesh. TrueZero had stripped his vest and shirt and sat coughing raggedly as a nasty bruise spread its way over his ribs. The other two operators knelt on either side of the rescued marines, checking them for injuries. Both hostages stared wide eyed at Britton, silent and terrified. One finally mustered the presence of mind to drawl a thank-you.

'You're welcome,' Fitzy answered for him. 'I'm afraid you've just become read into a rather classified government program. We'll go over the requisite nondisclosure agreements once you've been cleared by medical.'

Britton knelt in the gravel of the trauma tent, stripping off his gear, as a blue-scrubbed orderly approached him. 'You okay?'

'He's Shadow Coven,' Fitzy snapped. 'He's better than okay. He's the magic behind the magic.'

The doctor at last turned to Colonel Taylor and gave a thumbs-up sign. 'They'll live.'

Colonel Taylor sighed, his shoulders sagging with relief. He leaned over Sharp where he lay on the gurney. 'I can't tell you how grateful I am to you, son.'

Sharp nodded, clearly uncomfortable with the praise. Colonel Taylor turned to Fitzy. 'Chief Warrant Officer Fitzsimmons, I'm delighted with the capabilities Shadow Coven brings to our force. Keep up the good work.' Fitzy saluted as Colonel Taylor made his way toward the entrance.

'I've got to call General Hamilton and let him know we're out of the woods. You take it from here.'

'Sir,' said Fitzy, and turned to Britton. 'Don't go thinking you're a fucking hero all of a sudden, Keystone. You've got miles to go yet.' But Britton couldn't miss the grudging respect in the chief warrant officer's eyes.

Therese stepped from the gurney's side and reached a hand up to cup Britton's cheek. She stood on her tiptoes and kissed him on the side of his neck, leaving him tingling. 'I think you're a hero, Oscar. You're amazing, and you did a great thing today.'

'Jesus,' Fitzy muttered, disgusted. 'Let's get you the hell out of here before this mutual admiration society gets out of hand.' One of the operators shook Britton's hand before Fitzy managed to whisk him back out of the tent.

Britton was exhausted, the adrenaline of the action curdling in his veins, leaving him sick and shaking. But he was also overwhelmed with a sense of joy. He had done it. He had used his magic to save people's lives. He had controlled it to the point where it did good. People were alive because of Oscar Britton, because of what he could do. How could running ever be better than that? *Here is where you can be different from Swift*, he told himself. *Time to stop fighting it*.

'I get it now, sir,' Britton said to Fitzy.

'What is it that you get?' the chief warrant officer asked him, frowning.

'I mean I'll do it now. For real. You don't need the ATTD anymore.'

Fitzy was pensive for a moment as they walked along. 'Well, that's an encouraging thing to hear, Keystone. Very encouraging indeed. But if it's all the same to you, we'll just keep it there for the nonce.'

Britton nodded, and they walked on in silence, pushing the rest of the way through the cash and back out into the road.

'Sir, if you don't mind me asking, there was this . . . giant black thing I saw when we first flew in. It seemed to be on the same side as the Goblins. I saw it again in one of the videos in the SASS. They said it was one of the Apache's "Mountain Gods".'

'That's right.' Fitzy kept his eyes straight ahead.

'Well, what are they doing in both Mescalero and in the Source?'

'Let me answer your question with a question, Keystone. Do you think that the United States Army, in all its wisdom, would have missed such a connection?'

'No, sir.'

'And, given that we clearly wouldn't have, do you think we might have people working on what the significance was?'

'Yes, sir, you would.'

'And do you also think that if we felt your opinion on this particular matter was of any value, we would have solicited it by now?'

'I get it, sir,' Britton said.

'I thought you might. Seeing how these SASS videos are starting you down the road to thinking you work intel, let's get you off that particular slippery slope. You don't have to go to the SASS anymore,' Fitzy said. 'I think we can both agree that you're past that.'

It was Britton's turn to be pensive. 'I need to go back, sir. Just one more time.

'There's something I need to do.'

Chapter Twenty-Three

Unconvinced

Kind of changes your take on things, doesn't it? We're suddenly a world starving for conspiracy theories. The mysteries are all solved. The heads on Easter Island? Stonehenge? Bigfoot? The Bermuda Triangle? In the past we'd just shrug our shoulders, and say, 'Magic!' We're still sayin' the same thing, but nobody's shrugging anymore.

– Comedian Art Wilkes,
Live on Home Entertainment Network

Britton entered the SASS while the enrollees were lined up for basic control practice. As Britton looked around, he realized that both Fitzy and Therese had followed him from the raid-staging site, and stood a few paces behind him. The No-No Crew, Wavesign among them, stood leaning against the side of the Quonset hut, refusing to participate as usual. The yard seemed tiny to Britton, Swift's crossed arms and frowning face even more petulant and useless.

Salamander paused from his work with a young woman, busy raising rock walls from the mud at her feet, and stared frankly at him, arms folded. A moment later, the rest of the enrollees followed suit. *Can they see the difference I feel?* Britton wondered. *Can they tell that I'm beyond this now?* He glanced over at the flagpole, with its reflective black-and-orange US flag. As a member of Shadow Coven from the outset, he would never need to raise it, but he felt that he had the moment he'd stepped through the gate into that foul-smelling room and dragged the hostages to safety. Oscar Britton had a purpose. Oscar Britton had a home.

'Apologies for the interruption, sir,' Fitzy said. 'Seems Keystone here is owed a favor, and I'm helping him collect.'

Salamander shrugged. 'Orders came down from Taylor a couple of hours ago. Britton's disenrolled.'

'No,' Britton said. He marched to the flagpole and stood rigidly at attention. He locked gazes with Wavesign, then looked to Swift, Pyre, and Peapod, making eye contact with each of them as he slowly and deliberately pulled on the rope, raising the flag to the top of the pole.

He executed a crisp left face and saluted Salamander smartly. 'With all due respect, sir. *Now* I am disenrolled.'

Salamander's mouth twitched in what might have been a smile. He stood at attention and returned the salute. 'Why, yes, Keystone. I do believe you are.'

Swift started to say something, but Britton silenced him with a wave. He stalked straight to Wavesign, who looked left and right before he became unable to deny that he was the focus of Britton's attention and met his eyes. The rain cloud coalesced.

'Wavesign, Ted,' Britton said. 'Raise that damned flag. Do it right now.'

'Huh?' the young Hydromancer said.

'You fucking heard me,' Britton said. 'Go raise that flag right now. Quit messing around.'

'Don't listen to him, Wavesign,' Swift said. 'The second you haul on that rope, you belong to them. You'd be your own damned hangman.'

Britton wheeled on Swift. He raised one fist and rolled a gate open on the depths of the Vermont rock quarry where he'd learned to scuba dive in his teenaged years. The freezing water was mostly black, streaked with green, choked with rock dust. 'You shut your fucking mouth,' Britton seethed. 'You're the reason this kid walks around in a rain cloud all the time. You're a miserable, angry bastard, and you won't be happy unless everyone rots with you. Now shut the hell up, or I will toss your sorry ass through this gate, and you can see how well your Aeromancy protects you from thousands of pounds of subzero water.'

Salamander sputtered at Fitzy. 'Unauthorized!'

Fitzy smiled. 'With all due respect, sir, it's not. Keystone here is a duly contracted Sorcerer, using his magic for designated operations. He's no longer a SASS enrollee. There's no call to Suppress him.'

Britton turned back to Wavesign, his eyes imploring. 'Come on, man. This' – he waved his hand under the young Hydromancer's moisture cloud – 'is because you have a crew of pouty children watching your every move.' Peapod and Pyre bristled, but Salamander shook his head, and they made no move.

'That's why you can't concentrate,' Britton went on, 'it's why you can't get control of it. Raise the flag and get out of here. We can put you someplace where you can get this under wraps.'

'Why would I want to do that?' Wavesign asked. 'They'll just teach me to control it so I can hunt down innocent Selfers, or murder people for them.'

'That's Swift talking,' Britton replied. 'The SOC isn't perfect, but they do good things, too.' He gestured to Therese. 'Therese is in the cash saving people's lives. I just got to do that today as well. It's like no feeling I can describe. Working for the SOC is like working for anyone. It's like our system of government. For all its flaws, it tries to do good. Sometimes, it succeeds. That's a hell of a lot better than standing around here with your arms folded, raining on yourself. You're wasting your time and your talent. Raise the flag.'

Wavesign's mouth worked, he looked at his feet. *I've got him*, Britton thought. But the Hydromancer only shook his head. 'I can't,' he muttered.

Swift opened his mouth, and Britton whirled back to him. 'Say something,' he said. 'Go on, do it.'

Swift's mouth worked, his eyes wide, but no sound came out. After a moment, the burden of eye contact became too much, and he looked away.

Britton took a step forward. 'You want to spin in useless circles? Fine. But you're done dragging anyone else along with you.'

He turned back to Wavesign. 'Raise the flag.'

Wavesign looked terrified, but he shook his head.

Britton whirled away from him in frustration. 'Can't we just drag him out of here?' he asked Fitzy.

The chief warrant officer shook his head. 'Regs,' he said. 'Gotta do it of his own accord. No coercion.'

Britton thought of the ATTD in his heart and snorted. 'You can always change your mind,' he said to Wavesign. 'I'll try to come check on you, and if you ever do change your mind, I'll find a way to work with you. Remember that.'

Swift found his courage again. 'He's not coming with you, you fucking turncoat. Forget it.'

Britton stalked back to him, conscious of Fitzy's and Salamander's eyes on him. His magic surged on the tide of his anger, but he clamped down on it. The hard line wouldn't work with Swift. If he was to get through to him, and to Wavesign, he'd have to try something else.

'You want to wind up like Scylla?' Britton asked. 'You want to have pride of place in your own solitary hole?'

'Better than what you're doing,' Swift answered. 'At least she's on our side. The SOC are the only people that really need to be scared of her. She believes in all of us being free to rule ourselves. That's what we all want.'

'You were the color of bad cheese when they took you out of the hole,' Britton said. 'Doesn't sound like she was on your side then.'

'That's not what she believes anyway,' Therese added. 'She believes in enslaving non-Latent humanity. That's not the same thing.'

'That's justice,' Swift answered.

Pyre nodded agreement. 'Christ, what do you think they're doing to us here?'

'Slaves can't raise the flag,' Britton said. 'They can't choose to be free.'

'That's not freedom,' Swift said, his voice hardening. 'It's just a different kind of slavery.'

'Why do you hate them so much?' Britton asked. 'I understand that you have reason to hate them, but it goes beyond . . . anything.'

'That fucker Harlequin came to get me after I got stupid at a show I was playing, let a little magic slip,' Swift said. 'I had a girlfriend . . . we had a baby together. She got in the way when they hit my apartment. He killed them.'

'They probably gave him a fucking medal for it,' Pyre added.

They probably did, Britton thought. *Successful raids are exactly the thing you get commendations for.*

Britton was silent. What could he say? No words he could string together would recoup those losses.

But Therese voiced his thoughts anyway. 'I know you're angry, but fighting everything won't bring them back to life. Life sucks really badly sometimes, but you still have to live it. You have to pick up the pieces and try to do something with what's left.'

'Working for them won't do that,' Swift said.

'We have our honor, we have our pride,' Pyre added.

'The army uses those terms a lot,' Britton answered. 'Honor's one of our core values. That shit all goes by the wayside the moment bullets start flying, or someone's competing for a billet, or somebody is trying to get out of an assignment. Hell, you sound more army than the SOC.'

'I can look in the mirror each morning,' Swift said. 'Can you?'

And Britton was silent at that, because after this latest mission, he thought that maybe he finally could.

But Swift's smug expression helped him find his voice. 'How much longer do you think you'll be able to look in the mirror, Swift?' Britton asked.

'What do you mean?' Swift asked, cocking an eyebrow.

'You know what I mean. How much longer do you think they're going to put up with your brand of resistance? They get nothing from you; heck, you actively attempt to subvert others around you. Sounds like a lose-lose situation for the SOC. How much longer before they just up and decide you're disposable?'

'They wouldn't do that,' Pyre said.

'Wouldn't they?' Britton asked. 'You're the ones who go on and on about how horrible and inhuman they are.'

'We're useful,' Pyre offered.

'Look at Scylla, they just keep her locked in the hole . . .' Swift added.

'Scylla is an incredibly powerful Probe,' Britton said. 'Latency is rare, but I see no shortage of Aero- and Pyromancers around here.'

He thought of Billy again, gibbering, drooling, the leads trailing from his skull. 'Maybe they'll lobotomize you,' Britton said. What was it Harlequin had said? *We'll turn your body over to our medical research facility to see if they can learn anything from your tissues. Either way, you help us.* 'Maybe they'll just decide they want to keep you around for medical research.'

Swift looked shaken. 'They won't do that.'

'Or maybe you don't appreciate the seriousness of what you're taking on here. Swift, I learned a long time ago that if you want to change powerful organizations, you have to do it from the inside. You have what it takes to do that.'

Swift's voice was barely audible. 'You don't understand . . . I can't.'

My God, Britton thought. *Am I actually cracking him? If he raises the flag, the whole No-No Crew will follow suit.*

'I do understand. Your girlfriend and child would understand, too. I know what the SOC did to you, to them, but that doesn't mean that you have to throw your own life away trying to get revenge for it, especially when you're not succeeding. Your family would want you to survive. They'd want you to go on.'

Swift found his composure, and with it, his anger. 'What the fuck do you know about my family? I'd rather die than work for these bastards. If they decide they're tired of my free will, let 'em come and kill me. At least I'll die free.'

Britton looked at the razor wire and guard towers surrounding them and let the overstatement pass.

'I'll fight,' Pyre added, not looking certain at all.

'And you'll lose,' Britton finished for him. 'I know it, and you know it. Hell, Swift, you don't want to die.' He reached out to put his hand on the Aeromancer's shoulder. 'I don't want you to die, either.'

Swift shrugged the hand off and bit down on a curse that came out garbled. He stalked off, Pyre trailing him.

You lost him, Britton thought. He shook his head. Therese and Fitzy joined him as he moved toward the SASS gate, glancing at the pillbox's rusted door as he did.

As if Scylla had sensed his gaze, the panel slid aside. 'Won't I be seeing you anymore, my pretty Oscar Britton?' Her voice drifted out to him.

'No, Scylla. I'm done with you, with all of you. I'm done here.'

'Oh, but I think I will,' she replied. 'Yes, I do believe I will.'

As if sensing Britton's discomfort, Fitzy gave him and Therese their privacy, walking a good way ahead of them both. He was quiet for a long time, looking at his boot tops until Therese nudged him. 'What? You're going to let Swift get to you?'

'I just wish I could reach him,' Britton said.

'That's good of you, really,' she said. 'But it's not your job to save him.'

'I want to save him,' Britton said. 'We saved those hostages, Therese. It was amazing. That's what magic can do if we let it.'

'It was amazing,' Therese agreed. 'You're a hero, Oscar.'

Britton shook his head. 'No way. I killed my father, Therese.' It felt good to say it, as if admitting it dragged the fact out into the light and cleansed it in the Source's unnaturally bright sun.

Therese was quiet for a moment. 'Did you mean to, Oscar?'

He shook his head. 'I don't think so. I hated the man, but I didn't mean to kill him.' If it felt good to say it, it felt doubly good to know it was true.

'You ever heard of "Rending", Oscar?' Therese asked, her voice scarcely above a whisper.

Britton nodded. 'Physiomancy the other way. Instead of closing wounds, you make them.'

It was Therese's turn to look at her feet. 'That's how I Manifested. By the time the smoke cleared, I'd messed a guy up pretty bad.'

'Dead bad?'

She nodded.

Britton couldn't think of what to say to that, so he followed with a repeat of her question. 'Did you mean to kill him?'

She nodded again. 'Fucker was putting his hands on me. If I hadn't, he'd probably have raped me.'

'Bastard deserved it then,' Britton said. 'You did right.'

Therese shook her head. 'It was horrible. I don't care if it was right or wrong. I'm never doing that again. Now that I can control it? Never again.'

They walked on in silence after that. Fitzy, noting a break in the conversation, paused to let them catch up. The adrenaline charge Britton had felt at taking on Swift had faded, leaving him tired and vaguely ill. He turned to Fitzy. The smaller man kept pace at his side, his face fixed and eyes hidden behind his perennial aviator glasses. His stride was pompous, his carriage arrogant, but Britton put it aside. *He helped you back there. He didn't have to let you do that.*

'Thanks, sir,' Britton said. 'I appreciate you sticking up for me back there.'

Fitzy didn't break stride and kept his eyes fixed straight ahead. 'Don't go expecting a reach around, Keystone. I did that for one reason and one reason only – because there was the slimmest chance that I could get yet another malcontent to do the right thing and ante up for his country. Don't go laboring under the delusion that this had anything to do with anything approaching the slightest positive inclination toward your sorry ass.'

Fitzy's voice was a monotone command drawl. Britton couldn't tell if the man was being ironic.

'Well, thanks anyway, sir,' he tried.

'You can thank me tomorrow,' Fitzy said, glancing briefly at Therese, 'by stopping these sickening attempts at foreplay and actually putting in some work.'

Chapter Twenty-Four

The Body

So, is it a law enforcement or a military matter? A Selfer is a threat to national security, but they're also US citizens. Where do the cops leave off and we begin? Nobody has a good answer. We've got one finger on the trigger and the other on speed dial to our lawyers. Everything's changed. Most of the old-timers don't recognize this army at all.

– Staff Sergeant Jim Horan, SOC Fire Team Bravo
Law Enforcement Support Element, Jacksonville, Florida

Britton refused to give up on Wavesign. He enlisted Therese's help. 'He might need a woman's touch,' he mused. 'Who knows? Maybe it'd break him loose. You raised the flag, and I know he likes you . . .'

Salamander insisted they stay for the day's classes. 'Never hurts to have a refresher.'

Wavesign, for his part, ignored them with studied effort. Britton might have pushed the issue, but Therese's company mellowed him, and he sat at the back of the classroom, acutely aware that their knees were lightly touching and pretending not to notice.

They exited the schoolhouse, tired and cramped. They'd missed chow, but Salamander had ordered a small folding table set up in the mud, covered with brown paper lunch sacks. Wavesign left quickly and moved beyond their reach. Britton decided not to chase him. He waited as the rest of the

No-No Crew passed, then tapped Therese on the shoulder. He grabbed a sack from the table and tossed it to her, motioning at the cold dirt.

'As comfortable as any spot in this pit,' he said. He slid down the building side, winced as a splinter dug through his shirt, and settled on the ground, grimacing.

Therese smiled. 'Nice one,' she said, taking a step back and squatting beside him. 'You always this smooth with the ladies?'

Britton shook his head. 'That was actually pretty good for me.'

'Spend a lot of time by yourself, do you?' she asked, still smiling.

'Not really.' He quickly corrected himself as she arched an eyebrow. 'I'm not bragging or anything. I just stuck to my guys a lot.'

'You miss them?'

Britton was silent for a moment. Remembering Cheatham's grip on his arm. *Let me go, Dan. Christ as my witness, I will shoot you*. 'You have no idea.'

Now Therese was quiet for a bit. 'And . . . and no girl?'

'I never had a kid,' Britton said, knowing perfectly well that wasn't what she meant but stalling for time to wrap his head around the question.

She scowled at him. 'Never mind.'

'No, I didn't have a girlfriend. There was someone on the base I was going to ask out, but . . . I just focused on work. I figured there'd always be time.'

Therese smiled ruefully. 'I think you'll find life on the FOB limits your romantic options.'

I met you, didn't I? he thought. He met her eyes and held them, convinced that she was thinking the same thing.

'I . . .' Therese started to say.

A pillar of fire erupted just beyond the barricade wall. The siren began to wail in time with the pulsing recorded voice: 'Take cover, take cover, take cover . . .'

'Got to love Goblin timing,' Britton muttered, jumping to his feet. 'Don't worry, it'll be over in a sec—'

But the recording had been replaced by a live voice. 'Coven

Four and Novice Del Aqua report to Trailer B-6 immediately for action stations. I say again, Coven Four and . . .'

'What the hell . . .' Therese started to say, but Britton had already grabbed her arm, his boots pounding the mud and out through the SASS gate, the guards moving to let him pass. After a few feet, Therese shook off his hand and matched his pace. Another fireball rose close by, the force of it casting chunks of chilly earth over the nearest barricade to rain down on them.

An electric cart was parked outside the trailer, the back heaped with tactical gear. Truelove, Downer, and Richardson were already being strapped in by a knot of harried-looking Goblin contractors. Their human minder beckoned to Britton and Therese, holding up helmets that were clearly the wrong size.

Fitzy intercepted Britton before he could take another step. His normally hard mouth quivered at the corners. He waved a picture in front of Britton's face. 'Get us here, Keystone. We need to be there right now.'

Britton seized the chief warrant officer's wrist. 'Hold it still, sir! I can't see it with you waving it around!'

His stomach clenched as he expected Fitzy's knee to impact it, but Fitzy said nothing and held still. The picture was a rough printout of a poorly lit room. Flat cement floor, dirty gray tile walls, low fluorescent lights. Construction sawhorses, plastic mop buckets, and barrier posts were heaped in a corner. Britton stared at it, trying to fix the details blurred by the low-quality print job. 'Where is this, sir?'

'Just get us there!' Britton felt a helmet slam down on his head. He took a half step to the side as someone buckled a holster on his thigh.

'I can't unless I have a better idea of where we're going! You've got to give me something to work with, sir!'

Fitzy gritted his teeth and ground out his reply. 'It's a subway maintenance locker. New York City.'

Britton closed his eyes and pictured the image. He tried to conjure the sounds; the steady pounding of the train wheels and the click of heels on cement. He tried to imagine the sharp smell of ozone and garbage, of the sweat of many bodies in close proximity. He gathered the current and pushed it forward. When he opened his eyes, the gate shimmered before him, the rest of Shadow Coven already disappearing through it. He barely had time to see if he'd gotten the location right before Fitzy slammed a vest over his shoulders and pushed him hard, sending him stumbling through the gate.

Fitzy followed behind, then turned and beckoned behind him. A SOC Sorcerer, his body armor blazoned with the Suppressor's symbol, ran along behind, sweating and out of breath. 'I trust you remember Lieutenant Rampart?' Fitzy asked.

Britton stared for a moment. The Suppressor's face was flushed with running, but his flattop haircut and broad shoulders jogged Britton's memory. 'You escorted me in, when I first came over.'

Rampart nodded, his cheeks rising slightly. 'Chief Warrant Officer Fitzsimmons tells me you've seen the light. Glad to have you on board.'

The tiny space was crowded by the new arrivals, adding to the two dozen men already packing it. The majority were black-clad police officers in tactical gear that rivaled the Special Forces operators Britton had worked with before. Black balaclavas covered their faces, exposing only nervous eyes beneath the helmet rims. NYPD/ESU was blazoned across their body armor in subdued gray lettering. Two men in expensive suits stood apart from them, whispering in a language Britton didn't understand. The cops and the suits formed a wide circle around a pile of bodies in the middle of the floor.

At least, Britton was fairly sure they were bodies.

They steamed, raw and red, twisted funnels of meat covered with scraps of human faces, shredded uniforms, plastic buttons. One of the dead's bones had grown through his body, shaped into pointed barbs, cruel weapons turned against the flesh they once supported. One of the bodies had been twisted neatly into the exact shape of a ragged pretzel.

Britton gestured at a scrap of uniform in a camouflage pattern he didn't recognize. 'Sir, wha—'

'It's Russian,' Fitzy said, eliciting glares from the two men in suits. 'The Sahir aren't the only liaisons we've got at the

FOB. The Spetznaz Vedma are their Witch Corps.' He met the eyes of the men in the suits. 'We've got some guys in Russia, too,' Fitzy went on, keeping eye contact. 'A fine arrangement for the continued enhancement of bilateral relations between our two great countries. A veritable lovefest. Until now.'

The men in suits shook their heads, said something in Russian, and pushed past him, around the gate, and out of the room.

'And the clock starts ticking,' Fitzy drawled. He spun back to the police officers, still ostensibly talking to Britton. He stabbed a finger at the chest of one of the cops with subdued captain's bars on his collar. 'You see, Keystone, New York City does things differently. They've got their own budget, bigger'n lots of federal agencies, so they figure they can handle things on their own. These fellows are the Emergency Services Unit. They're the finest of New York's Finest. Security clearances, military cross training, all the bells and whistles. They know how to keep their mouths shut. Which is why they've been assisting the Russians in tracking down an illegal immigrant Selfer who fled here from Russia. They figured they could handle getting the Spetznaz where they needed to go, setting up a perimeter to keep anyone from getting out. Looks like they may have overestimated their capabilities. Never send a cop to do a soldier's job.'

'Now wait just a fucking min . . .' the NYPD captain began, but Fitzy shouted over him.

'New York's efforts at polis-style autonomy have resulted in a truly embarrassing mess for our vodka-swilling allies, and they want it dealt with quickly. And what they want done quickly, the president wants done quickly, and we all know who does things quickly where magic is concerned.'

'The magic behind the magic, sir,' Britton said.

Fitzy nodded, finally turning to face Britton. 'Those fuckers who just stormed out of here are on the way to the UN. We had damn well better have something to give them by the time they get a message to the White House. And by "we", I mean "you".'

'So, what are we up against here?' Britton asked, as he turned to take in Downer, Truelove, and Richards. All three looked steel eyed and ready, but Britton knew their stomachs must have been doing the same somersaults as his own.

'A Render,' Fitzy said, motioning toward the back of the room, where a couple of the NYPD cops were dragging the barriers out of the way, revealing a sizeable breach in the tile wall, with the sound of rushing water coming from beyond. 'Our little immigrant is possessed of a particularly nasty bit of Probe Physiomancy.' He motioned at the corpses. 'I don't need to remind you that what you're looking at are three of Russia's best magical operators and a sizeable squad of New York's Finest.

'One Probe did this, just one.'

Therese froze beside him, and Fitzy turned to her. 'You raised the flag, little lady. You drank the Kool-Aid. Time to make good on it. I'm afraid you're the positive to the negative we're taking down.'

He turned back to Shadow Coven. 'Rampart's in charge of this op. I've got to go play public-relations jockey. Seems when Coven Four deploys, important folks want to talk to the program head. You all set, sir?'

Rampart nodded, smiling. 'We've got the magic behind the magic, Chief Warrant Officer. What could possibly go wrong?'

Fitzy frowned.

'Enough already, let's get it done,' Downer muttered.

A light sheen of sweat had broken out on Therese's forehead. 'What about Hayes? I'm not the only Healer on the FOB.'

'Oh, right,' Fitzy said, motioning them toward the break in the wall. 'I almost forgot. Hayes asked that you bring tissue samples back for the Special Projects Activity. You know, for science. He was rather insistent on that point.'

'Tissue samples?' Britton asked.

Fitzy shrugged. 'Just slice off some chunks.'

'Let's go, sir!' one of the ESU cops shouted to Rampart, already disappearing through the opening behind his captain.

'And you're on. NYPD needs a chance to redeem themselves, so they're your fire support for this run. Besides, they know the sewers under this city better than any SOF operators we've got.' He leaned in close, his voice urgent. 'Get it done, Oscar. Get it done right.'

'Roger that, sir.' Britton nodded and stepped into the aperture.

Darkness swallowed them. Britton struggled with panic in the smothering blackness before it burst into illumination from tactical lights suspended from the barrels of the ESU officers' weapons. 'Jesus!' Rampart hissed. 'There goes our night vision! Shut those off!'

'We don't have time for this,' the ESU captain whispered as the lights went out amid muttered curses. 'She's got a fifteen-minute head start at least. We need to get on her, or we're going to lose her!'

So, it's a girl, Britton thought. *Seems to be a trend.*

'Settle down, Captain,' Rampart answered, his voice disembodied in the darkness. 'Slow is smooth, smooth is fast.'

'I've got it,' Richards said.

Britton felt Richards's current rise and billow outward. A soft, green glow began to spread across the walls and ceiling, from beneath the wide, rushing stream of water beside them. 'Some of the lichen here are phosphorescent,' Richards said. 'They just need a little coaxing.'

The light from the plants didn't blind them, but it cast all in a creepy green, raising dancing shadows off the water's surface. They stood on the catwalk of an old sewer tunnel. The vaulted ceiling arched away from them, old, pitted bricks slick with calcified plant growth. Rats squeaked in the distance, shadowed by the darkness farther down the catwalk, beckoning to them like some monster's gaping maw.

The captain snorted and gestured with the barrel of his submachine gun. 'She went that way.'

'Better take point then,' Richards answered. 'Spell casting is a rear-echelon occupation.'

The captain swore and motioned to his men, who advanced into the darkness, weapons at the ready. Richards lit the lichen as they passed, keeping them in a bubble of the sickly green light, darkness pressing at its edges. Downer motioned at the water. An elemental sprang from its rippling surface, a spined dog made of shimmering green liquid, loping alongside them.

'Nice,' whispered Truelove. 'All I've got to work with is dead rats.'

'I can feel something,' Therese said, her voice trembling.

'Stay cool,' Rampart whispered. 'Everybody keep it on lockdown until I get her magic Suppressed.'

Britton could sense it, too, a magical current, the eddying of it foreign beside the familiar touch of the rest of the Coven, distant but getting closer with each step they took. He glanced across the water. The sloping brick wall of the sewer tunnel was unbroken as far as he could see, the vaulted ceiling a pool of shadows. Long cracks ran through the old brick but nothing nearly big enough for a person to fit through.

Britton looked to Rampart, who shrugged. It was clear he could feel the current, too, but there was no one there.

'Captain, is there anywhere this Selfer could hide?' Britton asked.

The captain shook his head. 'Not unless she can crawl through walls. She's dead ahead.'

They advanced, the pulse of the foreign current getting stronger, until Britton felt it suffused him, so strong that it tickled his taste buds and buzzed in the back of his throat. There was nothing. The glowing lichen showed an empty corridor. They pushed on, and the current began to recede.

'Wait,' Truelove said, 'we've gone past her.'

'That's impossible,' the captain said. 'The water's not deep enough for anyone to hide in. She has to be up ahead.'

Rampart cursed. 'No, he's right.'

Britton shook his head. 'She's behind us.'

'How the hell can you know that?'

'We can feel her current, you moron!' Downer groused, her elemental scampering back the way they had come, nosing at the water's edge.

The captain gave a hand signal, and three of the police officers crouched back down the catwalk, flicking their lights on despite Rampart's complaints. The harsh white beams swept the dirty concrete and spoiled brick, scattering clusters of frightened roaches but revealing little else. One of them stood and adjusted his helmet. 'Sir, there's nothing here, it's only . . .'

His voice ended in a choked gurgle, his head twisting backwards, the black balaclava suddenly dripping and ridiculously skewed. An instant latter, the cop next to him simply folded in half with a wet snap, the light going out of his eyes before he even had time to scream.

Human flesh poured out of the wall beside them in a wave, piling into a mass that stretched across the catwalk and spilled into the water, growing and growing.

It seemed the Selfer could crawl through walls after all.

She had lost all human form. The flesh was completely protean, an amorphous mass of pink skin, flexing and pulsing. It was dotted here and there with eyes, fingernails, knobs of bone and hair. A mouth opened in the mass and began to burble something before it was smothered over by the gathering folds of flesh.

Rampart jumped forward, extending his arms. Britton could feel his current race forward, interlacing with the Selfer's flow . . .

. . . and shunted aside. Rampart stumbled backward, his own tide swamped by the Selfer's magic, far too strong for him to roll back.

'Oh, shi—' he began, then the Rending magic grasped the top of his head and folded his skull in on itself, compressing his head down into the trunk of his body with a thick, slurping sound. Rampart, headless, swayed on his feet for a moment before collapsing to the tunnel floor.

Downer's elemental leapt on the Selfer, tearing chunks from the growing mound. Two others sprang from the water to join it. The Selfer quivered under the blows, then simply flowed over them. The elementals vanished beneath the gathering mass, splashes of dirty water leaking out from between the folds.

Gunfire echoed in the tight space, making Britton's ears ring. The Selfer's mass nearly blocked the passageway behind them, impossible to miss. The NYPD officers knelt, pouring on the fire, bullets ripping through the mound of flesh, sinking into it with hissing thuds. The Selfer shook under the onslaught and slouched forward, rolling over herself, reaching out toward them.

And then, a brief and hideous silence broken by the sharp clicks of magazine releases as the cops reloaded. 'Ohshit-ohshitohshit,' one whined.

A bone spur, long as a spear, shot from the mass, catching him through the throat. Another cop simply detonated, spraying them all with the gobbets of meat he had suddenly become. 'Get the hell out of here!' the captain shouted, grabbing one of his men by the drag handle on his body armor and hauling him backward.

Downer stepped up, gesturing at the water again. 'This isn't going to do it! I need something more to work with!' Britton opened a gate and sent it sliding past the retreating cops. The blob didn't even make an effort to dodge, the lurching flesh barreling directly into it. The gate sliced it neatly in half, the edges peeling back to reveal a stack of gristle and organs that followed no anatomical pattern that Britton knew of. It fountained blood, shaking as if in rage, halting.

And then the flesh simply flowed over itself, growing back together and moving forward. A curtain of biting insects swarmed over its surface, magicked along by Richards. Britton thought he glimpsed slithering shapes in the water biting at the Selfer, snakes or rats. It hardly slowed. Another two cops went down, bent into shapes that made Britton nauseous.

We're outclassed, Britton thought. *Time to get out of here*.

But then Downer let out a wet shriek and collapsed, her pelvis and legs twisted into a bloody corkscrew. She twitched, screaming. Therese knelt at her side, eyes closed, magic pouring out over Downer's mangled body, rolling back the damage.

'Some of it's dead!' Truelove yelled, his own current reaching out. The Selfer froze, shivering. Deep within the recesses, flesh piled upon flesh, layers of it had turned gangrenous, necrotic strips marbling the lumbering whole. They spread, biting, squirming, the body attacking itself, dead and alive struggling to control the motion of the mass. 'It won't hold her forever, Keystone!' Truelove shouted. 'Do something!'

Do what? Cutting and shooting the thing wasn't going to help. The Selfer's body had been so completely transformed, he wasn't even sure if there were vital organs anymore. They'd have to burn it. Maybe that was why it was down where fire would never go? But he had no fire. Coven Four was without a Pyromancer.

The cops retreated past them, still futilely pouring bullets into the mound of flesh. The Selfer leisurely reached out with her magic, twisting them into screaming corpses, one by one.

Britton threw open a gate and barreled through into the SASS schoolhouse. He'd wagered right. Class was back in session, and he scattered desks and tables as he charged Pyre. 'Jesus, Britton! What the hell do you think you're . . .' Salamander began before taking in Britton's battle dress and the scene beyond the shimmering gate and lapsing into silence. Britton grabbed the young Pyromancer's lapels. 'Fire! Through that gate! Right now!'

'What?' Pyre squeaked. 'No! I can't . . .'

Britton raised a hand and clipped him across the face. 'Now, you fucker! Right fucking now! Downer!'

'I've got it!' she mumbled weakly, her legs untangling beneath Therese's ministrations, flesh coalescing, bones straightening.

Pyre's head rocked to the side and snapped back, his eyes narrowing. Britton ducked as the flame erupted from his chest, pushing over his shoulder and through the gate. It passed into the sewer and over Downer, who screamed with the effort of shaping it. Britton followed, shutting the portal behind him, not looking to see the reaction in the SASS.

Downer's work was done by the time his boots hit the catwalk. Five elementals had sprung from the blaze, hunched humanoids with flat heads on flickering shoulders. They leapt across the water, pounding the Selfer with burning fists, igniting patches of greasy skin with every blow. The Selfer screamed in earnest, pain howling from a dozen mouths opening for that express purpose, the teeth glowing and popping like gunshots as the elementals covered it. The corridor was quickly choked with greasy smoke. The stink of cooking meat sent the remaining cops to their knees, retching through their balaclavas.

Britton could feel the current of the Selfer's magic turn inward, focusing on reconstructing her own flesh. He glimpsed the bubbles of healing flesh through the smoke. The elementals strained, their bodies stretching as they spread their fire across her.

Britton glanced at Downer, the blood unpooling around her, leeching back into her knitting skin. Therese nodded at him. 'I've got this!'

Britton lurched forward, grabbing one of the cops by his shoulder and hauling him upright. He slapped the bottom of his gun, sending the barrel up to smack his chin. The cop turned to Britton, his eyes wide. Britton shook him, pointing at the Selfer's burning bulk. 'Pour it on! Now! We don't get another chance!'

The cop shook himself, raised his weapon, and pulled the trigger. The echo of gunfire competed with the roar of the flames. It galvanized the remaining cops, who turned and knelt, adding their own fire to the din. The bullets passed through the flame bodies of the elementals, ripping into the Selfer's solid flesh as it shrank beneath the flames. A low moaning erupted from the smoke, which began to overtake the corridor, until Britton could see no flesh at all. Britton pushed his flow deep into the thick wall of smoke and opened a gate. He couldn't see it beyond the tiniest flickering line in the smoke, and from that he worked it up and down, moving it like a cleaver, chopping into whatever remained of the burning bulk of the Selfer.

Her current waned. The smoke began to dissipate, the burning brighter. The conflagration shrank as the elementals consumed what fuel remained, smaller, smaller, until at last a misshapen lump smoked in the center of the shallow water, immobile, stinking.

There was no indication at all that it had ever been human.

Britton felt the magic current gone and rushed to Downer's side. The girl was sitting up, gingerly moving her legs. 'Sarah! Are you okay?'

Downer nodded, her lower lip trembling, eyes going wet.

'Oh God, it hurt so bad . . .' She looked at Therese, who leaned forward, gathering the girl into an embrace.

'No,' Downer said, breaking free, sniffing up her tears. 'I'm fine. I should secure the area.' She got to her feet, shaky and wobbling, and limped off, heading toward nothing in particular. The elementals winked out, dispersing into the remaining tendrils of smoke.

Therese made to follow her, but Britton stopped her with a hand on her shoulder. 'Don't.'

Therese looked at him and nodded. 'I know. It's just that, for a moment there, she was her own age.'

Britton nodded back. 'Magic makes you grow up fast. Nobody can fix that.'

Britton turned to Rampart's corpse, then back to Therese. 'There's nothing you can—'

'Nothing,' she cut him off. 'He's dead.'

'He saved me when I first got to the Source. Saw me through a firefight and got me to the FOB.'

Therese nodded. 'It was his job, Oscar. He knew what he signed up for.'

The NYPD captain moved among his remaining men, blubbering. Of the twenty ESU officers who had set out, four remained. 'Oh Jesus, oh Jesus fucking Christ,' he whispered, his eyes raw and red rimmed, from the smoke or the tears Britton couldn't tell. He knelt by one of his men, scarcely more than a pile of cloth and flesh scraps. He reached out a trembling hand, jerked it back, reached it out again.

'What the fuh, fuh . . .' he huffed, turning his dazed expression toward Britton. 'What the fuck did you do? What happened to my men?'

Britton shook his head, heading toward what remained of the Selfer's corpse.

'Where are you going?' the NYPD captain shrieked, waving his gun. 'What about my men?'

'Sir,' one of the remaining cops said, reaching out.

'Get the fuck off me!' The captain slapped his hand away. 'You!' he shouted at Britton, raising his weapon.

'He's off his rock,' Britton said. 'Somebody secure him.'

'Got it,' Richards said, gesturing. An outcropping of natural rock rose out of the water, flowing like liquid concrete into a fist around the captain's torso, holding him fast. 'Fuck off me!' the captain shrieked. 'The fuck off me! Sergeant Torres! Shoot that man!'

'I wouldn't do that,' Britton said, but the cops didn't appear to need the warning. They were busy clustering around their captain, talking in soothing voices.

Britton turned back to his task. 'To the captain's original question,' Richards said, 'where are you going?'

'Hayes wants tissue samples, right?' He slopped down into the water beside the hulk of smoldering flesh. Up close, Britton could make out the remains of severed vessels, half-formed organs. He conjured a small gate and cut out a brick-sized sample, thick flesh marbled through with half-formed remnants of Lord knew what. There was at least one cooked eye and something that Britton swore was a flexed elbow. The stench was overpowering.

He climbed back onto the catwalk and opened a gate back on Trailer B-6. 'Downer!' he called down the catwalk. 'Can you walk?'

The Elementalist turned, took a few steps, shaky but surer than before. 'I'm fine,' she said.

'All right, everyone back through. Tell 'em the job's done and to get a cleanup crew down here. I'll give a report to Fitzy.'

Richards and Truelove stepped right through without any hesitation, responding to the natural tone of command in Britton's voice. Therese hesitated at the threshold. 'What about you?'

Britton hefted the chunk of meat. 'Tissue sample. I'll be along once I deliver it. Promise. Thanks for everything, Therese.'

Therese nodded and stepped through, but Downer paused, facing him, eyes narrowed. 'Who the hell put you in charge? Fitzy's the Coven Commander.' Britton could see the whirl of emotions competing across her face, scarcely under control even with the Dampener's help.

He put a hand on her shoulder. 'You were very brave, Sarah. Hell, you pretty much saved us all. I'll make sure Fitzy knows it. I'm proud to serve with you.'

Britton could tell it wasn't what she had expected, but her face was stone otherwise. After a long silence, she turned and walked through the gate. Beyond the static shimmer, Britton could see medics and Goblin orderlies fussing over the team. Certain that they were safe, he shut the gate and opened a new one, stepped through.

The cold hunched his shoulders, and he wrinkled his nose at the chemical-preservative smell. Behind him, the plastic curtain rippled, gently ruffled by the currents of the giant chiller in the center of the room. All around him, corpses lay on tables in various states of dissection, a macabre review of the bestiaries he had marveled at as a child. The fauna of the Source spread out before him: giant eagles, horned lions, small dragons, double-headed serpents. Here was a leopard with a human face, its tail hacked off, the flesh avulsed to reveal the articulation of the bones. There was a unicorn of storybook legend, the skin around the horn flayed back to show the attachment to the skull. Colored dye had been injected into the major veins running beneath the surface.

And Goblins, everywhere Goblins. The desecration of their corpses shouted the central message of the Special Projects tent: just another animal. Source fauna.

Britton's lip curled at the sight. He had to get out of there. He cast about, looking for a flat surface on which to leave the tissue sample. The only flat surface proved to be a folding aluminum writing desk strewn with files. He placed the meat on the clearest portion. A stack of files had toppled over sometime ago, spreading each one out in a stepped path, the titles stamped in antiquated font theatrically stereotypical for the military. AMPHISBAENA, read one, SPITTING SERPENT. Another read UNICORN, HORNED EQUINE. Britton began to leaf through them, eyebrows rising at the identities of the corpses laid out around him.

Then he froze.

SCYLLA, one read. HUMAN NEGRAMANCER. Someone had written UNCOOPERATIVE/RECAL across the front in red marker. Britton took a glance over his shoulder, then peeled back the cover and began to read.

. . . remains steadfast in her refusal to act in her own self-interest. While it is impossible to be certain if Andrews's theory is correct regarding the elemental foundation of her magic, I see no harm in obliging him. We certainly lose nothing by trying, and, frankly, right now she is little more than a drain on the taxpayer resources necessary to house and guard her. We've had outstanding success in prefrontral cortex intervention with other subjects, and I don't think I'm overstating the case when I say that it has handed this army a functional Portamancer where we'd otherwise have had a serious problem. In this case, the use of the Orbitoclast rendered the subject particularly vulnerable to the influence of his mother, who, fortunately, is cooperative and patriotic. While there is no such influence in 'Scylla's' life, I respectfully request that a hard time limit be set to allow the PSYOPS team to finish their work. If IO isn't the answer here, then surgery certainly can't hurt us. We should set a deadline for prefrontal cortex interception and see where that takes us . . .

Footsteps. Britton slammed the folder shut and stood back from the table, his mind swamped with images of Billy drooling, his mother draping her pale arms around his neck, crooning in his ear.

Hayes stepped through the flap and squeaked at the sight of Britton, his jowls shaking. He took a step back and nearly tripped over himself. 'What the hell are you doing here!?'

Britton pointed at the chunk of meat on the desk, and croaked, 'Tissue sample, sir. Fitzy said you'd want it.'

And then he shouldered past the captain without another word, not trusting anything he might say.

Billy, drooling, compliant, opening and closing gates at their will.

They'd do the same to Scylla.

If she didn't play ball, they'd do the same to her.

Fitzy took Britton's report stone faced. He nodded curtly and sat Britton in front of a laptop, where he typed out in meticulous detail all the events he had just recounted. It took Britton over an hour to ensure he'd captured it all, Fitzy making low conversation into a radio while Britton typed.

Eventually, Britton stopped typing and turned, looking at the chief warrant officer while he paced the trailer. 'What's your problem?' Fitzy asked eventually.

'It's Rampart, sir. I just . . . I'm sorry.'

'Are you fucking kidding me?'

Britton was silent.

Fitzy paced forward, his shoulders bunching. 'Rampart was SOC in his bones. That man had more steel in his dick than you do in your entire body. He doesn't need your sorry.'

Britton was used to Fitzy's posturing by then, and after what he'd just been through, it failed to impress. He shrugged. 'Will there be a funeral?'

'There might be, but not for you. Rampart didn't know you and didn't want to know you. For you there's work, and that starts tomorrow at 0600 sharp.'

And 0600 turned out to be more MAC practice. When Britton arrived, Truelove stood beside a wooden pallet covered with a blue plastic tarp. Ashen toes and pointed ears poked out from beneath it.

Truelove looked embarrassed. 'Hi.'

'You okay?'

Truelove shrugged. 'It's what we trained for. I'll be fine.'

'What about Downer?'

'Physically? She's doing great.'

'Mentally?'

'I don't know,' Truelove said. 'She . . . she was hurt pretty bad. But she's not talking about it.'

'What . . .'

'You got a jump start on your GIMAC,' Fitzy cut him off. 'And if you're done socializing, we might as well get moving with that.'

'We're gonna MAC?' Britton asked in disbelief, then regretted his tone, as Truelove's face fell. Truelove was Fitzy's height and lacked the chief warrant officer's build.

He struggled to find something placating to say, but Fitzy interrupted him. 'Hell, no. Rictus couldn't MAC with a twelve-year-old girl. This is GIMAC for you, remember? Rictus has integrated MAC of his own.'

Truelove nodded nervously and dropped into a guard.

'We've been practicing on our own, while you worked with Fitzy,' he said, his voice apologetic. He raised his arms, and the pallet shuddered. The tarp flew off as ten Goblin corpses jerked their way to circle Britton. Their sightless eyes turned toward him, heads slewing on broken necks. Here, a nose was missing. There, a bit of jawbone protruded. Fresh from some meat locker, the corpses emanated cold. Britton could see traces of frost on what remained of their ears and noses. Truelove closed his eyes, spread his arms, and the zombies dropped into MAC guards of their own. 'Hee-yah,' one of them groaned. Truelove smiled.

'You've got to be kidding me,' Britton said.

'No joke,' Fitzy said. 'Feel free to gate in and out of Portcullis as needed. Richards's dog pens are full. Pluck from them as needed to even the odds.'

'Ready or not.' Truelove smiled. 'Here I come.'

They swarmed him with surprising speed. The first swiped for his arm, cold, dead fingers brushing his wrist, raising gooseflesh. He leapt backward, and one of the zombies grabbed him around the waist. They were small, but their dead strength was terrible and Britton felt the air squeezed out of him as the withered arms locked over his stomach.

He hammered his elbow backward, cracking the thing hard in the face, while simultaneously twisting his ankle behind it and sweeping its leg. It flew backward into another zombie, and Britton was already turning, pistoning a fist into the face of another opponent, seeking a way to break through the circle.

A zombie leapt into the air, kicking Britton hard in the chin, one frozen toe snapping off as his head rocked backward, knocking Britton into another zombie, which pinned his arms at his sides. Three more rushed him from the front.

He slid a gate open behind him, then pushed off with his thighs, driving himself and the zombie through the portal, crushing it against the hard concrete of the loading-bay floor. Two of the zombies stepped through the gate as he shut it, leaving a heap of half-faces and torsos dropping to the concrete.

The thing beneath him ceased struggling and he stood, stomping hard on its face, his stomach lurching at the crunching sound beneath his heel.

He opened a gate beside Truelove and emerged. Fitzy leapt between them, waggling a finger. 'He's off-limits. Go dance with the dead.'

Britton turned just in time to dodge another leaping kick. He slid to one side, opening a gate in midair. The zombie passed through it, and he let it shut, kicking the next one hard in the chest and driving it back into its fellows.

Britton began to find his rhythm, the magic integrating seamlessly into the dance of the MAC. A corpse punched at him, he caught its arm, opened a gate and flipped it through, closing the portal on its shoulder, leaving him holding the limb, which he turned to fling in the face of his next assailant. It fell backward, decapitated by another gate as it tried to rise.

The remaining corpses paused, spreading out to circle him again, advancing more cautiously. Britton backed toward Truelove, careful not to get too close. 'Can't we talk about this?' he asked.

'Not a chance,' Truelove answered, grinning, 'unless you want to surrender.'

One of the corpses took a tentative swipe at Britton, who chopped down hard on the wrist. The hand hung askew as the thing backed away. 'Nasty,' Britton hissed. 'Seriously, Rictus. With all due respect, that's disgusting.'

Truelove laughed hard, his hands dropping to his knees. The circle of zombies paused.

Britton threw open another gate, pushing the magical current through it. He felt the penned dogs and roped one easily. The gate shimmered and spit it out. It snarled at the alien smell of the animated corpses and sprang, seizing one by the throat. Britton dove over it, scissor-kicking a zombie in the face and sending it rolling. He spun as he landed, sliding a gate like a cleaver down the line of the circle, cutting through three more. He sprang after the gate, shutting it just as he emerged on the last corpse, grabbing it by the throat and lifting it off the ground. Its dead face was blank, its little legs kicked at him. He squeezed the thin neck, like chilled rubber. It stank of chemical preservatives.

He wrinkled his nose. 'We done here? I think I'm going to be sick.'

Fitzy nodded, and Truelove lowered his arms. The corpse went limp in Britton's grip, and he dropped it, wiping his hand on his trousers.

Fitzy began to gather the broken corpses and drag them into a pile in the corner, where two soldiers moved them onto the discarded tarp. A fresh pallet was wheeled in through another entrance. 'Give me a hand here, it'll go faster,' Fitzy said. A few of the corpses had traces of the white paint that dotted Marty's face and completely covered the Goblin sorcerers they had fought at the LZ.

When the floor was clear, Fitzy called for another round, doubling the number of zombies. Britton flew through the fight, the gates opening and cutting with fluid precision. 'Zombies are inefficient,' Fitzy commented. 'The real enemy will be smarter and harder. Remember that and don't get cocky.'

What real enemy? Britton thought. *What could possibly be nastier than that blob of flesh we just took out?*

But despite Fitzy's warning, Britton found it hard not to get cocky. He slid the gates around like giant razors, dispatching his opponents five at a time. *My God*, he thought, finally appreciating the power of GIMAC. *I am truly beginning to master this. I'm a one-man army. I have rescued hostages, I have taken out a Render who flattened an entire NYPD SWAT team.* By the end of the third round, he toyed with the corpses, gating in and out behind them. He pulled one into the loading bay, threw it to the dogs, then leapt out behind another, dropkicking it into its fellows before gating back out of sight.

By the end of the practice, he felt as if he were flying. Truelove threw his hands up. 'Enough,' he said, 'uncle.'

Fitzy clapped lightly, one corner of his mouth slightly twisted. 'Adequate.'

Britton nodded gratefully and clapped Truelove on the shoulder. 'That was kick-ass, man. Seriously.'

Truelove grinned, transforming his face, showing some of the confidence Britton expected in a man his age. 'You made pretty short work of the whole crew.'

'Yeah,' Britton agreed, 'but it won't be like that when you let 'em loose on a real enemy. Man, it's going to scare the crap out of them!' It wasn't idle praise. He remembered the dead faces circling him, empty eyes staring.

Truelove grew pensive. 'I've never been in a real battle. I mean, nothing beyond these little raids.'

Britton clapped him on the shoulder. 'Neither have I. I don't think wars are fought like that anymore. It's no big deal.'

'I think it's a big deal,' Truelove said. 'We still work for the army, you know? What if we have to fight hundreds of people, like the training we just did, only real?'

'Then we figure it out as we go,' Britton said. 'It's serious, but that doesn't mean it has to be heavy.'

'What was it like when you rescued those hostages?'

Britton thought about it for a moment. 'It's like what you think it would be like. Shouting, confusion, terror. But you just follow your training, and everything sort of snaps together and works.'

'It works for you,' Truelove said.

'It'll work for you, too.' Britton nodded. 'Hell, it already did.'

'What if it doesn't?' Truelove asked.

'That's why we work as a team. So we can lean on each other.'

'I wasn't a lot of help back there, in the sewers.'

'Are you kidding me? If you hadn't held that blob in place, I would never have had the chance to get Downer what she needed to finish it off. We did it together, Simon. It wouldn't have worked without all of us.'

'It wasn't enough to stop her . . .' He trailed off, but Britton knew what Truelove was picturing. Downer on the ground, her lower body twisted and bloody.

'That's combat, Simon,' Britton said. 'It's messy and dangerous, even when things go off perfectly. It's the business we're in. Downer is alive because of you. Remember that.'

Truelove looked silently back at him, eyes grateful.

'I'm going to shower and get changed,' Britton said. 'I'll meet you at the OC, then we can grab chow?'

Truelove nodded. 'I'm gonna stop by the cash first. That fight gave me a splitting headache. Lemme see if I can get a couple of aspirin first.'

Britton accompanied him, hoping to see Therese or Marty. They approached the hospital just as the flaps whipped open, a squad of MPs rushing through in helmets and body armor, carbines slung across their backs.

Struggling in their arms, hands zip-cuffed behind him, was a Goblin contractor. The squad dragged him away from the cash, long feet trailing in the mud.

Britton looked to Truelove, who shrugged. He turned to one of the orderlies, who was retrieving the tent flap from where it had snagged on one of the support poles. 'What the heck was that?'

The orderly shrugged. 'Entertech Goblin contractor. They busted him stealing from the cash.'

The worm, Britton thought. *Marty tried after all. That outstanding, sweet, fantastic little bastard. In spite of everything, he still tried, just because I asked him to*.

'What'll they do to him?' Britton asked.

'Fire him, I guess,' the orderly replied. 'He stole some kind of experimental medication from the Special Projects tent. You know Goblins. They're hooked on sugar, caffeine pills, any kind of stimulant. It was only a matter of time.'

Britton's stomach lurched. He turned to Truelove. The Necromancer had turned pale.

'They're firing him,' he said. 'Oscar, they'll kick him out of the FOB.'

'So?' Britton asked.

'So,' Truelove answered, 'he's a collaborator. This base is surrounded by hostile tribes. He'll be dead before he makes it twenty feet.'

Britton rushed through the flaps. He fumbled through the receiving area, pushing past several nurses who yelled at him, making his way to the urinalysis section. Marty was nowhere to be seen, but one of the Goblin orderlies recognized him and sat him on a folding chair while he disappeared. He returned a moment later with Marty in tow.

Britton gripped his elbow urgently. 'I need to talk to you.'

Marty nodded and pulled Britton through the back of the tent and out into a muddy, but private section.

'Okay,' Marty said, his eyes huge with concern. 'No anger. Okay.'

'It's not okay,' Britton whispered fiercely. 'That Goblin, you sent him? For the worm?'

Marty smiled.

'Thank you, Marty, but . . .'

'Thank you,' Marty interrupted. 'I thank you. You help me first.'

'Marty, they got him. They caught him.'

Marty nodded. 'Okay. He mine Logauk.'

Britton looked at him, uncomprehending. Marty tapped his eyelids, then put his hand behind his neck. 'My Logauk. He mine . . .' He paused, searching for the word. '. . . my contractor?'

'He works for you?' Britton remembered the respect Marty commanded among the Goblin orderlies in the cash, how he had threatened the Physiomancer with a work stoppage.

'But they caught him! They fired him! Truelove says he'll be killed!'

Marty shrugged. 'Sorrahhad fight. No like Mattab On Sorrah. We help.'

'These Sorrahhad will kill him?'

Marty nodded. 'Maybe he get home. Long walk.'

'Marty, thank you for trying to help me. But I didn't want anyone to die. For me, it's a big deal when someone dies . . . even when that person works for you. Even when it's your . . . Logauk.'

Marty's forehead wrinkled. 'No understand.'

'Just promise me. Promise me that you won't do anything else that risks getting someone fired. I can't . . . I can't have that.' He thought of the cop in Shelburne. He thought of his father.

'Forget the whole worm thing. I don't care about it anymore. God! I was such an idiot. I should have said something before you sent him to . . . we've got to help your Logauk . . . do you know any . . .'

'Spending quality time with your boyfriend?' Britton jumped as Fitzy's voice sounded from behind him.

'Got a little banged up in the training with Rictus, sir,' Britton said. 'Ma . . . this contractor has a knack for helping me out after I've taken a drubbing. I use him following most of our MAC sessions. I've come to rely on him.'

'Come off it, Keystone,' Fitzy said. 'I know this little piece of Goblin filth drinks with you in the OC every night. Do you think I'm stupid? I've allowed it thus far because I thought it might be good for you to learn a bit about the indig here, but I'm putting the hammer down now. No more fraternization. You know it's not allowed, and I'm done looking the other way. I catch this pointy-eared little terrorist in the OC, and I'm gonna have all your asses for breakfast. That clear?'

Britton boiled, leaning hard on the Dampener to keep his surging emotions in line. He pushed past Fitzy, heading for the exit. Maybe there was still time to help the Goblin.

'Don't even think about trying to help that little thief either,' Fitzy called to his back. 'He's been fired and turned loose. That's all, no punishment. Even someone as softhearted as you should be pleased with that.'

'He'll die out there, and you know it,' Britton said.

'Maybe he should have thought of that before he decided to get high off our supply,' Fitzy said, crossing his brawny arms. 'Anyway, it doesn't matter. He's a quarter mile outside the wire by now. There's no way you could find him if you tried. Let it go, Keystone. You told me that you'd made your peace with us, that you're a company man now. I believe you. Tonight, you're going to put your money where your mouth is.'

Chapter Twenty-Five
Raid

I get the whole right to protest thing. That's real nice. It's also real antiquated. This ain't Martin Luther King out there. Some of the people in that crowd have the ability to level a city block. You can worry about civil rights after the mission debrief. For now, civil disobedience is still disobedience. You bring order to this chaos any way you can.

– Captain 'Ridgebreaker' (call sign), Alleged mission prebrief
'Burning Man Incident', Black Rock Desert, Nevada

At 0200, Britton opened his hooch door to see an electric cart idling, with Downer behind the wheel.

'Ready?' the girl asked him.

Britton nodded, rubbing sleep from his eyes. 'What are you doing here?'

'Been working with Fitzy all morning. He said I could take liberty for the rest of the day if I came and got you. Apparently he's got a recon gig for you,' she said.

He looked up at the sky, lit by the weirdly large moon and spray of stars. 'You call this morning?'

Downer ignored him.

'You wanna drive?' She gestured to the cart and shrugged when Britton shook his head. 'Good, I like driving.' She arched an eyebrow at him. 'I am, after all, old enough.'

Britton smiled and huddled next to her while the cart bumped its way toward the flight line. He watched her, so excited to be driving a stupid electric cart, amazed by how young she was.

He looked down at her legs. Therese had done her work well. There was no sign of the damage the Selfer's Rending magic had done.

'Are you . . . okay?'

'Why wouldn't I be?' Downer asked.

'Come off it, you know why.'

'I'm fine,' Downer growled, her eyes fixed straight ahead. 'We did what we had to. I got a little sloppy is all. That won't happen again.'

Britton wanted to put his hand on her shoulder, to tell her he was her friend, that she wasn't fooling anyone with the tough-girl act, that it was okay to be who she was, a scared kid who had gotten badly hurt. But he could tell by her tone that it would only drive her further away. So, he nodded.

'What's the op?' he asked, keeping his voice businesslike.

'Damned if I know; I salute smartly and do my job.'

'Listen to you,' he said. *She wants to be treated like an adult, to be taken seriously. You can do that much for her.*

'What?' she asked.

'You sound like a military officer, saluting smartly.'

She grinned. 'I do?'

He nodded. 'Yeah. You've really come along. Dropped all that weight, too. You're a shadow of your former self.'

Downer beamed in the starlight as the cart jounced. Her short hair framed a face that would be pretty when she got a bit older. The fat was truly gone now, hard training and military chow making her lean. 'Thanks, Osc . . . Keystone,' she said. 'Kind of wish my mom could see me now.'

'Why's that?'

'She was always . . . you know, she was just really religious. She never found out I was a Probe. Well, she probably did, but that was only after she thought I was dead. She was a megabitch. She's probably glad to think I'm dead.'

'I know what you mean,' Britton said, thinking of his father.

'But now I'm doing good work, I'm helping out. I think if my mom could see that, it might . . . you know.'

'Change her mind about you.'

Downner nodded, her voice grew pensive. 'She never thought much of me. Used to call me her "little piggie". Mostly I think she was mad because I never took to church the way she wanted me to.'

'It was like that for me, too.'

'Your mom?'

'My dad. He was a real piece of work. He was pretty religious, too, and he never liked me.'

'Does he think you're dead?'

Britton waved a hand at the concrete barricade wall, hidden in the shadows beyond the rows of tents and converted trailers. 'He's out there somewhere, probably in some monster's belly.' He remembered Stanley's wide eyes as he looked beyond the gate, the keening of the approaching demon-horses. His poor mother. Where was she now? *I never got to say I was sorry to her, either.*

'You gated him out here?'

He nodded. 'In front of my mom. Right before I ran.'

She was silent for a moment. 'Well, it's all behind you now,' she said. 'You got a presidential pardon, same as me. Harlequin says we're all legal now. Totally in compliance.'

He shook his head. 'Why do you think this whole operation is so secret? The confidentiality agreements? Why we're contractors instead of SOC? This whole thing is completely illegal.'

She looked dead ahead, her lips pursed, searching for a reply. He regretted his words. She was a Selfer, same as he, ripped out of any sense of home. She'd found one there, and he supposed, so had he. And just like him, she'd proved herself. She'd used her magic to do some good. She deserved the absolution that brought.

'It's all right,' he said. 'This country was founded on breaking a law. Sometimes laws don't get the job done. Sometimes it takes brave people to do that.'

'Harlequin said we're all in compliance,' she repeated.

'He wouldn't steer you wrong.' He looked over at her. 'And he seems to really like you.' He had no evidence of that, but it had the desired effect, and Downer smiled broadly. Britton understood. Harlequin was an impressive figure even to an adult; how much more so to a young girl?

'You got a boyfriend?' he asked. He instantly knew he had erred. He had meant to flatter her, but she grew quiet, her face clouded. *Idiot*, he said inwardly. *Your team gunned him down.*

'I'm sorry,' Britton finally said. 'It was stupid of me.'

'Nah,' Downer said eventually. 'He was stupid. He was just a kid. He smoked and stuff. Things are different now. I'm trained, and I've grown up a lot. Tom was nice, but he wasn't really good with his magic the way . . . you know, the way some people are.'

The way Harlequin is, Britton thought.

'Being young doesn't necessarily make you stupid,' Britton said. 'He was probably doing the best he could, just like you.'

They rode in silence the rest of the way to the flight line. Three helos – two Apaches and a Blackhawk – were spun up and awaiting them.

Fitzy waved from the Blackhawk, motioning Britton to board, then dismissed Downer with a wave of his wrist. The Blackhawk held four soldiers kitted out for an imminent assault.

The helos launched skyward, veered sharply, and set off, leaving Britton to clip in and watch the landscape unfold from the open bay door. The barricade wall of FOB Frontier passed beneath them, marking the bustle of men and the maze of buildings from the rolling landscape, brightly lit by the stars. The plain gently rose, clustered with tangles of vegetation. Campfires burned here and there, too far below for Britton to make out their sources. After a few minutes, the plain gave way to thick forest. Spiky treetops clustered so thickly that Britton couldn't make out the trunks.

Fitzy signaled the flight officer, and the helo shuddered, the engine noises rising to a high whine, then suddenly dropping lower. Britton could see the rotor tips, the low blur shifting as the pilot made adjustments. The birds sagged in the air.

'Whaddya think?' Fitzy asked, grinning.

Britton started as he realized that he could hear the chief

warrant officer much more clearly though Fitzy still had to yell. The birds were far more quiet than before. He'd never heard of such technology when he'd been flying.

'It ain't silent running, but it'll do,' Fitzy said. 'We're going to make a recon pass over a Goblin fortress. It's causing us problems every time we want to reach the coast, and command wants it out of our backfield. You're going to get a nice, long look at the field inside the palisade. Once you feel confident, we're going to gate in and clear the place.'

The birds began to descend, dropping close enough for Britton to make out the pointed tops of the trees, sparkling with frost.

'No way this is quiet enough,' Britton said. 'They'll hear us.'

'But not until we're on top of them,' Fitzy said. 'Just keep your eyes open and get a good look. Less time on target, the safer we'll all be.'

'If it's such a problem, why not hit it from the air?'

'Because we want to capture the Hepta-Bak alive. Command thinks the other Sorrahhad tribes might fall into line if we can convince the leaders to negotiate.'

'The Hepta who?'

'It's their leader. Like a prince. You can tell him from the white dots on his face.'

Britton thought of Marty, the white paint on his eyebrows, forehead, the base of his ears.

Fitzy paused, as if considering something, before he spoke again. 'Remember when you asked me before about the Mountain God you saw when you first landed at the LZ?'

Britton nodded.

'Well, you just keep an eye out for anything like that.'

'What do you mean, sir? What am I supposed to be looking for?'

Fitzy frowned. 'Anything like that, I said. Anything big and black or anyone who looks like they might be buddies with anything big and black. Sharp teeth, booga-booga, whatever.' He flapped his hands, irritated, and Britton decided not to press the matter.

'We don't normally come in this low or this quiet,' Fitzy

said, 'so we should have a minute or so before all hell breaks loose. If that's enough time, we'll try to stay on the hop over the fastness. You keep looking until you have a good fix on the area.'

The helos swept low over the trees, their rotors still thudding loudly to Britton's ears. The sharpened stakes of a palisade wall came into view. The rough bark had been scraped off felled trees, their sharpened points adorned with wooden turrets at regular intervals. Small watch fires burned in some of them. Britton could make out squat Goblin silhouettes, cradling spears. The central keep rose on a grassy hill behind them. Huge turrets thrust into the sky, peaked towers roofed with spiraling patterns of slate. An enormous gate, at least four stories high, split the palisade. Larger turrets rose to either side, each hanging a long triangular banner down the wall's face, shrouded in darkness.

The helicopters put on speed, close enough that stealth was no longer a concern. Britton could see figures scrambling in the turrets. A horn sounded from one of them, deep and haunting, intensely loud even over the sound of the rotors.

One of the Apaches opened up with a rocket, and there was a short pop before the turret exploded, sending flaming shards of wood spinning. The helicopters raced over the wall and out over the swath of ground outside the keep. Britton could see scores of Goblins racing to and fro. A few fired ineffectual arrows. Some of the Goblins wheeled on the backs of huge, snarling wolves, shaking gleaming swords skyward. Small buildings dotted the ground, most with thatched or slate roofs. A pen teemed with some kind of livestock, squat and hairy, bleating in terror.

At the base of one of the towers, a smaller pen was built, its railing higher and topped with sharpened stakes. Colored paint gleamed from the posts, clustered thick with guards, big by Goblin standards. Banners flapped from the corners, showing the same winged wheel that Britton had seen on the banner where the Apache Selfers had kept their hostages. The center of the pen was empty, but Britton squinted as he looked at it. The air shimmered, as if a heat haze dwelt there in spite of the cold weather. The helicopter moved too fast for him to focus on it. He turned to Fitzy to mention it but was cut off by sharp reports from the ground.

Gunfire sounded as the few Goblins with stolen guns opened fire. The big guns on the helos held their peace, but the soldiers returned fire with their carbines, far better shots. Britton saw a few of the creatures plummet, screaming, from the parapet walk.

He turned to Fitzy, ready to tell him that he had a good fix on the keep. Anything to stop the slaughter and get them out of there. He saw a streak of white issue from the base of the keep. 'They've got a sorcerer down there!' he called to Fitzy, pointing. One of the Apache pilots had seen him and the cannon glowed on the undercarriage, the rounds churning the ground to mud. The white figure flung up its hands and vanished in the rain of lead.

'All right! All right! I've got it! I've fixed it!' Britton shouted. The ground was a blurry nightmare of shouting Goblins. The air stank of cordite. His ears rang from churning rotors and gunfire. He had no idea if he could gate back to the place. 'Let's get out of here!'

The flight officer nodded and shouted to the pilots. The Apaches fell into formation as the Blackhawk turned toward the palisade wall, gaining elevation.

And stopped in midair, wrenching so hard that Britton pitched forward.

His arms pinwheeled as he stumbled toward the open bay, the ground, hundreds of feet below, spinning under him. The soldiers cursed as they were thrown forward. A carbine went spinning through the air, tumbling to the ground below.

The carabiner, fixed firmly to the floor ring, yanked hard on his belt, checking his slide. Britton landed hard on his shoulder, one arm dangling out of the helicopter. Down the length of the bird, he could see the tail fixed firmly in a wooden grip. One tower burned brightly where the rocket had struck it. The other had grown outward, its wooden form budding, the planks sprouting leaves and branches. Fresh bark covered its gnarled surface, forming a massive fist that held the helo fast. A white-painted Goblin stood at the fist's base, a leather cape sewn with metal discs slung around his neck. He gestured, and the fist moved inward, hauling the Blackhawk down to the parapet walk beside a post with a giant bird skull, striped red and orange, affixed to the top, whence it glared balefully at the helo that shuddered against the wood.

Britton stared at the skull. He had seen it before. 'Sir, I . . .'

But there was no time. Goblin warriors raced along the walls toward them, brandishing weapons, shrieking.

Fitzy rose to a knee, reaching out toward the Goblin Terramancer, but an arrow shot out of the crowd, forcing him to break his concentration and duck away.

Fitzy cursed. The Goblins closed fast. The Terramancer walked along the branch, surrounded by five Goblins, big for their race, wearing long hauberks of metal rings with extended drapes that covered their faces. Their long ears pointed out from beneath conical steel helmets, pierced through with golden rings. Three brandished curved, broad-bladed swords. The other two held pistols.

One pilot shouted into the radio while the other spun up the rotors, straining against the magic that held them fast.

'Shut her down!' Britton called to him. 'You'll tear us apart!'

Britton turned to the soldiers, leaning out of the bay with their carbines leveled. 'Keep the parapet clear, and I can get us out of here!'

The Apaches wheeled above, opening fire, raining bullets on the ground. The throng on the parapet was too close to the Blackhawk for them to risk firing on them.

A bullet whined off the helicopter's side as the soldiers opened up, the rhythm of their fire slow as they took careful aim. In moments, Britton began to hear the drumroll of three-round bursts as the crowd of Goblins swelled on the parapet, a group so large that even indiscriminate fire would find a target.

Britton called to the pilots, 'Get your butts out on the parapet where I can gate you to safety! And wave the damned Apaches off! They can't do anything here!'

The flight officer began shouting into his headset as one of the pilots struggled with his harness. Fitzy ran to assist him, his face pale. 'Stay in the damned bird!' he called to Britton. 'We can't lose you!'

Britton ignored him, stepping out onto the parapet walk as the first of the soldiers began crying for ammo. One of them was firing one-handed, the gas tube on his carbine so hot that the plastic dripped from burned fingers.

They would be overwhelmed in moments.

The Goblins thronged the parapet, climbing over their dead as they scrambled for the helo. A few more rounds cracked from stolen weapons. Britton felt a hiss of air pass his head. He threw open a gate on Portcullis's loading bay and grabbed the soldier with the burned hand by his body armor, hauling him through.

'Leave it!' he shouted to the rest. 'Get in the damned gate!'

The air gusted violently. The hair on Britton's neck stood up as the smell of ozone filled the air. Another Goblin, painted white and wreathed in crackling lightning, looped over the helo's rotors, slowly spinning down. He shouted at the Goblins thronging the parapet in their own language, waving his arms, motioning them to move aside.

The Apaches hovered impotently, jerking higher into the air as the Goblin Aeromancer appeared.

Two of the soldiers turned and dove through the gate. The last one looked up at Britton just as an arrow hissed out of the advancing mass, catching him below his neck. He rose and stumbled, falling against Britton's thigh, tracking blood down his trousers.

Britton hauled him upright as Fitzy appeared out of the helo's open bay, firing his pistol just as the Goblins reached the helo's nose, swarming over it, stabbing at the windscreen with their spears. The plastic exploded as the pilots fired their pistols through it.

Britton threw the wounded soldier through the gate just as the first Goblin reached him. It snarled, clad in leather armor, face mostly hidden behind a mail drape hanging from a crude steel bowl of a helmet. It leapt forward, slashing downward with a two-handed axe.

It might as well have moved in slow motion. Britton

could see its strike rise, exactly where it meant to fall. The creature's movements, its eyes, the angle of its shoulders; all telegraphed the axe's destination. It was faster than an animated corpse.

But it was slower than Fitzy and far slower than Britton.

He sidestepped the blow, catching the axe's haft and torquing his arm, sending the creature banging into the helo's side before dropping off the parapet walk and plummeting to the ground below. The Goblin behind it was even slower, stabbing with a pike that dangled beads on leather thongs. Britton grabbed the weapon's head and opened another gate. He ran the creature halfway through it, then shut it, leaving half a Goblin shuddering in the Source.

Britton turned, leveled the gate horizontally, and sent it slicing down the parapet. Goblins were cut in two, leapt to their deaths, or ran screaming back to the turret.

Fitzy's words rang in his ears. *Once you have learned how to integrate your Gate Sorcery with MAC, you will be deadlier than an entire rifle company.*

But the other end of the parapet swarmed. The front of the helo was black with small bodies. They reached through the broken remains of the windscreen, hauling the pilots out.

The Terramancer appeared at the end of his wooden fist, striding triumphantly over the tail boom. He paused just outside the range of the slowing rotors, said something to Britton, and gestured. The parapet walk erupted, sprouting into gnarled branches, blossoming with buds. Hooked wooden fingers reached for Britton . . . and stopped. 'Get back in the damned bird!' Fitzy cried, gesturing at the Terramancer.

Britton raced back into the helo. The flight officer and one pilot held the other pilot's legs, engaged in a brutal tug-of-war with five Goblins standing on the nose of the Blackhawk. Britton rushed the cockpit, grabbing the pilot's ankle and adding his strength to the contest. They struggled for another moment, but at last the pilot came flying back through the windscreen, howling as he left skin on the ragged shards of plastic.

The Goblins reached, and Britton opened a gate in the middle of them, slicing them and the helicopter's nose in half, sending the remains spiraling to the ground. The gate looked in on Portcullis's loading bay, where the three soldiers were tending their wounded comrade. James the armorer stood over them, buckling on a tactical vest. A few soldiers milled around him in various states of readiness. Their eyes went wide as the gate opened. Britton motioned them back and threw the wounded pilot through.

'Go! Go!' he shouted to the remaining men, who nodded and jumped through. The flight officer paused at the gate, turning back to him.

'Sir, what ab . . .'

'I'll get him!' Britton shouted. 'Get out of here!'

Britton ran back to the parapet, where Fitzy stood over the Terramancer, slumped and bleeding. The chief warrant officer wrenched back and forth, Goblins hanging from his arms. One leapt and wrapped its arms around his neck while another grabbed his leg. Fitzy hauled the Goblin over his shoulder, hurling it into its fellows. Another Goblin threw its sword down, grappling his waist.

Slowly, Fitzy sank to his knees. Britton shouted and ran toward him.

Then he was ripped off his feet, spinning in the air, whipping through the helicopter's cabin. He came out the other side of the bird, his body whirling through hundreds of feet of empty air, the helo shrinking in the distance.

He hung in the air. A Goblin Aeromancer faced him, its grimace cracking the white paint that covered its body. It leaned forward, grinning, prying one eye open wide.

And then Britton was falling.

Terror unleashed a flood of adrenaline that threatened to swamp him. He felt the Dampener kicking in, shunting the terror aside. The wind whipped his face, his dry eyes too painful to keep open.

So he closed them and concentrated on the soft couch in the recreation area at LSA Portcullis.

He felt the shift in magical currents, the sudden change in smells, temperature, air pressure. He slammed into the soft couch, sprawling among soldiers who squawked, scrambling. His kicking boots knocked the TV off its stand. He bounced, his nose spraying blood from the impact, his shoulders and chest reporting the hit. He didn't think anything had broken, but couldn't be sure.

There was no time.

Britton sprang to his feet and leapt off the back of the couch. He heard the shouts of the startled soldiers, saw Don and the blond desk officer staring openmouthed, then he'd opened another gate and jumped through, slamming shoulder first into the Goblins swarming Fitzy, sending them flying. A few clung stubbornly to him.

The Aeromancer swooped over them, screaming, a dark cloud spinning behind him.

'Get out of here!' Fitzy screamed.

'Sure thing,' Britton said, locking his arms around Fitzy's neck. A Goblin squirmed between them, clinging to Fitzy's waist. The Aeromancer descended, cloud pulsing with light. Britton gripped Fitzy tight, pushing off with his thighs, opening up the gate behind him.

They slid on the loading bay's smooth floor, the gate shutting behind them. Britton's shoulder collided with James's shin, sending the armorer tumbling over them.

It took them a moment to scramble free, the Goblin crawling out from their midst, gasping. It scrabbled a few feet on the concrete floor, its fur cloak flipped backward over its head. Fitzy hauled himself to his feet and threw himself on it, grabbing the fur-covered lump of the Goblin's head and slamming it into the concrete again and again.

Britton moved to stop him, but hands gripped his arms, holding him back.

'Son of a fucking bitch!' Fitzy screamed over and over, punctuating each shout with the muffled wet sound of the Goblin's head striking floor. At last, the creature was still, a dark stain spreading across the cloak.

Britton looked around. Soldiers crowded one of the SOC soldiers from the helo. The arrow had been pulled from his collar, white gauze pressed to the wound. He stirred weakly, his skin white and sweaty. The injured pilot sat beside him, dressing his own wounds with the help of the flight officer. Radio chatter blared somewhere in the darkness.

'Sweet baby Jesus,' James whispered. 'What the hell happened?'

Fitzy whirled on Britton. 'Genius here pulled a bunch of heroics instead of getting himself to safety like he was ordered! You goddamned idiot! Do you have any idea what it would have meant if you had died? What if they captured you?'

'What the hell is wrong with you?' Britton screamed back. 'I saved your goddamned life!'

'You're not in the life-saving business!' Fitzy yelled, spit flying. 'You're in the shut the fuck up and do as your told business! When I want to be saved, I'll order you to do it!'

Britton shook his head. '. . . damned crazy.'

Fitzy leaned in close, his breath sour. 'You think this means I owe you. You think this means we're buddies. You remember one thing, contractor. I am not your friend. I am not your comrade in arms. I am here to make you into a righteous engine of war. Nothing more, nothing less.

'You're paid to be a weapon, not a hero. Remember that.'

Shadow Coven sat in their usual place at the bar. Britton slumped moodily over his folded arms, doing his best to ignore Truelove, who badgered him with questions. Richards and Downer sat beside him, trying hard not to look as interested as they were.

Britton couldn't concentrate on the flurry of questions his Coven threw at him. Fitzy's words echoed over and over in his mind.

A weapon. That's all I am, a tool. He had felt that once he raised the flag, he would be part of something again. He had watched his magic do good, rescuing American serviceman and putting down what could only be described as a monster.

But this last raid. Where was the good in that? Was that what he was? A weapon? An instrument wielded for whatever capricious whim the army chose?

'Fitzy was pissed,' Britton said, turning back to the conversation, trying to drive such thoughts away.

'Man, I bet. He just wanted you to leave him there to die?' Truelove asked.

'Yup. The Camp Commandant met him at the flight line when I gated us back in. Dressed him down right there.' Britton looked gloomily at his drink. He wasn't sure what the cost would be, but he knew it was coming and soon.

'You're all right, and that's what matters. Nobody got hurt,' Truelove said.

'Yeah,' Britton replied again, staring into his drink. His mind was full of images of burning wood, Goblins screaming to their deaths.

'He's right,' Downer said. 'You did good. You got them out of there.'

'What was it Harlequin said to you?' Britton asked. 'That we'd be fighting narcoterrorists? Enemies of our country? We slaughtered Goblins last night. We must have killed a hundred of them.'

Downer leaned toward him, sympathetic. 'Come on, man. They're not the same ones. They're not like Marty. There are good Goblins and bad Goblins. You went after a Defender tribe, Sorrahhad. Those are the same ones who attack the base every night! You know how many lives you saved by what you did?'

'No,' he replied. 'I only know how many lives I took. Sorrahhad means Defenders, right? What is it you suppose they're defending?'

'That's stupid,' she replied. 'That's just their name for themselves. Of course they're going to make it nice like that.'

The tide of mutters sounded across the patronage as it always did when Marty entered. The little Goblin made his way to the bar, smiling.

'Christ, Marty,' Britton said. 'You can't come here anymore. Fitzy is going to pitch a fit. He's laying down the law about us hanging out now.'

Marty wiggled his ears and mounted a stool. 'Fitzy is . . .'

Britton cut him off with a raised hand. 'Stop. Enough with that.'

He pointed at Chris, his finger mimicking a gun. 'Give him his usual, and be forewarned that I'm in no mood for your bullshit right now.'

Chris took one look at Britton's face and filled a cup with

sugar. Truelove helped Marty onto the stool, shaking his head. 'He's right, Marty. Fitzy's gone off the deep end lately. We don't want you to get in trouble.'

'You hurt?' Marty asked, standing on his stool and reaching out for Britton. 'Big fight, no?'

'Yeah,' Britton said. 'Big fight. Must have killed about a hundred of your countrymen, Marty.'

But Marty nodded sympathetically, clucking in his throat. 'I no anger, Uskar. Sorrahhad. They fight. No help.' His fingers found Britton's scalp and roamed over it, searching down the back of his neck, looking for hidden injuries.

'You see . . .' Marty searched for the word. 'Bird head? You see bird head?'

Britton nodded. 'Yeah, a skull. Painted red and orange. Marty, I saw that same symbol before. But I saw it . . . I saw it in my own world, when I rescued some of my own people.'

Marty nodded, smiling. 'Lost. You are lost people. I say you lost good. Sorrahhad say you lost bad.'

'What do you mean, lost bad? Even if you think we're good, and we hurt you . . .'

'Lost good. They Sorrahhad,' Marty repeated, nodding. 'They Heptahad On Dephapdt. They say you lost bad. They fight. Bad. You okay.'

'Marty, that's not the point!' Britton said.

'What's not the point?' Fitzy swayed in the doorway. In all their time at the FOB, they had never seen him there. Nor had they ever seen him drunk. Their instructor stank of whiskey, the fumes reaching them where they sat. His face twisted in rage, eyes swimming.

A SOC captain with confident eyes, young and trim, rose from one of the tables, walking carefully toward him, Britton could see the flash of his lapel pin, the Aeromancer's blowing wind. 'Chief warrant officer,' he said, 'these premises are off-limits to warrants.'

Fitzy ignored him, jabbing a finger at Marty. 'I thought I told you not to hang out with that little shit. Why can't you just follow orders, damn it?'

'You're not setting much of an example yourself,' the Aeromancer said, putting his hand on Fitzy's shoulder.

'Civilian contractors can drink here, but you can't. Besides, you look like you've had enough already. Why don't we get you outside, and some fresh air will . . .'

Fitzy brought a knee up into the man's crotch with explosive force. The captain doubled over in time to catch Fitzy's fist in his stomach. He collapsed on the floor, and Fitzy stepped over him. The other officers sat at their tables, looking down, up, anywhere but at Fitzy's eyes, roving the room in search of another challenge.

Fitzy turned back to Britton, pointing. 'Get him the hell out of here. I see you talking with him, I swear to God you're both meat, starting with him.'

'It's okay, sir,' Truelove began, 'we were just . . .'

'Nobody's talking to you, needledick,' Fitzy spit, his eyes never leaving Britton's.

'Come on, Marty,' Britton said, easing the Goblin off the chair. He took the creature's hand and began circling around Fitzy, moving toward the exit. Downer began chattering at him, but Britton missed her words, focusing on the door. Fitzy shouted something at her and turned just as Britton reached the exit.

'Where the hell are you going?' he shrieked.

'Following your orders, sir. Getting him out of here,' Britton said, and left, moving quickly.

He heard the door slam, then spring open again as Fitzy shuffled out after him, yelling at him to stop.

Britton picked up speed, half dragging the Goblin down the track toward the cash. The mud sucked at his boots, but Marty's long, three-toed feet spanned the surface as easily as snowshoes.

'Stop!' Marty said. 'He anger! I go! No problem, okay!'

'No, Marty,' Britton replied through clenched teeth. 'I am not leaving you alone in the dark with him. Not like this. He'll kill you. Once we're back to the cash, we'll be fine.'

Marty was silent as Britton dragged him along, Fitzy lurching behind, too drunk to catch up to them but too fit and fast for them to lose him, shouting obscenities in their wake.

Marty jerked his hand free, but matched Britton's pace as

they trudged the rest of the way, and the lights of the giant hospital tent began gleaming in the distance.

Britton stopped short. Marty kept up the pace, rushing forward and moving into the light of the tent, mixing with the crowd of orderlies, nurses, and medics who made the place a hive of activity day and night.

Britton turned as the Goblin shot him a thankful glance and disappeared inside. He suppressed the urge to run off on his own, even when the sloshing of boots and whiskey stink announced Fitzy's arrival.

'Where the hell did that rat get off to?' the chief warrant officer whispered in Britton's ear.

'He's gone, sir.'

'You're going to learn to obey orders, Keystone,' Fitzy slurred. 'God as my witness, I will make you. You've got potential, but it only counts if you play on the team.'

And that's what it comes down to, Britton thought as he faced off against the chief warrant officer. *No matter what good you do, no matter how much your magic affects the world, you will still belong to them. This drunken, teetering madman who treats Marty like dirt will be your boss until he's replaced by someone worse.*

Because Fitzy spelled it out for you. You're not one of them, and you'll never be. You're a weapon, Oscar Britton. You're a tool. This Coven may be becoming your family, but you're all just tools together, all pretending that you are loved by an organization that only seeks to own you.

He remembered the report on Scylla. They'd gladly cut into her brain, destroy her mind. Was that what had happened to Billy? Was that why he shook and drooled under his mother's arms? Was that what they would do to Britton if they decided that the tool was more trouble than it was worth?

These people can never be your family. This place can never be your home.

As if to accentuate the point, Fitzy tapped Britton's chest. 'Push it too far, Keystone, and we can always give you a little reminder, the last one you'll ever need.'

And that's why you have the ATTD. That's why they'll never take it out, no matter how loyal you become. Why earn your respect when they can own you outright?

You're no different than precision munitions or a fighter jet. You're an expensive toy, nothing more. You may have gained some skill at using magic, but it's not yours. You can still only do what they want you to when they want you to.

Deep in his heart, he rebelled against the growing kernel of feeling that maybe Scylla was right.

Chapter Twenty-Six

Decisions

Everybody knew she was Latent. That whole sudden, perfect storm thing at the video music awards? I mean, come on, man. A lot of people thought it was CGI, but not the folks who were there live. There's no way to fake weather on that grand a scale. Of course the SOC knew. But did they do anything about it? Hell, no. There's always been two sets of laws in this country – a set for regular folks and a set for the elite. Report your Latency or die. Unless you're a senator's kid, a famous actress, or an NBA superstar. In that case, we can work with you.

– Artie Welch, Friday Morning Krazytalk 98.2 FM

If Fitzy remembered the night's altercation, he gave no sign. But starting the next morning, the tempo of their training increased.

'It's time you stopped being useless,' Fitzy growled at them, as they gathered in the practice yard where they'd first tested out. 'You're going to be operating against Selfers, and Selfers use magic. You're soldiers . . . or as close as bloodsucking contactors can get to it. That's given you a range of skills in firearms, combat-casualty care, hand-to-hand combat, wilderness survival, not to mention the courage, leadership, and discipline necessary to get tough jobs done. Why, I'd hazard to say that even without your magic, you'd be a force to be reckoned with.

'The Selfer has none of these traits. All he has is magic.

Take that away from him, and you have a frightened child, helpless and ripe for the righteous punishment that you will mete out on behalf of the government of the United States and God Almighty upon whom our sovereignty depends.

'And that's what we're going to teach you now. How to take that magic away.'

Fitzy tapped the armored fist on his chest. 'Suppression is a highly sophisticated art. It is an act of intricate skill rather than power. This is why Rump Latents like me wind up assigned to it so frequently. If you can learn the knack, and I assure you that you can and will, you can interdict anyone's magical capability.

'And that's the thing, isn't it?' he asked, coming closer to Britton. 'We all know that my magic is ten times weaker than yours. But with proper training, that's just fine.'

As he spoke, three nervous-looking Novices filed into the compound. All three were male, broad shouldered, and tall.

'SAOLCC has seen fit to tap Cepheus and Camelopardalis Covens to loan us some Terramancers,' Fitzy said. 'These men were chosen because of their facility with nonsentient automatons, what we affectionately call "tar babies".' As he spoke, the men spread their arms, and the soil before them bubbled upward until roughly man-shaped piles of earth swayed before them, chips of rock sparkling from within.

'You may consider these tar babies as your incentive to get this right the first time. They will clobber the snot out of you until you can destroy them. The only way you can do that without getting me highly agitated is by Suppressing the magical flow that animates them. You will do this by Binding your own magical current to theirs, without giving it shape – such as a gate' – he pointed to Britton – 'or a sentient elemental' – he nodded to Downer.

'This is conducted, like most magical exercises, largely by feel. The only way to learn it is to do it, so let's start learning.'

The going was tougher than Britton expected. He stood across from the automaton. The Novice behind it saluted and dropped into a MAC guard, the tar baby following suit, the cut of its hips and shoulders mimicking its driver exactly. It lunged for Britton, throwing a rocky right cross at him that he easily blocked. But the automaton was made of hard earth and rock, and Britton danced backward, cradling a bruised arm.

Fitzy laughed. 'You won't get far that way.'

Britton reached out a hand and tried to visualize his current flowing through the automaton. Before he could blink, a gate had opened in the middle of the creature, cutting it neatly in half. The Novice behind backed out of his guard and raised his hands. Fresh earth flowed upward to fill the cracks, knitting the tar baby back together while Fitzy yelled. 'What part of "don't use your magic except to Suppress" didn't you understand?'

'Sorry, sir,' Britton said. 'I didn't mean to. This is new to me.'

'My boot up your ass isn't new to you,' Fitzy shouted, 'and that's what's coming if you keep this crap up. Do it right, Keystone!'

Beside him, Downer's tar baby was already a pile of loose rocks and clods of dirt. 'It's easy.' She beamed.

'How the hell are you doing it?' Britton asked.

'Umm. It's like . . . it's like there's a string from the Novice to the tar baby,' she said. 'Try opening your gate there.'

'It's not group therapy, Keystone!' Fitzy shouted, and nodded to the Novice, who charged the automaton forward, catching Britton off guard. He ducked backward, but not before a rocky hand swatted him hard on the ear, leaving his head spinning.

Britton focused on the image of a chain connecting Novice and tar baby and tried again. His mind flashed a vision of Portcullis's loading bay out of habit and for a moment, a gate flashed open in front of the Novice's face. He gasped and stumbled backward before Britton could close it. The automaton stumbled backward as well, raising its arms in time with its master to ward off the gate.

'Damn it!' Fitzy snarled, striding forward.

Britton sidestepped a few paces and concentrated on calling the magic, Binding it to the thread between tar baby and Novice, pushing all other thoughts from his mind. Fitzy reached him, raising a hand, then stopped as the automaton collapsed.

Britton could feel his flow pushed outward, intersected with the Novice's. The pressure of the foreign flow interleaved with his own, a gentle pulsing in his chest. As his mounted, it yielded slightly.

'I got it,' he said, raising his hands. 'I got it, sir.'

Fitzy nodded stiffly at the collapsed automaton. 'Lucky thing, too,' he said, and dropped his hand. 'Let's see you do it again.'

Britton couldn't do it again for much of the next round, but neither did he make the mistake of opening a gate. When he finally managed the Suppression, Fitzy simply called for another go. By the fifth fight, both he and the Novice were sweating. The fatigue made it harder to concentrate on rolling back the magic, forcing him to fight the tar baby as best he could, his forearms, shins, and chest quickly becoming a field of bruises. The pain made him long for a trip to the cash for more of Marty's healing leaves.

But by the end of the day, he was Suppressing as consistently as Downer.

The Coven's spirits were high as they wrapped up the day's session. They traded jokes and slapped one another's backs as they took turns rolling one another's magic back. Even Fitzy cracked a smile and pronounced their efforts 'something approaching competence', before giving them liberty and leaving them to their own devices.

But Britton's good spirits sank as quickly as they had risen. *What are you so happy about?* he asked himself. *Because you've learned a new skill that now belongs to your slave masters? You're all just tools in a toolbox, a good day of training won't change that.*

'I'll hit the showers and maybe catch up with you all in the OC,' Britton said, trying not to let the feeling show.

'Uh, negative.' Downer grinned at him. 'You are going directly to the cash. Do not pass Go.'

Britton looked down at the network of bruises covering his arms.

'Your face isn't much better,' Richards said.

'Thanks,' Britton said.

Truelove laughed and headed down the muddy track

toward the hospital. 'Come on, Keystone, let's get you fixed up.'

Britton felt pride surge in spite of himself. He was mastering his abilities, he was part of a team that was every bit as skilled and dedicated as he was. Even if the army owned them all, their affection for him was genuine enough. These people were still his friends.

'I think I'm going to get cleaned up first, maybe lie down for a bit.'

'Are you kidding?' Downer asked. 'You look like you got hit by a truck.'

'Yeah,' Britton said. 'I'm just kind of licked. A few bruises won't kill me. I'll catch up to you.'

'This isn't about Fitzy's new anti-Goblin-fraternization stance, is it?' she pressed. 'If you need to see Marty, go see him. You know I always say, regs are meant to be broken.'

Britton laughed in spite of himself. 'Do you always say that?'

'Well, no,' she admitted. Her face went pensive, then she flashed him a smile that showed the dazzling beauty she would one day become. 'But I'm learning to.'

But in the end he didn't go back to his hooch; his feet took him back down the same muddy lane, tracking slowly toward the cash. Why was he going? He wasn't hurt that badly. Despite Downer's mothering of him, he would do much better with a nap than a doctor.

It's Therese, he admitted. *You want to see her.*

And what was wrong with that? She was a beautiful woman. And so what if he ran into Marty? Screw Fitzy and his idiot no-fraternization policy. What was he going to do? Fire Britton? Kill him? The man was a drunken bully. Britton knew how to deal with bullies.

But as he searched deeper, he knew that he wasn't being honest with himself. He wanted to see Therese. There was something he had to know.

Britton pushed through the plastic flaps and between the rows of metal hospital beds that clustered under the canvas. He tapped a passing corpsman on the shoulder. The man turned, took in the Shadow Coven uniform, and took a hasty step backward.

'Sir?'

'Heard you've got a new Physiomancer on staff. I need to see her.'

'She's real busy, sir.'

'And our Coven commander is real insistent we get proper care. He's also real ornery. Your call.'

The corpsman paused a moment before nodding. 'Follow me, sir.'

Therese turned out to be in the Burn Unit, just a few paces away. A quick scan of the ward showed that Specialist Lenko had been moved elsewhere, but Britton only had eyes for Therese. She bent over an unconscious patient whose face, neck, and arm were a mottled mass of charred skin. Her eyes were closed as her hands roved over the burned tissue, leaving pink, healthy skin beneath.

He positioned himself on the opposite side of the bed and waited. In a moment, Therese opened her eyes, meeting his. A broad grin spread across her face, and she nodded at him.

'My hero returns.'

He grinned like an idiot. 'So, when do you get off?'

'I can take a few minutes if you'd like to get caught up,' she said. She crossed to him and began to run her hands over his bruised arms, which tingled with warmth as her healing magic penetrated into them. 'Oh God, Oscar. You look like hell.'

'They've been working me pretty hard,' he managed, closing his eyes and basking in the feel of her eddying magic and his knitting flesh.

'Come on,' she said.

He nodded, and she led him through a series of canvas-covered walkways to a heated tent, where long wooden tables had been laid out. Medical workers, military and contractor, human and Goblin, were spread out among them, eating and chatting. Britton sat down on a bench and was surprised when Therese slid along next to him, her knee bumping his.

There was a long silence as they stared at one another. Britton was surprised at how easy it was to be quiet with her, just sitting and enjoying the shadows playing over her cheeks and the hollow of her throat. At last, Therese blushed and broke the silence. 'I go back to the SASS about once a week to check up on folks, and you'll be pleased to hear that Wavesign's fine,' she said. 'They didn't allow it at first, but I put up a fuss, and they caved. You'd be amazed how much leeway they give you when you've got a rare and valuable talent.' She smiled.

'Tell me about it,' Britton said. 'You've been working with Marty?'

'The Goblin?' Therese clapped her hands. 'He's so great. He's been showing me around since I got here, helping me. I figured he was someone important in his tribe. The other Goblins pretty much bow to him.

'How's Downer doing?' she asked.

'Fine, I guess. She won't say a word about it. You're an amazing healer, Therese. There's no evidence she was ever hurt, but . . .' He tapped his head.

'She's a strong girl,' Therese said. 'She'll be okay.'

'You think?'

'She has to be; this is her life now.'

There was an awkward silence. Britton drummed his fingers on the table. 'Therese, I . . .'

'What, Oscar?'

'Are you happy that you, you know, raised the flag? That you agreed to cooperate?'

Therese was silent for a moment. 'On the whole, yes. I mean, Hayes is a bastard, and there's a lot of admin BS to put up with, but overall, I like it. Even if I disagree with the overall organization, even if they basically own my life, in the end my magic still helps people. People are alive and whole because of me. I can sleep at night knowing that.'

Britton nodded, silent.

'What about you?' she finally asked.

'I don't know,' he said. 'At first, I was sure I was doing the right thing. I mean, Swift is so stupid and useless, and he's dragging Wavesign down with him. After we saved those marines, I really thought I'd made the right call. When we took down that Selfer in the sewers . . . she was like a demon out of a nightmare. After that, I was absolutely sure we were on the right side. I felt like you do now, that I was ultimately doing good, that in the balance, it was right to cooperate. But they've got me killing the natives here now. They treat Marty like dirt. And in the end, I can't shake this feeling like no matter how much good I'll do, I'll always belong to them. Fitzy called me a weapon the other day. I don't know if I can live like that.'

'You sound like Scylla,' Therese mused. Britton's blood ran cold at the comment.

Because he knew he was Scylla to them, fine enough when he was cooperating but standing by to be lobotomized once they decided he was more trouble than he was worth.

She noticed his expression and squeezed the back of his neck. 'Oh God, Oscar. I'm sorry. I didn't mean it like that.'

He shook his head. 'It's nothing. I know she's nuts, and I know she's a murderer. But you have to admit that some of the things she says make sense. I guess that's what scares me.'

She asked me to help her escape. She can take this bomb out of my chest if I do.

'Therese' – Britton turned to her – 'you said before that you needed time to get good enough to get this thing out of my chest. Are you good enough now?'

She placed her hand on his chest and paused, eyes closed. 'I can . . . see it. Man, whoever put it in there was good. Molding heart flesh is tricky stuff, at least when you're trying to keep it beating.'

'Can you do it?'

'I don't know, Oscar.' She shook her head. 'To be honest, it'd be a long shot. Even if I was confident that I could do it, you'd need something for the pain. It's going to hurt like hell. You're not going to be able to gate anywhere if you die of shock.'

He winced. 'It didn't work out so well the last time I had someone steal from the cash.'

'Goblin contractors don't have the access that I do. I'd just need some time. I'd also need some time to do the work.'

He paused. 'What happened to Specialist Lenko?'

'Who?' she asked.

'He was in the burn unit . . .'

'Oh,' she said. 'They moved him. We've got the burns covered, but there's an infection. I boosted his immune response, but it's touch and go right now. You know him?'

Britton shook his head. 'Later. We've been talking way too long. I should let you get back to work.'

No sooner had he spoken than Captain Hayes appeared at their table. 'Everything all right in here?'

'Fine, sir,' she answered. 'We're just finishing up.'

'You disappeared from the floor, Therese. We just had a Humvee hit outside the wire. You're needed back in trauma.'

'Be right there, sir.'

'That fat bastard,' she muttered after he'd left. 'I haven't seen him help a single patient since I've been here. He's always back in the Special Projects tent. What the hell are they doing back there?'

Britton stood, thinking of the report he'd read on Scylla. 'Research,' he said. 'And they wonder why half the country-side is up in arms against them. We meet in the OC for drinks most nights. Can you make it there?'

'Things get insane here at night, Oscar. That's when most of the attacks happen, and the worst of the wounded come in.'

He paused at the exit. 'It's really good to see you again, Therese.'

She smiled. 'Get out of here. I'll get to the OC tonight if I can. If worse comes to worst, you know where to find me.'

And Oscar Britton grinned.

Because he did know where to find her, and while it wasn't a way out of there, it was something.

Chapter Twenty-Seven

Mescalero

Anticipating future theaters of war is the responsibility of every staff officer. The twenty-first century saw the addition of space and cyberspace to the traditional realms of air, sea, and land. It is time for us to begin consideration of arcane or magical space as an arena where operational preparation of combat environments should be considered. Much study is still needed to illuminate this developing field, but as a nation, we can only gain by getting out in front of the planning process before our enemies do.

– Lieutenant Scott Dyson, United States Navy
Final paper for Master's of Strategic Conflict Studies
Maritime College of the Armed Forces

Britton sat in the OC with the rest of the Coven, celebrating their new skill. Truelove flirted hopefully with Downer. Richards, more than a little tipsy, Whispered a tufted squirrel up onto the bar, where it urinated enthusiastically in Chris's direction while the bartender growled and idly threatened to chuck them all out. Britton's stomach churned as his eyes swept the Coven. These people were his friends, weren't they? The army might own them all, but they could still care about one another.

He brooded over his conversation with Therese. What if she could get the ATTD out? Did he really want to go? Britton felt the pride again, the sense of belonging. Despite the bomb in his heart, despite Fitzy's continued abuse, he was beginning to make a home there. He had raised the flag, he had made the decision to work with and for the army. Whether he was a weapon or a valued member of a team, what difference did that make? Wasn't this better than a life spent running?

From the moment he leapt through the gate from Dawes's bedside, his magic had owned him, driving him from hole to hole. He had saved the lives of those marines. When one really considered it, he'd saved the lives of everyone involved in that operation. He'd done it again when they'd battled the Selfer in the New York City sewers. He looked again at Downer's functioning legs. There were good people still breathing because of what the SOC had taught him to do with his magic. Despite the shock of the engagement, his skirmish at the Goblin fort had left his heart singing. He had mastered his abilities. He had, almost single-handedly, faced an army and beat them, getting his team out scarcely harmed.

The SOC had taught him how, and they still had more to teach him.

Was the SOC really so terrible? They hadn't murdered Downer after all. They had, in their own way, saved her. When he really thought about it, he supposed they'd saved him, too.

He stared moodily into his drink. But he couldn't ignore Fitzy's drunken threats against Marty, the useless murder of the Goblins in the fortress, or the report strewed on Hayes's desk, detailing plans to slice into Scylla's brain. Her words rang in his ear. How could he live as if he belonged to these people? Who knew what they would ask him to do next? It was only a matter of time before he was tasked to hunt down Selfers who weren't monsters like the Render in the sewers under New York, but decent people like him, saddled with abilities they hadn't asked for, who didn't want to be under the army's thumb.

His gut twisted. But how could he give up all he had learned? All he had yet to learn? And just when he was finally getting good?

He swore.

'You okay?' Truelove asked. Britton reflected on how far the small Necromancer had come, his confidence improving daily. Any irritation at being disturbed fled at the sight of his face, friendly and open.

'Yeah,' Britton said. 'Just thinking about when I was running is all.'

Downer looked at him quizzically. 'Why bother? You're not running anymore.'

Truelove punched Britton's shoulder, then blanched as Britton turned toward him. 'Sorry.'

Britton smiled. 'No, you're right. I'm not running anymore. It's okay.'

Truelove brightened instantly. 'Damn right it's okay. Chris! Another round.'

Britton's improved mood led them to drink enthusiastically, and they reported to trailer B-6 with slightly aching heads the next morning. Fitzy leaned against the whiteboard. A pale, thin-lipped man in a brown uniform stood beside him, the newcomer's shoulder patched with an eagle surmounting a buffalo. Gold script curled beneath the symbols – UNITED STATES DEPARTMENT OF THE INTERIOR. BUREAU OF INDIAN AFFAIRS.

'Morning, campers,' Fitzy said, pleased at their surprise. 'Allow me to introduce Captain Day from BIA's law-enforcement division. Command has, despite my better judgment, determined you to be at a stage in your training where you can be of use to your country in something more significant than mucking about sewer systems or beating up on the locals here.

'The Great Reawakening has given a lot of people some funny ideas. The funniest are held by the Mescalero band of the Apache nation, who occupy a substantial swath of New Mexico. These folks got the idea that not only is their territory autonomous, it's sovereign, and they fully seceded from the United States of America. The first thing their tribal council did was to legalize the use of magic in the confines of this supposed sovereign state, with results that you have seen. The death toll in this insurgency currently stands at over two thousand US armed services personnel, with an additional five hundred sworn law-enforcement officers and an undisclosed number of civilian advisors.

'Even worse, this minority of Selfers keeps the majority of law-abiding Apache from living in peace with us. They want to return to the "old ways", whatever the hell that means, and consider anyone who doesn't agree with them as an enemy collaborator worthy of death.

'Keep that in mind when you consider the crocodile tears of all these sympathizers who'd like to see these folks cut loose. Unregulated magic is a pretty idea for those who don't have to deal with it, but I'm sure Captain Day here will agree that the real thing is nasty business.

'You've got a rare opportunity to stop this death toll in its tracks, and Captain Day is going to tell you how.'

'Gentlemen.' The BIA captain's voice was high and nasal. Britton couldn't tell whether or not he deliberately ignored Downer's gender. 'We have a rare opportunity to make a serious dent in the enemy's order of battle. The tribal council's most important general is a Selfer called Chatto.' Captain Day turned to the overhead-projection image displayed on the whiteboard. It depicted a man with old eyes. His leathern, wind-scoured skin made his age difficult to discern, but his long black hair, tied with a red bandanna, looked thick and young.

'Don't get nostalgic for the noble savage getup. This man is personally responsible for the Ruidoso massacre, including taking out the airlift that went in for the survivors. It remains the biggest tragedy American first responders have ever suffered. Chatto's capture could lead to a ton of actionable information that we could use to wrap up this firefight once and for all. More importantly, Chatto is a rallying point, and taking him out of the fight would seriously lower enemy morale.'

'So, why now? Why's he suddenly vulnerable?' Britton asked.

'Chatto cast off his wife when she decided she wanted to join the modern world. Cut her up pretty bad.' He toggled the projector and the image changed to a young Apache woman whose beauty had been marred first by hard living and further by livid scars running up her nostrils.

'Apache custom is to slit the noses of women who betray

their husbands. They call her *Nalzukich* now. Means "slit-nose". That he let her live is amazing enough. But now he's shown a real soft spot. Their daughter just got her period, which gives them four days to have her blessed by their *Gahe*. Chatto invited Slit-Nose to the ceremony.'

Captain Day toggled the projector again. 'She got there early and sent us this video.' The screen displayed a wide stretch of dried badlands under a blanket of bright stars. Scanty scrub growth competed with dry rocks to cover the space. The image looped, again and again. Captain Day looked expectantly at Britton. 'We have no idea where it is. But we were hoping it wouldn't matter.'

Britton watched the video loop and imagined the freezing cold on that near-desert plain. He pictured the smell of dried sage, the allure of the distant stars. He felt his magic pulse expectantly and nodded. 'It won't.'

Captain Day grunted. 'In and out. We want Chatto alive if possible, but we'll accept his death if you can recover the body. It's critical that all the Mescalero people know he's down, but not how he got that way. Alive would be better because Chatto can hopefully confirm some ideas we have on where the heart of the insurgency is located. Slit-Nose will meet you at the infil point and take you to the ceremony. There'll be one *Gahe* there, but that shouldn't . . .'

'We don't speak Apache, sir,' Britton interrupted, to a frown from Fitzy.

Captain Day nodded. 'It's what they call their "Mountain Gods".'

Britton recalled a black form, nearly too fast to follow, flashing across a video screen. He shuddered, remembering flashing teeth.

Captain Day patted the air with his palms. 'They look scary, but their bark is worse than their bite. Trust me, this'll be a cakewalk.'

Cakewalk, Britton thought, remembering Dawes's burned body. *I've heard that one before.*

'I'll come along to translate,' Day went on, 'but once you make the assault, I'm hanging back. I wouldn't want to get underfoot.'

Yeah, I bet you wouldn't, Britton thought, seeing the fear in the man's eyes.

'Just remember,' Day said. 'Slit-Nose may be on our side, but she's still Apache. You don't trust her one inch more than you have to.'

'Why can't she just lead you to the ceremony?' Downer asked.

'BIA doesn't want in on this op. We've got enough of a public-relations disaster out here. Chatto's a wild animal who needs to be put down, but the press isn't going to spin it that way. He needs to drop inexplicably. It needs to look like . . . well, like magic.'

'How do you know she won't betray us?' Britton asked.

'We've been in touch with this particular person for some time,' Day said. 'The only person she hates more than me is Chatto. And we've got an added bonus. Puberty ceremonies are usually held in the presence of ancestors. They'll probably meet the *Gahe* on a burial ground.'

'That means corpses,' Truelove said.

Day nodded. 'Lots of 'em. The Mescalero have been using the same burial plots for centuries.'

The Necromancer smiled. 'Well, all right.'

'Last equipment check,' Fitzy said, as the Coven slammed magazines into pistols and tightened the straps on their body armor. 'Stay on my six and remember, these aren't Goblins, and they sure as hell aren't tar babies. These are Selfers and no friends of ours. Stay frosty, and for the love of all that's holy, do as you're fucking told. There'll be at least thirty men at this ceremony, and that's a conservative estimate.'

'Too easy,' Downer said, grinning. 'We're the magic behind the magic, remember?'

'Damn straight,' Truelove said, pale and sweating.

Britton glanced at the video one more time and opened a gate on the flat expanse. He felt a surge of pride at how easily it came to him. The video was clear, but the ground was almost featureless, yet with only a few minutes of watching it, he could guide them there effortlessly. But there was work to do. He could pat himself on the back later.

They stepped through onto the starlit plain. Slit-Nose greeted them, eyes defiant. '*Da go te,*' she said.

'How do you say hello in Apache?' Britton asked Day.

Slit-Nose laughed and smiled wider. 'No need. I speak English. We're not all dumb Indians out here, no matter what this asshole tells you.' She jerked a thumb at Day, who shook his head.

Fitzy swore. 'We do not have time for this bullshit. Let's get this show on the road.'

Day barked a few more words to Slit-Nose in Apache before nodding back to Fitzy. 'It's your show from here on in. Good luck.' He stepped back through the gate and was gone.

Slit-Nose surveyed Shadow Coven for a moment, then shouldered a hunting rifle and moved off into the night. The landscape was unbroken, dotted occasionally by burned-out cars or discarded piles of tires, and Britton felt naked in the open starlight.

'So, you guys are special army, huh?' Slit-Nose asked. Her voice was deep, worn.

'We're interested parties, ma'am,' Fitzy whispered. 'We want to see peace restored to the Apache nation.'

Slit-Nose laughed at his attempt at quiet. 'We won't be there for a while. Nobody can hear us here but rabbits.'

Fitzy cursed under his breath, and Britton had to stifle a chuckle. 'All the same, ma'am. We'd rather not talk. The sooner we take custody of your husband, the sooner we can return to peaceful relationships between our peoples.'

Slit-Nose stopped and glared at him. 'No peaceful relationships, white eyes. You get your man, then you *leave*.'

Fitzy looked as if he would reply, then considered Slit-Nose's hard look. At last he nodded, and they went on.

Britton recalled Fitzy's words. *This minority of Selfers keeps the majority of law-abiding Apache from living in peace with us.* At least one law-abiding Apache didn't seem to want anything to do with them.

They followed Slit-Nose in silence for about ten minutes before she stopped them just shy of a stack of abandoned cars strewn with trash. Firelight flickered on the horizon. Britton could barely make out the specks of black shapes around it.

In the center was a series of white domes – canvas wickiups.

'All right. Keystone, I need you and Prometheus on the far side of the ring. Can you sight it from here?' Fitzy asked.

Britton nodded. 'I can get off to the side. We should be well covered by darkness. Who's going to take care of you, sir?'

'Oh, I think we'll manage,' Richards said, spreading his hands. About his feet, a small throng of jackrabbits, spiders, and snakes had already gathered in silent, ordered columns beside four coyotes. As Britton watched, one stepped forward, sitting back on its haunches and saluting smartly.

'We've got more inbound,' Richards said.

Britton smiled and opened a gate on the MAC practice tent. 'Okay. I've got a good spot.'

Fitzy nodded, tapping the commlink in his ear. 'I'll radio when it's showtime. Warn me if you see anything from that angle that I should know about.'

A moment later, Britton and Downer crouched behind a broken boulder covered with painted handprints, barely discernible in the darkness. A small crowd of Apache, mostly men, were dressed in jeans and T-shirts. They surrounded a circle of white canvas wickiups and were chatting amiably, with no evidence of ceremony. He pulled night-vision binoculars from his belt and sighted down them. In the distance, he could make out Fitzy, Richards, and Truelove approaching at a crouch. Richards's small army of animals slunk along behind them. Slit-Nose must have bugged out. Britton's stomach went cold at the thought, but there was no time to worry about it.

Britton and Downer jogged to crouch behind an abandoned car that offered a better view of the circle. They were getting close, and Britton could hear snatches of conversation. He couldn't count the number of people around the canvas domes, but there were far more than thirty, talking in low voices around a raging bonfire. Downer paused, beginning to stand until he yanked her down.

'What the hell is wrong with you?' he asked.

'Something's . . . can you feel that?' she replied.

Britton paused, focusing. The cold air made his shirt stick to him beneath his armor, his ball cap itching on his brow.

The magical currents on the Home Plane were so much fainter than the Source that he had scarcely noticed them despite so many Selfers in one place.

But once he focused, he picked up one current stronger than the rest. And close.

He moved to open a gate as his magic rolled back, and an elbow crashed into his ear, smashing the commlink and sending him sprawling. Four men emerged from the car they had chosen as their hiding place. Two wore jeans and T-shirts, pistols in their hands. The other two were stripped to the waist, their bodies painted entirely black. Their heads were enclosed in horned wooden masks, carved surfaces painted with leering, fanged smiles. The magical current, now Suppressing Britton's own, came from one of them. The other reached out to Downer, Suppressing her as well. The Selfer Suppressing Britton reached down and unsnapped Britton's holster, retrieving his pistol. The other Selfer advanced on Downer, who had begun to backpedal.

Downer raised a hand to her commlink. 'One, one, this is Prometheus,' she said.

One of the other men raised his pistol to her face. 'Don't be stupid,' he said. His English was flat and slightly accented as Slit-Nose's had been. 'Give me your gun.'

He turned to the masked Apache Selfer Suppressing her. 'She's got a current?'

'They both do.' The Apache started forward, the mask leering. 'How many more of you are there?'

Britton scrabbled in the dust, groaning. Even if Slit-Nose hadn't sold them out, he should have known that they would have lookouts on the perimeter. Downer's commlink buzzed in her ear, but she didn't dare answer, staring at the muzzles of the guns, fingers tensed on the triggers. The Selfer Suppressing Britton kicked him again and again, then leaned over and punched him in the temple. Britton's head rebounded off the packed earth, and he saw stars, as he fought to cling to consciousness.

'You got nothing to say, white eyes?' the masked Selfer before Downer asked her. 'Maybe I'll fuck it out of you. Maybe you'll scream loud enough for your friends to come. Your boyfriend here' – he paused to add his own kick to Britton's stomach – 'can watch.'

One of the men pinned her elbows behind her back while the second covered Britton at a gesture from the masked Apache.

He nodded to the Selfer Suppressing Britton, who gave him a final kick, then turned his current to Suppress Downer while the other Selfer dropped his Suppression. 'Watch and learn,' he said to Britton, easing his manhood out of his trousers.

'That's too small to make me scream,' Downer snarled, struggling.

'Heh. White eyes bitch. I've got something for you,' the Selfer said from behind his mask, bursting into flame below the waist.

Britton's stomach was a mottled pit of agony. His own magical tide drifted far from him, hidden in a haze of agony. But he saw the Apache Selfer step toward her, his manhood and pelvis engulfed in fire, reaching for Downer. *If I don't do something, she's going to suffer. Dig Deep.*

Oscar Britton dug deep. His stomach twisted, his head swam from the effort.

But a gate snapped open through the neck of the Selfer standing closest to him. Blood fountained skyward, and Downer squinted as she felt the Suppression drop.

'Oh, you've got something for me all right,' Downer said.

Two elementals sprang from the fire around the remaining Selfer's crotch. The first leapt at the man covering Downer, who dropped his gun, screaming, as his skin began to bubble. The second darted between her legs. The man behind her released her arms, uttering curses that quickly became screams.

The masked Selfer held up a hand, flames rocketing toward Downer. She held up her own hand and five more burning human shapes surrounded her. Britton rose to his knees, still too weak to work any magic of his own.

The masked Selfer ran for the circle, calling for help in Apache. The circle erupted in response, and Britton could see the Apache running in the firelight and yelling. A few jumped into the air and others burst into flame or began to sparkle with gathered ice.

And something else. From within one of the wickiups came a high shriek, guttural and hissing at the same time, a horrid mockery of the Apache being spoken around it.

The night lit with muzzle flashes as the first bullets began to smack into the dirt around them. They took shelter behind the car just as Richards's animal army broke over the circle.

Britton held a hand over his stomach, willing the nausea to pass. 'Go! Go!' He waved at Downer. 'It's now or never! I'm behind you!'

Downer sprinted toward the circle, her elementals spreading out before her.

Britton came close behind. He put on speed as one Apache Selfer collapsed under the weight of a score of biting jackrabbits. A snarling coyote dragged another across the ground by his throat. Another coyote yanked at his arm.

Several coyotes and stray dogs yelped as rounds tore through them, and a few of the non-Latent Apache began to dance, stomping through a morass of spiders and snakes. One of the Apache Aeromancers blazed lightning through the animals, scorching them in droves. Britton felt Downer's current reach out, and that same lightning became a small pack of electric elementals, man-shaped and diving for the canvas domes.

Fitzy gestured at the Aeromancer, and he fell from the sky, shrieking. He turned his head and sighted Britton. 'Let's get this over with,' he shouted. He pointed at one of the wickiups. 'Secure the goddamn target, Keystone!'

The wickiup whipped into the air, support poles snapping, swept skyward by the casual sweep of a slender black arm. The Mountain God crouched, ten feet tall, its twisted man's body so dark that it absorbed the firelight. Its horned head reared, the real horror making a mockery of the Selfer's mask. Its dagger teeth glowed wetly.

Behind it, the air shimmered slightly, as if heat were reflecting off hot asphalt. Britton's eyes widened. There was no speeding helicopter to obscure his vision this time. There could be no mistaking the rippling in the air. What the hell was that? Some strange magic? But there was no time to worry about it. Richards's Whispered animals were recoiling from the thing, fleeing in a chorus of whines, barks, and squeaks. Richards frowned, focusing his ability with no result.

Fitzy knelt, drew his pistol, and fired three rounds into the gaping mouth; but the creature didn't seem to notice. It lashed out, so fast that it blurred, and Fitzy was flying backward to skid in the dirt, the plates of his body armor shattering. He struggled to his feet, shaking his head.

'Damn it, Rictus! A little help here!' he shouted.

Truelove spread his arms and the ground all around them erupted.

The Apache turned their guns to their feet as gray corpses swarmed upward, snatching ankles and thighs and pulling them flat. Britton heard shrieks and snapping bones.

Downer gestured at the bonfire, which erupted into a fountain of elementals. At twenty, Britton lost count of the creatures leaping into the center of the camp to throw themselves at the Mountain God, which shrieked but did not burn. Its black skin seemed simply to absorb the energy of their attacks. It took another lurching blur-step toward Fitzy, gnashing its teeth.

Britton knelt and snapped open a gate in front of its face.

It shrieked again, throwing an arm across its face and turning away. Britton hauled the gate backward into its path, the edges slicing through its trailing heel and cutting it off. Tendrils of black mist escaped from the wound as the creature howled. It turned and fixed Britton with a hateful stare. Then its eyes flicked to the gate as Britton brought it around and slid it toward the creature.

In a moment, it was upon him. Britton threw himself sideways, parrying a raking sweep of the thing's claws with his forearm. The collision made his shoulder shake, his teeth clicking together hard enough to make him grunt. He felt the bone fracture beneath the skin, and tears leaked from the corners of his eyes. The *Gahe*'s flesh was sleek as satin, a layer of softness stretched over iron. Cold emanated from its flesh, burning him where it contacted, and traveling up the reverberation of his bones to numb him to the shoulder. He fell back, teeth chattering.

Britton's eyes lit as a fire elemental darted across his path, but the Mountain God swept it away, gnashing its teeth with a sound like grinding metal. It leapt at him again.

Britton opened a gate between them as it snapped its jaws shut. The Mountain God cried out in horror, jerking back as Britton snapped the gate shut, but not before he severed one of the thing's horns, which vanished through the gate in a puff of black smoke. The creature stabbed forward with a clawed hand, overshooting Britton's head and catching him with the crook of its elbow, sending him spinning. Britton's head went numb from the impact, the cold spreading to his chest. He rolled over on his back just as the creature sprang after him, ignoring the bullets Fitzy poured into its side.

As its claws plunged toward him, Britton opened another gate, cutting off the arm at the shoulder, so that the black smoke of the wound, odorless, heavy, and unspeakably cold, covered him.

With a final shriek, the Mountain God turned and waved its good arm at the air behind it. The strange shimmering stopped, brushed over by the creature's fingertips. Then it turned and bounded out of the circle so fast that it practically vanished, its cries suddenly trailing into the distance.

All around them, the Apache succumbed, dragged to the ground and strangled by their own dead ancestors or cooked beyond recognition by the legion of elementals surging from the bonfire. Fitzy stepped among the corpses, leading with his pistol, poking into each wickiup, looking for his quarry. 'Spread out!' he shouted. 'Don't let anyone past you! Whisper those damned chickenshit bunnies back here and get a perimeter set up!'

But Britton didn't move. He looked around the circle as the warmth slowly returned to his body, aghast at the field of corpses. There had been far more than thirty, closer to seventy, he guessed. The long hair had fooled his military-tuned mind. They weren't mostly men at all.

There were women, at least a dozen girls. In a few places, Britton could see elderly couples who had clung to one another before one of Truelove's zombies had covered them. The few fighting men had died grimacing, but they looked nothing like the monsters he'd watched summon a plague of scorpions against their own.

Did you think they'd all be men? he asked himself. Did you think they'd all be the snarling killers you'd seen in those videos? Get real.

A stab of pain brought his hand to his shoulder. His fingers came away wet from where a round had grazed him. In the rush of battle, he hadn't felt it. As he recovered from the adrenaline, his broken arm began to throb with pain. He felt dizzy with revulsion as he looked back over the dead.

But horror competed with another emotion as Britton surveyed the carnage, and Fitzy emerged from a wickiup with Chatto, Suppressed and zip-cuffed.

Britton wrestled with this new emotion before finally giving in to it, blossoming as it did from having taken on a small army and a monster from the Source and emerging victorious.

Pride.

Chatto sat zip-cuffed in the chilly mud outside trailer B-6. Captain Day worked with two MPs, replacing the plastic with metal restraints before standing him up. Over his shoulder, two men in white lab coats were visible through one of Britton's gates. They stood around the spot where the Mountain God had first appeared, taking samples of the air and shaking their heads over laptop computers.

Captain Day turned to Fitzy. 'On behalf of the Department of the Interior, thanks. This is really going to help us peel the onion and get down to the root of this insurgency.'

'It's my pleasure,' Fitzy said, smiling at the Coven. 'I have to admit that even a stopped clock can be right twice a day.'

The rare compliment spread grins across all of their faces. Britton laughed, then felt instantly ashamed, recalling the faces of the dead.

'You laugh?' Chatto called to him, his voice old and careworn, as if sensing Britton's conflict. 'What have you done today? Killed men for the crime of wanting to be free? For using the talents given to them by the Creator?'

'Shut the hell up,' Day shouted, but Chatto ignored him, his eyes chips of flint as he glared at Britton.

'You're a slave,' he said. 'All you did tonight was cement your bonds. You will never know freedom. You think just because you can't see your prison bars they're not there? Pretty jail's still a jail.'

Day backhanded the Apache into silence. The MPs threw him roughly forward and walked him into the trailer, leaving Day shaking his head.

'Sorry,' he said. 'He won't be laughing in a couple of hours, and the tribal council won't be laughing when he rolls over on them.'

'That thing came from here, didn't it?' Britton asked him, remembering the strange shimmering he'd seen behind the snarling black creature. 'That's the real reason we went after him. There's some kind of link. That's what you want him to tell you about.'

'Now it's your turn to shut the hell up,' Fitzy growled. 'You've got some scrapes on you. Much as it would amuse me to leave you here in agony, you are government property, and it's my solemn duty to see you're patched up. I'll radio for a Physiomancer.'

But Britton wasn't listening. He was thinking of men who were really just tools. He was thinking of pretty jails.

The Apache had tried to hurt Downer, but was that so different than Scylla's reasoned murder? Or Swift's senseless rage? The outpouring of anger from a powerless and desperate quarry? A mad revenge for the bodies of the women and children they knew they would soon be mourning? Were they so different from the Goblins, fighting for their land?

Selfer criminal or government tool. He had to find a better way. He looked at the pride and sense of belonging in the eyes of the rest of the Coven. He felt it himself.

But Scylla's words kept returning to his mind. He would always belong to them. His magic would only be a tool for their purposes, for bringing people like these to their end. Fitzy's words followed Scylla's. *You remember one thing, contractor. I am not your friend. I am not your comrade in arms. I am here to make you into a righteous engine of war. Nothing more, nothing less. You're paid to be a weapon, not a hero. Remember that.*

Dead Goblins, dead women and children. Britton had been the tool the army gripped to bring about their end.

He realized with a sudden twisting of his guts that maybe he hadn't meant it when he had told Fitzy that he got it.

Maybe it was time to run again.

Chapter Twenty-Eight
Oplan

Physiomancy is frequently credited as a healing art. This reputation is deserved, as its primary application is the knitting of broken flesh. But most students of the arcane do not fully appreciate that Physiomancy is merely a neutral manipulation of live flesh. As readily as it can be used to knit, it can be used to tear. Such offensive Physiomancy is commonly known as 'Rending' and is among those magical practices specifically prohibited by amendment to the Geneva Convention and the McGauer-Linden Act.

– Avery Whiting
Modern Arcana: Theory and Practice

The screams kept him awake all night – high and shrill, almost childlike. He knew they were Chatto's.

Britton, who now had no trouble sleeping through the Goblin's magical attacks or the screaming return fire of the automatic defenses, was haunted by the tortured cries of this one man. He rolled back and forth in his hooch, pulling his pillow over his head. They hadn't bothered to take Chatto far; they'd gone to work on him immediately. Britton's schoolhouse by the P pods had temporarily become their base of operations.

This is the man responsible for the murders you saw in those videos, Britton reminded himself. *This is the man who would have gladly seen Downer raped.*

But the screams carried to him, and he realized that he

didn't care. *We're supposed to be the good guys. That's what gives us the right to judge Selfers. Because our way is better.*

The thought propelled him to his feet and sent him racing out of the hooch, pushing in the direction of trailer B-6. *Idiot! What do you hope to accomplish?* he asked himself.

But his feet wouldn't stop moving until the screaming became a gurgling sigh, followed by silence. He stopped, only a few hundred feet from the trailer, able to see the external sodium light glinting in the dark, beset by clouds of insects, drawn by its false-moon promise.

The light cast a sick, yellow sheen on the trailer door as it slid open, and two soldiers emerged, silhouetted against the blackness, dragging something lumpen and wet into the light.

A man followed them out, wiping his hands on his trousers, breathing heavily. He moved toward Britton, lighting a cigarette as he came. The man almost collided with him in the darkness, then fell back a step in surprise. The light from the cigarette showed the pale, doughy cheeks and blue hospital scrubs of Captain Hayes. The Physiomancer was covered in gore. His scrubs were so plastered with blood that they looked metallic under the moonlight. He gave Britton an exhausted smile.

'You should get to bed,' Hayes said. 'You're going to be a busy boy tomorrow.' He pushed past Britton and made his way out of P block.

Britton knew he should say something, impede Hayes's progress, do anything other than stand there dumbly, staring at B-6's now-closed door. But he couldn't move, couldn't speak. He felt drained of all energy. *I did this. As surely as I saved the lives of those marines, I cost that man his. People die in war. Criminals pay for their crimes, sometimes with their lives. So why does this feel so wrong?* He didn't know what Hayes had done to Chatto behind that trailer door, but he could imagine.

I can't do this anymore. I can't work with or for these people. No matter what Therese or the rest of Shadow Coven are doing, I have to go. I have to find a way out of here.

* * *

Britton didn't sleep another wink that night. His mind raced with escape plans. He couldn't go to Scylla, and Therese wasn't ready to help him yet. Where would he run to? After what he had seen at Mescalero, the Selfers trying to rape Downer, could he ever take refuge there? He lay awake, brainstorming, and was dizzy from fatigue when Fitzy finally came for him, near sunset on the following day.

'Got some more work for you,' the chief warrant officer said. 'Follow me.'

They mounted one of the ever-present electric golf carts and buzzed back into the training area, following signs for the Terramantic Engineering Range. The cart bumped to a stop just as the sun was dipping below the horizon, washing all in shades of simmering orange. A broad field was stripped bare of plant growth, the dry ground randomly soaring upward into earthen bridges and ramparts. A giant length of wall ran ten feet, trailing off into mud. A tank stood on it, empty and silent, treads peeking over the edge.

Fitzy got out of the cart and beckoned to Britton, making his way toward a long wall of raised earth.

'I was hoping for more time, but the old man says we've gotta be ready to jump as early as tomorrow.' He paused at the wall's edge. A white sign admonishing all that only authorized personnel were permitted behind it had been driven into the ground. 'Now, I know we normally use videos to give you a read on an area you're gating into, but this is an important run, and the brass wanted to be absolutely sure. So, this time we're giving you a simulated environment. You'll be gating in at sunset, so we need you to get it read now.'

The other side of the wall was a hastily constructed mock-up of a hotel entrance. Groups of contractors were still assembling a sweeping arc of broken pavement covered with sand and scrub cacti. The white paint on the broad awning was badly chipped and pocked with bullet holes. The sliding glass doors were covered with metal strips. A circular driveway, broad enough to host a fleet of vehicles, sported barricades of tires topped with barbed wire. Toppled statues, their arms adorned with bronze feathers, lay heaped beside the doorway. Wooden masks obscured their faces.

The SOC had gone so far as to pipe in smells. Britton noted the brimstone stink of diesel generators, burned rubber, and spent cordite.

'This is where the council is hiding out?' Britton asked. 'Or does this have something to do with how the Apache are getting their Mountain Gods over to the Home Plane? Maybe this is how they talk to the Goblin tribes?'

'It's not your job to worry about what it is or isn't, Keystone. It's your job to familiarize yourself with this set and gate your Coven to the infil point on command. You're lucky; we were going to use this to run exercises, but it turns out Chatto confirmed our suspicions, and we're going before his reporting gets stale. You have to admit, a physical mock-up beats the hell out of a video.'

Britton faced Fitzy. The chief warrant officer looked small, his bald forehead sheened with sweat.

'These aren't Goblins, sir. These are Americans.'

'You're goddamned right they're not Goblins,' Fitzy seethed. 'You'd better keep that thought foremost in your mind when we run this op, son. Grabbing Chatto is going to seem like a picnic compared to what we're going to face when we walk into the viper's very nest.'

'Americans, sir,' Britton repeated.

'Selfers,' Fitzy snapped back, 'and therefore dead. Did you forget ol' tons o' fun you tackled down in those sewers? Did you miss the point of those videos we showed you? You were not pardoned to pontificate. You were given a second chance to follow orders and do your damned job. Is that perfectly clear?'

A tool. A weapon. Not a person. Remember that.

Britton stared at him for a moment before turning back to the staged scenery before him.

After a moment, Fitzy shifted uncomfortably behind him. 'Got it?'

Britton nodded.

'Are you sure? You've got it fixed?'

Britton turned to face him again. He gestured to his eyes, letting the malevolence show. 'Solid, sir. I'm good to go.'

* * *

Britton brooded over his drink in the OC that night, the tension around him palpable. His mind wrestled with escape plans, all of them ending with his heart exploding. The rest of the Coven felt it. Truelove sat nervously beside him. He tried starting a conversation twice, both times with nervous platitudes, before Richards drew him off.

All the training. All the excitement. All the pleasure that had grown from mastering his magic. For what? Killing his own people? The darkness congealed in his mind. He'd half a mind to confront Fitzy, Suppression or no, and give him the drubbing he deserved. He'd die, to be sure, but it seemed that he'd have to choose between that and being a murderer anyway. Maybe death was more honorable.

Only the thought of Therese kept him seated and docile. He had her back. That was something. There was a possibility that, with time, she could get him out of there. But how long would it take before she felt confident to help him? And what would they make him do in the interim? Scylla had promised to help him right now. All he had to do was get the Suppression off her for five minutes.

He could feel Downer's eyes on the back of his head. He was killing the joy she felt at her own burgeoning skill, and she resented it. Please, he thought. *Don't say anything. Just leave me alone tonight.*

'What is it now?' she asked.

'I'm in no mood, little girl,' he answered.

'Excuse me?' she asked.

'I'm warning you. Leave me the hell alone,' Britton said, turning to face her.

Richards and Truelove stood. 'Easy, you two,' Truelove said.

Britton held the Necromancer's eyes. 'Shut the hell up.'

Truelove turned and swallowed. Richards stood still behind him, a hand on his shoulder.

'What is your problem tonight?' Downer asked. 'Are you still pissed about the assault? Because you need to get the hell over that.'

'Forget it,' Britton said.

But Downer's hackles were up. 'What, then?'

'Nothing.' He swallowed hard, trying to suck down the simmering resentment. *It's not her fault. Don't take it out on her*. But he saw her as she was – completely sold on the SOC's bill of goods. *A little while ago, you were running. There's no zealot like a new convert*. The thought infuriated him. She didn't care what she belonged to so long as she belonged somewhere. *Are you so different?*

'Tell me,' she demanded, 'or else get over yourself and apologize to Rictus.'

'Did you miss the screaming last night? Am I the only person on earth who heard it?'

Truelove looked at his feet. Downer's face fell. 'That's not our business.'

'What the hell are you talking about?' Britton asked. 'It's not only our business. It's our fault!'

'You don't know what happened,' she said, shaking her head.

'No, you're right, I don't *know* what happened. But I'm not retarded, so I can hazard a fucking guess. And, surprise, surprise! Fitzy had me prep for our next op.'

Downer's anger vanished. She pressed forward, Truelove and Richards coming with her. 'Seriously? What was it? When do we go? What are we doing?'

'That's what you care about?' Britton asked. 'Never mind the screams in the night. What's our next op?'

'Damned right that's what I care about!' Downer said. 'What is it?'

He shook his head. 'It's . . . forget it. Fitzy probably doesn't want you to know.'

'Fuck that! You can't pull that crap! You have to tell us now.' She tugged on his arm.

He jerked his arm away, standing. Downer leapt back, frowning.

'Don't pretend you don't know! It's fucking Mescalero, all right?' he said. 'Are you happy now?'

'What, the reservation again?' Richards asked.

Britton nodded. 'Yeah. I recognized that . . . casino or resort or whatever. You know, the one from the news.'

'I knew it! That's Apache Selfer HQ!' Downer jumped for

joy. 'Holy crap! Chatto talked! He rolled over and gave them up!'

Britton snarled. 'Are you kidding me? Do you realize what they did to him to get him to talk? You were crowing about protecting your country. You went on and on about narco-terrorists or pirates or whatever bullshit you were into.'

She looked at him, uncomprehending.

'These are Americans!' he raged. 'This is our own country! We're not going to China or Somalia, you idiot! We're going to New Mexico! They tortured that guy all night, and we lay there right next to it, and we didn't do anything!'

Downer shook her head. 'Sometimes you have to break eggs to make an omelet. Did you forget the videos? They're Selfers . . .'

'So were you just five damned minutes ago! And those videos are bullshit! Half the people we took out going after Chatto were girls! Little fucking girls!' Britton shouted, taking a step forward. Richards put a hand on his chest, and Britton slapped it away, sending him backward into Truelove. Both sprawled against the bar.

An instant later, the mud floor rose up into a fist that gripped Britton's throat.

'Don't,' Richards said, leaning against the bar. 'Not another step.'

Britton opened a small gate, severing the fist at the wrist. The dirt fingers fell away from his neck. Then Britton felt his magic roll back, and he turned to Downer.

'That's right,' she said. 'You think you're such hot shit because Portamancy is so rare? Without it, you're just a bruiser. And there are three of us. We can all Suppress now.'

A little girl, a pasty nerd, and a doughy older man. Britton thought they'd need three more if they wanted to take him on. An instant later, he regretted that thought. As badly as the anger choked him, what was he going to do? Pummel a little girl because she was doing as she was told? Because she'd found the home he wanted for himself? The SOC wasn't going to make him kill his own countrymen. But neither was it going to make him swat little girls.

'Forget this,' he said, turning to the door. 'You can go

rampaging through a reservation if you want. This isn't what I signed up for.' *And just what the hell do you think they'll say? "Oh, that's fine, Oscar. You can sit this one out. Maybe you'd prefer some other missions that you find more personally agreeable.' They'll pop that cork in your chest, or you'll wind up in a blue hospital gown like Billy.*

He hauled open the door just as Downer fired back a retort, but Britton didn't hear it; his attention was completely fixed on the scene outside.

Fitzy knelt over Marty, who sprawled in the mud that had frozen hard in the cold air. The chief warrant officer's fist impacted the Goblin's oversized head again and again, sending it bouncing off the ground. Marty's shoulders were limp, his eyes shut. His mouth trickled blood.

Behind Fitzy, two MPs stood impassively, carbines cradled in the crooks of their arms.

Fitzy snarled, incoherent words punctuated each blow. His face was a shade of purple visible even in the darkness.

And then Britton's legs were moving.

Behind him, Truelove shouted a warning, but Britton was already throwing his shoulder into Fitzy, knocking the Master Suppressor off Marty's chest and sending him sprawling. Britton could smell the whiskey even from that distance. The MPs started forward, noted the Shadow Coven uniform, and paused.

'What the hell are you doing?' Britton shrieked at Fitzy, who had begun to scramble to his feet. He knelt at Marty's side, chafing the Goblin's wrists. 'Marty! Are you okay? Marty!' The creature stirred weakly, groaning.

Britton looked up just as Fitzy's boot swung toward him. It was too late to dodge, but he managed to catch the blow mostly on his neck and shoulder. He launched over Marty and skinned his hands, choking on the dust kicked up by the impact.

'I told you he wasn't supposed to drink with you,' Fitzy said through clenched teeth. 'This little fucker was on his way here from the cash. Not sure what it is you people don't understand about orders, but we're going to get that straightened out right now.' He started toward Britton, who rose to his feet.

Out of the corner of his eye, Britton spotted Truelove dragging Marty out of the way. The MPs looked on, amused.

'You're going to beat him to death for trying to have a drink with his friends?' Britton raged.

'No, I'm going to beat him to death for eating the eyes out of the still-warm corpse of an American soldier!' Fitzy hissed. 'And when I'm done, I'm going to teach you some manners.'

He turned toward Truelove. 'Get the hell away from him, needledick. He's got dues to pay.'

Truelove dropped Marty and scrambled backward on his skinny buttocks. 'Sir, it's a custom! They do it to honor their dead!'

The wheels clicked in Britton's mind. He remembered the young specialist's burned body in the cash, Therese standing by. *Lenko must have died. Oh God, Marty.*

'Good,' Fitzy said, reaching down to grab Marty's ankle. 'You love them so much. You can eat this piece of crap's eyes right after I kill him.'

And then he was sputtering, with Britton's arm locked around his neck. He punched Fitzy hard in the kidney, and the chief warrant officer dropped Marty, grunting.

'You'll have to kill me first,' Britton whispered in his ear, then he pivoted his hip, slamming Fitzy face-first into the dirt.

The chief warrant officer lay there for a moment, stunned. The rest of Shadow Coven stood openmouthed. The MPs started forward, but Fitzy began to rise to his hands and knees. He waved a hand at them, and they stopped, looking askance.

Fitzy slowly got to his feet, shaking his head. He spit out a tooth, a trail of blood making its way slowly down his cheek. The face above it was scraped raw, mud caking the wound. One eye was already beginning to swell shut.

'If that's what you want,' he whispered, 'who am I to deny you?'

He spread his hands, and Britton felt the Suppression take hold as Fitzy started forward. Rage countered the alcohol, making him incredibly fast. He threw a jab at Britton's face and followed with a kick as soon as Britton had swatted it aside. The boot tip caught him in the thigh, sending him staggering backward, his aching leg buckling under him.

'You're fucking dead, you sack of shit,' Fitzy said, advancing. 'I tried. I really did. But some people absolutely cannot be taught.' He pumped a right uppercut at Britton's jaw, but it was a feint. The real blow hammered down from the other hand as Britton caught his right wrist. It collided with his ear, filling his vision with stars and sending him down to the mud again.

Britton kicked out blindly and caught Fitzy's ankle. Fitzy cried out in pain and dropped, breaking his fall with a sharp elbow colliding with Britton's ribs. Britton gulped for oxygen, drowning in nausea as he struggled to pull away from Fitzy's oppressive weight. The chief warrant officer sprawled on him, smothering him with his bulk. His hands, raw and mud-crusted, found Britton's throat and began to squeeze. Britton locked his hands on Fitzy's wrists, shaking left and right, but the chief warrant officer's grip wouldn't move. The gulping continued, the nausea intensified, the world shrank to a gray tunnel. The vise constricted until his neck registered only a steady fire that vanished beneath the desperate cry for oxygen.

Britton hammered his knee upward, finding soft flesh again and again. Fitzy only grunted, then shouted something to the MPs, and then all sight and sound was gone as Britton's lungs cried out for air. *He's really going to kill me. He's really that crazy. This is how I die.*

And then, suddenly, the pressure was gone. Pain awakened him. His neck was a ring of fire, his head stuffed with molten lead. Fitzy's weight lifted off him. Britton's ears filled with the sound of roaring blood, his eyes with blurry light. He rolled onto his stomach and retched, struggling to his hands and knees as vision returned.

The roaring sound in his ears resolved into words. Fitzy's voice. 'Do you have any idea what you're doing?'

Truelove answered, stumbling over the words. 'I can't let you do this, sir.'

Britton stood, his vision slowly coming clear. Fitzy had backed up to the corner of the chow-hall tent. Before him, bright tusks glittering, lurched the embalmed corpse of the silver boar from the OC. Truelove stood behind it, hand outstretched. Fitzy kicked at the animated corpse experimentally, then jerked his boot back, the sole gouged by the sharp, metallic bristles.

'You're an idiot, Rictus,' Fitzy said, extending a hand. 'I can switch that magic off.'

'But then you'd switch mine on,' Britton slurred through the clearing fog. He maneuvered around Fitzy's shoulder, just enough for the Master Suppressor to see him, but not close enough for a strike. 'And I will cut off your fucking head just as soon as I can open a gate . . . sir.' He spit out the last word.

The boar lurched forward another step, shambling on sharp metallic hooves. Its mouth worked, chunks of hardened yellow embalming fluid flaking out of the corners.

Fitzy jerked his head from the boar to Britton, then up to Truelove and back again.

His eyes widened and his jaw trembled.

Fear, Britton realized. *Holy crap, this is Fitzy afraid*.

Fitzy's gaze sawed left and right. Britton followed his eyes. The MPs were gone. Fitzy turned to Downer and Richards, standing wide eyed outside the OC's entrance. 'You two! Give me a goddamned hand here!'

Neither of them moved.

Fitzy's eyes narrowed again as he turned back to Truelove. 'I swear to God you will fucking pay for this. You all will. This is gross insubordination. This is fucking mutiny. You are all going to die.'

Truelove swallowed. Britton felt a cold lump in his stomach. The ATTD throbbed in his chest. He knew it was no lie.

But he would be damned if he'd show that to Fitzy. 'That'd be fine, sir. Now you run along and have a great day.'

He motioned to Truelove, who backed the boar off a couple of steps.

Fitzy took a hesitant step away, skirting the boar. He looked back at them, meeting each of their eyes in turn.

'I don't know what the hell you all think you've accomplished,' he said, 'but I assure you you've just earned yourself a world of hurt.'

He spun on his heel and stalked down the track, leaving Shadow Coven in stunned silence behind him.

They stared at Fitzy's shrinking back until it was swallowed by the darkness. Then Britton blew out his breath, and Truelove sat down abruptly, the boar collapsing in a broken heap.

'Oh shit,' the Necromancer whined into his hands, 'we're so fucking dead. I can't believe I just did that.'

Downer stared at him, mouth opening and closing.

'I've got to get the hell out of here,' Richards said, and took off after Fitzy.

'You saved my life,' Britton managed. 'Thank you.'

'You can thank me graveside,' Truelove said. 'Do you honestly think command is going to tolerate mutinous Probe contractors? Oh my God, we are so fucking dead.'

'He was going to kill Marty,' Britton offered.

'Marty's a fucking Goblin!' Truelove said. 'Do you really think anyone cares other than us?'

'Wait,' Britton said, looking around. 'Where is Marty?'

'The MPs took him,' Downer said, her voice stunned.

'Took him where?' Britton asked, panic rising in his throat.

'Where the hell do you think?' Truelove asked, tears streaming down his face. 'They're going to fire him. He's as good as dead. We didn't accomplish a goddamn thing.'

Chapter Twenty-Nine
Release

What is magic, really? It is the monkey wrench in the works. It is the great leveler. Suddenly, without warning, the kid who bags your groceries is stronger than an infantry division. The homeless guy you ignored for years has the power to cure your scoliosis. The criminal on death row can stop a forest fire or save a cruise ship trapped in a storm. Magic is the death of social structure. It has taken the completed puzzle, broken the pieces apart, and tossed them in the air. It's up to us to put them back together again. The new picture they form will be very different from the old one.

– Johnathan Tillich, *Magic and Society, Part VI*
Public Radio Network

Britton took off running, not looking back.

'Where the hell are you going?' Downer shouted after him.

He didn't answer. *To save Marty. To finish this.*

His boots pounded the semifrozen mud toward the cash. The scenery passed on either side of him, a blur of converted trailers, piled sandbags, soldiers turning their heads to take in the Probe contractor hurtling past them.

The cash was quieter than usual, but Britton didn't fail to notice the MPs patrolling the tent entrance. They noted his hurried entry but made no move to stop him as he burst through the flaps. The cash floor was equally quiet and guarded. Another small knot of MPs stood ready beneath the signs to the dental unit.

That's over where Marty works. That's where they took him.

What did he think he was going to do? Charge in there and carry Marty away? They'd shoot him dead. *No, my magic will stop them.* The feeling of power was heady, he could crush them if he wanted. He really could save Marty.

And drop dead in the mud, clutching a chest that slowly hemorrhaged purple.

The ATTD has got to come out. Therese.

No, she wasn't ready.

Scylla, then. But how could he?

But there was no time to ponder it. Scylla was the known quantity. Therese wasn't sure. Truelove's words echoed in his mind. *They're going to fire him. He's as good as dead.*

There was no time. If he was going to save Marty, he had to do this now.

Britton burst from the cash tent, making for the SASS.

Night was the SASS's slow time. The enrollees were all in their bunks beneath the corrugated-metal domes of the Quonset huts. The guards lazed in the parapets and towers, casting half-lidded gazes out into the semidarkness. Britton forced himself to measure his stride, to walk casually toward the gate, hands in his pockets. He briefly considered trying to whistle and abandoned the idea. The knot of panic passing between his stomach and throat wouldn't permit it.

It felt like it took an eternity to walk all the way to the gate at that maddeningly casual pace. Every step was a delay during which Marty's captors could push him outside the wire, thank him for his service, and leave him to die. He couldn't let that happen.

But neither could he hurry, not if his plan was to work.

One of the gate guards squinted in the darkness, began to salute, then dropped his arm when he realized that Britton was a contractor. 'Good evening, sir,' he said.

'Evening,' Britton said, doing his utmost to keep his voice even, unconcerned. 'What's going on?' It came out as a rasping croak, his words quaking. *Oh God, they'll know. They'll know something's wrong.*

''Nother day, 'nother dollar,' the guard drawled, unconcerned. 'What can I do for you?'

'I'm Keystone, Umbra Coven. I used to be an enrollee here.' Britton's confidence grew.

'I recognize you, sir. What's going on?'

'Chief Warrant Officer Fitzsimmons wanted me to drop something off with Major Salamander. Just take a second,' he said, flashing his badge.

He had nothing to drop off. What if the guard asked to see whatever it was? He would say it was a message. But what message? His mind spun as he tried to think of something, but the guard was already nodding and sliding the barrier out of the way.

Britton swallowed and trotted through, trying to look unhurried as he made his way toward the Quonset huts. The pillbox hung in his peripheral vision, two Suppressors on duty, one seated on a camp chair just outside the door.

Britton risked a look over his shoulder. The gate guards were already out of view. The guards in the towers barely spared him a glance, their bored eyes cast outward.

Britton broke off and veered to his right, moving toward the pillbox. One Suppressor stood in the darkness, his face illuminated by the tip of his cigarette. The other leaned against the wall, camp chair tilted back. He rocked it forward so it stood straight and waved distractedly. 'Hey.'

'Hey, guy,' Britton said, forcing himself to slow down. 'Life in the fast lane, eh?'

'No doubt,' the Suppressor said, 'what's going o . . .'

But Britton had crossed the last few steps between them and snapped open a gate behind him. The Suppressor began to turn, seeing the static shimmer of the light in his peripheral vision, as Britton planted a boot in his chest and kicked him through, sending him to sprawl on the floor of Portcullis's loading bay.

The other Suppressor had only begun to turn toward him as Britton pivoted on his leg, rocketing his foot up and over to send it crashing into his temple. The Suppressor crumpled, unconscious, the lit cigarette going dark in the mud. Britton looked back at the Suppressor he'd kicked through the gate.

'I'm sorry,' he said. The Suppressor only gawked at him, jaw gaping, from the other side of the gate, propped up on one elbow on the concrete floor.

Then Britton shut the gate, and the man was gone.

'Sir? Hello?' A call came from one of the towers beside the gatehouse, quickly followed by 'Oh, Christ!' A searchlight lit, the beam dancing crazily across the ground before him. Voices began to call out.

Britton turned and pounded on the rusted door. 'Damn it, Scylla! Wake the hell up!'

Her voice came from the other side, as calm and poised as if she had been awake, standing there the entire time. 'I'm awake, Oscar. Thanks for coming.'

The first bullet whined over his shoulder to tear a chunk from the concrete wall. Britton threw open a gate and crouched behind it as an alarm sounded. Bullets whistled toward him, whisking through the gate and out over the star-dappled field where he'd sheltered in Nelson's barn what felt like an eternity ago. Boots thudded in the mud, coming toward him. More shouting.

He tried to sneak a look around the gate to see what he faced, but was driven quickly back by the increasing hail of bullets around him. What the hell was taking Scylla so long? Maybe she had lied. Maybe she couldn't help him. Maybe she was cowering inside her concrete prison and waiting for him to die.

The boots thudded closer, almost on top of him by then. He could see the doors to the Quonset huts off to his left slamming open. Swift stood there, Peapod, Tsunami, and some of the other enrollees behind him, gaping. Major Salamander emerged from another door, his body already wreathed in bright orange flame. Britton felt a current reach out, snaking into his own, rolling it back, snapping the gate shut.

He crouched in the mud, eyes closed, waiting for the bullets to tear him apart.

And then the pillbox disintegrated.

One moment, Britton had crouched between his gate and the firmness of the concrete wall. The next, his back was coated in blowing concrete dust, and the rusted scraps of pitted metal that had once been the pillbox door. Scylla stood in the midst of the ruin, her pale mouth stretched in a vulpine smile. Her current was wild, intense. Britton felt it surging all around him, nearly suffocating in its enormity. The boots stopped pounding, the steady thrum of the bullets ceased. Britton's magic flooded back into him as the Suppression dropped. He stood and looked around.

The first thing he saw was Salamander, sprawling in the mud, clutching at his stomach, his flame out. A company of guards writhed in the dirt before him, also grasping their abdomens, shrieking. 'My, oh my.' Scylla smiled. 'I have been waiting for this for a very, very long time.'

Swift turned, pushed back against his fellow inmates, and retreated inside the hut, slamming the door behind him.

'Scylla,' Britton cried. 'Please. I kept my part of the bargain. Take this thing out of my chest.'

She looked at him, her eyes distant, distracted, as if noticing him for the first time. 'Indubitably. But first, let a girl stretch her legs.'

The SASS collapsed. The chain-link fencing shuddered, the polyurethane coating bubbling and cracking off, the metal first rusting, then melting, then blowing apart. The wooden towers sagged, wet-looking, and finally collapsed into black sludge that pooled in stinking bogs. The schoolhouse collapsed with the wet sound of a smashed cantaloupe. The guards writhed, then stopped screaming, their flesh turning transparent, then black, then fluid, seeping into the ground to leave purple skeletons, which soon followed suit, dissipating into a runny yellowish slime the color of turned egg yolks. A few fell from the heights of the parapets, silent, rotting as they went, splattering on the hard ground in sulfurous puffs. Britton tried to count the dead. Had they said she'd killed twenty? There must have been fifty gone at a stroke. The Suppressor he'd kicked into unconsciousness was reduced to a puddle of human sludge. Not a guard was alive as far as he could see. Britton's stomach spasmed in horror.

You did this, he said to himself. *You let her go.*

The Quonset huts, with the enrollees inside, so far as Britton could tell, were untouched.

Scylla strode toward Salamander, still whole and vomiting on the ground, clawing at his belly.

'I told you,' she crooned to him. 'I told you, didn't I? I told you that this was coming.'

'Oh, God,' the major managed, his feet kicking out. He vomited again, all blood this time.

'Scylla!' Britton shouted. 'Stop it! Jesus! This wasn't the deal! You were supposed to take the bomb out!'

'And I will,' Scylla said. 'Just as soon as I'm finished here.

'I'm going to leave you alive,' she said to Salamander. 'Do you know that? First, I'm going to mix up your guts so that no Healer can ever fix them quite right, then I'm going to waltz out of here right in front of your face, so you can see what comes of trying to hold your betters.'

Salamander's mouth worked, he was trying to speak, but nothing came out save for the thick liquid, black now, leaking from the corner of his mouth.

Britton shuddered. *You knew this would happen. This is your fault.* His eyes swept the fetid pools that had once been people, his mind already stretching to accept their deaths on his conscience. The only thing he could do was put a stop to it. Did the rest of the FOB yet know what had happened here? Would they set off the ATTD? At this point, would it be more than he deserved? How many dead because of him? He couldn't permit himself to think about it.

He gathered his magic and threw it out toward her, Suppressing the flow that flooded into the major. He felt for the string of magic, Scylla's outward flowing current, where it connected to Major Salamander's weakly stirring form, and directed his own current there, trying to override it. For a brief moment, he felt Scylla's magic roll back, then her tide surged through his, gripping the major ever more tightly. Her head whipped toward Britton, and she snarled.

'I told you to wait until I was finished.'

'No way,' he said. 'I can't let you kill him.'

'You can't stop me either, you idiot,' she said. 'You don't

fucking get it, do you? I am not in the habit of sparing cockroaches, Oscar. Nor do I take kindly to those who interfere with my efforts at extermination.'

'If you kill him, I'll never gate you out of here.'

Scylla threw back her head and laughed. 'I don't need you to gate me out of here, Oscar. I never did. All I needed was for you to get me free of the Suppression, and in that capacity, you have performed admirably.'

Britton gasped as his own gut clenched. He was overcome with nausea so intense that he felt his stomach was lurching inside him, kicking, expanding, struggling to escape. His throat hitched, trying to expel the burning bile that was rising within, but nothing would come out. He struggled to breathe, his knees going out from under him, and he fell on his side, the frozen mud blessedly cool against his cheek. A few feet away, Major Salamander was curled in the same posture, his eyes staring into Britton's own, seeing nothing.

'I understand,' Scylla's voice was untroubled, as if nothing had happened. 'It's Stockholm syndrome, or something similar. You're identifying with your captors, sympathizing with them. You just need a moment to see reason. You just need a reminder of what you are.'

She reached toward him, clenching her fist. He hadn't thought his stomach could get any worse, but he was wrong. His body locked, the nausea so powerful that it coursed through him until it felt as if the pores of his skin would vomit blood in an effort to vent the illness. He made no sound. Through his graying vision, he saw Major Salamander's head slumped in the mud, a thin trickle of bloody drool sliding down his chin.

'Feel that? That's your reminder. That's what you are, what I am. It's what's in us both. Can you feel that?' She paused, seeming to wait for an answer, but Britton could barely hear her, suffused as he was by a nausea that far transcended pain.

'That's power, Oscar. That's your birthright. Now, you understand what it is. You think the SOC has taught you anything? That Dampener has castrated you, Oscar. You have no idea what you're truly capable of. And now that you have a sample of it, can we kindly dispense with the moralizing and get the hell out of here?'

Just as quickly as her magic had gripped him, it was gone, and Britton sigh-retched his relief, shuddering with the taste of the fresh air, feeling his muscles slowly unclench. Major Salamander lay opposite him, perfectly still.

'We're wasting time, Oscar.' All kindness was gone from Scylla's voice. 'Let's go. I can still take the ATTD out once we're quit of this place. Show me that you've broken through their efforts to brainwash you. All you have to do is move us.'

Britton reached out a trembling hand toward Salamander, brushed his nose with his fingertips. No reaction. The major was dead.

'Come, Oscar,' she said, kneeling, 'let me help you up.'

Britton looked around him, leaning briefly into her hand under his upper arm. The SASS was completely laid waste. Only the Quonset huts where the enrollees lived stood untouched. Beyond them, the rotted wreckage was strewn around in the eerie silence, buildings, equipment, people.

Everywhere, puddles of vaguely man-shaped purple-and-black sludge. *Those used to be people.*

He shook off her arm. 'Fuck off. Kill me if you want to. I'm not opening shit.' He was still too weak to open a gate or try to Suppress her again. He could do little more than rise shakily to his knees.

'Don't be silly, Oscar,' she said, her voice matronly, chiding. 'Even now they're coming. What do you think they'll do if they find you here?'

'Fucking kill me, I hope,' he said. Her magic had released its grip on him, but his stomach still writhed with horror and guilt. *Escape was only her secondary motive*, he thought. *Revenge was the first.* 'I'm the idiot who freed you, who let you do this. Here's hoping they kill you, too.'

Scylla threw back her head and laughed. 'Pretty, but not too smart. They're not going to kill me, Oscar. If they were going to kill me, don't you think they would have done it already? They put a bit of explosive in your chest, and you quail and beg and do whatever they tell you. You never got it, did you, Oscar? I explained it plain and simple. They're not going to kill you unless they absolutely have to, unless you give them no choice at all. Only the tiniest fraction of the human population comes up Latent. We're too precious to kill. The corpses I left behind are all lost in the cost-benefit analysis.'

Britton got shakily to his feet but found he couldn't support his own weight, and crashed down again. 'They were going to carve up your brain,' he said. 'They figured they weren't getting enough for the cost of keeping you. They were going to make you like Billy. If I'd just waited a little while longer, they would have done it.'

Scylla turned to face the perimeter fence, with its open view of the plain beyond. The guard towers stacked just behind it were gone, reduced to piles of flaking crumbs, as if the wood had been ravaged by termites. She laughed, long and low.

'Well, I suppose I should thank you, then, shouldn't I? Because their return on investment is about to go way into the red.' She turned, bent down, placed her cool fingertips under his chin. Her face was serene, beautiful in the weird light of the Source's giant moon.

'One more chance, Oscar. Are you helping me? Or am I not going to get killed by the SOC on my own?'

For a moment, Britton's stomach fell. Her eyes, huge and welcoming, her mouth so steady, her voice so even. She knew something he didn't. It all made sense to her, there was no confusion, no doubt. Could she be right while the rest of the world was wrong?

But a stench curled in his nostrils, tendrils of stink, rotten, fetid. God knew how many bodies, the remains of people slowly dripping back into the earth. 'Fuck you,' he said, jerking his chin away from her.

'A pity,' she said. Britton could hear shouting, boots pounding in the distance, the whine of an electric motor. 'Well, I'm not going to kill you, Oscar Britton. Instead, I'm going to leave you to reap the rewards of your position. You're of no use to me if you're not going to open a gate, so you can keep that bomb in your chest. You clearly prefer it to freedom. I don't have the time to give you the education you so clearly need. I'm done mothering you, Oscar. If you live, if any of you live, perhaps you'll come to learn in time. When you do, I'd be much obliged of your company. Bye now.'

She turned back to the fence line and spread her arms. The strength of her gathering current overwhelmed him, and his stomach clenched anticipatorily, but Scylla was as good as her word, and the magic billowed outward instead.

The fence collapsed, rotting back to the mud like everything else inside the SASS. Scylla began to walk forward, her shoulders lightly dusted by swirling motes of rusted metal, disintegrating in the gentle breeze, as farther down the line, shouts erupted. Britton craned his head to one side, and his eyes widened. All along the FOB's perimeter, outside the SASS's boundaries, the concrete barricade walls were crumbling, the skeletal stubs of their rebar supports stuck out into the sky, briefly silhouetted against the moon before they, too, flashed into flaking rust and blew away in the wind. Machine-gun emplacements collapsed, antiair systems fell to pieces with light pops. Hundreds of men and women wailed and collapsed, before dripping into the earth, their bones laid bare in fetid clouds of what used to be their bodies.

It went on as far as Britton could see in both directions. An Apache, circling on patrol, highlighted Scylla within a bright halo of its searchlight before suddenly breaking apart, its component pieces wafting away on the breeze before they could even hit the ground, the pilots nowhere to be seen.

Britton saw a tank park off to his right vaporize, the neat rows of main battle tanks reduced to stinking hulks of desiccated ore. Buildings collapsed in rotting heaps. The wailing went on and on.

Scylla turned to Britton, winked, and waved, then turned on her heel and strode out of the FOB, disappearing in the blackness beyond.

As far as Britton could see in either direction, the FOB's perimeter had completely vanished. The base was entirely open, near as he could tell, to the countryside. Britton knelt, paralyzed with horror. So many dead, so much destruction. All because of him, because he had let her go.

And the ATTD still nestled in his heart, mocking him, reminding him that this swath of ruin had all been for nothing.

Movements in the grass beyond, small, hunched creatures rising out of the long grasses, calling to one another in their guttural tongue. Goblin spotters, Britton knew, from the hostile Defender tribes. They called in magical strikes every night. He'd seen the forward observers they used to direct them. Magic wasn't so different from artillery in that sense.

They stood in the saw-toothed, swaying grasses, their silhouettes betraying utter shock.

Then one of them blew a horn.

Another blast followed farther down the line, and another.

The line of destruction that Scylla had wrought was suddenly alive with clarion calls, low, rumbling blasts followed by shouts. Britton couldn't understand the language, but he knew full well what they were saying. *The defenses are down. The way is open. Come now, come now. We may never have this chance again*.

Panic-fueled adrenaline fired in Britton's heart and stomach, strength flowing back into him. He lurched to his feet, turning to the wasteland that had once been the SASS's gate, and ran with all he had.

Little Bighorn

The notion of Prohibited or 'Probe' schools is the root of the problem. What incentive do Probes have to cooperate, to turn themselves in? From the moment they Manifest, their very existence is illegal. When you relegate a class of people to pariah status, you are creating a ready-made insurgency. The problem here is that this particular one has the power to bring about a change in the regime.

– Loretta Kiwan,
Vice President Council on Latent-American Rights
Appearing on WorldSpan Networks *Counterpoint*

Chapter Thirty

Escape

You can call it blasphemy all you want, but the timing is perfect. Jesus Christ was an unusually powerful Physiomancer during the last Reawakening cycle. Your whole system of belief is based on a fluke of history. What you do with that realization is your problem, but it sure as hell should deflate your basis for oppressing homosexuals, outlawing abortion, and prohibiting magical schools.

– Mary Copburn, Council for Ethical Atheism

With every step, Britton's mind returned to his heart. He imagined that he could feel the ATTD bouncing, dancing in his ventricle, waiting for the signal that would tell it to end him. His feet pounded with the rhythm of his heartbeat. Pound, pulse, pound, pulse, pound. Boom? When would the boom come?

Maybe Scylla was right; maybe he was worth too much. But he wasn't taking any chances. The cash tent loomed before him, oddly quiet considering what had just happened.

In the distance, gunfire was erupting in the near-ceaseless staccato that spoke of real engagement. Several helicopters buzzed overhead.

Britton burst through the cash flaps, charging into the trauma unit. Several orderlies stared at him, but all the MPs were gone. *Probably busy guarding Marty*, he thought, *or gone to see what the hell is going on out there.*

Therese stood in the trauma unit, chatting sympathetically

with a young marine who was gingerly testing his shoulder, pressing his fingertips against one of the tent beams, then wincing in pain. 'Don't be such a baby,' she admonished. 'It won't even be sore by tomorrow.'

The marine grinned at her and opened his mouth to say something as Britton approached.

'I need to speak to you,' Britton said. His eyes bored into hers. *Don't ask, just come with me.*

Her eyes lighted on his bruised neck, his skinned hands and arms. Her nose wrinkled at the rotten stink on his clothes. She held his gaze for a moment before nodding. 'Follow me.'

She led him to the row of individual examination rooms, each kitted out with a long hospital gurney, complete with foam mattress, curtained off from the bustle of the main cash. As soon as she'd closed the curtain, he seized her elbows and drew her close.

'You've got to get this thing out of my chest, right now.'

'Are you crazy?' she whispered, shaking her head. 'I don't know if I can even do it, and I haven't had a chance to get the meds I need yet. The pain could kill you!'

He shook his head. 'I'm dead anyway, and so is Marty if you can't get me free of this thing in the next few minutes.'

'Oh God, Oscar. What happened?'

'It'll take too long to explain. Suffice to say that I fucked up big-time. This whole FOB is about to come down around our ears. They've got Marty, and they're probably going to kill him as soon as they realize what the hell is going on. While I'm at it, I need to get us all out of here. I can't do that if the SOC can track me. Therese, we don't have any time.' He took her hand and placed it on his chest. 'You have to try.'

She opened her mouth, and he caught her hands, hoping the intensity of his stare conveyed the urgency his words could not. 'Please, Therese. I need you to do this.'

She was silent another moment, then nodded. 'Get on the cot, hurry!'

She disappeared as he lay down, and returned again carrying a syringe. 'All I can get are some Benzodiazepines. It'll calm you down more than the Dampener, but it's not going to do anything for the pain.'

Britton thought of Marty and bit down. He felt his heart racing. *Still beating. That's something.* 'Let's get it over with.'

She looked at him, one hand on his forehead.

He held her eyes as he felt the syringe pierce his shoulder and the chemical wash into his bloodstream. It was followed by peace, a dizzy and relaxed euphoria. His heart slowed, the harsh sodium lights took on a halo of rainbows. Therese waxed more beautiful than ever.

'I love you,' he said before he knew he had spoken.

Therese smiled and leaned down, her lips brushing his forehead. He kept his eyes closed as she pulled away.

The doped fog washed over him, Britton's mind cart-wheeled, forming escape plans. Once the ATTD was out, and he could gate away, then what? Rescue Marty, bring Therese, somehow convince Umbra Coven to come with him, take them all somewhere the SOC could never follow.

But the SOC could always follow, couldn't they? Britton wasn't their only Portamancer. Billy's drooling face swam into his drug-addled vision. Anywhere Britton could go, the SOC could follow.

'Hang on, Oscar.' Therese's voice cut through his reverie. 'I'll do this as fast as I can.'

He felt something pressed against his mouth and opened to accept it. A small rubber ball. He bit down on it instinctively and heard a murmur of appreciation from Therese.

The warm ripples of her current intensified, dropping down into his chest, slipping behind his ribs and cradling his heart. They curled there, gripping the muscle. Britton could feel the tendrils moving through the valves and chambers. It tingled but didn't hurt. They probed. Britton could feel the magic gather, pause.

'There it is,' Therese said. 'Here we go.'

Agony. Pain like he had never known before. Scylla's assault on him had been nothing compared to this. His breath vanished, his vision gone white for the second time in less than an hour. A vise gripped his heart, each beat hammered so hard he felt it would pound him to fragments. He could feel the ATTD migrating, the flesh spasming to push it upward. The muscle shuddered, threatened to stop, but the tendrils of magic kept it beating steadily. But Therese couldn't keep the body's natural rhythm. Waves of agony sounded across his body as every cell cried out in rage at the flow of oxygen suddenly interrupted.

He tried to scream, but he couldn't move muscles completely locked in spite of the drugs coursing through him. His jaw clamped shut, teeth digging furrows in the rubber between them.

Pain became the whole of his universe, eternal, all-encompassing. Oscar Britton lay in it and prayed to die.

And then, mercifully, he did.

Stanley Britton stood naked, his wiry body strong as ironwood, the muscles mapping a rolling landscape beneath the skin. Only his face and silver-threaded hair betrayed his age. He hovered above the saw-edged grass, weird stars drifting overhead. Demon-horses cavorted around him, nuzzling his thighs, crooning affection. His fingertips touched lightly over their shaggy backs.

A huge stone resting on his chest, Oscar lay on his back and looked at his father. The weight crushed him. Blood lapped the edges.

'Dad,' he croaked. 'Dad, get it off. It hurts.'

'Sir,' Stanley said in Fitzy's voice. 'Show some god-damned respect.'

'It's killing me.'

'Funny how that works,' Stanley said. 'Just deserts, I'd say.'

'I'm sorry,' Oscar managed. 'I didn't want to . . .' The stone dug deeper, he felt his ribs give way beneath the weight, his lungs compressing. He could barely manage the air to speak.

'You always were a little slow on the uptake,' Stanley said. He gestured over his body. 'Do I look hurt to you? If I were any better, I'd need rubber pants. No, no. I'm just fine. You're the one who's dead.'

Snow swept around him, the air suddenly chill. The fat flakes rained down around the stone, soaking the blood, burying him. The cold swept into his veins, freezing him, making him leaden. A black shape blossomed behind Stanley's head, extending long slender limbs over his shoulders.

Oscar strained to make it out, but the blizzard picked up, obscuring his vision. Stanley vanished in the deluge until all Oscar could see was his head, leaning back into the crook of another's neck. The shadow behind him nuzzled him affectionately, like a lover.

'See you soon, son,' his father said, then the snow took Oscar, leaving only the crushing weight on his chest, constriction and lingering agony.

'Oscar.' The snow began to clear. The cold and agony remained.

'Oscar.' Not his father's voice. Someone else. Someone good.

'Oscar, come on.' Something battered his cheeks, he tried to move his head away from it, but the slaps continued.

The snow resolved into a canvas ceiling supported by metal poles. Harsh sodium lights.

The cash.

'Oscar, look at me.' Therese's almond eyes, wet with concern, filled his vision. She waved a hand in front of him.

Balanced on her fingertips was a steel insect, its segmented carapace still glossed with his blood. One end dangled a long wire, stingerlike. The other housed a clear plastic dome, pulsing a gentle blue light. Black numbers had been stenciled on the side.

'We got it,' he croaked. His voice burned in his throat.

'We got it,' she said, biting back tears. 'How are you?'

He began to sit up, the ball of pain in his chest expanded. His head swam with drugged bewilderment and nausea. He leaned over the table and dry-heaved, the spasm aggravating his agony.

'Oh, God,' he said.

Therese put her hands on his chest, whole and unscarred. 'Oscar, lie down. You can't move yet.'

He shook his head, the motion nearly made him pass out. 'No time. We've gotta get Marty.' *And after that? Later. Take it step by step.*

He swung his feet over the edge of the cot. They slammed down on the ground, and he nearly vomited again, but the solidity of a hard surface made him feel somewhat steadier.

'Oh, Jesus, you're crazy,' Therese said, putting her shoulder in his armpit to support him. The smell of her hair soothed him, then made him sick again. His vision faded and returned in time with the pulsing agony in his chest.

'They'll kill him,' he said, and forced his weight onto his feet. His knees failed him, and he sagged against Therese, who steadied herself with one hand on the cot.

She couldn't carry him. He'd have to dig deep. He took a shaking step.

It took them nearly a minute to get halfway across the tiny room, but they made it. Therese still dangled the ATTD between two fingers.

'No,' he croaked, 'get rid of it. It could go off any minute.'

Outside, the cash was erupting in noise and chaos. The word must have begun to arrive. A loud buzz of helicopters sounded overhead. Deep booms, some sounding like magic, some not.

Therese set the ATTD down on the cot and helped Britton walk. 'What's going on?'

'Later, we've got to move.'

'Where are we going?' she asked.

Britton slouched toward the dental unit. 'Just look for MPs.'

They found them in abundance. A knot of them swarmed the urinalysis section, carbines pointed earthward but fingers braced tensely over triggers. Marty stood placidly inside a protective ring of surly Goblin orderlies. They snarled in their language at a translator who sat behind a laptop, shouting questions. The tent thronged with onlookers, furious Goblins, soldiers, and orderlies alike. Half of the MPs faced inward, keeping the angry Goblins from assaulting the translator. The other half faced outward, keeping the equally enraged humans from storming Marty.

Truelove and Downer stood outside the ring of MPs, lending their shouts to the throng. Truelove spotted Britton and ran to him.

'They're trying to see if he had any accomplices on the staff,' the Necromancer said. 'I've been trying to tell them it's just a custom, but nobody is list— Wow. Are you okay?'

Britton nodded. 'Need to talk to him.'

Truelove glanced nervously from Britton to Therese and back. 'They're not going to let you.'

Boom. Boom. The crackle of gunfire. 'What the hell is going on out there?' Truelove asked. He took a step away from the circle, then looked nervously back to Marty.

'Stay here, I'm begging you,' Britton whispered as Therese helped him forward.

He tapped one of the MPs on the center of his body armor and pointed at the Goblin. The soldier wrinkled his brow. 'Shouldn't you be lying down?'

Therese gestured to Marty. 'Please! We all know what you're going to do to him, just let us say good-bye?'

'Fine by me, ma'am,' the MP said, 'so long as you're willing to pay for the lawyer when they write me up for disciplinary action.' He took a half step to better block their progress.

The Goblins continued to shout. The linguist typed furiously on his laptop, shouting back.

No time.

'Marty!' Britton bellowed. His lungs flexed with the effort, and the balloon of pain swamped him. He stumbled against Therese, and Truelove raced to help her hold him up.

Boom. Boom. Thup. Thup. Thup. Three MPs listened to their squawking radios, then took off, running for the cash entrance.

Marty looked up, eyes widening as he noticed Britton. He began to shout.

The Goblins around him surged, throwing themselves at the MPs. The ring widened in reaction, the linguist scrambling backward, snatching up his laptop. The crowd of onlookers stumbled backward, and the tent shook.

'I see him!' Marty shouted. 'I see friend!'

The MP officer, a pale-faced lieutenant who looked almost as young as Downer, pulled out his pistol, leveling it at Marty. 'Calm down! Now just calm the hell down!'

But Marty would not calm down. He called for Britton as the Goblin contractors clawed at the MPs, a few of whom began to flail with the butts of their carbines.

Britton managed to raise his head. 'This is getting out of

control, Lieutenant. I'd put that gun down if I were you. You take a shot in here, and you're going to hit a friendly anyway.'

The lieutenant snatched his pistol backward as one of the Goblin contractors lunged at it, and cursed.

'Damn it, let him through!' he called to the MP in front of Britton.

A boom sounded. Closer that time. Had the ATTD gone off? No, it wasn't that close.

Yet.

The crowd of Goblins immediately calmed, stepping back and surrounding Marty again as the MP stepped aside, allowing Therese and Truelove to help Britton into the ring.

He shrugged off their grip, kneeling before Marty. The Goblin placed his hands on Britton's shoulders – huge eyes looking into his. The white spots of his face were smeared, his breath sour. 'You hurt.'

Britton rested his head on Marty's narrow shoulder and whispered in his ear. 'Yeah, but it's going to be okay. We have to go now.'

The lieutenant looked on nervously, and the ring of MPs began to tighten.

Another boom shook the cash this time. The MPs looked around nervously. The lieutenant shouted into his radio. 'Shovel, this is six. What the hell is going on?'

When Britton raised his head, Marty looked at him, eyes wide and uncomprehending.

Downer was still outside the ring. Britton turned to Truelove. 'We're leaving. Come with us.'

Truelove took a step back, slowly shaking his head.

'What are you doing?' the lieutenant shouted, turning away from his radio. 'Pick him up,' he called to one of his men.

They were out of time. 'I'll come back for you,' Britton said, and extended a hand. A gate opened behind Marty. Beyond it, he could see a bowl of rose moss where he'd gone on his first camping trip in the mountains of Vermont's largest state park. The current of his magic soothed the pain in his heart but brought a dizziness that nearly knocked him out.

He pushed Marty through the gate with one hand and swung Therese into it with the other. Then he pitched forward, falling halfway into the portal, his face down in the soft plants, his nostrils filling with the scent of frostbitten red clover.

'Come on,' he whispered to Truelove, knowing the Necromancer couldn't hear him.

He felt Therese's hands dragging him the rest of the way through the gate, turning him over.

The other side was a maelstrom of yelling soldiers surging toward the gate. The Goblins flung themselves against them, blocking their progress. Truelove stood still, mouth open and head shaking. Downer was behind him, arm draped across his chest and holding him back, her face contorted and screaming. The lieutenant raised his pistol and fired a shot into the gate. It dug a trench in the frozen ground beside him, sparking off a rock.

Britton yanked his knees to his chest and shut the gate.

He lay still for a moment, letting the biting cold chase the fog from his mind, leaving only the pain in his chest.

The silence was overwhelming. He had forgotten how strong the sense of constant magical current was in the Source. Back on the Home Plane, he felt barren, his own current lonely and isolated. The wind picked up, sending a scattering of dead leaves in a rasping dance somewhere nearby. Marty let out a low sigh of amazement, gawping at his surroundings.

Therese broke the quiet, digging furiously in her pocket. 'Oh my God, Oscar, they'll blow it up. I left it in the cash.' He had no idea how powerful the explosive was, but it wouldn't need to be too strong to do a lot of damage in such tight quarters.

And Britton knew the cash was about to be overwhelmed with work.

He fought to his knees. 'I'll take care of it.'

He swallowed hard, dug deep inside himself for the energy to open another gate, staggering to his feet and lurched back into the room where Therese had extracted it. He snatched the blinking device off the cot, then jogged down familiar pathways, until he stumbled into air as cold as the bowl of rose moss where Therese and Marty awaited him.

He dropped the ATTD in front of the stainless-steel surface of the industrial chiller. He swept his eyes past the Goblin corpses in their various states of dissection and his eyes alighted on a rack of winter parkas bolted to one of the tent-support rods that held up the cold chamber. He snatched three and pushed himself back through the gate, collapsing beside Therese again.

He managed to lift his head and shut the gate.

But not before the flash of orange shocked his eyes and the low growl of the explosive shock wave whispered faintly in his ears, the tremors sending him off into peaceful blackness.

He gave up the fight and surrendered to it.

Because he had escaped FOB Frontier.

Because, at long last, he was free.

Chapter Thirty-One
Last Stop

You can dress it up any way you like, cover it with laws and fancy proclamations. None of it can change the truth, which is simply this: you're terrified. Humans are in the presence of creatures that look just like them but are to them as humans are to insects. This is why the SOC is so utterly disgusting. Why the hell would you work for cockroaches? They should be working for us. Hell, they should be slaving for us. And, in time, they will.

– 'Render', Houston St Selfers
Recorded 'Message for SOC Sorcerers' distributed
on the Internet and the streets of New York City

They lay in silence for a few minutes before Britton shook himself and stumbled to his feet. He shrugged the parka over his shoulders and tossed one to Therese. She helped Marty into his, draping it over his oversized head so he looked like a small child bundled up for the cold. He winced at the touch of the ground, lifting the splayed toes of his thickly callused feet, but there was nothing to be done.

Therese placed her hand on Britton's chest and he could feel the magic beginning to do its work again. 'Just let me double-check . . .' she said.

After a moment, she raised her hands to his shoulders. 'Oscar, you've got to send me back.'

He shrugged off his exhaustion, pushed through the pain. 'What? I just got us out of there.'

Therese shook her head. 'There are sick people, hurt people. I have to help. You're safe now, but I'm not going to run with you. They need me there, Oscar.'

You have no idea, Britton thought. The sounds of explosions and gunfire echoed through his head. He could picture the Goblins swarming through the collapsed perimeter. *They are going to need you more than ever now.*

'Therese, you can't. They'll kill you. How long do you think it's going to take them to figure out how I got the ATTD out? Do you honestly think they'll turn a blind eye to that?'

Therese nodded. 'Maybe they won't figure it out,' she whispered. 'Maybe I can explain.'

'Don't be ridiculous. What do you think they're going to do?'

She shook her head. 'Oscar, what the hell was going on there? Something was happening, something started this all off.'

Britton was silent. He looked at his lap. She shook his shoulders. 'Tell me, damn it.

'There's a problem, isn't there? People are being hurt.'

He nodded.

'Send me back,' she said firmly. 'I have to help.'

His heart caught in his throat as the image of the intact Quonset huts flooded his brain. They stood, untouched, in the middle of the devastated SASS. The occupants were still inside, Britton knew. Swift, Pyre, Peapod. Tsunami. Wavesign. The Goblins would be pouring over that ground first.

And that wasn't even counting the other Goblins, Marty's tribesmen who worked on the FOB. Would they be punished for helping Marty escape? Maybe. But there were hundreds of them spread all over the FOB. Britton knew he couldn't save them all.

But the SASS enrollees were all in one place, and that was a start.

'You want to help?' Britton asked. 'Help me.'

He stood up, shaking slightly, exhaustion gripping him.

'Where are we going? What are we doing?' she asked.

'Marty' – Britton looked down at the little Goblin – 'I need you to stay here.' He shuddered to think of what would become of the creature, stranded on the Home Plane, if they didn't return for him.

Marty shook his head. 'Come with you,' he said.

'Oscar, what's this about?' Therese asked.

'Marty,' Britton said. 'Please. Just sit tight and don't move. You won't be able to help us where we're going, and I can't stand having gotten you out of there only to get you killed. I promise I'll be back.' *What if you're not?* 'I promise.' He unclipped his pocketknife and handed it to the Goblin. It looked larger in his small hands, but still woefully inadequate.

'I'll be back.' He turned to Therese. 'I freed Scylla,' he said. 'I thought I had to. I was a fool. She gutted the FOB like a piece of rotten fruit. I don't know how bad it is, but I assume the neighboring Goblin tribes are hitting it hard right now. That's what all that noise was. She left the SASS enrollees alive, but they're right in the path of the advance. If there's any chance of helping anyone, Therese, it should be them. I'm not happy that the SOC has a fight on its hands, or that people are going to be hurt, but I'll be damned if I'm going back to them again. You want to help someone? Help me help Wavesign and the rest of them. I put them in this position, but the SOC put us all in it first. I can't undo what I've done, but I can try to fix some of it, and I can do it better with your help.'

She stared at him, mouth gaping. 'Please, Therese,' he said. 'There's no time. We need to go right now. I don't even know if they're still alive, but we've got to try.'

'Goddamn it, Oscar.'

'You want to chew me out? Fine. Do it later.' He opened a gate just outside the scattered remains of Scylla's pillbox. 'Now or never,' he said. He jumped through without looking back.

But when he looked up, Therese was behind him.

And the Quonset huts were still standing, awash in a sea of Goblins.

The battle had pushed on beyond the SASS's borders. Britton could make out army fire teams in the distance, firing from behind the cover of a few armored personnel carriers.

Apaches wheeled overhead. Aeromancers danced in between them. The sky was clouded with Rocs, circling over the fray, their backs loaded with Goblin crews discharging clouds of javelins on the battle below them. Squadrons of wolf-borne Goblins charged among the soldiers, swinging halberds. White-chalked sorcerers ran in their midst, their flowing currents sensible to Britton even from that distance. As Britton watched, one armored personnel carrier was engulfed in magical fire. The ball turret gunner leapt screaming from it, beating at the flames. A dull thud heralded the arrival of a mortar round, bursting in the midst of the advancing Goblins, sending a few spiraling into the air. Britton crouched as the shrapnel tore in his direction, but he was too far away to be harmed.

A helicopter flew low over the fight, miniguns blazing. A white-painted Goblin sorcerer spread his arms and the earth erupted into a lurching spike that clipped the spinning rotors, sending the helo spinning erratically into the line of APCs, exploding in a bright ball of flame.

He heard Therese suck in her breath beside him. *Later*, he thought. *For now, do what you can.*

Swift floated above the Quonset huts. A few of the enrollees had gathered around the No-No Crew on the roof. A big, bearded man in cargo pants lifted a Goblin over his head and threw him down into the crowd below. Swift spread his arms, and lightning cracked among them, sending them scattering. Wavesign knelt on the curved dome, his perennial rain cloud gone. He managed short bursts of carefully controlled magic, sharp tendrils of ice that spread to scattering storms as they buffeted the Goblins below, driving them back. The stress of the conflict had again focused the young Hydromancer's magic, and Britton marveled as the shards of deadly ice rained down on the throng. The havoc seemed to have had the opposite effect on Tsunami. She crouched behind Wavesign, hugging her arms around herself, crying. Pyre swept his arms over his head, sending balls of fire arcing down into the mass. A few met targets among the Goblins that gripped the Quonset hut's superstructure, trying to scale it. Peapod gestured, and earth exploded in the midst of the

Goblins, a gaping crater that sucked dozens of them in, burying them as the ground coiled on itself and closed back up, chomping like hungry teeth. A javelin burst from the throng and caught another enrollee in the chest. He fell screaming off the roof, disappearing into the surging mass below.

A cry sounded. Britton watched as a Roc banked toward Swift, its back brimming with Goblins, leveling stolen rifles at him. Swift's attention was riveted on the assault from below, oblivious to the airborne threat moving toward him.

Britton exploded into motion, running forward and extending a hand. A gate sliced open alongside the giant bird, severing one wing. It shrieked, flapped once, experimentally, fountaining blood onto the creatures below it, then tumbled over on its side and pitched to the ground.

'Come on!' Britton was shouting. 'Swift! Clear a fucking lane and come on!'

Some of the Goblins to the rear of the mass surrounding the hut were beginning to turn, their eyes narrowing. An arrow thrummed through the air, narrowly missing Therese. Britton opened a gate on the roof of the Quonset hut, but the enrollees spun to face it, disbelieving.

'Go through! Go through, you idiots!' Britton shouted, then shut the gate to open it again in front of Therese to intercept a spear hurtling toward her belly.

A group of the Goblins had turned toward them, the muzzles of their wolves plunging and snarling, while the riders brandished swords and pistols. A wolf coiled on its haunches and sprang toward him. Britton caught it in midair with a gate and sent it sliding down through the mass of the creatures, forcing them to dive to either side.

Britton's skin began to itch, suddenly, maddeningly. His throat swelled, his tongue feeling as if it had been rolled in dust. He blinked, his eyes burning. A Goblin sorcerer moved toward them, splitting the white paint across its face as it screamed at them. It thrust its arms forward, and Britton felt his whole body cry out for water, as if he'd been wandering a desert for weeks. He swept his arm to one side, sliding the gate toward it, but the sorcerer threw itself backward, and he shut the gate to follow its progress.

Another Goblin raced toward him, a huge bearded axe waving over its head. Britton managed to drop to his side, aiming a kick at the creature's abdomen, and sending it flipping forward, the axe tumbling away from it. An arc of lightning plowed through the Goblins, raising shrieks and the stink of burning flesh to Britton's nostrils, but the Goblin Hydromancer's grip on him was still tight, and he crawled in the dirt, feeling his skin begin to peel away.

Suddenly, the magic's grip released him. He struggled to his feet to see Therese standing, her lips peeled back, fingers extended. She snarled, and the Goblins before them liquefied, flesh melting onto quivering trunks. Bared teeth dripped away, sliding into running gums that vanished to reveal shrinking jawbones. The cry that went up was unholy. What remained of the wolves and their riders danced bloody jigs. Broken hindquarters turned spastic circles. *She had sworn she'd never Rend again*, Britton thought. *This is going to leave a mark.*

For the moment, the circle of Goblins surged back, horrified by the carnage. Therese's current relaxed, and Britton could see her face fall, horrified at the damage she'd wrought. *Can't worry about that now.* He snapped the gate open on the roof again and motioned to Swift. 'Go! Go!'

Swift gaped at the carnage beneath him for a moment before lighting on the roof and herding the remaining enrollees into the gate. Wavesign stumbled, nearly slid off the roof as a javelin flew past his calf, but Swift caught him under the armpits and shoved him through.

Rotors whined overhead as two Kiowas appeared on the horizon, banking sharply toward them. The Goblins broke their paralysis and turned to face the new threat. Britton closed the gate and opened it in front of them. Therese stood, dumb, her eyes fixed on the field before her. Her mouth worked, silently. *She's no Scylla*, he thought. He draped his arm around her shoulder as gently as he could and walked her through the gate, stepping into the bowl of moss where the enrollees had gathered around Marty, shivering in the cold. Swift stared around him at the woods, cradling his elbows, stupefied. Wavesign crouched at the base of a tree, shivering in his own cloud of vapor.

Marty had been busy in their absence, his arms full of mushrooms. A small pile of sampled plants had been gathered on a rock beside him. Now he stood and dashed among the SASS enrollees, clucking over wounds and producing his worn leather pouch.

Therese paused a moment, then joined him, turning first to Britton. 'Nothing I can do for you,' she said, her voice distant, clinical. 'You need a Hydromancer, not a Healer.' She walked off, squatting by a young woman with a gash across her face, cupping her cheek and letting her magic knit the wound.

'Therese . . .' he called after her. But she ignored him, losing herself in the bustle of her work.

Later, he thought again. *It's not safe here. You're in a state park not too far off the beaten path. The SOC still has a Portamancer. They can be here in an instant. How long before you are discovered? Before these people freeze?*

He looked back toward the crowd of enrollees. They squatted, miserable and shivering, muttering in low voices, most looking too shocked to do much. But Britton knew it wouldn't last long.

This is your fault. You got them into this. Now, you have to get them out.

Chapter Thirty-Two
A Safe place

. . . of course the muj had that crazy Muslim total prohibition on magic use. So they were reduced to packing all their gear in through those tight Waziristani defiles, little more than goat paths, really. They were counting on the cloud cover screening them from our air-assault teams. But they didn't count on the Aeromantic support getting the skies cleared up in a matter of minutes.

– Interview with Col Alexander Keifer, 101st Airborne Division
Excerpted from Robin Hamdan's *100 days in the FATA*

Britton stood, stunned. He had done it. He had fled the SOC, he had gotten away. Swift looked up at him, his eyes wide. *You're thinking the same thing. You have no idea what to do either. You were so focused on getting free that you never gave a minute's thought to what you'd do once you got there.*

But Britton remembered running before. He remembered his world spinning away from him and keeping on regardless. He remembered staring at a hanging pay-phone receiver, smelling like stale beer.

Baby steps, he thought. *The first thing this crew needs is a leader*. The crowd continued to mill, shivering.

Peapod alone seemed to have any presence of mind. She swept her arms upward, and the trees bowed, extending branches to shelter them, keeping off the worst of the wind. Pyre stooped and heaped a pile of stones, running his hands over them until they glowed red-hot, sparking and cracking, warmer and brighter than any wood fire Britton had ever seen. The enrollees shivered around it, arms draped around knees. Britton worried that the light might alert the authorities but figured that the comfort was more needed at the moment. For now, panic had been staved off.

'Thanks,' Swift managed. 'What happened back there, with Scylla?'

Britton almost told him, then decided to keep it to himself. *You can't afford a fight over that just now*. Instead, he ignored the question. He glanced nervously skyward as the sound of a plane thrummed far overhead. Through a gap in Peapod's shelter of trees, Britton could make out blinking red lights on the wings.

'Where are we?' Swift asked.

'Vermont,' Britton said. 'State park. I went camping here once.'

'We can't stay here,' the Aeromancer said.

'No, we can't,' Britton replied.

'We could head to Mexico,' Pyre piped up, 'or Canada.'

'So we can get rounded up and handed over as part of the reciprocity agreement?' Peapod asked. 'Mexico is a damned vassal state.'

'You got a better idea?' Pyre snapped.

'Why can't we just stay here? Or maybe go to some other wilderness? What about Alaska?'

'We're not survivalists!' someone in the crowd said.

'We don't have to be,' Peapod replied. 'We've got magic.'

'That won't do us any good once the SOC starts hunting for us,' Swift said. 'They're better than we are.'

'Bet you wish you'd spent a little more time practicing with Salamander when you'd had the chance, eh, No-No boy?' Tsunami groused.

This is getting out of control, Britton thought. *Someone has to lead before things come totally apart.*

'That's enough,' Britton said, his voice taking on the tone of command he'd used in the army. The group responded to it, looking up at him expectantly. *What now?*

Britton felt fingers brush his own and looked down to see

Marty at his side, looking wide eyed at him. 'Much angry,' the Goblin said. The others stared at him, and whispers ran through the clearing.

'Why?' Marty asked, ignoring them. 'Why angry?'

Because I hurt them, Britton thought. *I didn't mean to, but I did. And now I have to make that right, Marty. Now I have to help them*. But he didn't say it. The group needed a commander, and it was not the time to show weakness or remorse. He only looked at Marty, his gaze level. 'We have to find a place to go where the SOC can't find us,' Britton said to Marty, his voice loud and full of confidence he didn't feel. 'That place can't be in this world. It has to be in the Source, and well away from the FOB. We don't know what else the SOC knows about the lay of the land there, but they will have a harder time finding and reaching us.' He made a point of not mentioning Billy, whose ability made reaching them no problem at all.

We'll just have to stay hidden, then.

Marty pursed his lips and wiggled his ears as if to say *of course*. He punched Britton's chest lightly and nodded. 'We Mattab On Sorrah,' he said, tapping his eyelids and bowing. 'We always help.'

'This is my Mattab On Sorrah now,' Britton said. 'The army is going to come for us.'

The Goblin nodded and smiled. 'I know.' He leaned in close, smiling and tapping Britton's chest again. 'Safe place.'

'Yes, Marty, a safe place,' Britton said. 'We have to take them there.'

Marty paused for a moment, thinking. 'Remember, bird head?'

Leering in the torchlight, the striped bird skull, hung on the Goblin fastness where Britton had saved Fitzy's life and been punished for it, rose in his mind. The Master Suppressor's voice rose in his mind. *You're paid to be a weapon, not a hero. Remember that*. 'I remember,' he said to Marty.

'Go there, I take you safe place.' The Goblin smiled.

'Man, I really don't want to go back there,' Britton said. He racked his brain for any image that he could recall well enough to gate to. But the landscape beneath the helicopter had blurred by too fast. The only thing he remembered well enough was FOB Frontier and the fortress. He could take them in some distance from it, but it would have to be in sight.

'Can't I take us back somewhere else?'

Marty shook his head. 'If not there, then not know where safe place. Go bird head. Then safe place.

'Safe place,' Marty repeated, giving his ear-wiggling shrug.

'This is your tribe? This is with your Mattab On Sorrah?'

Marty nodded.

Britton felt his emotions well up at the creature's quickness to help strangers, but now was not the time to show it. He swallowed hard, hoping no one would notice how much the gesture affected him.

'Uskar,' Marty said, gently tapping his own eyelids, then Britton's. 'Okay. Okay. Always help. You important.' He smiled gently, then leaned forward and imitated the human gesture, hugging Britton about the waist as best he could. 'Important. Everything okay.'

Britton patted the Goblin's shoulders as he mastered himself. At last he turned to the remnants of the tribe and spoke, hoping his voice wouldn't break.

'Marty knows of a place we can go. Someplace safe in the Source. We're going to take fifteen minutes to get everyone patched up as best we can, then we're out of here.'

'Back to the Source?' Pyre asked. 'We just escaped from there!'

'This is only temporary,' Britton said. 'Do you honestly think there's a place in the entire US safe for us? Or in any bordering nation? Besides, I can only gate us places I've seen. Or did you propose we walk to wherever we're going to hide out? I know this isn't ideal. I'm not offering you an end to running, just another place to run to.'

'What the hell happened anyway?' one of the enrollees shouted. 'How the hell did that Witch get free in the first place?'

Swift looked frankly at him, arms folded across his chest.

You'll have to tell them eventually. If they're going to follow you, it has to be under honest terms. 'That's my fault,' Britton answered. He paused, letting the stunned silence wash over him. 'You want to blame someone, you can blame me.'

He shouted down the chorus of protests that welled as the group began to grasp the impact of his words. 'That's enough! I've been soldiering long enough to know that if we're going to live through this, it's going to take discipline and teamwork. You may have done things however the hell you wanted to when you were on the run, but that changed in the SASS, and it's not going to change back just because you're free of it. You want to judge me? Judge me later. After we are all safe, after this latest round of running is at an end. I can't bring the dead back to life. All I can do is save the lives that are remaining. What we need is a safe place, someone to shelter us until we can figure out what you want to do next. Marty can provide that safe place, and I can take us there. It's the only chance we've got, and for it to work, you're going to have to trust me and let me help you. You may not like it, but it's the only way.'

And what do you do once you get to Marty's tribe? he asked himself. *We rest, we get ourselves fed and patched up. Then we make plans. The first thing we need is a place to regroup, rest up, and rearm.*

'What if we stand and fight?' Swift asked, but his eyes showed he already knew the answer to his own question.

'If you stand against the SOC, you will die, make no mistake,' Britton replied. 'You have great heart, but you are too few and too poorly trained. The SOC are professional warriors. They make a study of killing with magic. I have trained with them far beyond the basic exercises you learned in the SASS. I've seen what they can do. Bravery isn't enough. Skill beats will, every time. You've learned something of discipline and self-denial in your SASS training. That'll give you a leg up over the average Selfer, but not nearly enough of a leg up.'

'Yes, Oscar.' Therese spoke from beside a SASS enrollee with a broken javelin shaft protruding from his thigh. 'Get us out of here. Do whatever you have to do to make us safe.' But her eyes were hard. *Don't think there won't be a reckoning later.* Britton nodded, his eyes scanning the group for a challenge. Swift turned away. Wavesign shivered, and Pyre gave a resigned nod.

'All right,' Britton said. 'If we're going to function as a unit, we need a commander. That's me unless anyone else thinks they can do a better job.'

A quick glance around the ranks showed him that nobody thought they could, or if they did, didn't have the gumption to challenge him. 'First things first, many of you need healing and a chance to catch your breath. I'm going to have to gate us in outside a stronghold of creatures like Marty, but who are not friendly to us, and I can't have wounds or exhaustion slowing us down. Fifteen minutes, then we go.'

Marty worked tirelessly alongside Therese, enduring his frozen feet in silence until Therese noticed his pained expression. Britton used his pocketknife to cut the bottom third of the parka away, wrapping the fabric around Marty's feet after Therese used her magic to repair the worst of the frostnip beginning to form on the Goblin's soles. That had the added advantage of making the parka fit correctly. No longer tripped up by the long coat, Marty was soon moving around more easily.

Fifteen minutes turned to twenty. Swift waved at the hot air emanating from the fire, sweeping his arms and circulating it through the small shelter of the bent boughs, warming the air to a comfortable temperature. Peapod bent to a small patch of wild onions and strawberries, gesturing until the fruits and vegetables responded to her magic. She gathered armloads of the swollen produce, distributing it among the group.

Therese leaned against a tree in exhaustion when the group's wounds were healed, but Marty would not sit still. He scurried about the clearing, lifting his giant feet high to avoid catching the tied-on fabric on roots and rocks. He high-stepped off into the underbrush, his breath hitching in excitement.

'Marty! What the hell are you doing? Get back here!' Britton called.

The Goblin stopped suddenly, staring intently.

'What is he . . .' Therese asked, but was cut off by a furious squirrel perched on a pine branch directly above Marty's head. It twitched its tail, chattering in rage at this strange creature invading its territory. Marty stared, wide eyed and delighted, until Britton grabbed his hand and led him away.

'Come on, Marty,' Britton said. 'I know it's interesting, but there's no time for this now. I promise we can go on a hike once we've got everything settled.'

Marty came along reluctantly, making petulant-sounding clucks deep in his throat and straining to look at the squirrel over his shoulder as they went.

While the others rested, Marty examined the new world with absentminded curiosity. He nearly danced with delight, his ears quivering, pointing at a cluster of juniper berries, before gathering them and pressing them into the pockets of his parka.

'Can eat!' Marty said, racing back to them with a handful of shriveled and frostbitten-looking mushrooms. Britton looked at the Goblin doubtfully.

'I don't know, Marty . . .'

The Goblin cast a worried eye at Therese. 'Must eat,' he said more urgently, then sniffed the mushrooms, wiggling his ears and smacking his lips. 'Can eat!'

'Do you think they're safe?' Therese asked, raising an eyebrow. 'He does have a knack with plants.'

Britton frowned. 'He has a knack for medicinal plants, but these are plants he's never seen before. He's in a totally different world. Being hungry is bad, but getting sick right now would be a lot worse. Better not to risk it.'

He looked at Marty and shook his head. 'Sorry, buddy. I think you need to curb your enthusiasm here.'

The Goblin looked annoyed and began to gesture wildly.

Britton sighed. 'Please, guy. You're at a ten. We need you at around a four.'

Therese giggled, and Marty stuffed the mushrooms into his pocket with a resigned wave of his hand.

A few of the enrollees had sagged against tree trunks in the magically heated air. Britton looked at Therese, sitting Indian style on the ground, her eyes drooping. 'We're exhausted,'

Britton said to Swift. 'Let's give everyone a half hour to grab some shut-eye before we move.'

'You sure that's safe?' Swift asked.

'No,' Britton answered, 'but it's probably smarter than blundering back into the Source ready to drop dead. Can you keep the air heated without that fire?'

Swift nodded, and Britton turned to Wavesign. 'Can you get that put out, buddy?'

Wavesign's effort was as uncontrolled as ever, but the fire was quickly doused, the rocks splintering further and hissing loudly. Swift quickly dried the damp patch that the young Hydromancer had left. 'All right, people,' Britton said. 'Grab some shut-eye if you can manage it. We go soon.'

He slumped alongside Therese and leaned against her shoulder. She didn't respond, but neither did she push him away.

'I'm sorry,' he whispered. 'I tried to do what I thought best . . .'

'Later, Oscar,' she said, her voice exhausted. 'Later. Let's get out of here first.'

He nodded and drowsed, grateful for the smell of her, the soft warmth of her shoulder against his.

The moon made a sparkling show of the trees and rocks as the enrollees gathered together for warmth. Swift's heated air made that largely unnecessary, but Britton knew that the closeness to one another kept the panic at bay. They weren't alone, and that was a start.

Britton closed his eyes and listened to the sounds of the night – the frost crackling, insects foraging, Marty making an effort at quiet and failing miserably. The little Goblin was far too excited to rest, and he paced the small enclosure, staring at his surroundings. Britton himself thought he couldn't sleep, the adrenaline keeping him awake and alert to sounds; turning each frost-snapped twig into the footfalls of an approaching enemy, but fatigue won out in the end.

He didn't know how long he dozed, drifting in and out of consciousness against Therese's shoulder. Fear and pain were momentarily forgotten. Britton sank into the warm glow of her nearness and drifted off to sleep.

* * *

A cold wind brushed his cheek, lifting him from the warm comfort of sleep and Therese nestled against him. The warm air had dissipated, replaced by the reality of winter cold. Britton buried his face in Therese's hair and clung to the fleeing threads of his slumber. Beyond it lay cold and hardship, and if he could stave it off for just another moment, he would. But the chill breeze blew again, bringing a regular rhythm to his ears, a gentle and familiar pattern that called him to wakefulness. Whup whup whup whup whup.

Britton shot awake. It was the sound of a helicopter. He reached out his arm and accidentally swatted Marty, who must have crawled to snuggle up against his back. The Goblin stirred weakly, and Britton reached over and pressed a finger to his lips.

Whup whup whup. The sound grew louder, closer.

Therese stirred. 'What's . . .'

Britton shushed her fiercely and pointed upward.

As the sound of the rotors passed into the distance, Britton propped himself up on his elbows. All around their small makeshift camp, the enrollees were crouched in silence, casting terrified eyes skyward.

'What the hell was that?' Swift hissed.

'I don't know,' Britton answered. 'Could have been the Weather Channel, could have been the SOC. We can't stick around to find out. Let's get moving.'

He turned to Marty. 'You ready?' *Just where is this 'safe' place you intend to take them? Will Marty's tribe welcome you? Is anywhere really safe for any of you now?*

Why was he there? Why was he doing this? He shuddered as he realized that he already knew the answer.

Because you don't know what else to do. Because if you don't move forward, you'll just lie down and give up, and you've fought far too long and hard for that.

The group froze as the rotors pounded the air overhead again. They stood still, necks craned skyward until the helo passed overhead again, and the sound faded in the distance.

'They must be flying a search pattern,' Britton said. 'It's the only reason they would be going that slow.'

Britton was grateful for the thick clouds that had blown in while they slept. Little moon and even less starlight penetrated the forest canopy, leaving a black sea whose rocky bed was dotted with the gnarled columns of tree trunks. Night was thick around them.

'All right.' Britton used his best command voice, loud enough that the group winced and snapped their gazes to him. 'Nothing more to be gained by hanging around. Let's get this show on the road.'

Chapter Thirty-Three

Betrayed

It is challenging to make a study of the effects of Latency on genetics. For one thing, Manifestation is extremely rare, and it is rarer still for two Latent individuals to mate and produce offspring under conditions that can be monitored for the purpose of scientific study. That said, there is promising statistical evidence to indicate that the children of Latent parents are much more likely to Manifest, and to do so at a very early age.

– Avery Whiting
Modern Arcana: Theory and Practice

The gate yawned across the clearing, eight feet high, its shimmering static surface offering a glimpse of the palisade wall in the distance. Long triangular banners draped down its surface, hidden in the darkness. Britton knew they were crudely painted in the likeness of a bird skull, striped red and orange.

'Heptahad On Dephapdt,' Marty whispered, his voice grave. 'Sorrahhad. Much fight.'

Britton turned to the enrollees. 'All right, the folks behind those walls may look just like Marty, but they are not friends. We get caught by these guys, and we're done. But if we keep together, keep quiet, and keep moving, I'm confident we can get past them unnoticed. It's a chance, but as rough customers as these folks are, they're a cakewalk compared to the SOC, and it's a far better bet than staying here. Everybody tracking?'

Swift nodded. 'Peapod, I need you at the rear of the group, keep folks moving,' Britton said. She nodded and took up her position.

'All right, let's do this.' Britton turned and stepped through the gate. He was briefly swamped by the intensity of his senses but shrugged it off, sighting the palisade wall and scanning the darkness for any movement. All was cloaked in shadow. Torchlight flickered from the turret that the creatures had repaired long since the rocket from one of the raiding Apaches had destroyed it. A new wooden structure jutted from one of the towers like some kind of cancerous growth, braced by roughly hewn crossbeams, crowned with a peaked slate roof. Its sides glistened wetly.

A water tower, Britton thought. *They don't want their Pyromancers busy putting out fires. They want them ready in case we come back.*

Peapod ushered the last of the group through. They stood gaping at the giant palisade wall, pointing and whispering to one another. Britton shut the gate quickly and began herding them away from the fortress. Tired and injured, the group made slow going. Wavesign's cloud pulsed with chunks of ice and hail, his terror magically palpable.

'It's amazing,' Swift whispered to Britton, running his hands over the saw-toothed grass.

Britton put a hand in the small of his back, pushing him along. 'Later. If we're caught here, it's going to get ugly.'

Swift slapped the hand down. 'All right, all right. I'm moving.'

Britton opened his mouth to say something, and all words fled.

Directly before them, just a few meters away, a rickety tower had been erected. Wooden crossbeams supported a slate-covered platform some thirty feet from the ground. Above the platform, three logs rose, lashed together to form a crossbar.

A massive Roc sat astride it, black talons gripping the tree-trunk thickness tightly. Its feathers were fluffed outward against the cold, making it look even larger.

Not a crossbar, then, a perch.

Of course. It's a watchtower. They want to be able to warn the main stronghold if another flight of Apaches comes in.

The group froze at the sight, but the giant bird had already sighted them; it cocked its huge head at an angle, and a single unblinking golden eye, the size of a dinner plate, fixed them.

About its neck clung a Goblin, his face buried in the creature's feathers, body entirely covered in white paste.

For a moment, both Roc and human stood in stunned silence, broken only by the wind whispering over the grass and hissing through the wooden tower slats.

Then the Roc shrieked, spread massive wings, and exploded off the perch, circling over them.

A horn sounded, deep and sonorous. Britton remembered it blowing when the helo force had swept over that same fortress with him on board.

'Run!' he cried, pulling at the group, hauling them away.

They scattered as the bird swept low. It made a pass, claws reaching out to snatch at Swift, but Pyre pumped his fist, sending a gout of flame to singe its underbelly, forcing it to rear back, wings beating strong enough to sweep a gust of wind that knocked the group to their knees.

Britton could hear the fortress gates creaking open in the distance.

Peapod stood forward and placed her hands on her hips, concentrating. The massive bird recovered from the burn and dove again, straight at her, huge talons reaching.

Then it paused, and Britton felt a surge in Peapod's flow as she Whispered desperately, competing for control over the Roc with the Goblin Terramancer on its back. The giant wings beat the air, and it swung its head side to side in confusion, crying out in alarm. But what little practice Peapod had ever had in Whispering was no match for the Goblin. Britton could see sweat breaking out on her forehead, her teeth gritting. Cries sounded from the fortress, and Britton saw that three more Rocs had taken flight, moving toward them. It wouldn't take them long to arrive.

He stepped alongside Peapod, reaching out for the Goblin's magical current. It was difficult to pick it out from all the others around him, but eventually he felt it, a foreign flow in the midst of so many familiar ones. He focused, Drawing the magic hard to him, then Binding it to the Goblin's flow, cutting it off. In an instant, Peapod's Whispering won out, and the Roc hurled itself skyward, righted, and launched itself toward its brothers as they winged toward it, shrieking a battle cry.

Peapod blew out her breath, placing her hands on her knees. 'Whew, that was close.'

Britton panted, nodding. 'Where'd you learn to Whisper?'

'A bug here, a sparrow there when folks aren't looking. You figure it out.' Her voice was hoarse.

Britton smiled. 'Good thing.'

The smile faded quickly. Even if they ran now, they would never outdistance the pursuing birds, and Britton couldn't Suppress three Terramancers at once. Even if they could defeat the Rocs, it would slow them enough to bring the entire Goblin tribe running to the attack.

He spun on Marty, who was busy gathering up some of the enrollees cowering beneath the tower.

'Marty! Which way is your tribe?' Britton asked.

Marty blinked at him for a moment before pointing out across the field toward a long line of snowcapped trees. Britton sighted the line, imprinting it on his mind. He turned and opened a gate back on the clearing.

'Everybody move!' he shouted, grabbing the nearest of the group and nearly throwing him through. All came quickly this time, and Britton shut the gate behind them just as the first sweeps of the Rocs' wings sounded nearby.

The group milled around uncertainly, some collapsing in the grass from terrified exhaustion.

'Now what the hell are we supposed to do?' Pyre said. 'We're right back where we started!'

'Hold on a second,' Britton replied. *Man, I hope this works.* He opened another gate as far as he could into the tree line that Marty had pointed out.

They reentered the Source deep among the trees. The Sorrahhad fortress was screened by the thick mass of trunks, but Britton could hear the cries of the Rocs as they circled the area where their quarry had suddenly vanished.

'Marty,' Britton said, but the Goblin was already pointing before he could ask the question. Britton memorized a distant hill before returning them all to the glade, then gated them out to it.

'Outstanding,' he said, clapping Therese on the back as soon as they returned. 'This works. We won't even have to hike it.' She stiffened at this touch, looked at her feet, then walked away.

Britton's heart sank, but he pushed the emotion aside and gated them back. Leapfrogging between worlds, Britton carried them what he guessed was many miles in just a few steps. When they finally emerged on a low, rocky rise after the tenth hop, Britton saw a small hamlet in the distance. Mud houses crowded narrow dirt tracks, the roofs thatched with dried saw-toothed grass. A log wall, much smaller than the one they had just fled, surrounded it. Square blue banners dotted it at regular intervals. Even from that distance, Britton could make out the image of a gnarled tree embroidered into the surface.

Beyond the wall, small garden plots stretched alongside sheds. Low wooden pens enclosed the same squat, hairy livestock that he'd seen when he'd attacked the Goblin fastness. Smoke rose from cooking fires beyond the palisade wall. Britton thought he could hear faint music, rhythmic and atonal.

Marty let out a sound that could only have been a sigh and pointed again. 'There. Mattab On Sorrah. Home.'

Britton laughed out loud, then choked as it quickly became a sob.

Because, for now, he had saved them.

The Goblins met them some distance outside the gates, astride the backs of giant wolves. A few Goblin Druids, their skins painted white, walked among them, but the wolf riders were warriors with dotted faces less elaborate than Marty's. They held spears, swords, and US military-issue carbines far too large for their small bodies, and wore leather jerkins studded with a pattern that resembled the tree from the banners.

At their head was a giant of a Goblin, still smaller than even Wavesign by a head; a mail hauberk was draped around his shoulders and he carried a huge spear bearing a banner matching those on the walls. His face was patterned in white dots that matched Marty's exactly.

The group paused, uncertain how to proceed, but Marty strode to the front of the group, shrugging off his parka and squaring his shoulders, suddenly oblivious to the cold. He seemed taller, radiating a confidence that Britton had never seen in him before. Gone was the curious, childlike creature that had shivered in the woods just a little while ago. He barked out a few words quickly in his language, his voice resonating the command that Britton knew the best military officers could invoke.

The Goblins' eyes widened. Marty barked another word, raising his hands, his ears standing up straight over his head. The Goblins reacted, the riders leaping off their wolves and dragging at the reins until the creatures lay down on the ground. The entire party tapped their eyes, bowing deeply. The white-painted Goblin sorcerers also bowed, but only slightly and from the waist, also tapping their eyelids. When they looked up again, their faces were joyful, and a few cried out what Britton only guessed were greetings, coming forward to brush their fingers against Marty's closed eyelids or the tips of his ears. Marty endured it all with an air of entitlement, his hands on his hips to allow the group to get close.

All except the spear bearer, who stood, clearly unsettled, the weapon resting in the crook of his arm. One of the sorcerers remained with him, exchanging whispers. When the greetings were complete, Marty turned back to Britton. His lordling face was gone, and he was friendly Marty again, grinning like a happy child.

'See?' he asked, beaming. 'Important.'

Britton laughed, clapping Swift on the back. 'No doubt, buddy. Important as hell.'

Marty wiggled his ears and led them into the gate, the wolf riders falling in as escorts around them, the spear bearer going in front, crying out what Britton guessed was a heralding of their arrival.

* * *

The village clustered around a broad plaza, the ground flat and covered with a carpet of moss that looked dry and comfortable. Ten glass-smooth stone chairs were arranged in a semicircle around a huge and ancient tree, wide and stunted like some giant bonsai. Britton recognized it as the tree from the banners on the palisade wall. Ten blue-robed, white-painted sorcerers, their ears sprouting tufts of long white hair, were already taking their seats. Ringed around them were scores of Goblins, large and small. Britton recognized tiny children, as cute in their minority as they were ugly as adults. Females stood around the perimeter of the circle, wearing brown shifts that exposed single, long brown breasts. Some of them had the nipples pierced with a sparkling jewel of some sort, their faces painted with dotted patterns. The other females clustered around them in deference.

The huge spear bearer stood forward and began a speech in his language that seemed to go on for a long time, while the seated Goblins listened, nodding occasionally. Britton turned to Marty to ask him what was going on, but was silenced with a wave. Whatever was happening, he was not to interrupt. At last, the spear bearer gestured back to Marty, who stepped forward, cutting him off. He launched into his own speech, bowing and tapping his eyes.

The spear bearer bristled at his words and started forward, but Marty intercepted him, reaching a hand down to the sole of his foot, then placing his hand against the spear bearer's chest. The assembled crowd gasped collectively. Whatever Marty had done, it was a grave insult or a challenge.

Britton stepped forward, unsure of what was going to happen, but Wavesign's voice rang out from the gathered tribe. 'Okay, looks like everyone's here.'

Humans and Goblins alike froze, the Goblins fixing him with angry stares. Wavesign grinned and raised his hands, flashing them his middle fingers. 'That's nice, you fucking rats. Suck on this.' The boyish uncertainty was gone from his voice. He sounded cocky, commanding.

'Wavesign, what the hell are you doing?' Swift asked.

And that was when Britton noticed that the young Hydromancer's perennial vapor cloud was gone. He could feel the boy's current, steady, disciplined, gathering solidly around him.

Wavesign produced a small black box from his waistband and thumbed it. A red light blinked on the surface, emitting a regular beeping sound. The group backed away, but Britton knew that whatever it was, it was too small to be a bomb. It looked more like a pager.

Or some kind of transmitter.

Britton's mouth went dry.

'You sold us out, you bastard,' Britton said.

Wavesign grinned, his fists shrouded in a cloud of whirling ice crystals. He nodded to Britton, the confidence in his eyes making him appear much older. 'Just following your lead, sir.'

He leapt aside as a massive gate slid open behind him. Through it, Britton could see Billy, his mother gentling his shoulders. Around him, a SOC assault team was scrambling to their feet, racing forward, chambering rounds.

Harlequin led them through the portal, his body wreathed in crackling electricity. Shadow Coven followed, Fitzy grinning at its head.

'Too smart by half, Oscar,' Harlequin said. 'You forgot you're not the only one with a gate.'

Then he leapt airborne, the storm erupting around him.

Chapter Thirty-Four
Last Stand

Sir, the president is completely clear on this issue. If Colonel Taylor's theory is correct, then there is a tangible link between the Goblin Defender tribes and the Mescalero insurgency. More importantly, there is a connection between planes inherent in the environment and independent of Portamantic magic. If true, this represents a cross-planar threat to the security of this nation and possibly the world. It must remain secret, and it must remain your top priority.

– White House Briefer to the Chairman of the Joint Chiefs of Staff

Twenty-five soldiers burst through the gate, carbines leveled. Along with Shadow Coven and Harlequin came two more SOC Sorcerers, pistols drawn and ready.

Marty barked an order, pointing, and the Goblins surged forward to meet them, brandishing spears. Several of the white-painted sorcerers sprang from their chairs, leaping into the sky or bursting into flames.

But it was Fitzy who fired the first shot. His pistol belched smoke and spun Pyre in a tight circle. The Pyromancer sat down hard, gripping his stomach, blood flowing from between his fingers. Britton cursed and Therese shrieked, rushing to Pyre's side as more carbines cracked, throwing back escapees and Goblins alike. A patter of bullets churned the ground between Therese and Pyre, and she was forced to throw herself in the opposite direction.

Britton raced forward, slapping down one of the carbine barrels so the soldier fired uselessly into the dirt. He snapped open a gate directly in the middle of the soldier, slicing him neatly in half, his dissected body sliding slowly apart. Britton leveled the gate horizontally, sending it arcing through the ranks of the SOC assaulters. They threw themselves to either side, but not before three more were cut in half. He pivoted neatly and crouched as one soldier moved past him, grabbing his ankle and yanking him off his feet. The soldier grunted as he went facedown in the dirt, his helmet flying off. Britton opened another gate and dragged his leg back through it, closing it like a cleaver about the man's hips before turning to lunge for Fitzy.

But Harlequin appeared overhead and dove at him, lightning springing from his fingertips. Britton opened a gate to receive the burst and began shifting it into the Aeromancer's flight path, edge turning outward toward him.

Then suddenly he was freezing. Wavesign grinned at him, hands extended. A cloud of swirling frost cloaked Britton, numbing his limbs, his teeth. The Hydromancer's voice was confident, precise, mature. All of his uncertainty, his childlike affectation was gone.

Britton recognized it as the voice of a trained solider.

'Once a traitor, always a traitor, I always said,' Wavesign said. 'I knew we couldn't trust you, Keystone.'

'I'm the traitor?' Britton yelled at him, his teeth beginning to chatter. 'You sold out everyone who trusted you!'

Wavesign shook his head, his wry smile reminding Britton of Harlequin's. 'I've never betrayed anyone,' Wavesign said. 'I've been carrying out my assignment, just like good soldiers do. But you wouldn't know much about how to be a good soldier, now would you, Keystone?'

The cold began to overwhelm him and Britton swore, shutting the gate and opening another one on the sauna in the Air National Guard base where he'd been assigned. He dove through it, but not before a bullet whined past his head, tearing a notch out of his ear. An inch to the right, and he would have been dead. He slammed against the cedar wall and collapsed, shivering, willing the heat from the stifling chamber into his frigid bones.

He looked up at another soldier who sat, wide eyed on one of the wooden benches, clutching a towel over his privates. Britton smiled at him, working his fingers and stamping his feet, feeling sensation slowly drift back into them. 'It's all right,' he said. 'I'll be out of your hair in a minute.'

The soldier got to his feet and ran past Britton, bursting out the sauna door and yelling for help, admitting a blast of room-temperature air that felt freezing to Britton. Britton took another moment to suck in the hot air, the silence, the pleasant smell of the cedar. The heat was as delightful as the absence of battle around him. No time for that. He opened a gate behind where Wavesign had stood a moment before and stepped back in, reaching for his neck. But the Hydromancer had moved on and he grabbed empty air, then suddenly Britton's magic rolled back, and his head rocked forward, somersaulting him face-first into the dirt.

As he rolled over, he caught a glimpse of Harlequin and Swift grappling in midair, with Swift getting the worst of the beating, his skin blackening with electrical burns from each of Harlequin's charged punches.

'Thought you'd get away, didn't you?' Fitzy said, stomping at Britton's face. He rolled out of the way, catching the chief warrant officer's boot and kicking up to catch him in the small of his back. Fitzy winced and fell on Britton, dropping an elbow into his shoulder joint that knocked it out of socket. He howled in pain and threw Fitzy's bulk off him, scrambling to his feet. Fitzy was up in time with him, pointing his pistol at Britton's face. A grim smile spread across his face as he pulled the trigger.

But the bullet flew wide, for Fitzy was suddenly swept aside by a branch of the gnarled central tree. He saw Peapod gesturing to it as the Master Suppressor went flying through the air, slamming into Downer, who had just completed animating a bolt of frost that Wavesign had produced. The elemental bounded into the press of Goblin warriors, knocking them aside with great sweeps of its arms, sending them staggering, blue lipped and freezing.

The elemental plowed toward him, and Britton backpedaled, calling up his magic for a gate. Then the elemental was gone, disappearing in a cloud of vapor. Britton sawed his head toward Pyre, his hand still smoking from the flame bolt. Satisfied that Britton was safe for the moment, Pyre dropped to one elbow, his face pale and sweating. The blood had stopped flowing from his gut and came in weak spurts. After a moment, he collapsed.

Around him, wolves darted, snarling at their former masters. Britton spotted Richards standing among the SOC assaulters, Whispering the animals on to greater ferocity.

Fitzy sprawled facedown in the plaza. A Goblin warrior raced to him as he rose and thrust its spear through his arm, pinning him to the ground. Fitzy shrieked and hauled on the spear, gritting his teeth as he moved up the shaft to reach his assailant. The muscle of his biceps squelched around the shaft, oozing bright blood. The Goblin quailed, openmouthed, at the chief warrant officer's bald ferocity, too terrified to drop the weapon. By the time it recovered its senses and released it, Fitzy had hooked his fingers into its eye sockets and slammed its head down into his knee. As the creature collapsed, Fitzy spun on Britton, ripping the spear from his arm and casting it aside. Britton goggled. Even with a Goblin-sized spear, the feat was impressive. Fitzy howled, covered in gore, looking like he had stepped out of hell.

Britton staggered toward the edge of one of the smooth stone chairs and slammed his shoulder into it, screaming as the joint popped back into place. The pain flared and ebbed as Britton tried his shoulder and found he could move it with some pain.

All around them, the battle raged. The sky was riven by streaks of lightning and gouts of fire as the Goblin sorcerers joined the fight. The sharp reports of gunfire and the stink of cordite thickened the air.

Britton still felt his current blocked by Fitzy, who charged him, screaming. He snapped a kick at Britton's face, but Britton sidestepped, catching the chief warrant officer's leg and pulling him into a solid punch on Fitzy's wounded arm.

Fitzy grunted and spun away, only to be grappled by the Goblin spear bearer, who snarled and sank his teeth into Fitzy's shoulder.

Britton felt a hammerblow to his thigh and collapsed, clapping his hands to his leg. He didn't see where the round had originated, but someone had shot him. He rolled on the ground, biting back the pain and trying to see how bad it was. It was impossible. If he released pressure on the wound, he might bleed out in moments.

A shadow fell across him and he looked up to see Wavesign standing over him, wreathed in a halo of spinning frost. He grinned. 'Hurts? Maybe I'll numb it for you.'

He raised his hands, runnels of water snaking down his arms to ball around his fists, where they spun, violent and sharp-looking, tiny waves tipped with icy razors. Therese stepped between them. 'No way, Ted,' she snarled.

Wavesign's face twisted. 'Move,' he husked. 'I'm not going to hurt you, and you're not going to hurt me.'

'Wrong,' she said, and laid her palm across his face.

The Hydromancer shrieked as his head wobbled and stretched, losing shape and running down his shoulders. His scalp unfolded, taking patches of the skull with it, opening like a blossoming flower. Gray matter churned beneath. Ice exploded from him, and Britton could see Therese's skin turning blue under its impact. Her beautiful hair crumbled away in chunks, snapping off with the sound of breaking twigs. She pushed Wavesign away to collapse in the dirt, and turned to Britton, her magic already repairing the damage to her face, the skin losing its pale, frostbitten color. She placed her hands over his thigh, and he felt the magic warm him, the bullet sliding forward and popping out the rear of his leg to lie in the moss.

Soldiers raced toward them, leveling their carbines, then shrieked and doubled over, their hair crumbling and skin flaking onto the plaza as one of the SASS enrollees advanced, snarling. She extended her hands, drawing the water out of them until they were nothing but piles of blowing dust.

Then she staggered backward, a fireball exploding into her chest and sending her sprawling, shrieking and beating at the flames. A Pyromancer advanced past his fallen soldiers. Britton recognized his perfect black hair and smug smile from the raid that first took down Sarah Downer. At his side shambled two dead Goblins and a soldier, his head mostly severed, and attached to his body only by a scrap of flesh. Truelove came behind them, arms extended and brow furrowed with concentration. Around him, dead Goblins tangled with their living fellows, stabbing with broken spear shafts or kicking and punching with mute resolve.

And then Britton looked up and all hope died.

A huge gate opened again, LSA Portcullis's bay a black maw behind it. With a whine and belching of diesel fumes, an armored personnel carrier rolled through behind the SOC forces. Atop the turret, a gunner hunched behind a fifty-caliber machine gun, the muzzle already blazing as rounds spit in the combatants' direction.

The fire was withering. The huge bullets churned the earth, tore chunks from the smooth thrones, spun Goblin and human alike, leaving them in bloody heaps. All around them, the Goblins fell back. A few of the white-painted sorcerers weren't even bothering to fight, and instead herded their folk away from the plaza, making for the gate on the far side of the palisade wall. Britton had no time to make a count, but many of the remaining enrollees lay sprawled in the dirt. One of Richards's Whispered wolves lay dead beside him. Peapod lay facedown in the dirt, smoke rising from her back.

We can't win this, Britton thought. *Not anymore. I have to get us out of here*.

Guilt rocked him. *They thought I was helping them, and I've only led them to their deaths*.

Therese screamed at the Pyromancer and rose to meet him, then fell away as a bullet clipped her shoulder and sent her stumbling backward. She clapped her hand to the wound, her brow furrowing as the magic worked.

Britton could hear Tsunami screaming and thought he caught a flash of the Hydromancer crouching behind one of the stone chairs, bullets whining around her.

Swift fell from the sky, hitting the plaza hard enough to bounce in front of where another enrollee knelt, cradling his face. Fitzy stood over him, blood streaming from his fist.

Fitzy motioned at the SOC force, and they began to fall back around the APC and its giant, smoking gun. With the SASS enrollees and Marty's tribe battered and pinned down by the stream of fire, there was no need to risk his men in close quarters.

Harlequin landed beside the Pyromancer, suppressed Britton's magic, and smiled. Behind him, the line of SOC soldiers advanced into the square in front of the APC. The Goblins had fled. Those of the enrollees who remained ducked behind the stone chairs.

'No pardon for you this time, Oscar,' he said. 'I'm afraid you're all out of chances.' His voice grew sad as he drew closer. 'A shame, really. I had high hopes for your redemption. You might have been able to make at least some of your crap right. Now we'll never know.'

And then he was reeling sideways as Therese charged him, shrieking. Britton felt his magic return as Harlequin transferred his current to Suppressing her.

'Never say never,' Britton shouted, and dove forward, spreading his arms. One caught Harlequin about the waist, checking his flight. The other caught the Pyromancer around the neck. A gate snapped open behind them. Britton knocked both men through and onto the top of the flight observation tower back at his old base at the 158th. The structure loomed nearly two hundred feet above the flight line, its hexagonal roof barely eight feet across and covered with slick tile. He threw himself backward as the Pyromancer screamed, tumbling over the edge, his shriek abruptly cut short by a wet thud. Harlequin somersaulted in the air, landing on top of an adjacent water tower beside the flight-line fire station. Britton turned the gate and slid it sideways after him, but Harlequin stretched out his arms, and the gate vanished as the Suppression canceled Britton's magic.

He grinned, muttering into the microphone clipped to his lapel, too low for Britton to hear.

'You blew it, pal,' he shouted across the distance to Britton. 'Unless you've learned how to fly, that is. You can just cool your heels up there while my crew mops up the rest of your pals.'

'Screw you!' Britton shouted at him, circling around. The top of the tower offered no way down, with only the huge drop to the concrete flight line below. There was no hatch through the roof. Harlequin was right. Unless he'd learned to fly, there was no way down. 'Go ahead and keep me Suppressed! So long as you do, you can't come after me. We're going to just sit here until we get old?'

Harlequin laughed. 'Nope. Got plans for you, pal.'

The rotary whine of helicopter blades sliced the air. The sound was deeper than a Kiowa, and Britton recognized the low pitch as one of the larger Blackhawks. They were usually on practice flights or patrols around the base. It wouldn't have taken the pilot more than a few seconds to respond to Harlequin's call and divert to his position. Britton could see the minigun barrels pointing out the sides of the helo as it flew toward him.

It made no effort to go broadside as it approached at high speed, no effort to bring the guns to bear.

Then Britton noted that Harlequin's pistol was still in the drop holster strapped to his thigh. He stood with a clear shot and all the time in the world to aim, but instead had his arms crossed, waiting.

He wants to capture me again. Maybe he was willing to kill me if he had to, but I still have value to these people.

Hope blossomed in his chest.

Britton turned and sprinted for the edge of the tower, putting a mad look of fear on his face.

Harlequin cried out and leapt off his perch, dropping the Suppression and flying to intercept Britton's fall.

At the edge of the tower, Britton dug in his heels, abruptly reversing direction and throwing himself back onto the tower roof. He spun to face the Blackhawk.

A gate opened right before its nose.

Directly on the other side stood the APC, its gun silent for the moment. Fitzy and the bulk of the SOC force gathered around it.

Britton could see the pilot through the helo's windscreen, hauling on the cyclic controls, but it was far too late to pull up. The Blackhawk passed neatly through the gate, the ends of the rotors shearing off and spinning over the flight line below. A grinding boom sounded from beyond the portal.

Britton closed the gate and leapt off the tower as Harlequin screamed, tackling the Aeromancer in midair and opening a gate beneath him just before the stone chairs.

Harlequin's body cushioned his fall, but both men still hit the ground hard enough to jar them apart, just as the explosion of the crashing helicopter caught them. The blast drove them against the base of the great tree as the Blackhawk slammed into the SOC force, turning over and catching fire as it spun among their ranks, its half rotors ripping themselves to fragments on the ground and tearing the soldiers apart. The shock wave struck Britton like a massive hand, forcing him up against the tree trunk and singeing his eyebrows. His head fetched up against the hard trunk, and he saw stars. His whole ear filled with a ringing buzz, and the angry wound on the other side of his head wept blood and rang in agony.

He sat against the tree trunk, all strength gone from him, shaking his head. As his sight cleared and the ringing began to fade, he noticed something strange.

Silence.

No gunshots. No crackling of arcing electricity or whooshing flame. The field of battle was quiet, with the occasional moan coming from the gory path left by the Blackhawk's ruined impact. The aircraft was buried halfway through a small two-story hut, which had collapsed over it, the thatching burning brightly. The APC had been knocked over on its side, the turret popped off and smoldering. Sarah Downer scrambled in the wreckage, her enemy forgotten, desperately trying to haul broken beams off the crushed bodies of soldiers.

Britton slewed his head to the right. Harlequin stirred weakly on the ground, blood running from a gash in his head, half-conscious. Behind them, Therese, Swift, Peapod and a few others had begun to stand, their faces streaked with blood and filth, their mouths open in shock.

Harlequin began to prop himself onto his elbows. Britton shot out a bootheel and caught him in the temple, knocking him back into oblivion.

Pyre lay a few feet before him, sprawled on his side. His eyes were open, seeing nothing.

Fitzy. Fucking Fitzy.

Britton launched himself to his feet, running to the wreckage.

He found Fitzy lying on top of two dead soldiers. His wounded arm had been burned to a stump from the elbow down, the wound mostly cauterized, but still leaking blood. Ribs protruded from his ruined side. He groaned, his eyes darting around, his good arm scrabbling in the dirt, searching for a weapon. Truelove was pushing himself to his feet behind him, swaying, blood streaking his shredded uniform. Richards sprawled beside him, his charred body cut neatly in half by a chunk of the helo's tail boom.

Britton staggered a few more steps and collapsed on top of the chief warrant officer, his knee slamming into the broken ribs and eliciting a weak moan.

'Kill you,' Fitzy whispered. 'Fucking kill you.'

Britton leaned in and whispered back, 'You're done killing.'

Fitzy grinned at Britton's closeness, then moved his good arm with sudden speed to his belt, hauling out a small knife and lunging for him. Britton twisted aside, and the slim blade found his thigh instead of his side, gouging out a furrow of flesh.

He screamed and head-butted his former instructor, who sprawled in the dirt, spitting blood. He tried to open a gate and found that Fitzy, for all his injuries, could still Suppress him. He looked around for a weapon and settled on a fragment of the helo's rotors, its jagged edges sharp. He snatched it up as Truelove regained his senses, and their eyes met. They held stares for a moment while Fitzy flailed weakly beneath him.

Finally, the Necromancer nodded and turned away.

Britton raised the rotor fragment over his head.

'Fuck you,' Fitzy snarled.

'No,' Britton answered. 'Fuck you.'

He brought the sharp edge down across Fitzy's throat, suppressing the instinct to look away as the hot blood washed over him. The magic tide rushed back to him as Fitzy gurgled his last.

A few soldiers began to rise from the ruined swath left by the Blackhawk's path, but were set upon by Goblins, screaming and dragging them back down to the ground, spears leveled at their throats. One of the Goblins dashed from the crowd, a chunk of stone held high over his head. He moved to one of the soldiers, raising the rock to dash his brains out. Marty barked an order from his position behind the stone chairs. The Goblin paused, looking askance, and Marty repeated himself until the creature reluctantly lowered the stone.

Britton examined the knife wound in his thigh. The gouge was deep, gently oozing blood around the edges, but he wouldn't bleed out anytime soon. He tried to stand and found that he could, though his legs shook. Therese could heal him later. For now, he reached out, grabbing Truelove's arm.

'Stay with me,' he said, as the Goblins converged on the survivors.

He looked for Downer, but was distracted by Harlequin, who had begun to stir against at the base of the tree, pushing himself onto his elbows. Britton took a limping step toward him, savoring the trip.

Somehow, they had won.

Swift reached Harlequin before Britton, leaping over the stone chairs and putting a bootheel on the Sorcerer's neck. The flames were out, but they had left Swift's chest badly burned, the swallow tattoo disappearing under charred skin. His black hair had melted to the sides of his face. One eye drooped into a track of burned skin that Britton knew would scar terribly.

Peapod appeared behind him, Marty at her side. Swift winced with each step, the side of his face twitching uncontrollably.

Therese knelt at Pyre's side, weeping.

The Goblins had rounded up what remained of the soldiers and were dragging them into the plaza. They came without protest, shaking their heads in disbelief that they could have been beaten. One stumbled and was rewarded by a jab from a spear in his buttock that drew blood. Downer stumbled along with them, a Goblin helping her along with thumps of his spear butt.

Britton could feel the Aeromancer's flow, but Harlequin was in no condition to muster any magic. Swift put his boot on Harlequin's throat and loomed over him.

'You recognize me, you fucker? Look at me.'

Harlequin groaned, opening his eyes but managing little more than slits. He tried to raise his head and failed, dropping back in the dirt.

Swift rotated his foot, tearing away skin. 'Open your fucking eyes! Look at me!'

Harlequin managed to open a single blue eye, but there was no recognition there.

But Swift only went on. 'It's me. Remember? You killed my girlfriend and my child. I killed myself trying to fucking earn somebody. When I was about ready to give up, I met Shai. So you killed her. Do you like me now? I'm a fucking product of your goddamned system.'

He spoke so quickly that drool escaped from the corner of his mouth, his words running together, scarcely understandable as his voice rose. 'But here's the best part. You lose. I've got you, and I'm going to kill you so slowly and horribly that before I'm done, you'll spit on your precious laws just for a momentary break in your suffering. You fucking son of a bitch. I am going to kill you. I am going to kill you. I am going to kill you.'

Britton paused, stunned by the depth of Swift's hatred. He could feel Swift's current gathering like a tidal wave, a well of potential energy bubbling beneath his skin. He must have been burning with it. Would he go nova? Harlequin seemed to feel it, too, and began to thrash weakly back and forth under the pressure of his heel. The Goblins had returned to the plaza and stood staring frankly at him, waiting for his next move.

Britton had no love for Harlequin, but he felt Fitzy's blood still warm on him. The sensation made him feel ill, weak. Harlequin was a bastard, but he was not Fitzy. Britton opened his mouth to say something but stopped. Swift's scarred face and insane rambling made him terrifying. If Britton spoke, he might divert some of that insensate rage onto himself. He didn't know what Swift would do.

Downer had no such compunction. She shrieked and shook free of her captors, racing to Harlequin, her hands outstretched. 'Don't you hurt him!' she screamed. 'Don't you hurt him!'

Swift's eyes never left the Aeromancer, who had recovered enough to prop himself onto his elbows, his head bending back under the weight of Swift's boot. Swift merely stuck out one hand, pointing at Downer.

A bolt of lightning sprang from his hand, catching her full in the chest. The Elementalist flipped over backward, her screams abruptly becoming a choking croak. She slid in the mud, the stench of cooked meat rising from her.

'No!' Britton cried, interdicting Swift's magical current. The strength of it nearly overwhelmed him, and it took him several seconds to properly Suppress Swift.

Downer writhed on the ground, alive but hurt badly. Truelove rushed to her side, cradling her in his arms.

Swift felt the Suppression take hold and whipped his head toward Britton, snarling. He bent, in one fluid motion, grabbing Harlequin's throat with one hand and yanking his pistol from its drop holster with the other. He stood again, the pistol barrel hovering rock steady over the Aeromancer's face.

'I don't need magic to do this,' he said. His finger tensed on the trigger.

'Don't!' Therese raced between them, hooking an arm under Harlequin's armpit and hauling him upright. Harlequin Drew magic to him, but Britton met his eyes and shook his head. 'You do, and you're dead, pal.'

Harlequin didn't release the magic, but neither did he Bind it to anything.

Swift didn't move, pointing the gun doggedly over Therese's shoulder. 'Get out of the way,' he said. 'You saved our lives, and I don't want to shoot you, but he's not getting away.'

Therese only stood, shaking her head silently.

Britton looked down at Fitzy's gore splashed across him and felt sick with himself. Rage had overcome him, and he had murdered the chief warrant officer. Therese wouldn't permit that. Not when a man was too weak to defend himself. She was better than that.

'No, Swift,' Therese said. 'We're letting him go.'

She gestured at the few remaining soldiers, hemmed in by Goblin spears and staring wide eyed at the confrontation. 'We're letting all of them go.'

Swift's voice was flat, the rage gone stale. 'I'm not kidding. Get the fuck out of the way.'

'We came here to escape,' Therese said. 'We've done that. Killing more people won't accomplish anything.'

Britton spoke up, hoping the words would shrug off some of the shame he felt. 'That's what Selfers do. We're not Selfers, Swift. We're not the SOC. We're the real good guys, and it's high time we started acting like it. I'm through with magic as a bludgeon. It stops here. He goes free, back where he came from. They all do.'

He met Marty's eyes as he said it. He knew he couldn't speak for the Mattab On Sorrah, but he also knew he couldn't permit them to kill captured prisoners, no matter how angry they were over the attack on their village. 'All water baby, right?'

But Marty only nodded, speaking quickly in his own language. There was a chorus of angry cries from the assembled Goblins, with a few of the white-painted sorcerers stepping forward, flapping their hands at him, but Marty silenced them with a few barked words, his command presence back again.

'All water baby,' he said. 'Always help.'

'We've all lost something,' Therese said to Swift. 'Killing him won't bring anyone back to life.'

The pistol didn't waver. Swift's face was inscrutable, his voice a tired croak. 'You're going to have to kill me if you want him to live.'

Therese paused, shook her head, then stepped away from Harlequin, spreading her arms and moving to stand beside Britton. 'I've had it with killing,' she said. 'You do what you have to, Swift, but you can't fight the whole world, not forever. Sooner or later, you have to accept things as they are, stop bitching, and start the hard work of changing stuff.'

Swift's lip curled, he pressed the gun forward, and Britton tensed for the ringing shot, for Harlequin's body to jerk and slump. He closed his eyes and sighed.

Silence.

When Britton opened his eyes Swift had lowered the gun. His eyes were on his feet. Two drops tapped on his boot tips. *Tap. Tap.* Tears, Britton realized.

'Fuck,' was all he managed to say, barely a whisper.

'Don't think I don't appreciate the gesture,' Harlequin slurred through split lips. 'But it's not my call. I'll be back, Oscar, for you and your friends. This won't change anything. I'll come for you.'

Britton crossed to Swift and took the pistol from his hands. Swift gave it up willingly, his grip limp and spent. His eyes remained fixed on his feet.

Britton swallowed. Felt his gorge rise.

Because there was one more killing that had to be done if they were ever to be safe.

Britton turned, dropping Swift's Suppression to open a gate directly before the chair where Billy sat, his mother's elephantine arms pale around his neck. His vacant blue eyes widened, his mouth working in shock at the sight of a gate not of his own making. He whipped his head from side to side, pulling one of the leads loose. His mother fumbled to reconnect it, her cat's-eye framed glasses going askew. Harlequin stiffened, but he lacked the strength to do anything.

'I'm sorry, Billy,' Britton said. 'It's the only way.' He made his single shot count, putting the bullet squarely between the Portamancer's eyes. His head snapped back, coating his mother's floral print dress with gray matter. Britton shut the gate before her screams could reach him.

He dropped the pistol as if it were diseased. 'No,' he said to Harlequin, when he could finally bring himself to speak. 'I don't think you're coming for anybody. Not anymore.'

Therese approached Swift, placing a hand on his burned face, the magic flowing out and smoothing the skin into shiny pink patches. 'It's okay,' Therese whispered. 'It's going to be okay.'

'How can it ever be okay?' Swift whispered.

Therese was silent, as was Britton. *I don't know how it can ever be okay,* Britton thought. *But at least now we've got a chance to try to get it there.*

Britton pictured a trip to Washington, DC, he had made in high school. He snapped the gate open, the image of his memories playing true. The front lawn of the White House was clearly visible through the shimmering surface of the portal. Crowds of onlookers gawked and pointed from beyond the iron fence.

'Off you go,' he said to Harlequin, shoving him toward it. The Goblins followed suit, prodding the remaining assaulters forward at spearpoint. 'Maybe you can explain to them what you've been up to. I'll be watching the newspapers for your quote. Best of luck with that.'

Harlequin glanced over his shoulder at Britton as he went. 'Just what the hell do you think you're doing?'

'Something new,' Britton answered. 'Go back to your masters. Tell them that their precious regulations are no longer valid. Tell them there's a new way.

'From now on, Latent people get a real choice. And I don't mean a choice between soldier and Selfer. Tell them if they don't get my message out, I'll do it my damned self. You can't stop me from doing the one thing you fear the most: telling the truth. I can make sure that people know about the Source, the FOB, what you really do with Probes, everything.

'And this. Tell them I'll be visiting them real soon to discuss the new order. President Walsh, Senator Whalen, all of them. They have this one chance to do the right thing. After that, I'll visit the newspapers and TV stations. They don't get to decide how magic is regulated anymore. You know why? Because I can be anywhere at any time, I can spread the word. I can show everyone the world they're so desperately trying to hide, and there's no way they can stop me.'

Harlequin nodded, the corners of his mouth rising slightly. 'You're one hell of a dreamer, Oscar. I'll be seeing you real soon.'

'I'll be ready,' Britton said, as the Aeromancer stepped through the gate, the rest of the assault force in tow. Sirens had already begun to sound outside the White House fence, and Britton could see white-shirted police pushing their way through the crowd.

When the last of the soldiers was safely through, he closed the gate and stared out over the ruins of the village. Already, the wreckage of the helicopter had begun to cool, and several Goblins picked through it or hauled off the small children who were playing too close to the remaining fires.

Behind him, Britton could feel the gazes of what remained of the group he'd led out of the wreckage of the SASS: Therese, Swift, Tsunami, Peapod. He could hear Marty speaking in soothing tones to his tribe, who were crowding closer. Truelove cradled Downer, still unconscious. Britton could feel the tension of their expectation, waiting for his attention.

But he took a moment before that next step, inhaling the intensified smells of the Source. The air was still thick with the stench of blood, fear, oil, and spent gunpowder, but underneath it was something sweeter, a light odor that spoke of the hearths in the houses still standing, of the buds on the old tree behind him that had been spared the fire, of the acres of grass and foreign trees just outside the palisade wall.

Oscar Britton took a deep breath and turned to face the coming dawn.

Glossary of Military Terms, Acronyms, and Slang

This novel deals largely with the United States military. As anyone familiar with the military knows, it has a vocabulary of acronyms, slang, and equipment references large enough to constitute its own language. Some readers may be familiar with it. For those who are not, I provide the following glossary. Many of these terms are fictional. Many are not.

ANG – Air National Guard.

AOR – Area of Responsibility.

APACHE – An attack helicopter, also known as a helicopter gunship.

APC – Armored Personnel Carrier.

ATTD – Asset Tracking/Termination Device. A beacon/bomb that can be placed inside a person to track their movements and, if necessary, to kill them.

BLACKHAWK – A utility/transport helicopter.

BUTTER-BAR – A second lieutenant in land- or air-based service, or an ensign in maritime service. The lowest commissioned officer rank in the United States military.

CAC – Common Access Card. A government identification card used across all five branches of the US military.

CARBINE – A shortened, lighter version of the traditional

assault rifle used by infantry. It is better suited for tight spaces common in urban operations.

CO – Commanding Officer.

COMMS – Communications.

COVEN – Replaces a squad for organizational purposes when magic-using soldiers are concerned. A conventional squad contains four to ten soldiers led by a staff sergeant. A Coven contains four to five SOC Sorcerers, led by a captain. Training Covens are led by a warrant officer.

CSH – Combat Support Hospital. Pronounced 'Cash'. A field hospital, successor to the MASH units of TV fame.

DFAC – Dining Facility.

DRUID – Selfer slang for a Terramancer.

ELEMENTALIST – A person practicing the prohibited school of Sentient Elemental Conjuration. This is the act of imbuing Elementals with self-awareness. This is different from automatons – Elementals with no thought, who are entirely dependent on the sorcerer for command and control.

FOB – Forward Operating Base.

GIMAC – Gate-Integrated Modern Army Combatives – MAC integrated with Portamancy. Also known as 'gate-fu'. See MAC definition below.

GO DYNAMIC – Command given to assault a target without regard to stealth.

GO NOVA – When a magic user is overwhelmed by the current of their own magical power. This results in a painful death similar to burning. A person who has 'gone nova' is sometimes referred to as a 'magic sink'.

HEALER – A Physiomancer. They are sometimes also referred to as 'Renders' in deference to their ability to damage flesh as well as repair it. Offensive Physiomancy is prohibited under the Geneva Convention's magical amendment. Offensive use of Physiomancy is also known as 'Rending'.

HELO – Helicopter.

HOOCH – Living quarters. Can also be used as a verb. 'You'll hooch here.'

HOT – Under fire. Usually refers to an arrival under fire. A 'hot LZ' would be landing an aircraft under fire. Also refers to a state of military readiness where personnel are prepared for immediate action.

INDIG – Indigenous.

INDIRECT FIRE – Sometimes shortened to simply 'Indirect'. An attack, either magical or conventional, aimed without relying on direct line of sight to the target. This usually refers to artillery, rocket, or mortar fire, but also Pyromantic flame strikes and Aeromantic lightning attacks.

IO – Information Operations.

JAG – Judge Advocate General. The legal branch of any of the United States armed services.

KIA – Killed in Action.

KIOWA – A light reconnaissance helicopter.

KLICK – A kilometer or kilometers per hour.

LATENT – Any individual who possesses magical ability, detected or otherwise.

LITTLE BIRD – A small helicopter usually used to insert/ extract commandos.

LOGS – Logistics.

LSA – Logistical Staging Area.

LZ – Landing Zone.

MAC – Modern Army Combatives. A martial art unique to the United States Army, based on Brazilian Jiujitsu.

MANIFEST – The act of realizing one's Latency and displaying magical ability. Latent people Manifest at various times in their lives – some at birth, some on their deathbed, and at all times in between. Nobody knows why it occurs when it does.

MINIGUN – A crew-served multibarrel machine gun with a high rate of fire, employing Gatling-style rotating barrels and an external power source.

MP – Military Police.

MWR – Morale, Welfare, and Recreation center.

NIH – National Institute of Health. Among many other services, NIH runs a Monitoring/Suppression program for those Latents who refuse to join the military but don't want to become Selfers. Participants are monitored continuously and have virtually no privacy. Most are treated as social pariahs.

NODS – Night Observation Devices.

NORMALS – Selfer slang for those who are not Latent. The term is respectful. The term 'human' is sometimes substituted in derogatory fashion.

NOVICE – SOC Sorcerers still in training, before they graduate SAOLCC.

OC – Officers' Club.

ON MY SIX – Directly behind the speaker.

OUTSIDE THE WIRE – Area beyond the secure perimeter of a military facility.

PROBES – Short for 'Prohibited'. Those Latents who Manifest in a school of prohibited magic such as Negramancy, Portamancy, Necromancy, or Sentient Elemental Conjuration.

PSYOPS – Psychological Operations.

PX – Post Exchange. A store selling a variety of goods located on a military facility.

READING – Slang for the military practice of using Rump Latents to 'read' the currents of other Latent individuals in an effort to discover their magic-using status.

RENDING – Offensive use of Physiomantic magic. See Healer definition above.

ROE – Rules of Engagement. The conditions under which members of the military and law-enforcement communities are permitted to employ deadly force.

RUMP LATENCY – A person who Manifests magical ability that is too slight to be of any real use. Such a person can only use magic to a very slight degree but can feel the magical tide in another person. Rump Latents are not commissioned as full SOC officers but make up a small percentage of the enlisted and warrant-officer support in the corps.

SAOLCC – Sorcerer's Apprentice/Officer Leadership Combined Course. Basic training for SOC Sorcerers. This rigorous training regimen teaches Latent soldiers the basics of magic use/control while simultaneously preparing them for their duties as officers in the US Army.

SCHOOL – A particular kind of magic, usually associated with a mutable element (earth, air, fire, water, flesh, etc.). Latent individuals only Manifest in one school.

SEABEE – Colloquial pronunciation of 'CB' – construction battalions of the United States Navy.

SELFERS – Latent individuals who elect to flee authority and use their magical abilities unsupervised. Selfers are usually tracked down and killed.

SF/SOF – Special Forces or Special Operations Forces. Used interchangeably.

SOC – Supernatural Operations Corps. Not to be confused with Special Operations Command (or SOCOM, under whose auspices the Supernatural Operations Corps falls). The SOC is the corps of the US Army responsible for all magical use. The SOC is a joint corps, which means it handles magic use for all US armed services to include the Air Force, Navy, and Coast Guard (though the Army is the executive agent). The Marine Corps does not participate in the SOC and runs its own Suppression Lances.

SORCERER – A SOC magical operator – an officer of the SOC who employs magic as his primary military specialty. The term is also used to refer to those contractors certified to use magic in support of SOC operations.

STRYKER – An armored combat land vehicle.

SUPPRESSION – The act of using one's own magical current to block that of another. This is typically a one-to-one ratio. The strength of a Suppressor's Latency must exceed that of the individual he is seeking to Suppress.

SUPPRESSION LANCE – A US Marine Corps unit that employs a Suppressing officer to block the magical abilities of the riflemen in the unit.

TAR BABY – SOC Slang for elemental automatons. See Elementalist definition above.

TOC – Tactical Operations Center.

UCMJ – Uniform Code of Military Justice.

WHISPERING – Terramantic magic used to control the actions of animals. This is prohibited by the US Code. SOC Terramancers are not permitted to Whisper.

WIA – Wounded in Action.

WITCH – Selfer slang for a Negramancer. Male Negramancers are sometimes called Warlocks.

Acknowledgements

A novel is a group effort for which one person gets all the credit. Let me try to amend that. I'd like to extend special thanks to my family, and in particular my brother Peter, who taught me that art is a thing worth striving for. Also thanks to my beta readers Tamela Viglione and Joel Beaven, and my agent and dear friend Joshua Bilmes. Thanks to my editor Anne Sowards, who believed in this project from the start. Thanks to my ad hoc readers Jay Franco, James Kehler and Kikki Short (who is also my Sister-in-Law, so I suppose I should thank her for marrying my brother too). Oh, and Mom, even though she admits to having no clue as to what I'm going on about.

Thanks to Stephanie, Mike, Wendy and the rest of the crew at the Potomac Yards Barnes and Noble, in whose cafe the vast majority of this book was written. Thanks to House Bloodguard, who taught me that discipline is the better part of valor, and to the Every Day is Wednesday Hash House Harriers (DC), who kept me in wine, women and song during the rocky post-deployment adjustment periods.

Special thanks to Chief Warrant Officer Andre Sinou, United States Marine Corps, who didn't break faith when I went to ground, and to Major General Edwin Spain, United States Army (ret.).You were right, sir. The last quarter second made all the difference in the world. Thanks also to Lieutenant Colonel James Wanovich, United States Army, who stilled the jitters when indirect fire came danger close. Small round, big base, sir.

Very special thanks to the men and women of United

States Coast Guard Sector Hampton Roads and the graduating ROCI class of 02-08 (especially Alpha Company, 1st Platoon). My first unit and graduating class, respectively. When you have such people to lean on, it's impossible to fail.

On the other side of the pond: Special thanks to Mark Lawrence and Joe Abercrombie (and Lou 'Applecrumble'). Thanks to John Berlyne and John Parker at Zeno. Thanks also to Gillian Redfearn for introducing me to the wonders of haggis. Thanks to John Wordsworth and the gang at Headline for believing in the project enough to give it a chance. Thanks to Dave Fields, whose eagle eye kept improving the book right into the eleventh hour. Thanks to Larry Rostant for his excellent work on the cover of the UK edition. Thanks to Marc Aplin and the crew at Fantasy Faction for early and fervent support. Thanks also to the King's Own Border, the Irish Guards and some gentlemen of Hereford who know who they are. Rule Britannia!

And last, but certainly not least, to Peter V. Brett, my Professor X. How could I have ever done it without you?

Read on for a sneak preview of

FORTRESS FRONTIER

The next book in the SHADOW OPS Series

Out February 2013.

Bookbinder still burned with humiliation when he went for breakfast the next morning. He kept his eyes on the dirt floor of the chow hall, ashamed to meet anyone's gaze. *You're being ridiculous*, he screamed at himself. *Hold your head up!* But every look seemed to hold an accusation.

The hot line was crowded, so Bookbinder headed for the cold food section, piling his tray with fruit amid the relative quiet. *This is stupid. You want bacon and eggs. Go get on the damned hot line!*

I can't bear to look at anyone right now. Besides, this will help me lose weight.

You don't need to lose weight, you fucking coward! Go get the breakfast you want!

But while Bookbinder's mind raged, his body moved with the same wooden rote that it had when he'd gone to his office after Taylor threatened him. He took a foam bowl off the stack, filled it with bran flakes that he didn't even like, then opened the mini fridge to get a container of milk. But the mini fridge door didn't budge.

The unexpected resistance brought Bookbinder out of his reverie. He looked up to note that the fridge was locked and unplugged. A paper sign was taped to the front. NO MILK UNTIL FURTHER NOTICE.

Bookbinder had eaten in military DFACs his entire career. In all that time, none of them had ever run out of milk. He looked at the juice case. It was powered at least, but three quarters empty.

Bookbinder turned to one of the goblin contractors wrestling a stack of cardboard boxes from behind the refrigerated cases. 'What's up here?' he pointed at the fridge.

The creature gave him a blank look, then turned to a navy non-rate, who stuffed his clipboard into his armpit as he approached the colonel. 'Can I help you with something, sir?'

'Yes, what's up with the milk and the juice? I'm the J1 here, and I didn't see any reduction in the standard food order.'

'I know who you are, sir. There's been a rationing order put out for all perishables, effective immediately. Came down last night at eighteen hundred.'

'A rationing order? Why?'

'I don't know, sir,' he gestured to the fruit and salad bar. 'That's starting to run low too.'

The comms blackout. Fitzsimmons' sudden vacation and now this.

'Who runs food services here?' Bookbinder asked. 'It's Major Holland, right? I didn't tell him to ration anything.'

'No, sir. He got it straight from Colonel Taylor himself.'

Taylor. That meant if he was going to get any answers, it would mean yet another confrontation, and Taylor had made it clear what he could expect from another one of those.

Something is very wrong. Supply issues are your problem. You have to find out what's going on. Even if it meant facing Taylor? He was terrified of the man's threats and rage. But he was angry that he had to worry about either one.

Bookbinder threw his tray down on top of the mini fridge in disgust and stormed out.

As he moved through the entryway, he noted the corkboard clustered with slips of paper thumbtacked over one another, advertising the various events on the FOB. Announcements for the perimeter 5K run and the Sunday morning prayer breakfast were crowded out by the official notices, warning FOB residents of the dangers of Source flora and fauna (IF YOU DON'T RECOGNIZE IT, DON'T TOUCH IT! REPORT TO YOUR FIRST SERGEANT IMMEDIATELY), reminding them to report suspected Latency or negligent magical discharges.

But one sign dominated the board's center, stopping him dead in his tracks.

BY ORDER OF THE CAMP COMMANDANT: ALL NON-ESSENTIAL RANGE USE IS CANCELLED UNTIL FURTHER NOTICE. WAIVERS WILL BE EXTENDED ONLY FOR WEAPONS REQUALIFICATIONS. UNIT ARMORERS ARE TO REPORT TO SFC SCOTT FOR INSTRUCTIONS ON AMMUNITION CONSERVATION AND DISPENSING.

It was dated that day.

Perishable food. Ammunition. I don't care if he does kick my teeth in. We've got a severe supply problem here.

Bookbinder marched out onto the plaza, looking for Taylor. With each step he took, his legs grew heavier as the cloud of fear around him coalesced into molasses. *And then I will keep kicking you, until you piss blood for the rest of your natural life.*

Of course, Taylor was trying to scare him. But fear robbed Bookbinder of all perspective. All he could smell was the sour taint of Taylor's breath, all he could feel was the pulse pound of the man's tangible anger.

He was almost glad when the indirect hit.

A deafening bang rocked the plaza, as a pillar of flame shot up over one of the blast barricades not fifty feet distant. A loud succession of booms sounded off in the distance. Bookbinder could see a cloud of circling rocs in the distance. The giant eagle-like birds looked small from here, but he knew up close they were bigger than a tank.

The SASS perimeter again. The goblins were launching another attack, maybe hoping to break through before the defenses were fully repaired.

The siren began to wail, calling all personnel to action stations. Men and women raced past him, pulling weapons off their shoulders and checking magazine wells. The low growl of helicopters spinning up echoed in the distance.

Well, you were going to get in a fight anyway. Might as well get in one where you actually stand a chance.

Since the last attack on the SASS, Bookbinder carried three loaded magazines as he was supposed to do at all times. He drew his pistol. It looked unfamiliar in his hand; heavy, thick. He took the weapon off safety, kept his finger off the trigger and raced in the general direction of the chaos. En route, he spotted an electric cart heaped with helmets and body armor, two goblin contractors jogging behind, keeping the heap from tumbling off.

'You! Stop! I need gear!' he shouted. The driver stopped the cart, hopping out and saluting. The soldier sized him up, pressed him a vest and helmet, saluted again, then jumped back on the cart. 'Good luck, sir!'

Bookbinder donned the gear, still amazed at what a little yelling had done, and followed behind. The crowd jostled as he moved closer, pushing through a wall of dark smoke, blanketed by noise; screams, gunfire, explosions, the sizzle and crackle of magic. In the midst of the press, choking on the brimstone stink of powdered concrete and cordite, all the people blended together. In this darkness and confusion, there was no branch, no rank, not even faces. There were just people, lots of them, all moving towards a common goal. Here, Bookbinder wasn't an administrative colonel, he was just another grunt, doing his part.

The peace it gave him would have been shocking if it weren't so soothing. He was smiling as he stepped out of the cloud of smoke.

And into hell.

He'd thought the indirect fire had hardened him. He'd shuddered through loud explosions, smelled the ozone stink of impacting magic, heard the screams and even seen the charred corpses of the dead.

It was nothing.

The SASS perimeter was a broken jumble of cracked concrete barricades and burning heaps of razor wire topped fencing. The newly erected guard tower had collapsed, igniting the magazine of the Mark-19 grenade launcher. The crew's remains were strewn about the wreckage, hands, half a torso, smoldering boots.

Two SOC Terramancers crouched in the wreckage, calling up a shelf of earth that provided much needed cover from the sea of goblins surging beyond. Bookbinder hadn't known that so many of the creatures existed in the entire Source. They trooped forward, many mounted on enormous, snarling wolves. Their sorcerers came with them, skin painted chalk white, hands crackling with magical energy. The horde hummed with rage, a drone so loud that it competed with the steady stream of gunfire mounting from the defense. Clouds of arrows, javelins and bullets erupted from the goblin throng, undisciplined bursts of fire that were effective through sheer volume. A woman beside Bookbinder coughed blood and collapsed.

A SOC Aeromancer streaked overhead, lightning arcing from his fingers and plowing into the goblin mass, setting scores of them alight before a roc crashed into him, sending him spinning, catching him in its beak, cracking his spine.

The rocks in the earth barricade glowed red-hot as a goblin Pyromancer arced a pillar of flame across it, sending one of the Terramancers and three other defenders screaming, beating at the flames.

A Stryker crested the rubble behind Bookbinder, the gunner letting off a brief stream of rounds from the fifty cal, then pausing as Colonel Taylor appeared, climbing the Stryker's standoff armor and yelling at him, waving frantically.

And then Taylor's eyes widened. He dove off the turret just as the gunner tried to duck below. A massive chunk of a barricade wall, rebar jutting from its jagged edges, knocked the turret clean off, sending it tumbling through the defenders, eliciting a chorus of screams. The dull thudding of approaching helicopters was momentarily drowned out by a roar of rage.

Taylor scrambled to his feet as Bookbinder turned.

Two huge creatures advanced through the goblins, each taller than any of the FOB's low buildings. They looked much like the goblins that barely reached above their shins; the same brown, gnarled skin. The same pointed ears and hooked noses. But there the similarity ended. Where the goblins were lean, these things were as thick as iron girders.

One of them roared again, swinging an oddly-shaped club. Bookbinder realized it was the shorn turret of an Abrams tank.

One of the helicopters swooped low, miniguns opening on the creature, then began to spin as a summoned wind knocked it in a tight circle, a goblin Aeromancer rising over the creature's head. The giant snatched the helo's tailboom, stopping it in mid-air, leaning dramatically to avoid the spinning rotors. The pilots and crew tumbled out the side, screaming, disappearing in the horde of goblins beneath them. The giant roared and cast the helicopter into what remained of the Terramancer's barricade, flipping it over and tumbling into the defenders, who fell back.

'Come on!' Bookbinder shouted, striding forward. He leveled his pistol and squeezed off a few rounds, certain he wasn't hitting even the massive targets presented by the giants. 'You scared of a couple of big goblins?' *You sound like an idiot. A scared idiot.*

But a small company of soldiers looked up at him, shamefaced, then took their knees, finding cover in the broken rubble, firing into the approaching mass. An arrow whizzed close enough that he felt the fletching cut across his cheek. *Get down!* His mind screamed, but he forced himself to walk among the defenders, shouting encouragement. What would Patton say at a time like this? Oh Christ, he had no damned idea. 'Pour it on, people!' He tried. He was terrified, but the wooden feeling in his limbs was gone. *Well, at least if the goblins kill me, I don't have to face Taylor.*

Pillars of flame erupted in the goblin ranks as SOC Pyromancers secured positions in the wreckage. A figure rose out of the ground and wrestled with one of the giants, some Terramancer's automaton, taking the drubbing from the swinging tank turret, but reforming just as quickly, its rock fists giving as good as it got.

Bookbinder tried to keep his shoulders back, his chin up. He fired more shots in the enemy's direction. 'You're going to let a bunch of pointy-eared rats overrun your position? Show 'em what you've got!' Could they hear the quaver in his voice? Around him, knots of defenders were coalescing. Here was a group of Suppressed marines setting up a belt-fed grenade launcher. There was an army sniper team, picking targets quickly, the need to aim obviated by the enemy's clustered formation. Were they actually taking heart from his theatrics?

He heard Taylor shouting at some unfortunate soldier. 'Conserve your ammunition, damn it!'

Conserve ammunition? In the middle of this?

Suddenly the world spun around him. Something slammed into his head, rattling his teeth. A moment later he realized it was the ground. The stink of ozone and blood filled his nostrils. Sound vanished, replaced by a ringing-whine. He scrambled in the mud, his vision gone. Was he blind? No, he could see light, make out shapes. *Get up! Get up!* But his limbs moved as if through thick water, and he was hot . . . so very hot. The brimstone smell gave way to the acrid stench of burning plastic and hair.

His vision returned and he rose to his knees, bringing one arm into view.

It burned brightly. He was on fire.

Bookbinder screamed, rolling on the ground, beating at the flames.

'I've got you, sir,' someone said. He saw a navy sailor running towards him, shouldering his rifle and pulling a water bladder off his back. There was a whoosh and a blazing ball of fire caught him in the chest, sending him tumbling in a heap.

The heat subsided as Bookbinder rolled in the mud, until he bumped against the shins of a goblin. It was painted entirely chalk white, its wizened features contorted with hate. It bent over and gripped the front of his smoldering body armor, hauling him to his knees. The goblin's magical current eddied out from it, so strong that it nearly overwhelmed him.

Well done, he thought. *You were the only one walking around while everyone else was taking cover. You were so brave, you managed to attract one of their Sorcerers.*

The creature's fist ignited in a ball of flame. It spat something in its own language, raising its hand.

Bookbinder's current surged forward, borne on his panic. It interlaced with the goblin's. Where it tugged at other magical currents during testing, now it wrenched, and Bookbinder felt the creature's magic break free, funneled away from it. The goblin's brows knit in terror and it dropped him, jumping backward, its fire fizzling out. There was an odd silence. The goblin stared at him, its expression horrified, as if to say *how could you?*

Bookbinder raised his pistol and shot it.

For all his lack of practice, he caught the creature in the middle of its forehead. Its look of horrified violation turned to surprise, then emptiness, then it fell over on its side, shuddered and was still.

And then Bookbinder noticed that the tide of battle had turned.

An avenue of gore opened through the goblins, wide as two-lane road. The ground churned to mud beneath a carpet of lead, chunks of earth the size of a man's fist bouncing skyward to mix with the shredded flesh of goblin, wolf and giant alike. The sky was dark with summoned clouds and drifting smoke, but Bookbinder knew that an A-10 Warthog had gotten airborne and begun its strafing run.

The withering fire added to the mounting defense, raining bullets on the attacking horde. At last they began to buckle. First in ones and twos, the goblins sprinted back into the fields, falling under carpets of Aeromantic lightning. Bookbinder could practically feel the fear sweeping over the attackers. In moments, the trickle became a flood as the enemy fell back to the cheers of the defenders, fleeing.

Bookbinder watched them run. He lightly patted his hands over his body. His gear and clothing were melted and smoldering, but apart from what felt like a bad sunburn, he didn't feel too badly hurt.

The scuff of boots in the dirt in front of him brought him back into focus. He looked up at a battered marine staff sergeant, his gear streaked with dust and blood.

'You all right, sir?' The man asked.

'Um, I think so. How do I look?'

The man smiled. 'Like a steely eyed dealer of death, sir. Oorah.' He saluted, then headed off.

Bookbinder stared at his back. A *real* marine, the kind that ate nails for breakfast, had just complimented him. After a battle. Bookbinder's mind swirled, the smoke, the terror, the goblin standing over him, all threatened to overwhelm him. *Later.*

But a notion was leaping in his gut. Colonel Alan Bookbinder, fit only for processing spreadsheets and pay statements, just fought in a battle and held his own.

Taylor's voice cut through his thoughts. The colonel held an army private by the collar and shook him vigorously. 'Full auto!' Taylor screamed. 'You're firing on full fucking auto! Did I not expressly order you to conserve rounds? Is that how you treat government property?! Is that what you do with the tax-payer funded ammunition entrusted to you?'

The scream was not the low growl of rage Taylor confronted Bookbinder with before. It was high, bordering on hysteria.

Bookbinder was amazed at Taylor's lack of control, amazed

he had survived a real battle. Another amazement overshadowed them all.

Bookbinder was amazed that he no longer feared this man who was big, but thick around the middle. Who was angry, but screaming with the whining hysteria of a man succumbing to panic.

Before he knew it, Bookbinder had crossed the intervening distance. 'Colonel Taylor, I think this young man has had quite enough.'

Taylor turned to face Bookbinder, hysteria yielding to surprise. His eyes widened as he let go of the private, who immediately saluted, grabbed his weapon and jogged away.

It took a moment for Taylor to put on an authoritative expression. 'Just what in the hell are you doing here?'

'Same as you, rallying to the defense of this base.'

'I thought I told you . . .'

'You told me a lot of things. And now I need you to tell me something else. What the hell is going on here? There's some kind of supply issue and all I know is that it's sudden and severe. We've got sundries issues at the DFAC, and you're shaking down a private, a fucking *private*, instead of leaving it to his first sergeant. And for firing on the enemy? Now quit fucking around and tell me what's up.'

'I fucking warned you . . .'

'Then do it!' Bookbinder screamed, mashing his forehead against Taylor's, driving the bigger man back a step. 'Go ahead and kick me in the blood piss, or whatever stupid shit you were going on about before. But you better fucking *kill* me, because if you don't I will keep coming back until you won't be able to get a lick of work done because you'll spend every hour of every day fighting me.'

Taylor gaped. Some predatory instinct deep within Bookbinder surged, carrying the magic with it. He struggled as he fought it down. Taylor stood in shocked silence.

'Now, there's two ways we can do this,' Bookbinder began again, anger yielding to fatigue. 'You can bring me into your confidence and we can try to solve this problem together. Or, I can order a complete inventory of all ammunition reserves, which is well within my authority as the J1 here. This will tie up all ammunition distribution. Nobody will get a single round without my say so. That won't be a problem if new stores are inbound, but they're not, are they Colonel Taylor?'

Taylor's shoulders sagged, the fight totally gone out of him. *I can't believe it. I was so certain he would crush me. Is this all he is?*

'Are they?!' Bookbinder asked again through gritted teeth.

Taylor looked at the ground. When he spoke, his voice barely above a whisper. 'No, Alan. They're not.'

The predatory sense of victory melted away at the sound of that voice. Bookbinder the alpha male was gone, replaced by Bookbinder the father and husband. He put his hand on Taylor's shoulder.

'Why?' Bookbinder asked. 'What's going on?'

'We lost contact three days ago,' Taylor said. 'I'm not sure if it has to do with Oscar Britton's escape or not. All I know is that Billy's not opening the portals any more. We've got no comms with the Home Plane. Nothing is coming through; no food, no ammo.

'We're cut off.'